Second Wave

Gaea Ascendant 2

Eric S. Martell

Second Initiative Press

Second Wave

Second Initiative Press

Printed in the USA

ISBN: 978-0-9989805-8-4

Cover art by Krzysztof (Kris) Krygier

Vox audita perit littera scripta manet.

This is a work of fiction. All the characters and events portrayed in this book are fictional, and any resemblance to real people or incidents is purely coincidental.

CONTENTS

Earth has been Invaded!

An alien invasion destroyed human civilization. Even though the invasion was stopped by "security consultant" Declan Dunham, the aliens set human technology back to the seventeenth century. Now they are threatening to return to finish the job, and Dec must take up arms again. He does so with his usual aggressiveness, but not without worry about leaving his family behind in a lawless wilderness.

In the process, he finds there are other victims of the invaders. With their aid, he steals a spaceship and sets out to locate the only race that fought the invaders to a standstill. His goal is to enlist their help in finding a way to finally defeat the aliens, and neutralize their threat.

The story is full of adventure and conflict. The alien races range from cuddly to horrific, and the fierce alien beasts of Tukoli will have you looking over your shoulder in the dark.

Dedication

This book is dedicated to Morghan and Jordan.

Thanks to Krzysztof (Kris) Krygier for the original cover art.

CHAPTER 1

We hold these truths to be self-evident, that all men are created equal, that they are endowed by their Creator with certain unalienable Rights, that among these are Life, Liberty and the pursuit of Happiness.

The Declaration of Independence – July 4, 1776

"Freedom is never more than one generation away from extinction. We didn't pass it to our children in the bloodstream. It must be fought for, protected, and handed on for them to do the same."

Ronald Reagan

I was unable to sleep. It was awful. I tossed and turned all night and it seemed like the sun would never rise over the Divide. I don't know how Liz put up with it, but she was quiet and, I assumed, sleeping, while I rolled around like I was lying in a bed of fleas. First, it was too hot and then too cool. The cabin window was open and I could hear the mountain stream gurgling along with an occasional chuckle and splash. That sound always helped me get to sleep, but tonight, the energy field just seemed to conflict with mine. I knew what the problem was, but I didn't want to face it.

That damned falling star last night – I knew it wasn't a meteor. It fit everything I had learned on Titan from the Ancient-One, the old alien mastermind of the Pug-bears' invasion, prior to killing him. I was certain that it was some kind of shuttle, bearing – and I knew this for a certainty because it was what the aliens had done the first time – a matter transporter. I remembered the Ancient-One's memories that I'd inadvertently hijacked from him as he tried to dominate my mind. The original transporter had been sent down with programmed instructions to locate a radioactive ore deposit. There had been one, far underground, in Rocky Mountain National Park.

The deposit was still there and the Pug-bears and Pugs knew where it was. It only made sense that they set their shuttle to return to the same location. I figured that the transporter network blowing up hadn't damaged the ore deposit. After all, it was deep in the rocks under the ridge where we'd found the transporter link to Titan.

If the falling star Liz and I had seen late last evening was a spacecraft, then the Pug-bears had made very good time in returning to Earth. I had been certain that they would need several more years to return. It hadn't been long enough to suit me. NASA's Cassini spacecraft had taken approximately seven years to make the journey. It hadn't even been four full years since we'd blown the Titan base and destroyed the transporter network. Yet, here the invaders came again!

The worst thing was that humanity hadn't even slightly begun to recover from the damage that the aliens' high-altitude nuclear blast had done. If anything, our society was still going down. The resulting electromagnetic pulse had destroyed all of the unshielded electronics on the face of the globe and most of the electrical grid also. It had resulted in a massive die-off of the human species. Oh, sure, primitive people across the globe hadn't been affected that much. They didn't rely on just-in-time inventory supply or any of the other "modern" conveniences that our culture had burdened itself with. They just got up the next day and went out and caught some more fish or went hunting or picked some...

Damn it! My mind was wandering. I kicked off the covers and when I opened my eyes, I realized that I'd actually been sleeping lightly. There was a faint suggestion of daylight coming in our bedroom window and the breeze coming through the window screen carried the wet lumber smell caused by the morning dew on the sides of our log home.

I took a deep breath and prepared myself to face the day, then stretched and rolled over to find Liz staring at me with her eyes open. Her face was ten inches from mine and I thought again – for about the ten-thousandth time – how lucky I was that she had fallen in love with me.

She smiled and my mood lightened up in response.

"You didn't sleep at all, did you, Dec?" It was more of an observation than a question.

"Not very well. I kept worrying about that falling star," I responded reluctantly. I knew from her slight frown and the little wrinkling between her eyebrows that she'd made up her mind about the thing. I didn't want to start talking about it, because I knew what her decision would be. It would be the same as mine and I didn't like my decision one little bit.

"You and I both know that wasn't a falling star," she said, frowning. "It was the Pug-bears returning to Earth. They have to be stopped quickly and permanently, Dec. If they aren't, well, we won't have a future."

She looked over at the window and then turned her face back to me to speak. "We've got to plan for Michael. He needs a world that's safe to grow up in," she said.

As usual, her face softened when she said his name. For such an independent woman, and Liz was as tough as they come and a good fighter, she had fallen completely for her little son. It must have been catching, because I, too, would do absolutely anything to protect him.

It's amazing what having your own child will do to your attitude. I can remember that I used to think that other people's kids were just a nuisance, crying in restaurants and ruining the atmosphere just when I was trying to have a nice meal. These days, I've got an incredible amount of patience for what the little ones go through now that I've put up with some major crying bouts myself. You get used to it and it becomes natural to give comfort and try to make things better. When they're happy, it's like the whole world is aglow.

My mind was wandering again. With a mental jolt, I returned to the source of my worry. I knew what I was going to do and I didn't want to do it, but there wasn't any option. I was the only one who knew enough about fighting the aliens to be able to make a difference. I'd proven deadly to them in the past and I was now even more prepared. The mental changes that had started under the Ancient-One's attack had continued and I was better at both mental communication and remote sensing.

Liz and I were always in a low-level mental-linkage. You'd probably call it telepathy, but it wasn't really like that. It was as if her thoughts were just part of my own thought-stream. I didn't have to pay attention to them, but they were always there in the background. This continuous communication made us very close and we each seemed to know what the other needed. Right now, I needed some encouragement and she knew it.

"Look, Dec, we both know that was the Pug-bears coming back. It was obviously some kind of spaceship or lander. Now, it may not have brought any aliens. It might be only a robotic ship, but you can be sure that it has a working matter transporter in it. They'll be back as soon as they can get their transporter link re-established," she was speaking softly as her eyes locked with mine. "You know that something has to be done to disrupt their plans again."

"Yeah, but why couldn't someone else do it?" I was arguing a lost cause and had already made up my mind, but I still wanted to have her convince me.

"You know you're the only one with the experience and ability to seriously screw them up. They took a beating the last time and they're going to be more ready this time, but so are you," she was referring to my maturing psychic abilities.

I knew she was right. My ability to insert thoughts and emotions into another mind had greatly increased since the time when I resisted the Ancient-One's control. So had my remote-sensing ability. It was handy since it made me a better hunter. In the post-electronics world caused by the alien's EMP, being able to put food on the table consistently was a blessing.

"I don't want to leave you and Michael!" I complained, "And – and, I know that you can't come with me. There's too much danger on the eastern side of the Divide from humans, let alone aliens!"

At this, she sort of kicked her feet to untangle them from the bedclothes and to get them clear of our cat, Jefferson.

He'd been lying between her feet. It's a bad habit he has. He was a street cat, used to hardship and unused to human contact. However, he'd decided that living with us was the greatest thing that ever happened to him. He just adored sleeping in the bed with us. He would sometimes try to get between my feet, but I was a little too restless and would usually kick him off. Liz, on the other hand, seemed to tolerate the heavy, hot lump that he made.

Now, she kicked and he got up and stretched, then jumped down and went into the other room. After a minute I heard the cat flap rattle and knew he'd gone outside to do his morning duty and check the homestead. He was at least as good a guardian as a dog. He'd alert me to anything amiss even if I had forgotten to check things out myself by mentally extending my perception.

I did and there was nothing dangerous in the vicinity. I judged that Jefferson would be fine. He'd learned to steer clear of coyotes and cougars. There were also a few wolves and bears that had found their way into the area and he left them strictly alone.

I was pushing my mind out a little farther into the aether, searching the general energy level for problems, when I was suddenly interrupted. Liz slid closer to me and put her arm around my shoulder. Her other hand was between us and it suddenly found a sensitive part of my anatomy, and... Well, it's not necessary to tell everything.

A few minutes later, Michael started crying from the other room and we got up, arranged our clothes and began the morning routine.

During breakfast, we discussed what needed to be done. Liz and Michael would have to stay in Grand Lake at our homestead. Jefferson, for all his alien fighting ability, would have to stay with them. I couldn't see trying to carry him over the mountains on horseback. The whole task was going to be up to me.

I needed to get the place prepared for Liz to run. We had a lot of wood already cut, although not enough to last through the entire winter. The chickens and rabbits were usually her task to care for. The fowl created enough eggs that we used the extras for barter. The rabbits were just about self-sustaining now that it was moving into summer. I was satisfied that the livestock wouldn't be too much of a chore for her to handle by herself.

We'd rigged some movable hutches with wire cages attached and all you had to do was pull them along on their small wheels. The rabbits moved along inside without panic. They'd been through the process often and knew that after the brief movement, they'd have access to a fresh batch of grass. As soon as the hutch and cage was in place, they hopped eagerly around and began to graze on the untouched grass.

Rabbits are great. They produce more meat per acre than cattle and they produce more rabbits at a rapid rate. Just look up Fibonacci's formula and you'll see how fast they can reproduce.

The chickens were almost as easy. The only problem with the animals that required much care was the lesser predators that were attracted to them. Coyotes, foxes, raccoons, weasels, the odd Fisher-cat, and, once, a wolverine had all fallen to my .22 rifle. The darned things were always optimistically thinking that they could get an easy lunch at our place.

I had finally figured out how to place a mental barrier around the farmyard that would generally keep them out. It was an area of gradually increasing unease. As they approached, they would begin to sense fear and it would increase. Few of them came on in after I set that up. The ones that did found there was an actual justification for the fear.

I'd taught Liz how to do the barrier and she was working on it, but not really facile as yet. She made up her short-falling by being at least as good a shot with the little pump rifle as me.

We took inventory of the supplies we had on hand and concluded that she was well set. It wasn't as if she would be totally alone either. We did live out of town a few miles, but we had many friends in the area that would be happy to help out if she needed anything in my absence.

During the entire time we'd lived in Grand Lake, there had only been a few intrusions from the outside world. We knew that the Denver area and most of the front range was under the control of some warlord who mostly ensured peace as long as he got his way. His gang or tribe or whatever you want to call it had never come over the mountains. From what we heard, he had his hands full ruling the people that were left on the eastern slope.

Starvation had come quickly to the cities when the trucks stopped bringing food. Denver had lost almost all of its population in the big die-off. As a result, the warlord's land was sparsely populated and that meant that he had frequent problems with wandering tribes or migrants who raided his villages.

Despite the massive death count, lots of humans had survived the EMP. The few radios we managed to get going again told us that. People were gradually beginning to rebuild in various enclaves around the country and across the world. Kansas City seemed to be doing pretty well. The Kansas wheat farms were still producing, although at a level comparable to that of the nineteenth century. They had begun to build steam engines and lately had managed to get some oil wells producing again. I judged that things would be back to normal in about forty or fifty years, provided that the Pug-bears left us alone.

As for the monstrous Pug-bears, we understood that they'd all been killed. The ones left on Earth after the transporter network blew were strictly feral. They had shipped cases of the symbiont eggs to Earth, but the Pug-bears wouldn't eat them unless they were caged and forced to eat the things. The few intelligent Pug-bears had supervised the Pugs in that activity. The symbiont life-form eggs were not very viable. They would infect the Pug-bear only once out of several thousand eggs eaten. When an infection occurred, it resulted in the Pug-bear developing a large cranium to house the symbiont. The minds of the two creatures merged and the conjoined organism became capable of rational thought. Capable enough that they'd now completely dominated fourteen planets and were giving signs of trying to dominate ours once again.

The Pugs, the humanoids that I'd thought were the only aliens for a long time, were a warrior race that the Pug-bears dominated mentally. They had all died off soon after we'd destroyed their transporter network. They were biologically incompatible with our atmosphere and needed breathing masks and protection for their skin. When their respirators failed, they died. We hadn't been bothered by them for several years.

There was something that still puzzled me. I had searched the memories I'd accidentally ripped out of the Ancient-One as thoroughly as I could and I still only understood a smattering of its knowledge. I knew the Pugs weren't capable of creating technology. They were used mostly as slaves and soldiers by the Pug-bears. The Pug-bears didn't have the physical capability to manipulate things. They were all teeth and claws combined with a tough carapace, but they had no hands.

What puzzled me about the aliens was that I didn't know where they got their high level of technology. They had space-flight capability that was far better than man's. Their transporter network utilized quantum entanglement and torsion waves – things which we'd only just begun to understand – and their weapons included the anti-matter "eraser" gun and anti-matter bombs along with the poisoned glass splinter shooting gun, two of which we still had.

The splinter-shooters held what seemed to be an incredible number of shots, but we'd still been carefully preserving ours. Both magazines were down to about ten percent at this point and we kept them back, just in case a Pug-bear showed up. They were the only weapons, short of a fifty-caliber sniper rifle that would lay a Pug-bear out with one shot, as long as the poison splinter was placed right down the alien's gullet.

I decided that I'd have to go into town to let the Sheriff and some others know what I was going to do. After breakfast, Liz and I saddled my horse, "Paint." Not a very original or creative name, but it described him. He was about as colorful a pinto as there was in the area.

Waving goodbye to Liz and Michael, who was too busy pulling Jefferson's tail to respond, I set out for town.

CHAPTER 2

It didn't take Paint long to carry me into town. He crossed the creek, his hooves clacking on the water-worn stones and his legs splashing in the fast running, shallow water. As we crossed, I could see some brook trout hovering in the eddies near shore, waiting for an insect to land on the water. I glanced back at Liz and saw her waiving again. I could see her mouth open, but the gurgle and chuckle of the water kept me from hearing her shouted, "Goodbye!"

We took the old jeep trail and followed it into town, finally arriving at the town center. The first person I saw was William Smith.

He had showed up a couple of months past, claiming that he'd come over the pass from the area west of Vail. A couple of the dedicated downhill skiers in town had spoken with him and they thought that he didn't seem to know enough about Vail to have come from around there. It didn't matter, though. In this post-apocalyptic world, people sort of reinvented themselves and he wasn't the only one who had changed their background story.

He greeted me congenially and inquired about Liz and our homestead. He'd been nothing but innocuous in all of our interactions, but for some reason, I didn't have a good feeling about him. Perhaps it was due to the shifty feel of his energy field.

I should explain that my enhanced mental ability doesn't allow me to read thoughts accurately without others knowing about it. I can sense general energy fields, but in order to read a person's thoughts, I'd have to intrude in a way that they would consciously recognize. It's a lot easier to link with those with whom I have an emotional bond. Tapping into a stranger's conscious level of thought is difficult for me. Invading a stranger human's mind hadn't been difficult for the Ancient-One, but I thought that the Pug-bears naturally had very powerful psychic abilities. I believed that they must be be stronger that way than humans, even though I hadn't met any humans with my mental ability, at least as yet.

William said that the Sheriff was over at the Courthouse and I headed that way. As I rode off, he ingratiatingly said, "Tell Liz 'Hi' for me."

I nodded and thought, "As if she'd be even slightly interested in hearing from you!" His idea of friendliness just grated on me. He was over-familiar without any basis for it and I didn't like it. I also didn't like the way he looked at Liz. A couple of times I'd observed him looking covetously at her when he thought I wasn't watching.

When I got to the Courthouse, the Sheriff was just coming out. "Hi, Dec!" he greeted me with a smile.

"Hey, Dave! What's up today?"

"I'm getting tired of being called into court on account of Mrs. Perkins' chickens," he wiped his forehead with a stained handkerchief. "She keeps losing them to coyotes, but every time she claims that it's Ralph McKinley's dog. She keeps trying to get the judge to order me to put down the best varmint dog in the area!"

The Sheriff and Ralph McKinley had a kind of varmint hunting club. They'd get together one or two nights during the week and go out with their dogs to run various wildlife. Raccoons, mostly. The dogs didn't care. They just loved to chase things. Dave and Ralph didn't care either. I suspected that they mostly used it as an excuse to get drunk and stumble about in the woods. I just hoped that Dave didn't fall in a hole and break his neck some night. He was a great Sheriff, not given to getting too excited, but very effective at keeping the peace.

"Sheriff, I've got a favor to ask of you," I told him.

He turned serious, instantly, "You know that I'd do anything I can for you and your wife, Dec."

"Did you see that fireball that crossed the sky about ten o'clock last night?" I looked up and traced an imaginary line along the path the thing had taken.

"No, but I heard something about it from several people. A couple of the guys were coming out of the tavern and they were kinda excited about a meteor. I just thought they'd had too much to drink," he said, deprecatingly.

"Liz and I saw it cross the sky. I'm sure that it landed over around Estes Park. You know that was where the aliens landed on Earth originally," I was just stating a fact that I was sure he knew.

"Yep! I remember that's what you told us when you first got here," he recalled.

"OK. Well, I'm dead certain that wasn't a meteor. It was a spaceship that they sent back to the same place. There's a reason that they landed there in the first place and it has to do with some kind of radioactive ore deposit deep underground. I believe that this landing will re-establish their matter transporter link to Earth and, if I'm right, we'll shortly see them coming back in force."

It was asking a lot of him to believe that I was correct, but he knew enough about me to realize that I wasn't joking about it.

"You're kidding, aren't you – No, I can see that you're not!" was his response.

"No, Sheriff, I wish I was joking, but I'm afraid that we're going to be up to our necks in aliens unless something is done."

"What can we do? The last time, only a few of the Pug-bears showed up around here. Are you thinking that there will be more? Will they try to take over and what kind of force will they have?" He took his hat off and mopped his brow again.

"That's just the problem. I don't know for sure that they'll bother us in force very soon, but I do know that the damned things have taken over at least fourteen planets and eradicated almost all of the life on them."

"Wait a minute! How could you know such a thing? It doesn't seem likely, now, does it?" He looked at me carefully with his law-enforcement expression.

I knew that I needed to be very precise with what I said next. I'd told him before about my encounter with the Ancient-One, but I hadn't gone into details about the mental battle we'd fought and the resultant effect on my mind.

"OK. Dave, I haven't told you this yet, because it sounds unbelievable, but when I killed the Pug-bear's leader, he was trying to dominate my mind with some kind of mental linkage." He nodded as he recalled the story. "When I found the strength to resist, it shocked him and he accidentally opened his memories to me."

"Well, but you couldn't have learned much in that short a time, could you?"

"That's a good question. The time was short, but thought is very fast. What happened was that a large number of his memories, I think maybe all of them, leaked into my subconscious and were stored. All I have to do is to ask the right question now and I can usually recall enough information from him to answer it."

"But, how do you know which question to ask?" Dave was sharper than he looked, no question about that.

"That's the issue. I often don't. I don't know what I know until something cues the recall, but here's the point. I do know that the aliens are deadly and mean us no good. Even if they let some of us live, we'll be no better than slaves at best and probably more like beef cattle, since they will eat humans along with just about anything else that moves."

"We've got to do something about this!"

"That's what I was getting to," I responded. "I'm preparing to go against them again."

"Well, what do you want me to do?" he asked, getting back to specifics.

"I'm going over the pass to see if I can't stop them from coming back," I said. "I'd just like you to keep an eye on Liz and Michael. They're going to stay at our place. It's too dangerous for me to risk her going with me and she has to take care of the boy anyway."

"That's no problem! You know I'll keep an eye on them. You've got a lot of friends in this town and we've learned that we either stand together or we won't survive," he responded.

"Times have been tough, haven't they?"

"Yeah! I've got to admit that I didn't believe everything you told us when you first showed up, but things have gone just about the way you said," he shook his head in regret.

It was true. Times had been tough. We lived in an isolated community and we'd had to develop our own food sources. There was no way anyone would send supplies to us. There wasn't really even anyone who knew or cared where we were.

"Listen, Dec, are you sure you should go alone? I can get some of the boys and we can – " he started.

I held up my hand and interrupted him, "No, you can't. You're the Sheriff here and the town needs you and all of the able-bodied men available for defense. I know that no one has attacked us in the last few years, but there's always the possibility that the Eastern Slope Warlord or some other gang will decide to move into the North Park area. I'd like the help, but I'd rather you and the guys stayed here and protected the town and my family. Besides, I'm experienced at fighting the creatures and most of the people here aren't."

He bridled a bit over that, "Now, hold on a minute. We've killed our share of Pug-bears."

"I know you have, but none of them have been the smart kind and, if they're coming back, that's what will come along with a lot of their soldiers. Those are the man-like ones I call Pugs. You haven't seen them, but they're tough and hard to kill and the big thing is, they can shoot back. The Pug-bears can't."

"OK. You've made your point. I'll just make it my business to keep a close eye on your place while you're gone."

"Thanks, Dave! You're a real friend. I knew I could count on you!" I turned Paint and rode off towards the general store. I'd promised Liz that I'd get some woolen fabric so she could work on winter clothes. You don't know how convenient it is to simply buy clothes off the rack until they aren't there any longer. Grand Lake had run out of garments a couple of years ago. Fortunately, a couple of the locals had developed fairly sizable flocks of sheep and we'd all learned to make do with woolen clothes. They didn't even itch much due to the colder climate in the mountains.

We'd learned that wool is a great survival fabric. You can get it wet and it still keeps your body heat in. Cotton will kill you in sub-zero temperatures if it gets wet. Wool won't; it will keep you warm and, even if not totally comfortable, it will keep you from freezing. We all wore wool shirts, pants and socks as a matter of necessity.

While I was selecting some cloth in the store, I overheard a couple of young women talking. They were from the far side of town and I didn't know their names although I'd seen them a few times. They gave the overall impression of less prosperity than the average. I mean that, given the circumstances, we were all poor in comparison to where we'd been prior to the alien attack, but these two had threadbare clothes and their moccasins were just about on their last mile. One of them had holes in both toes where the leather had given out. This was not usual in town. Most of the people took good care of their clothes and equipment, so these two stood out.

Anyway, they were chatting excitedly about William Smith. One of them seemed to have romantic aspirations for him and the other was encouraging her.

"He's just so handsome that I could just die when he looks at me," she said.

"I'll bet that he'd be a good provider, too. He told me that he always has meat on his table," her friend chipped in.

"I hope that he asks me to the next dance. He told me he would," the first enthused.

The clerk who was assisting me just shook her head and spoke quietly to me, "Those girls don't have the first idea about that guy. I've heard that he's made a run at every single woman in town, especially if they have some nice property. Neither of those two has any prospects and their fathers are both kind of shiftless, so they won't have anything that would really attract him." She was shaking her head in disparagement as she spoke.

"Well, Molly, I don't know them or their fathers, so I can't say, but I've been keeping my eye on Smith. His story didn't seem square when he first arrived in town and I can't say that he's been an outstanding addition to the community, for all his talk about his hunting," I was, perhaps, a little over-doing it. He hadn't been a liability to the town and he did bring in the odd deer or elk. He worked mostly as a hand for one of the sheepherders and didn't have a place of his own.

"Nothing good will come to those girls if they get to hanging out with him," she said as she measured my selection. "That will be five dollars, Dec."

We had continued to use the old currency. There wasn't any government backing it, as far as we knew and the paper and coins were worthless, but they'd been mostly that way before the attack. It was a convenience that allowed us to keep track of transactions. We simply pretended that the currency had value and it did, as long as people were willing to trade it for food and supplies. Of course, we'd also take food, gold, ammunition, and anything else of value in barter, but we always tried to reduce the transaction to dollars and cents to make it easy to balance out.

"Here you go, Molly, and thank you," I said as I handed her five silver dollars and left.

On the way back, I rode past the school. It was in session and I could see Nancy standing in front of the chalkboard through the window. She and Mike's decision to stay in Grand Lake before the EMP had proven to be a great benefit to the town. They had taken over the school and the local children were getting a great education as a result.

She looked out the window and I waved, not expecting a response, but she waved back. I could see some of her students turn curious faces to the window as she did.

It wasn't long before I got back to our place.

Chapter 3

Liz and Michael were having lunch by the time I'd unsaddled Paint and gotten him settled in the corral. Jefferson had complicated things by greeting me and parading around between my feet and rubbing on the horse's fetlocks. Paint didn't mind. He and Jefferson were friends and the cat often spent hours in the barn, largely, I suspect, due to the mice that made their hazardous living gleaning pieces of grain that the horses spilled.

I went up the steps, stomped the dust off my boots, and entered to find my wife and son sitting at the table. A third plate waited for me.

Over lunch, we discussed our preparations for my upcoming odyssey. I'd decided to dress in my worn buckskins and try to look like a wandering mountain man. I figured that if I didn't look prosperous and also gave off an aura of competence, most likely, I'd be judged as not being worth the hassle of trying to rob. Liz agreed and we went on to talk about how she'd manage while I was gone.

After we'd eaten, Michael and I went through my kit and packed the things I'd need. Warm clothes, a compass, a topo map, sleeping bag, fire starter, my Sig and a couple of boxes of ammo along with all eight magazines. I decided on taking the .300 Win Mag. I didn't have much ammo, but the thing was a great shooter and easily reached out to ridiculous distances accurately. It was just a little too much gun with too much recoil for Liz to use anyway. I could have taken one of our M-4s, but those just wouldn't kill Pug-bears. I also rejected the old bolt-action .338 as too heavy and slow. As an afterthought, I took down my snowshoes and set them beside the door. It had been a cold winter and the snow wasn't off the peaks yet.

Over Liz's protests, I left her both splinter-shooters. I pointed out that she could use them to defend the cabin and they'd easily kill aliens if any showed up. Besides, where would I, as an indigent mountain man, come up with such a weapon? They'd cast some suspicion on my cover, assuming that I needed cover. I convinced her that I could always scavenge one of the alien weapons if the opportunity presented itself.

I busied myself for the rest of the day, cleaning, rubbing waterproofing into the leather, and arranging my gear for easy packing. I finished my work in the early evening and spent the time after supper playing with Michael. Liz would occasionally give me a rather forlorn look, but we didn't discuss my upcoming journey or my low probability of survival and success.

I had another restless night and so did she. We finally fell asleep, huddled together under the down comforter and content with each other's closeness.

Dawn finally arrived. Liz had gotten up and had coffee on by the time I'd gathered my things. As we ate, I tried to memorize everything, because it promised to be my last family dinner for an unknown length of time.

It wasn't more than an hour later that Paint and I were crossing the creek. I'd had a little trouble with Jefferson. He had given every indication that he was going to come with us. He obviously recognized that I was preparing for a lengthy journey and he did his best to complicate things, pacing around and yowling periodically. The yowls got on both my nerves and Paint's. The horse actually seemed glad to get across the creek and away from the cat.

I thought that Jefferson was going to try to swim across the quick-running stream for a moment, but Liz and Michael had walked down with me. She grabbed him, just as he was preparing to make the plunge and I urged Paint to cross.

I paused as we came up the bank on the far side of the ford and turned in the saddle to wave one last goodbye. Paint took that exact moment to try and shake some of the water off and it kind of ruined my seat. Michael laughed and Liz smiled and that gave me a good mental picture to hold in my mind while I was away.

Within an hour, we were heading up the road past the ranger station and moving into the park. The road hadn't been maintained since the EMP and it was falling apart. The asphalt was cracked and pot-holed and weeds were growing up through the cracks. Nevertheless, it gave us a slightly more level path, and Paint gradually wended his way around the obstacles as we began the long climb.

I'd hoped to reach the top and be partway down the other side by dusk, but I ran into an unfortunate complication. The snow was packed high and the pass was still blocked. At about the ten thousand foot level, I pulled up. My horse had been making heavy going of it for the last ninety minutes and I knew he wasn't going to be able to continue. The snow was just too deep. It was also getting too dark to go on due to a front that was coming over the front range. We paused in the wind as I looked around at the desolate scene. After a moment, I led him off into some low trees and made a camp for the night.

I figured that I'd have to send him back down tomorrow, but I didn't want him wandering around in the dark. Paint was a smart horse and I knew that he'd go right back to the barn. Life there was too good for him to ignore. The thought of regular feedings of cracked corn (hard to get in our valley, but worthwhile) would be enough to ensure his return.

I tied him to a spruce and stomped a level area out in the snow. Then I unpacked my kit and set about gathering squaw wood for a small fire. I had a tarp and my sleeping bag and didn't need the fire to last all night, but I did want a warm supper and some hot tea.

In short order, the flames were crackling and I had a small pan full of snow melting. The wind had picked up and there were snowflakes on the breeze, so I was glad I'd stopped. I fed Paint and then myself, then got my sleeping arrangement set.

I gathered some fresh branches and laid them out into a rough bed. Then I spread the tarp and laid my bag out on it. Taking off my boots, I climbed in the bag and sat watching the fire, my rifle at my side. My Sig was, as it always is, close at hand inside the bag.

The flames died down and the snow came in more heavily as the night progressed. The wind was blowing up a half-gale, but most of it was above the spruces. I'd picked a spot where they were thick and the heavily needled branches shielded me from most of the storm. Paint slept standing up and everything was peaceful, until sometime in the small hours of the night.

I awoke instantly as Paint snorted. I didn't sit up, but lay there, surreptitiously putting my hand out on my rifle. As I grasped the weapon, I pushed my senses out into the aether. I was immediately aware of a presence there and the signature was definitely feline.

As I worked on sensing the creature, I gradually resolved the signals I was getting to an area to the south of my camp. That was the way I'd come into the trees and the sensation of stealthy approach was localized along my path.

The problem with mental contact is that you don't always recognize the source. Contrary to what you'd think, animals are somewhat indistinct in their mental signatures. Deer and elk give off generalized browsing and vegetarian auras with timidity and caution mixed in. Predators, on the other hand, are a little more difficult. It's relatively easy to tell that they're interested in hunting and killing prey, but it's harder to tell exactly what they are.

An animal doesn't know that it's a "deer" or a "wolf." It does have a sense of self in relation to other creatures, but, if you could read its mind, you'd understand that its personal identification doesn't have elements that relate to human categories. It only knows that it's predator or prey and aggressive or timid.

A dog, even the smallest Yorkie, thinks it's every bit as tough as a wolf. The wolf may give off a bit more stealthiness, I don't know how else to describe it. They're more sneaky, but so are coyotes and foxes. I found it really difficult to tell them apart based on their mental auras.

The sensation I was now getting was that of a cat, but, aside from the fact that I knew it wasn't Jefferson, it could have been a house cat, a lynx or bobcat, or a cougar. It approached and I gradually understood that it was interested in Paint. That level of interest keyed my understanding and I realized that it was a cougar.

It was suspicious of my scent, but it was hungry and the horse smelled like a good meal. I read in its thoughts that it had eaten horseflesh before and had found it good. It was stealthily preparing to attack in a manner that it had calculated held the highest probability of success. The darkness and gusty wind served its purpose admirably. I could sense that it was confident that it couldn't be detected as it slunk nearer.

Now that I knew what I faced, I wanted to frighten it off permanently and not have to worry about it sneaking around for the rest of the night. It knew that horses and men didn't have the night vision ability it had and it depended on not being visible. I thought that I could frighten it off fairly easily.

I began to push out a general feeling of unease and danger into the surrounding energy field. I built up the projection, trying as I did to bypass Paint. I didn't want to frighten him into the jaws of the cougar. He shifted uneasily as I created the sense of a large bear, just awakening and angry.

I could tell the cougar was beginning to feel a deep sense of unease. The prey that it had marked was already the property of a bear. It might try to face down a bear, but it knew that it had no chance against one. I kept pushing my energy into the aether and suddenly, I became aware that the cougar's energy field was gradually fading. It was softly retreating, using the gusts of wind as cover for its moves. I kept up the bear projection and then tried to implant it into my mind where it would reside at a low level with only a minimal conscious effort.

The cat was gone and, I hoped, not coming back for the rest of the night. I sent a mental probe out to it and realized that it was now quite far away and moving out across the valley, searching for other prey. I relaxed gradually. The wind continued gusting and I finally went back to sleep.

Chapter 4

Morning came early. The wind had fallen during the night, but the snow had kept up for a while and I had a couple of inches covering the half of the tarp that I'd drawn over my sleeping bag. I kicked off the tarp and set up, shaking the snow off as I did.

Paint stirred and shook, in turn, sending snow flying off his back. Our paths would part today, but first I probed the energy field surrounding us, finding nothing to cause alarm. It seemed clear all the way back to our homestead and I placed the image of the warm barn and cracked corn into his mind. He snorted and perked his ears. I could see that he was hungry and the idea of corn was very tempting.

I climbed out of my bag and pulled the halter over his ears, taking the time to scratch behind them, affectionately. While I did, I reinforced his idea of heading for the barn, then I let him go.

He took a few tentative steps back towards the road, pushing through the hardened snowdrifts under the trees. As he reached the road, he paused and looked back at me where I stood in the embrace of the spruces. I mentally pushed him down the road and without another glance he turned and waded through the deep snow to the asphalt, heading down the hill.

Returning to my tarp, I restarted the fire and cooked a couple of pieces of bacon that I'd brought. As I did, I mentally followed the horse to ensure that he continued back. I checked again after I'd eaten and cleaned my utensils in the snow. He was a long way down the road and it seemed likely that he was speeding up.

Then I had a sudden thought. What would Liz think when he came back alone? I crouched in front of the small fire and concentrated on her. She was asleep, but presently she was in touch with me on some half-sleeping, half-waking level. I did my best to convey the idea that I was fine and had sent Paint back. She seemed to understand. I finished by projecting a sense of love and concern for her and Michael, then withdrew from the deep level of contact.

I gathered my kit and heaped snow on the coals of my breakfast fire. It took me a moment to strap on the snowshoes and then the work began. I had to climb a couple of thousand feet through the snow and I wanted to be down the other side and into the tree line before night fell. It wouldn't do to remain exposed above the trees overnight. It might turn out okay or not. The weather at this time of year was unpredictable, but last night's snow had warned me that I shouldn't take chances.

I'm going to skip over the next few hours. They were unpleasant, involving a lot of walking, resting, gasping for breath, and curses about the snow. It was packed underneath and last night's snow had served to cover up hollows and icy patches. I had a devil of a time avoiding stepping in a hole and the ice made it harder, causing me to slip at the most inconvenient times.

I was more than ready to quit climbing by noon. The day was clear, so that was a blessing. I paused and took off my pack in order to pull out some jerky that was stored inconveniently in a back pocket. Stuffing a huge bite in my mouth, I looked around.

I'd been focused so closely on taking the next step and then the next that I'd neglected to notice how high I was getting. When I looked around I realized with pleasure that I was at the top of the pass and only had a few hundred yards to go before I started down the other side.

I shuffled along with the bow-legged stride the snowshoes necessitated and was shortly looking down the eastern side of the pass. I paused to consider my course of action. If I continued down the main road, I would probably miss the site where the lander had come down. I expected to find it close to the ridge where we'd previously found the transporter that led to Titan. A vague sense of disquiet intruded into my mind as I thought about the possibilities.

Finally, realizing that I was getting more and more uneasy, I paused and tried to open my senses to the general energy field. As soon as I did, the source of my disquiet became obvious. I hadn't sensed it earlier due to being mostly exhausted from the climb and simply concentrating on putting one foot in front of the other.

There was a concentration of humans about three miles away from me. They were somewhat to the east and down about two thousand feet. That was just about where I judged the lander would be.

This was going to be harder than I'd hoped. I hadn't planned on having other people around, but it looked like the Eastern Slope Warlord's gang had seen the landing and had come up to investigate. The thought patterns that I was sensing were a combination of curious and aggressive. It wasn't a nice kind of aggressiveness, either.

After thinking about the situation, I decided that it would be better for me to head eastward. To accomplish what I wanted was going to be a real chore. I needed to come across a huge snowfield on the northeast side of Old Fall River Road and pass Marmot Point. Then I'd have to climb a steep spur of the mountain, cross through a heavily wooded area, and eventually descend to Chapin Creek. I could follow the creek until the trees closed in and then I'd be near the end of Chapin Creek trail. I presumed the trail would be marked by the Park Service, although the condition of the markers at this point was likely to be poor.

Assuming I could find the trail, I'd reach Chapin Pass and be able to head south. Then I'd be more or less due east of the location where we'd found the alien installation four years ago. I'd try to come up to it from that direction.

This approach gave me, I hoped, plausible deniability. The people I'd sensed were undoubtedly surrounding the lander and I was going to have to interact with them in order to accomplish my goal of sabotaging the aliens' transporters again. With any luck, I'd be able to enlist some of the people to help, but whether they would prove to be helpful or hostile, I still wanted to give no clue that I'd come over the pass from Grand Lake. They'd left us alone for the past few years and I wanted that to continue.

Getting across the snowfield was a chore. My foresight in bringing my snowshoes was something that proved to be very helpful. It was mostly hard snow covered with a couple of inches of wet, fresh snow, just as it had been coming up the west side of Trail Ridge. I took my time with the traverse and checked with a spruce pole that I'd cut to make sure there were no buried crevasses. I didn't want to fall due to sheer carelessness.

After a couple of hours, I reached the tree-covered ridge. It was steep, but by zig-zagging through the forest, I eventually came to the top. Then I had to work my way down to Chapin Creek. That part of the journey was dicey. It was even steeper and the snow was wetter on the south side of the ridge. The net effect was that I was constantly in danger of slipping out of control. I found myself grabbing spruce branches for assistance about every third step. After a lot of work, I came out of the trees onto a steep and barren slope that led down to the creek.

It looked like the trees had been repeatedly scoured away in this area by avalanches and I kept a wary eye upslope as I descended. I needn't have worried, though. The underlying snow was icy and the deposit from last night's fall wasn't thick enough to create any avalanche danger. I finally got down to the creek and was pleased to find that it was running and even had a few stretches of open water in the steeper sections.

I lumped along, clambering over boulders and fallen trees that were racked up beside the creek. It seemed like it took me forever to descend the thousand feet or so to where the trees closed in on the creek. Apparently, the avalanches hadn't reached down this far, since the terrain flattened out. Once I got into the trees another problem arose. I couldn't find the trail! I cast around a bit, but there was just no sign of it. How quickly man's marks on the wild fade!

There was nothing for it, but to follow the slope downward, so I did. In another thousand feet, I came to what looked like a reasonable ascent to a small pass I saw above me to the south. Climbing it, I finally did find a marker set into the south side of a boulder. It said "Chapin Pass Trail" and I knew I was in the right place. I crested the ridge and was able to see a series of rocks that looked like they were in the right location.

There was another, more obvious cue. I could see the smoke from a fire or fires rising over the ridge from the far side. I figured that whoever it was had made a temporary camp there. It was almost certain that the people I'd find would-be gang members, or whatever they called themselves.

Thinking ahead, I paused while I found a crack between some large rocks to store my backpack for later retrieval, then I started off again on my downhill hike. I was working my way around a series of boulders when a rifle shot plowed into the snow a few feet to my left. I stopped and held up my hands and waited.

It didn't take too long before I saw a couple of raggedly dressed men coming out of the rocks about a hundred yards away. They had me covered with rifles and I assumed that there was probably another one or two that were providing back-up from some hidden location. It didn't matter. I wasn't there to fight.

When they got close enough to talk in the light breeze, the uglier one of the two shouted, "Who are you and what d'ya want?"

I called back, "Name's Dec. I'm just coming down out of the high country and heading for Estes. I've about had it with this crazy weather."

Both of them laughed, "There ain't anything at Estes anymore! What kind of ignorant fool would head there? Everyone around these parts was et up by the aliens years ago."

I tried to look surprised as I replied, "I didn't know. I came out of Wyoming this spring and I've been working my way south through the mountains. I thought I'd get down to Denver for the summer."

"Well, if you're going to Denver, that's where we're from." They laughed and eyed each other surreptitiously. "You'll have to come with us. We've got a camp over the hill by the spaceship that come down the other night. You'll have to talk to the Warlord's assistant, though." They paused and one elbowed the other while they both laughed again as if at some private joke.

I didn't know what was so funny, but I answered, "OK. That's no problem with me. I've got no grudge against anybody around here, so I'm happy to talk."

"You might as well save your breath," the one with the ready elbow answered. "You'll have to square accounts with the Red-Head and that usually takes some doing. Follow us and don't start acting funny."

From their general look and the level of their conversation, they obviously weren't on the high end of the IQ bell curve. Even so, I didn't want to give them any ideas. I judged it best to try and seem friendly, "You going to let me keep my rifle?"

"Yeah, you can carry it, for now, I got enough to carry. But, keep your hands off it; you're covered from a couple of locations," the smaller one answered. They seemed confident in their backup.

We hiked down to the ridge-back and around to the downhill side. I remembered the area well, even though I'd only seen it once. There were still some signs of the transporter explosion, broken rocks, and debris. I could even see a bit of the door frame where it had been set into the rocks.

A little farther down was an open area and the aliens' lander was there. It wasn't at all what I'd thought it would be. Instead of looking like an engineered spaceship, it appeared to be slightly organic. It was covered in some dull-black material that didn't reflect light so that it looked sooty. It was as if it were covered with lamp-black. And the shape! It wasn't entirely smooth but had ridges and coils of unknown function crossing the roughly dome-like object.

I started to head towards it, but they stopped me. "You'll have to get straight with the Red-Head 'fore ya get anywhere near that thing."

The other added, "Yeah! You better be convincing about where you're from and what you're doin' here. She ain't in a real good mood this morning."

"Why would that be," I wondered, more to keep them talking than curious. They'd already given me some good information and I hoped for more. The mental energy field in the camp area was confused and gave off equal parts of fear and hostility and aggression. I couldn't get any useful sensation beyond that.

"Ain't nothin' she's tried that can open that thing up. It just sits there grinding," the ugly one answered.

"Grinding?" That aroused my curiosity.

"Yeah. It makes a kind of grinding noise. You can hear it if you put your ear against the boulders around here," was the answer.

"OK," I paused and thought, "Maybe it's grinding up rocks or drilling."

The instant I said "drilling" I knew that was what the thing was doing. My Ancient-One memories told me that the lander was equipped to drill down to the radioactive deposit in order to extract ore so that it could power up the transporter it was carrying. The process was automatic and was controlled by a series of fairly simple relays and a low-order computer system. I didn't think their cybernetics was on a par with ours, or, I should say, the way ours used to be.

My thinking about the lander was abruptly interrupted as we approached the fire. There was a large clot of men standing around, all carrying weapons ranging from rifles to swords and spears. There was a sudden, sharp exclamation from the middle of the group and the standing men scrambled aside, leaving me facing a beautiful, red-headed woman.

She was dressed in some good quality mountaineering gear and from that, I judged that the supplies in Denver hadn't run out yet. Despite the rather shapeless down jacket she had on, I could see that she was about my age and in good – no, great physical condition. She would have been a pleasant sight, except for the angry frown that was displayed on her face.

Chapter 5

I stopped and waited as the red-headed woman approached. She had incredibly clear, green eyes, but they weren't welcoming.

"Who are you?" she demanded.

She had an air about her of control and authority as if she wasn't used to being denied. I found this a challenge but realized that she'd undoubtedly met this attitude from a lot of men in the past. She'd probably developed a mechanism to deal with the rebellious male ego, so I took a different approach from the one that I'd been planning on. If I read her correctly, she was intelligent and intensely curious about the lander.

I smiled and explained why I had come down from the mountains.

"I saw the fireball caused by the spaceship the other night and I realized that I had to come down here and see if I could stop the aliens from attacking us again." There was a gasp of collective amazement from the group.

The woman drew back a bit and then stepped forward, "How do you know this thing?" She pointed at it and asked in a testing manner, "Do you think it's something that 'the aliens' sent?"

"It's a long story, but I'm sure they're trying to come back and finish the job they started. Their goal is to kill all of us and take over the planet."

"That's not very likely, Mister! We know them better than that! They came here to try and help us elevate our civilization," she put her hands on her hips.

That was new! I had to know where it was coming from. "What do you mean, they're here to help us? How do you know that?" I asked.

"We rescued one of the big ones and he's told us everything," was the amazing answer.

"How does he talk to you?" I was coming to a surprising conclusion but wanted more information before I decided what to do.

"With his mind, of course!" She tossed her head and her hair shifted, spilling over her right shoulder.

I carefully probed her mind and encountered no barrier at all! It was shocking at first, but I realized that extended contact with an intelligent Pug-bear could result in the lack of normal mental barriers. Taking a chance with her, I formed a mental statement and sent it into her mind, "So, he talks to you like this?"

She staggered back, making a warding motion with her arm. There was a general stir and clicking of safety's coming off as the men pointed various weapons at me. I held up my hands in a non-aggressive way.

"No!" she recovered quickly and motioned them to put their guns down. "We're not going to kill this one, not yet, anyway."

That wasn't very reassuring, but it promised me some kind of opening for discussion.

"Take his weapons away and bring him over to my tent," she ordered.

Rather than fight a useless fight, I handed one of my captors my rifle and my forty-five. I hated to let the Sig go, but there was no choice at the moment. I looked the man in the face and with a mental emphasis that let him know I was dead serious, I said, "I expect them back in good condition. I'm pretty attached to both of them."

He took them in a moderately respectful manner. I judged that was the best I could hope for. A couple of the fellows that had been standing near the woman stepped forward. They were both wearing football helmets and they looked like NFL players. Both were huge, towering over my six-foot-two with inches to spare.

One of them cracked an astonishing bright small which lit up his dark face, "You-all best come along with us with no trouble. It'll be alright, you'll see."

I appreciated the reassurance. He seemed friendly, but his friend had a frown on his face that drew his blond eyebrows together in a threatening manner. I held up my hands to show that they were now empty and followed them through the crowd to the far side of the fire.

There were a number of tents set up in a more level area there and they led me to the largest. The white man held open one of the flaps and I walked into the large tent. Their red-headed leader had composed herself on a portable camp chair, sitting as if she were a queen on a throne. I stepped through the door and stopped, waiting for her to speak.

"How..., how did you do that?" she was plainly nervous about my mental communication. "No one but the Master can speak that way." She paused, then continued, "What are you? Are you one of them?"

She looked at me closely and then answered her own question, "No. You're just a man. How can you do that? Did they train you?"

Projecting a reassuring energy field cautiously, I answered her question with a question of my own, "Do you worship the Master?"

She jumped up, her eyes flashing, "No! He needs our help and we help him..."

Her voice trailed off as if some memory was trying to come to the fore in her mind.

Sensing that her thoughts were open, I inserted my mind into hers again, "You help him because you can't help yourselves. You find that you want to do what he says, correct?"

She didn't notice that I was communicating mentally now. Her thought-stream filled with images of the Pug-bear. It lived in Denver and was a kind of second leader to their tribe. They looked up to it and, here I shuddered mentally, they fed it prisoners found guilty of capital offenses.

The Pug-bear was working to guide the tribe's leader, the Eastern Slope Warlord, in a quest to dominate as much territory as possible. She was in awe of the creature but disliked its intrusions into her mind.

I thought it over and realized that the alien had to have acquired its symbiont while on Earth. That's the way it worked. The symbionts couldn't travel through the transporters without dying. A Pug-bear could, but it would come out the other side without its passenger. That meant that Pug-bears had to come to Earth in a lander in order to preserve their intelligence or they had to eat symbiont eggs while here. One out of several thousand eggs would hatch and embed in their brain, eventually yielding a high level of an alien-sort of rationality to the creature. The one that her people had saved must have arrived as a feral Pug-bear that gained its rationality on Earth. That would mean that it didn't have the complete set of knowledge about their culture that an older one might have. It very well may have decided to assist the Warlord, not knowing about its species' invasion plans and goals for dominating planets.

"Look, I'm a friend. I know about these creatures and learned to communicate from their greatest leader years ago. I can help you with the spaceship," I sent, adding a reassuring emotional overtone to the message.

As I did, she took a deep breath and I could sense that she'd decided to try and work with me. Her previous hostility was gone, leaving just a sense of hardened aggressiveness, which I judged was her way of dealing with men who might challenge her position.

"I was sent up here with all of these fighters to try and open the spaceship. The Master thinks it is very important to him. He doesn't want it damaged and he wants it operational, but I don't know what to do. Nothing we've tried has had any effect on it and none of my men are any help whatsoever!"

Her attitude had ranged from querulous to anger as she went on.

"I've got to get it open and running somehow. Nobody even knows what it does, but we've got to get it going. If we don't, the Warlord will be very disappointed in us and it won't be good," she added.

I got a quick mental glimpse of a prisoner tied to a wooden frame and being whipped. Obviously, the Warlord wasn't the patient kind.

"I know what the spaceship does and I've got an idea about why it won't open yet," I told her. "It has got to reach a source of power and it's drilling down through the rocks to access some uranium that is buried deep in the mountainside. Once it reaches that, it will extract what it needs to power up and it will open then." She was listening carefully and I added, "but, I might be able to open it sooner if you'd like."

She considered, "If you can open it now and you know what it does, it would be a great help to me. But, first, how do I know I can trust you? And, how do you know how to open the thing?"

I'd broken through her normal defenses and she was being open with me. It was an entirely reasonable doubt that she was expressing, so I answered in a reasonable way, "I'm familiar with their technology and may be able to see something you missed that will allow me to open it. As for trust, you don't know me, but I'll bet that you have a sense that I'm trustworthy."

It was cheating, but I did it anyway. Trying not to be detected, I carefully inserted a sense of trust and friendship into her subconscious as I spoke. I didn't like to do it. I'd only previously communicated with Liz in this fashion and it felt as if I was being too intimate with this strange woman. I felt like I was somehow being unfaithful to my wife.

The tactic seemed to work. She sighed and stood up, "Let's go out and see if you can figure out how to open the thing."

Since I'd already pushed emotions into her subconscious, I figured that I might as well go on with the exercise. I inserted a sense of foreboding into her mind and explained "I'll need my weapons. There might be one of the enemy inside. They've been known to hitch rides in the Master's ships."

This was totally false, but I wanted my guns in case it came to a parting of the ways and also in case the transporter started and a bunch of Pugs came through. My intent was to convince her that I was watching out for the "Master" and also to convince her that there was some danger involved.

"OK, but I'm going to have Ted and Frank watch you closely," she responded.

We stepped out and she snapped her fingers as if she were calling a pair of watchdogs, "Oh, boys! Come over here and watch him. We're going to look at the spaceship."

The two helmeted men trotted over from the fire and we made our way to the matte-black, slightly organic-looking lander. On the way, I collected my rifle and pistol. Their weight felt reassuring.

As we approached the device, I could feel a grinding vibration coming through the rock beneath my feet. The thing was drilling down in some fashion. It had been doing so since it landed and was probably near the ore deposit by now.

We stopped and looked at the thing and I asked her, "How have you tried to get inside so far?"

"We've pushed and poked everything, but nothing happens," she answered. "We even tried cutting and shooting it, but nothing scratches the surface, not even the biggest rifle. Everything just bounces off."

Ted frowned darkly and added, "That's right. I hit it as hard as I could with my sword and I didn't even leave a mark." He paused and then added, "It almost broke my hand, though."

Frank snickered at that but said nothing.

We walked around the lander, looking at the striations and rope-like curls covering its surface. On the side away from the fire, I noticed a slight depression with a shallow slot beside it. For some reason, the slot reminded me of Liz showing me how to open one of the Pugs' door locks. As I remembered, I stuck my thumb and index finger into it and spread them apart.

There was a hiss of pressure-equalizing and a bad smell as the surface in the depression slid backward into the hull of the lander. My companions jumped back in alarm and I drew my pistol, just in case. As I did, Frank pulled out a well-oiled, three-foot-long sword. It looked small in his hand and he pointed it at me, "Don't try anything funny or I'll have to hit you with this."

I nodded and waited for the door to finish swinging back. It was difficult to see into the shadowed opening. The matte-black of the surface blended smoothly into the shadow and I couldn't be sure that the door was completely through with its movement. Then I heard a small click indicating that the mechanism had completed its cycle. I stepped forward into the opening and waited while my eyes adjusted.

The three of them crowded in behind me as I waited. There was plenty of space in the interior, although the roof was low. The sound from the men speaking outside was muffled. Perhaps the matte-finish of the outside was used inside also and it deadened the space. I waited to be able to see.

Chapter 6

My eyes gradually became accustomed to the darkness inside the lander. As they did, I realized that the sunlight reflected off the snow outside faded out as it touched the walls inside the doorway. It didn't offer any illumination and it was as if the walls just sucked the light in and absorbed it.

I carefully extended my arms and felt the surface of the inner walls. It was surprisingly smooth and must have been covered with some form of nano-coating. My hand slid on the wall easily as I inched forward, carefully moving my feet as I attempted not to run into or trip over anything. The others stayed where they were, just inside the entrance.

As I progressed deeper into the shadow, my eyes finally adjusted and I realized that there was a faint glow coming from directly ahead of me. I moved toward it and passed through a doorway. As I did, the interior lighted up with a faint bluish glow. It wasn't very bright, but it did offer enough illumination for me to be able to see where I was.

The surroundings were similar to the exterior of the lander. There were ropes and knots of organic-looking tubes and structures on the bulkheads and ceiling. The ceiling was low, barely offering me enough space to stand upright. The two guards would undoubtedly have to crouch in an uncomfortable position in here.

Just as I thought of them, Frank called to me to stop and wait for them. They groped their way in and then exclaimed as their eyes revealed the strange structures inside.

"Wow! This looks like something out of a movie I saw where those alien things killed everyone!" Ted exclaimed.

"Let's explore this place and look for something that looks kind of like an elevator door," I instructed. I'd already extended my mental senses and found no sign of anything living in the interior. "It's probably safe enough, as long as you don't accidentally activate any controls or break anything."

"OK, Mama!" Ted said, sneering at my caution.

"Knock it off!" the woman said and he shut his mouth with a snap. She certainly had the men under control. I assumed from this that the Warlord backed her implicitly.

"You know, you never told me your name," I said to her.

"It's not important that you know, but just for convenience, you can call me 'Ms. Ní Mhaolagáin.'"

I stopped and turned towards her, "Despite my first name, I'm not good with Gaelic and that's too much of a mouthful to use in an emergency. What do your men call you?"

She blushed. The light was dim and blue and made it difficult to see, but I could distinctly make out the color change across her face.

"They call me 'Red' I guess," she said quietly.

"That's not very flattering. Do you have a first name?"

"Yes," she was thinking it over. I couldn't understand her reluctance to give it to me, but then I got a sense that she felt her first name made her vulnerable in some fashion.

"My mother called me, 'Erin,'" she finally said, after some additional hesitation.

"I don't use it very often," she added as an afterthought.

"With your permission, I think that's what I'd like to call you. I'm Declan, but you can call me 'Dec'," I smiled.

"Don't take this as permission to be familiar with me!" she warned. "I'm still in charge here!"

"You think!" I mentally added, but I didn't argue the point.

We moved on into the lander. It seemed larger inside than outside. I guess the perspective of the surrounding mountain peaks had made it seem smaller.

We progressed through a short, curved hall and then came out into the central chamber of the thing. There were some odd-shaped devices that were attached to the floor. I presumed that I was looking at the engine system, but I couldn't really make much out of it. The lander was designed for one specific job and there wasn't any provision for passengers. The space was designed around the machines and it was filled with cases and equipment of unknown use.

We sidled around the outside edge of the room, sliding between the larger machines and the wall. The NFL players made hard going of it. They both outweighed me by at least a hundred pounds and the available space didn't accommodate their thick girths.

I could sense a grinding vibration through the soles of my feet. The thing was still busily working to get at the ore deposit. I couldn't see why it didn't use the energy it was expending on drilling to activate the transporter, but then I remembered from the Ancient-One that the transporters required an improbable amount of energy to set up their first linkage. After that, they worked with almost no energy expenditure. It had to do somehow with establishing quantum entanglement, but I wasn't able to understand the memories that came through to me on that score.

We moved around the largest machine in the compartment and there was the transporter door. It was open. I inspected it in the dim light and suddenly realized that it didn't even have a door. It was just a bare frame that led into a small compartment in the body of the machine. I guessed that it was protected from accidental intrusion and the door wasn't actually required.

I turned to Erin and said, "This is the transporter that will link this lander to another planet. I believe that it will connect to Oberon."

She looked puzzled and I hastily added, "That's a moon of Uranus and I think that's where the aliens are located."

Frank let out a surprisingly high-pitched giggle and repeated inanely, "Uranus!" stressing the last syllable.

Ted laughed at the middle school humor but quickly became silent when Erin glanced at him.

She turned to me and asked, "How does it work?"

"I think that the machine is still in the powering up phase. That vibration we feel is it reaching out for the radioactive ore that's buried below us. Once it reaches the deposit, it will extract what it needs and then it will power up." I was only half-guessing about the process.

"The interior is where the transportation takes place?" she asked, stepping through the frame and turning to face me through the opening.

"Yes," I started to tell her that it might not be a good idea to stand inside the thing, but Frank suddenly shoved me and I stumbled into the opening also. The two guards came in right after me.

"It's too tight out there!" was Ted's comment.

Needless to say, the dratted machine chose that exact moment to power up. The grinding sound abruptly stopped and we looked at each other in dismayed surmise. Then there was a flash of blue lightning around the door and I felt the disorientation of the passage through space. It was a feeling that I'd hoped never to experience again.

The passage seemed to take longer than I remembered. There was a blur of lights that streaked by the front of the door and the air got quite thin in the compartment. When the lights stopped flashing, we were facing a closed-door where there had been none before. From its sudden appearance, I knew we were at our destination.

Erin gasped and the two guards let fly with expletives simultaneously.

I pulled my Sig and faced the door in a shooting stance. As I did, Ted grabbed my arm, but before he could try to disarm me, Erin snapped, "Leave him alone!"

"Thanks – " was all I got out before the door opened with a familiar punctilio.

We emerged in an empty space. There were no windows and the room's entrance was closed and locked. I tried my two-finger trick in the adjoining slot, but the lock was inactive, at least from our side. We were trapped!

"What are we going to do now?" Erin plaintively asked.

I looked at the inside of the transporter box. There was a single button there, but nothing happened when I pushed it. I thought that maybe our combined mass had exhausted the initial energy of the thing, but maybe it was just designed for a single trip before it required recharging.

I suspected that the transporter's arrival would have set off an alarm somewhere and figured that we'd shortly be up to our necks in Pugs or Pug-bears or both!

"You guys had better get ready for a fight! Now!" I commanded.

"Won't they be glad to see us?" Erin asked.

"They're not friendly at all. The Master you've got in Denver isn't one of this group. Anything that comes into this room is going to try and kill us," I said, patiently.

In response, Frank and Ted drew their swords with their right hands. Frank pulled a pistol from his belt with his left hand, while Ted drew a long knife. Erin looked like she was in doubt about what I'd said for a moment, but then she pulled her own pistol.

"The pistols won't have much effect," I said. I had drawn mine in the transporter because there just wasn't room enough for me to unsling my rifle. Now I re-holstered the Sig and pulled the long weapon off my shoulder, preparing to shoot when the door opened. It was anticlimactic. The door didn't open, so we waited.

Chapter 7

It took about thirty minutes before the door to the room began to open. When it did, we had another surprise. The two beings that opened it were like none I'd ever seen before. They were humanoid but much smaller than Pugs. They were about four feet tall and covered with a smooth pelt of fine fur. They somehow reminded me of an otter in their sleekness. Their hands weren't webbed, though. They had well-defined fingers. There were other differences also. They had a rounded head that was larger, in proportion to their body, than that of an adult human. It gave them somewhat the look of a human baby. Their mouths were small and so were their noses. They also had two large, dark-black eyes. Altogether, they were about as attractive a creature as I could imagine an alien to be.

Judging from their fur and overall look, they seemed to be a very close analog to mammals. In this I was wrong. They turned out to be egg layers. However, they did have some of the attributes of Earth's monotremes. They carried their young with them for months after hatching until they were able to get around on their own. They didn't have a fleshy pouch but simply carried the babies in their arms. They also turned out to be quite intelligent.

Frank and Ted had been standing flat against the wall on either side of the door and as the two furry creatures came into the room, the large men jumped at them. The creatures responded by leaping straight forward, directly towards me. They belatedly saw Erin and me standing right in front of them and both of them made a loud chirping noise in fright. One was so overcome that it fell on its back as it tried to stop from running into Erin. As it did, it dropped a small, rectangular, metal box that clattered across the floor. The other collided with me and I caught it as gently as I could. It felt warm and soft, but it was shivering in fright.

As I restrained it, I probed with my mind and made contact. "We're not going to harm you," I sent.

It froze and looked up at me, then I received a weak thought back, "They're from the third planet in this solar system." It recognized my species, then.

I thought back, "Where are the – *Large, fierce, clawed things*?" Not knowing their name for the Pug-bears, I improvised and visualized one of the large aliens.

What came back was confused. The creatures worked for the Pug-bears as some kind of slaves. You'd have thought that they would resent their slavery, but they couldn't take any actions that would go against the Pug-bears' interests. I probed deeper. The small creature was still frightened, but its mind was open. I could tell that the Pug-bears had systematically destroyed its natural mental defenses. It was completely vulnerable to mental contact.

"What do you call your kind?" I asked.

The answer carried an overtone of pride, "We like the light of the Sun, our own, beautiful yellow Sun, not like the other two-legged slaves (I presumed it meant the Pugs by this). We thrive in the light and we call ourselves – – – ."

The concept came through, but not the sound. The best I could come up with was the word 'Sunny' as in sunshine. I spoke out loud to the others, "They call themselves something that translates as 'Sunnys' because they love sunshine. They have a mental aura that is non-aggressive and I'm sure they won't attack us."

No one spoke for a moment. Suddenly, the Sunny I'd been restraining, stopped shivering and placed its hand on my arm, trustingly. It chirped and the other one climbed slowly off the floor and stood up. Their mental energy was now calm and all overtones of fright had gone. It was a change like night and day. One minute they were frightened, the next, everything was just fine.

It turned out that they were incredibly optimistic and joyful by nature and, as long as they weren't being physically abused or assaulted, they were able to remain happy. I renewed my attempt to connect mentally and found that their thoughts were still puzzled. They were wondering how we'd gotten into the room and what our intentions were.

"We're not going to harm you," I sent. "We came through the transporter from the third planet. It powered up unexpectedly while we were inside and we came here."

They chirped back and forth about that for a moment and then the one that I'd caught drew a deep breath through its mouth and then actually spoke to us in stilted English.

"I ken dat you're humans, but you're in dire danger in this place at this time."

Our mouths dropped open in astonishment. Its voice wasn't very loud and didn't carry far, but we could understand it.

"Do you understand our language?" Erin gasped.

"Yes, dat we do, but not well."

His mispronouncing "that" was a mistake that set Frank and Ted off into a joint fit of semi-hysterical laughter.

The Sunnys started at the sound and clung to each other for a moment. When it became apparent that the huge men weren't going to attack, the little creatures relaxed.

"What manner of feeling be dis?" the speaking one asked.

"Amusement coming from relief of stress," I sent, thinking it would be easier for them to understand my thoughts than a verbal description.

"Oh, I make a mistake in my 'peech." His mouth didn't seem like it was structured correctly to properly enunciate our words.

"You're speaking very well. How did you learn our language?"

"We been in contact with you long, long ago," was the surprising answer. "You called us 'Wraiths,' then."

I knew that name had originally referred to water spirits in the Scottish highlands.

"Do you live in the water?" I asked.

"We live near water, if we can. We swim good. De Great Ones don't like it. Dey don't swim at all. We have no good water here. Dis not a happy place."

I read a sense of regret in its mind at the thought. Taking the moment, I probed deeper and found a surprising structure embedded in the creature's thought pattern. It was reminiscent of the control that the Ancient-One had tried to use on me. I explored in the not-here, not-there, dimensionless, mental space.

The Pug-bears had implanted some kind of control mechanism composed entirely of emotions and thoughts in the small creature's mind. I tried to trace the winding pathway of energy. It took a moment, but it suddenly resolved into the distinct sense of a knot and I pulled on one of the loose ends in a way I can't properly describe. The knot first tightened and then fell apart as the compulsion disintegrated. The small creature staggered and then rushed over and embraced me.

"You freed me! Freed hims, too," it cried, pointing at its compatriot.

It was easier the second time. In just a few seconds the two Sunnys were hugging each other and spinning around in a kind of wild dance of joy. We all four watched them with amazement.

Erin looked at me and slowly said, "I could tell you were somehow talking to them. What did you do?"

"I just broke a compulsion that they had in their minds, that's all," I answered, in a kind of distracted fashion.

"What did it compel them to do?"

"They were under the control of the Pug-bears, uh, aliens." I tried to smoothly correct myself. She probably hadn't heard my name for the large creatures.

"You mean the Masters?" she asked in a hostile tone of voice.

"Look, Erin. You've got to get control of your attitude about those creatures. Just because you think the one in Denver is good, doesn't mean they all are. As far as I know, all of the rest of them just want humanity dead."

"Maybe they've got a good reason," she snapped.

I started to speak but then paused to think. There must be some reason she was so distrustful of me and so aggressive. I was tired of her attitude, so I rather rudely read her thoughts.

There it was, buried in the background, but still accessible! She'd been treated horribly as a young girl. She'd been abused; not sexually, but beaten repeatedly.

I carefully sent a reassuring message into her mind, "Not every man is evil; not everyone enjoys violence. But, the Masters want to dominate Earth."

She shuddered as the thought took hold, "I – I don't..." her voice trailed off for a moment. "I have to think about that," she finally said.

Leaving the question of what motivated her, I turned to the now quiet Sunnys. They were standing close together and I saw that the one that had fallen had retrieved his box. Looking closer, I saw with astonishment that it was a metal lunchbox of obviously human make. It had a cartoon drawing of a large, floppy eared Great Dane standing beside a long-haired teenager. I recognized the characters and was mildly amused. The Sunny was clutching the box as if it were quite valuable.

I pointed at it, "Where did you get that box?"

"Oh. We found it in the other dome, the one where the Great Ones live. It for adjusters holding." He opened it to show me some odd-shaped, hand tools.

The answer wasn't exactly to the point, but it did set my mind off on a tangent.

"Are there any 'Great Ones' in this dome? Or, are they somewhere else?"

"Dey off in the other one. Der none of them here. I see dat you don't like them."

"They want to control our planet and kill all of us."

"No, not all of you. Dey keep some to do their works. And, to eats."

"We don't want to work for them or be food, either. I want to stop their invasion," I answered.

"Now dat you freed us, we want other Sunnys free too. We can helps yous. Will you help us?"

"I'll helps yous uh, I mean help you." Listening to their speech had gotten me feeling confused. Much more of it and I was going to start talking just like them.

Chapter 8

S ince the door to the room was now open, courtesy of our two, furry friends, I stuck my head out to look around. The room was apparently one of several, semi-free-standing, cube-shaped structures that were spaced regularly around one of the aliens' clear domes. I could see a large planet with a visible ring system in profile against the sky. Although not as well-defined as those of Saturn, the rings were still spectacular.

From the view, I judged that we were, as I'd thought we'd be, on Oberon, one of Uranus' moons. The Pug-bears had a base on this moon that was isolated when we destroyed the matter transporter network a few years ago. Their main base on Titan had suffered a huge atomic explosion caused by the stored nuclear bombs we had set off. The explosion had destroyed the base and the resulting damage to the transporters had blown up the one on Oberon. The aliens had now recovered from the damage and were starting to mount their second attack.

As I turned my attention to the dome and the surrounding area, I saw no Pug-bears and none of the Pugs. I looked inquiringly at the Sunnys and they seemed to understand the import of my glance. The talkative one hastened to assure me that we were in no immediate danger. The Great Ones, he informed me, were in another series of domes on the far side of the moon. There was only a single transporter that went from their domes to the Sunnys' habitat dome and that one was isolated from our present location physically, in case there was another mishap.

It looked as if the Pug-bears were taking no chances with their last base. My informant's energy field practically radiated candor, so I told the others not to worry and that we should try to find out what the Sunnys knew about the overall situation. What followed was a very informative mental conversation, punctuated by their unusual language usage in occasional attempts at clarification.

The little creatures were quite sharp, easily as quick on the uptake as a human, and probably smarter in some ways. They were, unfortunately, totally pacifistic, having no more ability to defend themselves than a baby. They started by giving me an abbreviated history of their race. The mental flow was a little easier to understand, not being constrained by their improbable speech.

The talkative one narrated, "We developed space flight a long time ago."

"What do you mean by 'a long time'?" I interrupted.

We had a little trouble communicating regarding time. Their measure of time differed from mine. They understood the idea of measuring it by the rotations of a planet around a sun, but they didn't like that method, arguing that it was too variable from solar system to solar system. Instead, they measured by the time it took light to go a set distance. I thought that might be variable also, depending as it did on the distance. They had some kind of concept about it that they couldn't quite make me understand. I got the conversation back on track by the tactic of simply agreeing that it was a long time ago.

The one without the box sent, "Our people are good at working with things. We're technologically oriented and when we developed space travel, we set out to explore the stars. We had some initial success. We explored five solar systems that held planets compatible with our form of life. We set up colonies on these planets, being careful not to interfere with the local ecology, although none of the planets had much on them by way of native life. We eventually had large populations on each of the planets and we engaged in trade back and forth. Each of the planets had its own specialty in manufacturing and agriculture, so our trade was very useful and benefited everyone. This was a golden age for us and we thought that we'd continue gradually spreading out as our populations grew."

"We also found several planets that weren't at all attractive. Some had carbon-based, oxygen-breathing life, but it was antagonistic to us in one way or another. We left those planets alone to develop on their own. Other planets had poisonous gasses or too heavy gravity and then there were the ones that had silicon-based life-forms. We can't survive on silicon-based planets. It takes too much life-support and costs too much, so we just cataloged those planets and left them alone."

"One of the first planets we explored was very near our beautiful home star. It orbited a dim red dwarf sun and was the home of the Pugs."

The Pugs were biologically different from the Sunnys due to their use of silicon in their skeletal systems. That was something that I already knew, but what I didn't know was that Pugs had an early iron-age society with a grave scarcity of resources. They were violent and fought with edged weapons for both food and breeding rights; a fact that made the pacifistic Sunnys very uncomfortable.

The Pugs had been locked in this conflict-based mode for what the Sunnys described as a long time. They didn't like change and the other part of their problem was that they didn't live very long; only about twelve of our years. They died before they'd had much of an opportunity to learn anything beyond how to kill each other and to breed. With such a short generation span and their antipathy to change, they showed no signs of developing further along the road towards a civilization with which the Sunnys could co-exist. The peace-loving Sunnys had taken a brief look at the Pugs' violence-ridden society and quickly left.

"When we left the Pugs' system, we placed an orbiting beacon in a solar orbit. It warned against landing on their planet. We wanted to warn other exploring Sunnys and any other intelligent species that might happen by to stay strictly away. We didn't think the Pugs would ever know that the warning sign was there."

I interrupted at this point, wondering if Earth had been quarantined by them at some point in the past, but they assured me that we were relatively new to their experience. They'd been on Earth briefly about three centuries ago based on their description of our lifestyle and culture of the time. They'd stayed long enough to recognize that, although we were violent and not highly advanced, we had the potential to both advance and become a species that would be compatible with them.

They had been most impressed by our literature and seemed to have some knowledge of poets of the period, mentioning in particular John Donne – a fact which seemed to square with their having been in Scotland long enough to be known as Wraiths. Our poetry had appealed to their sense of spirit and as a result, they felt they recognized some underlying aspect of our make-up that resonated with their conception of a potentially good neighbor.

"Everything was good for us. We had a trade network and our ships were gradually exploring the surrounding stars. Then disaster struck. We landed an expedition on the Great Ones' planet. It looked safe. There was no civilization that we could see, only animals. We thought that the dominant life-form (the Pug-bears – to use my name for them) was simply a dangerous beast. Up until that time, we had never considered that there could be such a thing as mental control. We had previously researched thought transmission, but we had no genetic talent for it and, as a result, we discounted it as a potential problem."

I resolved to learn from their oversight. I, too, might have some blind spots in my mind that could be exploited in a totally unfamiliar situation. I'd have to be more careful in the future. The Ancient-One had almost caught me, but I hadn't realized the existential danger on the level that the Sunnys had faced.

"We thought the Great Ones were animals that posed no more danger to us than any other predatory, oxygen-breathing, carbon-based life-form. We were wrong. The carnivorous Great Ones evolved in a highly competitive environment where there was little prey. They laid eggs that hatched into their immature form (the things I called 'spiders') and they left the little ones to fend for themselves. It was 'eat or die' for them and somehow they evolved a powerful mental ability to emotionally control prey."

I could see how it would be easier to simply cause a prey animal to freeze into immobility than to chase it down. The Pug-bears had taken that ability to a fine edge and apparently had no problem dominating the defenseless Sunnys. The feral Pug-bears simply ate the Sunnys they captured. However, there was a complicating factor. The Pug-bears' planet also had another form of life; a non-motile creature that filled the role of a symbiont to the Pug-bears.

"This creature has a complex life-cycle that involves laying eggs that hatch into small worms. The worms go through several phases and end up as parasites to a small, ecologically-unimportant herbivore. When they could catch it, the Great Ones would eat that creature. They eat anything they can capture and the herbivore, while not plentiful, was just another meal to them."

"When they consume the parasite-infested herbivore, the parasite sometimes migrates into the Great One's brain. Once there, it blends its circulatory and nervous systems with those of its host and then increases in size, effectively becoming an ancillary brain for the Great One. This blended brain gives them a different level of mentation and they become far more intelligent. This only happens rarely, so the Great Ones are normally a feral, unintelligent species with only a few, sporadically occurring, intelligent members."

"The intelligent ones are driven towards dominance since their intelligence simply magnifies their feral nature and gives them a huge sense of ego. Prior to our arrival, the few intelligent ones had used their advantage to control as much territory and breeding rights as possible. The older ones were respected, due to their survival abilities and were given some deference by the younger, intelligent ones, as long as they could still fight. Those that become too weak to fight are soon killed."

"Our expedition had the ill-luck to encounter one of these 'smart' Great Ones. It immediately saw the potential that our technology offered. It recruited other intelligent ones and they forced us to help their species. They read our minds and understood that there were many planets available and they want to conquer as many as possible. Even the weakest of them wants to control its own planet."

"We were mentally controlled and driven to research the symbiont's life-cycle. We eventually were able to bypass the intermediate steps that involved the herbivore and we learned how to compress the symbiont eggs into wafers containing thousands of eggs. When the feral Great Ones eat the wafers, one in about ten thousand of the eggs develops into the mature symbiont, thus conferring intelligence upon the Great One. Part of our duty for them is to make sure there are more and more intelligent ones. The feral ones won't eat the eggs voluntarily. They have no conception of the change the symbiont will instill. We have the Pugs capture them and feed them only on the egg wafers until the infection takes hold. Once the young ones gain intelligence, the old ones mentally instruct them."

In this laborious fashion, the Pug-bears had built up a sort of society. The normal life of a Pug-bear was violent and they were likely to die from any number of natural causes as they matured. They naturally equated success with longevity and recognized intelligence as an important advantage. They valued experience as a key component of leadership and, to the small degree they cooperated, they appointed the oldest to be their leaders. These leaders had conceived a plan to use the Sunnys' technology and ability to manipulate tools to expand to other planets.

"Technology and tool using were totally unknown to the Great Ones prior to our arrival," the other Sunny added.

I had been attacked by the one that called itself 'Ancient-One' and I also knew that the more immature ones had only a modicum of psychic ability. Until they developed a high level of intelligence, they weren't able to communicate or dominate humans. It seemed that we were more naturally immune to the feral Pug-bears low power commands than the less fortunate Sunnys. Even a young, feral Pug-bear could freeze a Sunny.

The first step for the Pug-bears was to take over the planet of the Pugs. They'd found out about the Pugs from the Sunnys and had immediately realized that these fierce creatures could be molded into their slaves. The Pugs would make good soldiers and provide the Pug-bears with an unquestioning slave that could use hand-held weapons, something that the Sunnys were constitutionally incapable of doing.

"We tried to escape the Great Ones, but, just as we can't fight physically, we can't fight them mentally. We just aren't mentally constructed that way. We are completely trapped and we ended up yielding all five of our colonized planets to the control of the Great Ones. They also took our beautiful, home planet! We have been prisoners, no, slaves for the past two centuries. The only possible thing was for us to aid the Great Ones' expansion plans and wait for some miracle. We hope that you humans could be that miracle."

The Pug-bears had seemed unstoppable. They'd successfully taken over fourteen planets in twelve different solar systems. Of the fourteen invaded planets, five had held civilizations of various degrees of development. The Pug-bears and Pugs used the Sunnys' spacecraft and their knowledge of quantum physics. The Sunnys had eventually developed the matter transporters for short-range travel. With the spacecraft and transporters as their modes of travel, they had access to other planets. The initial lack of FTL travel didn't bother them, since they didn't think of extended travel time as an obstacle to their plans.

They'd also forced the Sunnys to develop weapons. The Sunnys couldn't use them, of course, but the Pugs could. The Pug-bears had no manipulative ability and they preferred to kill with their poison claws or jaws, but they rapidly saw the utility in weapons.

I was familiar with the splinter-guns, the antimatter rifles, and bombs, and the electro-bolt shooting weapon. There were also some varieties of projectile shooting weapons, similar to human arms that were developed for the Pugs' use. With the development of the splinter-guns and the anti-matter weapons, the projectile shooters had been abandoned.

These constituted the entire armory developed by the Sunnys. The Pug-bears saw no reason to force the Sunnys to create any additional types of weapons since these had proven to be enough to destroy the five civilizations they'd encountered. The other nine planets they invaded only had animal life that was easily dominated. The Pug-bears found some of these planets to be paradise for them, since there were few Pug-bears and plenty of prey, giving them lots of room for expansion.

I asked the Sunnys if there were any natural pathogens or toxins on any planets that could cause the Pug-bears a problem. Their answer was complex, but, in their experience, there was nothing to worry about on other planets other than chemical toxins. The native viruses and single-celled life-forms couldn't attack a non-native life-form.

This surprised me until one of them explained. We tend to think of a virus as an elementary, not-very-evolved particle on the edge of life. In fact, our viruses are highly-specialized to attack the creatures with which they evolved. Given an alien life-form that the virus had never before encountered, it was less than a one in a trillion chance that the virus would find something in the alien's physical make-up that it could exploit. H. G. Wells' common-cold defense would never work in real life.

"We thought the Great Ones had met their match on one planet. They invaded a jungle planet that we believed contained only animals. There were no signs of civilization that showed up in our initial survey. Once the Great Ones established a beachhead on the planet, they met implacable resistance."

They always used the same technique in their invasions. They'd send a robotic probe to establish a transporter on the surface. The large, interstellar spaceships were unable to land and the Pug-bears didn't care for the idea of physically landing in shuttles. If the civilization being invaded used electronics, they would use an EMP to destroy the target's communications.

I knew from my past experience with their first invasion and from the Ancient-One that the symbiont would die when it passed through a transporter unless it was in egg form, but I didn't know why. The Pug-bears recognized that their source of intelligence would disappear when they transported, so they normally just sent young, feral ones through the matter transmitters. They directed the Pugs to ship the symbiont egg-wafers to the planet for feeding to the feral Pug-bears on the surface. This strategy, although cumbersome, eventually created enough intelligent Pug-bears to dominate the local environment.

The Sunnys explained, "The transporter technology limits the usable distance, not because the quantum waves can't travel farther, but because the transporter mechanism is susceptible to interference. It sometimes interpolates other waves into the signal. This is a function of the distance the signal has to travel; the distance between the two stations. When the distorted waveform reaches the destination transporter, it reassembles the signal to create the transported item and the result can be very unfortunate. The creature that tries to travel too far often comes out as a real mess; not a mutant, but just too distorted to live. Short distances like those found in a solar system are not a problem, except for the symbionts. They are extremely sensitive to even small distortions of their energy wave structure and even a short transporter jump will kill them."

An intelligent Pug-bear wouldn't travel through a transporter under normal circumstances. I'd seen them do it, however, and realized that they would sacrifice their symbiont if the circumstances were important enough.

"The fifteenth planet that the Great Ones attempted to invade turned out to be the home of an animal that was far more fierce than any they'd previously encountered. Even more dangerous than the Great Ones themselves. The animal was intelligent to some unknown degree. Although it had no visible signs of civilization, the members of its species would organize and work together to set elaborate ambushes for the Great Ones and the Pugs. Given the general lack of intelligence of the newly arrived Pug-bears, the ambushes were very successful."

The armed Pugs had also been outclassed. Some of their weapons were adequate to combat the enemy, but generally, they were killed before they even became aware that any danger was near. Stealth and cunning seemed to be the winning combination and neither were the natural attributes of either the Pugs or the feral Pug-bears.

I asked, "Why don't the intelligent Pug-bears come to the planetary surface in shuttles? I can understand why not transporters, but why not fly down?"

The answer was that they did, but they never went anywhere in force. There just weren't enough intelligent ones to go around. Instead, they relied on growing symbionts on the invaded planetary surface. There might be only one or two intelligent, older individuals on any planet at any one time.

The Sunnys resumed their history,"They made us leave that planet and we abandoned it except for an observation station. We left it orbiting the world, just in case the denizens developed some ability to strike back or to get into space."

So far, the Sunny observers and the Pug warriors had seen no activity that would indicate any technological advances made by the inhabitants of that planet.

This was a lot of information to absorb and it nearly exhausted me to find it out. It was made worse by the speed of the transmission. The actual 'conversation' only took a few minutes; thought is faster than speech, after all. My human companions were getting restless and I had to pause a few times to ask them to restrain themselves. Ted and Frank finally stretched out on the floor and closed their eyes. Erin just kept watching me, somewhat suspiciously as the Sunnys brought me up to the present situation. It was very interesting.

Chapter 9

The Sunnys had a spaceship propulsion system that would move at almost light speeds, but it was still sub-light with all that implied. Travel of any distance was necessarily a multi-generational thing. This didn't bother the Pug-bears, since they lived for about one hundred and forty years. It was more of a problem for the Sunnys. They lived for a span that was roughly human-equivalent.

The first Sunny explorers that had arrived on the Earth had come from one of their colonized stars that was located about ten light-years away. It was probably Epsilon Eridani, but I wasn't sure about that. I missed Liz's astronomical knowledge. She'd probably know the star name for sure. When I thought of her, I had a poignant vision of my wife and little son waving goodbye to me at the stream by our homestead. I'd come a long way in just a few days.

The original Earth invasion by Pug-bears had come from a different planet that was located about thirty light-years away; not the closest one the invaders occupied, but then they didn't do things systematically. The Pug-bears had traveled through sub-light space for about half of their lives to invade the first time. They'd raised many generations of Pugs along the way. The Sunnys were well into their third generation before they arrived. It was a very long-term operation, but the Pug-bears didn't think of it in that way. It was only the next step in their plan to dominate all of the planets, everywhere.

I reflected. This is what you get when you give power to creatures that are mostly ignorant of facts about the universe. They had no true sense of the immensity of our local galaxy alone. Of course, it might not have made any difference to them if they did. They were just out to take over planets and expand.

During the time that it took the invasion force to make that thirty light-year voyage, the Sunnys on their home planet had made a technological leap. On the whole, they were incapable of resisting the Pug-bears. Although their scientific research had slowed as a result of their subjugation, it hadn't stopped and they'd finally developed a Faster-Than-Light drive.

The lunch-box carrying Sunny was quite knowledgeable and tried to educate me on how their normal space drive worked, but the best I could figure was that it was sort of like a microwave oven, except that it somehow grabbed virtual quantum particles from the underlying zero-point field and accelerated them to near-light speeds. The particles could be ejected in controlled directions and that provided the propulsion. The FTL drive was a modification or off-shoot of that. Once it kicked on, it converted the normal particles of the ship into waves in the quantum plenum and the sub-light drive was turned off. This change of state somehow allowed the ship to ride the existing torsion waves of the universe, but I didn't get that part at all.

What I did get was that the sub-light technology was almost within the spectrum of human knowledge. It was a direct outgrowth of their normal space-drive and that was something that we were almost ready to invent. We just needed to have the right discoveries and we'd be able to utilize the technique. I had actually seen something on the internet years ago which described a so-called EmDrive. That was the basic idea. Of course, we'd dropped it when the EMP destroyed our electronics.

An adjunct discovery to the FTL technology allowed them to create an instantaneous communicator. They now had the ability to send messages instantly back to the homeworlds. That mechanism was a first-generation development and was currently dependent on a large gravity source and could only work from the surface of a planet; spaceships couldn't use it at the present time, although my furry friend thought that would change.

The possibility of an Ansible-like device that made instantaneous communication was something that I didn't like hearing. I had to ensure that no calls for help went back. With the FTL drive, the Pug-bears could be back on top of us quickly.

Now able to travel faster than light, the Pug-bears goals for universal conquest were accelerated. They made the Sunnys create more large spaceships. One such had been equipped with the FTL drive and sent out as a follow-up to the original Earth invasion. It had just arrived at Oberon about four or five of our months ago. The newly arrived Sunnys had been working madly since that time to help the few surviving Pug-bears rebuild their base.

"Dey eat us Sunnys, most of us, and all the Pugs," my talkative friend informed me, speaking out loud for once.

The Pug-bears had nom-nomed their way through the surviving Pugs and had started on the less important of the original Sunnys in the years since their source of human protein had been severed by my actions. I felt somewhat guilty at having condemned the little, furry guys to be eaten, but I'd have still done the same thing. Blowing up Titan had been the logical step in our resistance.

The FTL ship had brought more Pug-bears of the intelligent disposition and plenty of Pugs. There was only a small contingent of Sunnys along to manage the ship. The Pug-bears were more about fighting than technology as long as the technology was there when they needed it.

Once they'd arrived on Oberon, the Sunnys had created another robotic probe to carry a new transporter to Earth. Their science had increased here, too. The new probe traveled much faster than I had remembered with my Ancient-One memories.

They hadn't the foresight to include an initial landing probe when they equipped the second expedition. They'd assumed that the initial expedition had been successful and didn't need a backup device, so they'd been forced to work hard to rectify that oversight. The new probe had been completed in the first three months after arrival of the second ship. Once completed, the probe was able to make what I'd assumed would be a seven-year trip in under a month. Solar system distances were equivalent to driving from city to city for their latest space drive.

The landing had been programmed for the same location as the initial one. They were sure that the necessary nuclear fuel could be created from the ore located under the mountainside.

The Pug-bears were unprepared to find an almost complete failure of the first expedition. This had never happened before and it infuriated them. On arriving in our solar system, the Sunnys had sent out sophisticated, quantum signals that had been returned by the Oberon base. They had found no signs of life on the bases on Titan or Io or the Earth and its Moon. My demolition job had been effective, sparing the Oberon aliens only due to the extreme separation of their domes from the dome where the transporter exploded.

Finding life on Oberon, the Sunnys had maneuvered the FTL ship into orbit around Uranus and simply parked it in a Lagrange point. The calculations for the point were complex, due to the additional moons orbiting the planet, but they were up to it.

The Pug-bears were unsophisticated in many ways; they'd left the FTL ship parked, completely unattended when they transported through the link to the surface of Oberon. The Sunnys hadn't wanted to leave the ship vacant, knowing full-well that it was a bad idea, but the Pug-bears had wanted all available Sunnys on the job on Oberon.

In a way, the Pug-bears' notion of leaving the ship vacant was understandable. No Pug-bear would take it. They couldn't do so without help, anyway. They had no manipulative ability and relied on the Sunnys and Pugs to do things for them. The Pugs were too non-technical to fly it and the Sunnys weren't allowed to leave Oberon. The clincher was that, in all of their travels, they'd never met another space-faring race. They couldn't imagine that anyone would happen along and steal the vessel.

I was inspired when I received this information. In the words of an old cartoon character, a carrot-chewing bunny, "They don't know me very well, do they?" Stealing the ship was the first thing that came to my mind. I just had to figure out how to go about it. Once we were in control, figuring out what to do with the ship would be easy.

I could see us arranging to drop a rock or something on the Pug-bears' base. Even a small asteroid would make a real mess.

They'd never had to worry about space warfare. Of course, neither had humans, but we had the habit of making up for our lack of experience with our creative imagination. It was my goal to teach them a hard lesson. As soon as that idea hit my mind, I'd asked the Sunnys to tell me the location of the transporter that connected to the FTL vessel.

It was in a dome that was over the horizon. The place was normally used only for material storage. They'd brought equipment from the FTL and left it near the connecting transporter until they needed it. There were only a

couple of Pugs guarding the link since the Sunnys normally requested parts
be brought to them by the Pugs and almost never went into the storage area.

I asked where the rest of the Sunnys were, but the answer I received wasn't
too helpful. They were in another dome on the other side of the planet,
adjacent to the main one occupied by the Pug-bears. The only link to them
went right through the Pug-bears' habitat. I regretfully dropped the idea of
rescuing them, until the lunchbox-carrying Sunny suggested that they call
the other Sunnys for assistance. He didn't think the Pug-bears would even
bother to come along with them when they came over.

I asked Erin what she thought, but she just said that she didn't want to see
any of the Masters right then. She looked at me and said, "I understand what
you told me about them, but I'm not sure that I can face one without giving
in to its control. I still think they might be good and mean us well."

"They certainly haven't dealt with these people very nicely," I retorted with
some heat. The thought of the little Sunnys serving as a snack was not a
pretty one and I felt my old antipathy towards the Pug-bears flare-up.

"OK. I give you that," she answered. "Let's just try what you said. Let's see if
we can steal their ship. The Warlord would like that."

I'd forgotten about her loyalty to the Warlord. He was a trivial worry in the
back of my mind at this point, but it looked like I'd have to deal with his
hold on her and her henchmen sometime soon. I nodded and responded,
"I'll bet he would." Luckily, she didn't notice the sarcasm.

I turned to the Sunnys and gave them the go-ahead to send for assistance.
The one with the lunch-box pulled out a small communicator and whistled
into it for a moment. While he did, I asked the other one what their names
were.

"Me's named," here he emitted a shrill series of chirps and whistles.

There was no way I could duplicate those sounds. I resolved to call him
Whistle from that point on. When I told him what I wanted to call him, he
seemed pleased and agreed that would be his name. Then he pointed at his
friend and asked what I intended to call him.

After a moment's thought, I realized that my initial impression of the lunch-
box Sunny was that our presence had frazzled his nerves so much that he fell

down. Remembering that thought, I answered back that I wanted to call him, "Frazzle." That name, too, was accepted in good grace.

The transporter link to the Pug-bears' dome was in the cube-shaped room directly across from ours, so we moved over to it to greet them. I had Frank and Ted flank the door, just in case a Pug-bear or Pug came through with the smaller creatures. We had just gotten set up there when the door opened and seven Sunnys came out.

I saw that they weren't all the brown shade of Whistle and Frazzle. Some of them had coats of other colors. They seemed to run the gamut from black through brown and golden to white in their coloration. A few were multicolored, mostly dark brown, golden. and white.

They were frightened of us and started to retreat into the cube, but the two guards jumped in front of the door. There was a burst of chirping as Whistle explained the situation. Six of the Sunnys immediately stepped away from the seventh and pointed at him. I saw that he was carrying a kind of backpack made up of mesh. He also had a sort of vague air about him that keyed my mental senses.

I probed his mind immediately and saw that he wasn't all Sunny. The backpack held one of the symbionts. It was somehow in control of him and was trying to mentally signal for help as I sensed it.

I jumped forward and ripped the pack off the small creature. The others whistled in horror as I pulled it off. There was a kind of nerve-like cord coming from the pack and attached to the furry one's spine. I slashed that with my knife and then threw the pack on the ground. The Sunny gave a cry and collapsed as I did.

I jumped forward and simply stamped on the creature in the pack. It crushed with a crunching sound that reminded me of squashing a roach. Noxious fluid leaked out of the net-like openings and a nasty odor assailed my nostrils. The thing was obviously dead. The Sunny, meanwhile was lying on the ground shuddering. I turned to look at him as his fellows came up to surround him. They didn't try to assist him in any way. He continued to shiver for a moment more and then stilled in death.

Whistle looked at me and said sorrowfully, "We die when the mind creature dies. We don' live long when they attach to us anyways."

They weren't angry with me, only resigned to the death of one whom they'd known was dead from the moment he donned the backpack. At least he died free from the creature's control and they appreciated my freeing him.

Remembering the mental control structure that I'd destroyed in both of my friends' minds, I inspected the minds of the six remaining strangers. Only one had a mental device embedded in his emotions and it only took a moment to destroy that. The others were apparently free of compulsions. Their only control was that their species was so used to obedience that they would not think of defying the Pug-bears.

I wanted to keep the Pug-bears from calling for help and with that in mind, I asked Frazzle if they could leave a message for them, thinking that we could make up some story about the Sunnys' absence. He assented, but said that it could only be mental – they had no conception of writing – that was something that only the Pugs and Sunnys did. He said that if we didn't want the Pug-bears to come after us, we'd better not send them anything right now.

I decided that our next move would be to attack the two Pugs guarding the link to the FTL ship. If we could get through to the ship, we'd send a message to the Pug-bears that the Sunnys had detected an asteroid that was on an orbit intersecting that of the ship's. The ship would be destroyed unless it was moved immediately and the Sunnys had gone to move it. This was pretty weak as a story and I wasn't very happy with it as a plan.

I was saved from even trying it when I asked Frazzle where the FTL communicator was located. It turned out to be conveniently set up in the storage dome with the two Pugs. With any luck, we could destroy the thing so the Pug-bears couldn't call for help.

We entered the cube-shaped structure and crossed to the transporter door. I pressed the call button and we were on our way to the storage dome.

Chapter 10

We were shooting when we came out of the transporter in the storage dome. The two Pugs had been faced away from us and, although I don't like to shoot people without giving them a chance, the blasted Pugs were just too resistant to bullets to let any advantage slip away. I fired off my Win-Mag and the muzzle blast literally knocked all of the Sunnys to the floor. They lay there in shock, holding their ears.

The Pug that I'd shot actually managed to turn around and look at me. He had a large hole clear through his chest but still had enough strength to move. I prepared to shoot him again, but he suddenly dropped.

Frank and Ted had jumped to the side when I shot and then rushed the other Pug. He was trying to draw his splinter-gun, but was already missing an arm. Frank was really fast with that large sword he carried.

The Pug finally figured out that he'd have to use his other hand, but just at that time, Ted shoved his smaller knife into the thing's chest. It let out a hiss and grabbed his arm and I could hear his teeth grind in pain. I was trying to get clear where I could shoot without hitting either of the men, but Frank beat me to it. He stepped past Ted and made a back-handed chopping motion and the Pug's head dropped to the floor. It instantly released Ted's arm and collapsed.

Erin was still back in the transporter with the Sunnys. I hastened to hold the door open and motioned them out. The Sunnys were still in shock. Their pacifism didn't prepare them well for this necessary violence. Erin had also been stunned by the wicked muzzle-blast of my rifle and her eyes were practically rolling around in their sockets. She shook her head and tried her best to recover as she helped shoo the Sunnys out.

They came out in a bunch, trying to avoid both the dead Pugs and the weapon-carrying humans. I took a moment to try and allay their fears and repulsion mentally, "Relax. It was necessary to do away with those two. We're safe for a moment and there will be no more violence."

That last was probably a lie, but I wasn't intending to shoot anyone else, at least at the moment.

As I walked by the dead Pugs, I stopped to gather up both of their splinter-guns. The other humans watched me incuriously. I don't think they realized how deadly the small, plastic-like things were. The two big men obviously had been too successful with their current armament to want to exchange it for a toy gun and Erin wasn't oriented towards weapons, being used to her guards.

The transporter link to the ship was on the other side of the storage dome and we threaded our way across the littered space, avoiding miscellaneous boxes of carelessly stored items. The Sunnys might have been technologically adept, but they didn't seem to have the concept of organized storage down very well. This transporter was set in the face of one of the standard cube-shaped rooms. There was a door leading to the inside of the cube and when I opened it to inspect the inside, it contained an intricate mechanism resting on a bench.

Whistle looked under my arm and said, "Dat be the communicator. Breaks it now."

I pulled my Sig and fired several shots into the most sensitive-looking part of it. There was a flash and some kind of energy glowed around it for a moment. Then it disintegrated into a pile of rubble. That solved one potential problem. The Pug-bears were now without any means of communication and I didn't care if they knew that we had stolen their ship.

We lined up, humans and Sunnys, in two lines and then entered the transporter when the door opened. It was a larger one than I'd previously seen, perhaps due to it being required to transport cargo and equipment of various sizes. Regardless, it easily held all ten of us. The six Sunnys only taking up about as much space as the four humans.

As I reached out for the go-button, I asked Whistle once again, "Are you sure that the ship is vacant?"

"Yes, me sure. No one would go der without permission of the Great Ones."

"OK. Here we go, then!"

The door closed and the walls shifted as they do and we came out in what might have been the cargo bay of the FTL ship. I was excited! This was my first time on a spaceship. I realized that I'd been traveling through space using the transporters, but this was somehow different. It was more exciting in a way. I'm too much of a romantic for my own good and the thought of flying through space was distracting.

The reality wasn't quite as awesome as I thought it should be. We were in a fairly large space – about a hundred feet long and about half that wide. The overhead was curved with cables and tubes mixed with metal girders like ribs following the curve up from the floor and disappearing into the vertical wall at the far side. Looking around, I realized that the transporter was located against a flat wall that was the front of a closet-like structure placed against the curved outside of the ship. It was remarkably like the cube-shaped storage rooms in the domes on Titan and Oberon. That made sense, since the same people, the Sunnys, were responsible for the construction.

The Sunnys had been here before and led the way across the vacant space to another transporter on the opposite wall. I thought to myself, "Of course, they'd use transporters to get around in the ship. Why walk, when you can dematerialize?" I found out later that there were also passageways around parts of the ship, but they were mostly in the areas where the Pug-bears resided. The sensitivity of their symbionts to the transporters was a huge weakness that meant they had to physically travel wherever they wanted to go. They could take a transporter across the ship, but that would kill their symbiont and they'd come out the other side as unintelligent, feral beasts. Not a useful outcome for most purposes.

We came out on the bridge. It was a large space, but the ceiling was low, due to the short stature of the Sunnys. The two big men both had to walk partly bent over. The overhead just cleared my scalp by a half-inch, so I had to be almost as careful as them.

The bridge held a few rows of stadium seating that overlooked some consoles in a 'U-shaped' formation around a single Sunny-sized seat. The consoles had video displays and something like a matrix of flat keys on their surface. The most stunning part of the place was a huge, transparent window that curved, seamlessly around the entire front of the room. It currently provided a view of Uranus showing that we were orbiting the planet in an inverted and bow-down orientation. It was a little disconcerting to me and I noticed that the other three humans carefully kept their eyes averted from the view. I guess they didn't feel too secure. It was a bit much. They'd started out the day standing in snow halfway up their calves in the Rocky Mountains and now we were preparing to leave the solar system. When I thought of it that way, it was a tribute to human nature that we were all still functioning.

I hadn't noticed previously, but there was something funny about the place – I weighed about Earth-normal! The ship had some form of gravity control. I asked about it and Frazzle explained. The ship had its own gravity as a result of the FTL drive technology. It had something to do with the power core and wasn't dependent on the FTL engines to be running. It was always on, even in this unoccupied vessel. Frazzle tried to describe the mechanism, but his description was over my level.

As Arthur C. Clarke said, "Any sufficiently advanced technology is indistinguishable from magic." It was a true statement. Frazzle's explanation was full of concepts that I had no words for and no background to begin to understand. It reminded me of an elderly professor trying to explain an advanced math concept to a preschooler. What I did get from his effort, though, was the fact that their discovery of the FTL drive had made gravity control possible.

The ramifications of that thought boggled my imagination. "You mean that the early ships, I mean before FTL, didn't have any gravity?"

"No, dey used centrifugal force to keep all on the floor. Der living spaces rotated," he explained, adding a visual image in his imagination of a weight spinning on a string.

"I'm glad we have gravity in this ship," I responded, somewhat inanely.

"Wait! This isn't normal?" Erin was slow on the uptake since she hadn't been able to follow the mental aspects of our conversation, but now she was upset.

"It appears to be normal for this ship," I said.

"I don't like it! It could stop or be turned off and we'd float!"

She was just too tightly wound and it was starting to bother me. "It won't be turned off. Stop worrying so much!"

The woman was a ball of fun. She was simultaneously fearful and aggressive; not a great combination in my opinion. I regretted having her along. Frank and Ted were useful and the good thing about them was they were normally so impassive that they didn't say much. That made them just about perfect companions in my judgment. Of course, I was going to have to deal with the Warlord issue sooner or later. That might prove to be a fracturing point for our loose group, but I was able to relegate that event to sometime in the future.

As if my thought cued her, Erin started, "Let's take this ship to Earth and get the Warlord – "

I interrupted, "And, what would he do? We've got to stop this invasion or Earth won't be ours for much longer. The Warlord might just want to use the ship to intimidate other people and expand his domain. We need to find a way to put a halt to the Pug-bears' expansion and this ship is just what we need."

She started to speak again, but I'd had enough. I held up my hand in a stopping motion. As I did, I surreptitiously inserted a copy of the Pug-bears' controlling mechanism into her mind. I had been studying it during the moments since I'd disabled it in the Sunnys. It wasn't very complex, but then the Sunnys had no defense. It might not work for long in a human, but I wanted her to go along with the idea that I'd been formulating. I also didn't want trouble with Ted and Frank and they were looking at me suspiciously.

She shut her mouth and then opened it to say, "I guess you're right. What do you want to do?"

Both Frank and Ted's mouths dropped open at this unexpected capitulation.

It was exactly the result I'd intended and I felt proud of myself for having learned to use another mental technique. I didn't like the idea of controlling another person against their will and I expected that she'd be resentful if she figured out what I did, but it was easier than arguing.

"Here's what we'll do. I've been planning on our actions and this makes sense to me. We'll fly to one of the Sunny planets to see if we can help them start a revolution to distract the Pug-bears."

I admit that I knew it wasn't one of my best ideas, but my two furry friends both exclaimed excitedly about it.

"Ders a group of us that are working to overthrow them! We can signal them to break things," was their explanation.

That was good to know. They did have an underground resistance and they apparently were capable of breaking things, if not capable of violence to other living creatures. I decided that we could work with that. Anyway, we'd have to. There wasn't another option that I knew of.

CHAPTER 11

You'd think that starting on a long space voyage would require a lot of preparation and checking. It didn't. The Sunnys just didn't do things the way humans would. Frazzle sat down and pushed a button that caused the entire vessel to make a kind of low humming noise. Then he keyed a few coordinates in with one of the flat matrix keyboards, checking the video screen as he did. He finished up by pushing a button. The entire time, he didn't seem the least concerned that we were standing behind him. I don't know if he even thought about it.

Suddenly the view in the forward window started to shift and Uranus moved out of the screen. I had already forgotten the Sunnys had told me that there was artificial gravity on the ship, so I started to look for somewhere secure or something to hang onto at the least. Then I realized that I didn't have to worry. Despite the obvious movement of the ship, it felt as if I were remaining perfectly still.

Obviously, Newton's laws were held in abeyance by the Sunnys' technology. The artificial gravity not only maintained our weight, but the field did something else. It negated the effect of a change in momentum on our mass. We were perfectly cushioned and immune to any movement, no matter how abrupt.

I looked at the two guards and they seemed oblivious. They hadn't even realized that they might have been in danger. Erin, on the other hand, was clinging to the back of another seat with a death grip. She suddenly saw me and realized that I was standing unassisted. When she did, she released her grip and tried to act as if she were nonchalantly just leaning on the seat. I let it pass. She had an attitude problem when it came to men and there was no sense in aggravating the situation.

The ship smoothly rotated until it was pointing upwards, orthogonal to the plane of our solar system and then it began to accelerate. There wasn't any flash or dash about it. The thing just started moving. I could see the Sun from the edge of the window and it was rapidly getting smaller. In just a few minutes we were moving at a significant fraction of light speed. Once again, there was absolutely no sensation of movement. I might as well have been standing on the Earth or even lying in bed. The Sunnys had conversed among themselves and then each carefully occupied one of the seats in the rows behind the control station. They had the expectant attitude of a group of theater-goers just prior to the curtain-raising.

I was disappointed. I'd kind of hoped for some kind of fanfare or an impressive blast-off or something. In fact, I wasn't sure what was disappointing about it. The ship moved so effortlessly that I was impressed. It would probably get us where we were going rapidly.

Even though we were moving rapidly and it looked as if we were going to continue accelerating, I wondered what would happen when we got to light speed. Einstein had made some predictions about that speed limit that indicated that nothing good would come of the exercise. I caught Frazzle's eye and asked him, "What happens when we get to light speed?"

He answered with a series of clear mental images rather than trying to speak English. It seemed that the ship wouldn't actually cross the light speed barrier in normal space. Once it reached a critical speed, about three-quarters of light, the FTL system would engage. This system created a special field that had the effect of converting the matter composing the ship and contents into a waveform that was similar to the quantum energy waves of the universe. We'd become, in essence, frictionless waves. The ubiquitous virtual particles wouldn't interact with those that made up our form. When that field took effect, the effect somehow allowed us to almost surf on the faster-than-light torsion waves in the quantum field.

I tried but failed at understanding what was going on. I sent Frazzle my conception, but he rejected my interpretation. He tried again, laying out the same series of images, but more slowly. It was kind of like the way humans tend to shout when they are trying to communicate with someone who only speaks another language. Being yelled at mentally didn't help my understanding either.

I gave up and resigned myself to my feelings of inferiority. Then I had a cheering thought. Just because I didn't understand the technology, didn't mean that I couldn't use it to good effect. I just had to know what the specs were, so I could make sensible plans. I didn't have to know how it worked.

That thought made me feel better. I mean, I normally think I'm pretty smart, but this required a jump beyond anything human science had come up with to date. Maybe I was being too hard on myself. Expecting to grasp it without the appropriate background was kind of silly.

I regrouped and asked Frazzle, "How long will the ship take to travel to your planet?"

This time the answer was a little simpler, but I still had difficulty. He answered definitively with a single visual image. It came through to me as if I were seeing him holding a yardstick with another, much shorter one beside it. The short stick was quite short compared to the longer one. I suddenly realized that the longer stick was his conception of how far light traveled in a certain length of time. The short stick then must represent the length of our voyage.

I started to say, "I see," but then I realized that I really didn't. How long was the long stick, anyway? Was it one of our light-years or maybe a much shorter distance? I didn't understand the scale and therefore I didn't understand how long a time the short stick was supposed to represent. I asked for clarification, "Can you tell me how long it is in Earth days?"

This request was met with puzzlement. He knew what I meant, but he'd never been to Earth and hadn't studied it much either. He didn't really know how long a period of revolution Earth had. We compromised, or rather, I should say, he compromised and I just went along with the idea, by visualizing the distance from Earth to the Sun. I knew this was what he meant because he showed me the solar system and indicated the third planet as a base point. The short stick image was much longer than the Earth to Sun scale. I tried to mentally estimate the difference but finally gave it up as a bad deal.

The best I could do was to guess that the voyage was going to take a time that could be measured in our days, but how many, exactly, I couldn't quite figure. However, thinking about being confined in the ship made me realize that I'd better learn about the thing. We needed food, places to sleep, and toilet facilities. I also hoped fervently that there would be at least some weapons available on the ship. With the latter in mind, I looked around for Whistle. He wasn't in sight, so I walked back to the command chair and asked Frazzle where he was.

"He in the place where eats," was the response. I was starting to get used to their English if it could be called that.

"OK. Where is that place?" I responded, realizing that at least my worry about food might be solved with the answer. He simply pointed at a transporter on the left wall. I left the bridge through that exit and found myself in what was obviously a dining hall.

There was a large bank of machines that reminded me of a similar bank of human vending machines. Whistle was squatting on a bench near one of them, consuming some kind of fish-like thing. He'd finished eating before I got close enough to identify it.

Seeing me, he made some unidentifiable noises in his own speech and then pointed at a sub-group of the vending machines, "Dose gives food humans can eats."

I inspected the displays dubiously. The operation seemed simple. You determined what you wanted and then pressed a button by the item's picture. The dish popped out immediately and, voila, dinner was served. Unfortunately, it wasn't really that good. The one that I selected looked kind of like a bowl of meatballs, but it turned out to be some rather oily vegetables. I tried them, but they weren't anything I'd ever seen before. They didn't taste very good, but I don't like broccoli either.

"Are these from Earth?" I asked.

"No. Dey from other planets like yours. Humans eats those before."

"Where did those humans come from?"

"Dey captives of Great Ones. Dey all dead now." He moved his hands back and forth in a negating gesture that somehow conveyed sadness and sympathy at the same time.

Obviously, the Pug-bears had captured enough humans and held them long enough for food to become an issue. My previous conclusion, that the aliens' captives didn't live very long, was apparently incorrect. The Sunnys' had been forced to find food for the captive humans and this was to our benefit.

I was assuming that Whistle wouldn't steer me wrong on this issue. I had a moment's hesitation before I started eating, but I was hungry. In the calculus of survival, I knew that I'd have to eat sooner or later. I trusted Whistle enough not to worry overmuch about the quality of the food.

I didn't finish the vegetables. Dumping the dish in what proved to be an advanced type of garbage can, I inspected the other 'human' vending machines. One served some sort of fish and another yielded up something that looked like yogurt but tasted like meat paste. It was actually rather good and I ate the full serving. I noticed that it was quite filling and I cocked an inquiring eye at the Sunny.

He was sitting quietly, watching me try the food and he instantly caught my meaning.

"Dat meats with other things human bodies need," he volunteered. "It keep you healthy."

"It's good, too," I responded. "Did your people come up with these types of food for humans or do you eat these also?"

"No, we eats other things, not those. We studied human bodies and fixed these foods specially for you."

Not only were the Sunnys way ahead of us engineering and physics-wise, they were also far advanced in the biological sciences. I couldn't imagine a group of human researchers coming up with food for a strange alien life form, especially a recipe that tasted so good.

I had been worried about water, but that problem was easily solved. There was a surprisingly ordinary sink and faucet assembly beside the machines. It was paired with a human-made paper cup dispenser. When I saw it, I laughed and pointed. Whistle made some noises of his own and then informed me that, in his opinion, humans weren't totally hopeless. He thought the dispenser was a useful design and the Pugs had simply lifted a few of the things in between trying to take over our planet.

Turning to my primary concern, I asked him about weapons. This elicited a series of whistles and clicks that I couldn't make anything of. I moved to mental communication and got the sense that there were plenty of weapons on board. These were stored in a central location.

I didn't think too highly of the idea. My immediate thought was that there should be weapons lockers disbursed in convenient locations, but he indicated that wasn't necessary and sent me a visual of the passage into the ship. There was really only the transporter link that was used. It wasn't like there were numerous ports that could be broken into by boarding crews. Everyone normally came aboard through the transporter and that served as a choke-point that could be easily defended. As we talked, my train of thought was distracted by another idea; could we trust the other Sunnys? I didn't think they were directly antagonistic to us, but there was something about them I didn't quite trust.

We went on a short walk and he showed me the armory. It was a small room that held enough weapons to arm twenty or thirty Pugs. There were plenty of the chemical-powered, poison-splinter shooting hand-guns, but I was more excited about the five anti-matter rifles that I called 'eraser-guns.' These were just about the ultimate in no-muss, no-fuss hand-held weapons. You could shoot them at anything and it would crackle and disappear. The longer you held the trigger, the larger the effect. The only problem with them was they were often too powerful. I remembered that I'd inadvertently destroyed some of the transporter links by shooting incautiously in the past.

There weren't any of the electo-bolt shooting things. These were larger weapons that required a tripod for support. I supposed they amounted to a sort-of crew-served weapon for the Pugs, although a single Pug had taken a shot at my group with one in the past. He'd missed, fortunately. It was probably because the weapon was a little too large for a single individual, even one as strong as a Pug.

Towards the back of the room, I found two things that really made me happy. The first was a case of the anti-matter bombs or grenades since that was their approximate size. These were incredibly powerful little bombs that I'd used to good effect before. They released a wave of anti-matter that caused a very strong implosion when it came into contact with normal matter.

I immediately stuffed two in the pockets of my vest. You just never know when a good bomb will be necessary. It had been quite a while since I'd had one of these things and, under the circumstances, I found their weight very comforting.

The other discovery was a different type of pistol. It was about the size of the splinter-shooters, but it looked like it had more in common with the eraser-rifle. I held one up, displaying it to Whistle. His aversion to violence made it difficult for him to actually look at it, but he glanced at it briefly.

"Dat, whoosh, disappears things," he muttered, turning away partially, so as not to have to look directly at it. "It same as dose long shooting things." He waved in the general direction of the rack of eraser-rifles. If it was a pistol version of the anti-matter rifles, it was a very welcome discovery.

I took one of the eraser-rifles and one of the eraser-pistols, finishing off with a splinter-shooter. Together the things didn't weigh as much as my hunting rifle. There was definitely an advantage to the advanced alien weapons. Something struck my mind at that point. I had some difficulty conveying the idea to Whistle verbally, so I gave him a mental visualization of two spaceships shooting at each other. The thought nearly gave him a conniption-fit. His return thoughts were first of vehement denial and then of impossibility.

It turned out that the spaceship wasn't armed. The Pug-bears had encountered no other space-faring races and the idea of space combat hadn't come into their consciousness. Of course, the Sunnys couldn't conceive of such a thing either.

Whistle was somewhat aggravated with me. "You has bad ideas, now I got bad thoughts, too," he said, with an air of regret.

I felt guilty for giving him the idea of space combat, but it made perfect sense to me. I was only regretful that the ship itself wasn't armed. That was something that I resolved to rectify as quickly as I could.

Chapter 12

W hen we returned to the others, there was considerable tension there. The two big guys and Erin were lined up on one side of the room, somewhat nervously fingering their weapons. The rest of the Sunnys were grouped together on the far side of the stadium seats, whistling and clicking to each other and looking fearfully over their shoulders at the huge men. Frazzle was still sitting in the command chair, but had turned and was glancing back and forth between the two groups.

"Where the Hell did you go?" demanded Erin, the instant she saw me. "We can't trust these things!" She gestured at the defenseless Sunnys.

"Whoa! What's the problem?" I was taken aback. It seemed like I couldn't leave her alone for a moment without something coming up that set her off.

"They wouldn't talk to us and kept making those noises that you said were their speech. They were probably plotting how to get rid of us!"

"Calm down, Erin and you guys, too!" I glanced at Ted and Frank. "You should be ashamed of yourselves. These little people are our best friends and allies in this mission."

"Listen," she paused for breath, obviously trying to calm herself before continuing. "We don't know anything about this invasion or war or whatever you call it. We were supposed to find out about that spaceship thing that landed and then report back to the Warlord and the Master. Now, you get us involved in some kind of outer-space trip and we don't know what to think!"

"OK. I can see your point, but, remember, Earth was attacked. You know that. You've had to fight off the Pug-bears – "

She interrupted me, "Only the wild ones. The Master said that some of his kind were smart and would help us just as he does."

"Erin, you, yourself heard what the Sunnys had to say about their slavery and the plans of the Pug-bears. They're dead set on dominating every planet they can locate." The blamed woman was just as difficult to deal with as a porky pine. Nothing seemed to calm her down. Of course, considering my track record with women, at least until Liz came along, I didn't expect much by way of success.

I tried the two men, "Look you guys, you've seen that the Sunnys don't mean any harm. They can't even fight; they're simply unable to engage in violence." An inspiration hit me, "I found where they keep the food!"

"Oh!" they both said, simultaneously. "Show us! We're starved."

That finished the discussion. I sent a calming thought to the frightened Sunnys and led the trio to the cafeteria (I don't know what else to call it.) Once they got some food in them, they mellowed out considerably. Even Erin admitted that things could be worse.

I was mildly encouraged by their change of attitude, but I realized that they were too confused at the moment to be an asset to our mission. On top of that, I actually was rather unsure about the Sunnys. My first two contacts were reliable enough and their mental auras were strictly friendly and upright. I couldn't detect any dubious feelings in them. They seemed more than committed to the idea of trying to sabotage the Pug-bears' rule over their race. On the other hand, the six remaining members of the second group of Sunnys somehow didn't have quite the same sense of honesty about them. I couldn't actually put a finger on what it was, but I, too, distrusted them.

Putting that line of thought into the back of my mind, I suggested to the other three that we look for some cabins. They were tired and the thought of someplace to sleep was welcome. Together we went back to the bridge.

We surprised the Sunnys when we came through the transporter. Frazzle and Whistle were engaged in what appeared to be an argument with the other six. They stopped instantly and the six filed out through the transporter that we'd just exited. I looked inquiringly at Frazzle and he glanced at Whistle before speaking. Whistle made some kind of motion to him and he apparently took it as an assent to address my prior concern, "Will you make mind-talk with me?"

I indicated that I would, but I needed to find a place for my companions to rest before I engaged in an extended dialog. Whistle pointed at the back of the bridge and started walking that way.

I was surprised to find an ordinary door there. It opened into a long and wide hallway that reminded me somehow of the corridors at the Stanley Hotel in Estes Park. There were rows of closed doors on both sides of the hall.

Whistle turned to me and said, "Dey can sleep in any of these rooms. Dey all good for Sunnys or humans."

We investigated and he was correct. The rooms weren't terribly large, you wouldn't expect that on a spaceship, but they offered enough space for even Ted to lie down. The floors were cushioned with some fur-like covering and the lights dimmed automatically when the occupant of the room lay down. It was a good sleeping arrangement, although there was a noticeable absence of places to store personal possessions.

The Sunnys didn't require much by way of clothes, sometimes wearing nothing and other times wearing a kind of light-weight pants. They also didn't have much of a sense of ownership regarding the small tools they had. Frazzle was an exception with his metal lunchbox. He held onto it carefully. It represented some kind of rarity in his mind.

Despite the lack of a chest of drawers or closets, all three of my fellow humans exclaimed at the softness of the floor and had soon picked out their own rooms. Erin made me promise to rouse her if anything happened and I agreed that I would, although I assured her that we were going to be traveling for a number of days. Ted and Frank just stoically laid their weapons aside and lay down. The lights in their rooms dimmed and I shut their doors.

Now, I was alone with Whistle. We returned to the bridge and he changed places with Frazzle, taking the control seat.

Frazzle came back and sat in the stadium seating while I sat cross-legged on the floor. It was time for us to make some plans. I sank into the half trance that I had found was most effective and sent an image that I was willing to communicate.

He wanted to keep the discussion mental, even though it was difficult for him. I had to do the work of both parties since all he could do was to try and control his surface thoughts so that I could glean a coherent meaning from them. The cause of the disagreement quickly became clear. He was afraid that my companions would become aggressive if they understood that the majority of the Sunnys were dubious about our goals.

The other six hadn't totally rejected the idea that we could provide some assistance to their race, but, in self-protection, they were actively exploring the possibility of capturing us and turning us over to the Pug-bears. They had been arguing with my two friends about this subject.

It was funny that I'd had those exact same thoughts while in the cafeteria. Thinking it over, I decided that I was doing some type of unconscious monitoring of them and had possibly sensed the discord.

I realized that Whistle was also paying close attention to us, even though he was excluded from our mental conversation. I carefully extended my thoughts and contacted his mind also. It wasn't any harder to communicate with both of them than it had been with one.

I assured the two that I meant what I said about attempting to help. Their minds lit up with gratitude and I knew that they would be reliable and helpful in the effort. They let me know that the others were from a different Sunny world, one that had suffered the depredations of the Pug-bears for far longer than theirs. The Sunnys on that world were now an endangered species and the six were suffering from a version of what I'd call Stockholm syndrome. They had become so fearful of the Pug-bears that they partly identified with them as a self-defense mechanism.

Whistle gave me an insight into their thought patterns. "When your people have been mostly killed and eaten by another group and there is no justification for the destruction in your own philosophy, it becomes easy to assume that the predators are correct. There must be something wrong with your people that makes them deserve their fate. If you think you're wrong, then everything the others do must be correct and you should help them because the greatest good is for correctness to triumph," he thought.

"The greatest good is actually in our favor! Your people have become victims of the Pug-bears and their will to destroy all other races. You must help me do something to stop them," I responded.

They agreed in principle but weren't sure how to go about opposing the Pug-bears. I questioned them at length about the planet that was our destination. It was very similar to Earth but had more water and less land. The major continent was a band around the center of the planet. The two oceans dominated the north and south hemispheres. There were two large, coastal mountain ranges that divided the landmass in rough halves, north from south and as a result, the climate was very different from that of Earth. The ranges were separated by hundreds of miles and the land between was desert and very dry. The clouds banked up against the sea-side of the mountains and dumped their moisture there, but none ever got over the high peaks.

Each hemisphere had two main seasons: winter and summer. Spring and fall were very short. In addition, the mountain ranges largely kept the winds circulating in two discrete climate patterns and hurricanes were common. The temperature range was wider than our average and I judged that there would be times of the year that would be distinctly uncomfortable for humans.

The Sunnys had large cities that stretched out on both shores of the central continent. The cities were connected by transporters, so if winter got too onerous for you, you could easily go to the summer side of the landmass. The Pug-bears hadn't yet finished dominating the planet, having only invaded about twenty of the local years ago. They lived close to the mountain ranges and rarely approached the seashore. They didn't like the higher humidity, especially in the summer. However, they ranged broadly in the long, dry winter and no location was safe from them at that time of year.

The strip of inter-mountain desert provided a perfect breeding place for the Pug-bears. Their eggs were sensitive to humidity and, as I'd seen in Carlsbad Caverns, high humidity caused most of them to rot before hatching.

The Sunnys had tried to build barricades to keep the Pug-bears away from their homes, but the combination of the Sunnys' pacifism and the Pug-bears' mental control made it easy for the Pug-bears to dominate the weaker and smaller creatures. There had been an initial slaughter when the largely feral Pug-bears had killed and eaten many of the Sunnys. The survivors had lived through this period by locking themselves in impregnable buildings and placing the keys out of easy reach. They'd suffered tremendously from the mental compulsions inflicted on them by the hungry aliens. If they'd been able, they would have taken the keys and opened the doors, placing themselves at the disposal of the Pug-bears. Hiding the keys and leaving the access codes in code that required considerable rational power to decipher kept them from giving themselves up.

They had finally determined that the feral Pug-bears didn't like high humidity and they set up huge systems of sprinklers that sprayed ocean water over their cities. This meant that it was always raining on their homes. The Pug-bears that carried the mature symbionts allowed this minimal defense since they wanted to preserve enough of the Sunnys to create weapons, transporter, and spaceships.

At times, they allowed the ferals to enter the cities and prey on any Sunny unfortunate enough to be caught. This random predation kept the Sunnys' numbers low and had been responsible for greatly slowing their technological development. The situation had degenerated into an unstable balance with the Pug-bears gradually increasing in number while the Sunnys slowly decreased.

The Sunny birth rate was much lower than that of their enemies. The Pug-bears laid eggs in mass and left them nearly anywhere. As often as one would defend its nest, others would simply walk away and leave the eggs and hatchlings to survive as best they could. They had no strong instinct to preserve their genetic lineage in the way that humans would.

I had understood from our prior conversation that the Sunnys had some sort of resistance movement and I had entertained great hopes for that, but the reality was discouraging. Their idea of resistance was to place locks on the sprinkler timers so that they couldn't be turned off at the Pug-bears mental command. This irritated the Pug-bears but didn't seriously deter them if they were truly motivated to come into the city.

The Sunny resistance had also been building up a stock-pile of weapons, all the while knowing that they couldn't really make good use of them. There had been an effort to condition some volunteers to the idea of violence, but it hadn't worked well.

I suggested that they should make automatic controls for their weapons so that they could set them to destroy anything that moved. It turned out that they'd tried that, but the scheme had met with the disapproval of the intelligent Pug-bears. They'd forced the Sunnys to turn off the control systems. The weapons were still in place, but inactive as of the last news my friends had received.

The planetary geology wasn't conducive to some grand strategy such as dropping a large rock on the heads of the Pug-bears. I'd considered towing an asteroid towards the planet, but the creatures were disbursed along the mountains all around the globe. Dropping high-velocity projectiles on their heads was attractive, but it seemed impractical. The Sunny cities, distributed along the seashores, would probably suffer more than the Pug-bears.

There was one possibility that I could think of. If I could somehow increase the humidity on the planet, it would discommode the aliens. Frazzle seemed to think that high humidity would ensure that their eggs wouldn't hatch. I wasn't sure about that, remembering how damp it was in the cave at Carlsbad where we'd first realized the Pug-bears and the spider things were related. Some of the eggs we'd discovered there had hatched, so I thought that some would be able to survive higher humidity.

I considered that memory and suddenly the memories bequeathed me by the Ancient-One generated an image of new hatchlings that were suffocated by high humidity. I knew from this that they were sensitive enough that my plan might at least slow down their expansion.

It was kind of naive of me, I guess, but I had somewhere read that comets were largely composed of ice. I reasoned that I could find some large icy interplanetary mass and use the ship to pull it to the point where it would fall on the mountains. The resultant vaporization of the ice should greatly increase the humidity of the entire planet.

I explained my thinking to the Sunnys and they were initially aghast at the idea of deliberately dropping something that could kill large numbers of living creatures on their planet, but after they calmed down and thought it over, they admitted that it might just have the effect that I hoped it would.

I asked if their cities could survive the heavy rain that was likely to be generated by such a strategy. They discussed it rapidly in a series of clicks and whistling sounds. Then Frazzle told me that they believed their people would be able to shunt most of the water out into the ocean, provided that they had some advance warning. They believed that their people could set up a series of dams across the city streets that would allow most of the water to pass through without damaging too much of the infrastructure. The thing that gave me hope for this plan was that the Pug-bears didn't monitor everything the Sunnys did, as long as they created the items the aliens demanded.

We agreed that we'd give the idea a try. As Frazzle put it, "We got nothings else to do."

It was indirect violence, but I suspected they justified it by pretending that they were dropping water on the mountain rocks with no intention of harming living things.

CHAPTER 13

After the initial excitement of the acceleration and after we got used to the ship's environment, things seemed to move slowly. The voyage to the Sunnys' system took longer than I liked and we'd had time to be bored for almost a day. My concern about time measurements was borne out when I finally managed to understand that the voyage would take about fourteen days.

Shortly after I'd finished conversing with the two Sunnys, I found my way to a cabin and fell asleep. After a couple of hours, I became conscious of a difference in the background sound of the ship and it woke me up. I hadn't satisfied my sleep requirements and was feeling as if I couldn't fully wake up, but I decided to go investigate.

The cabin I'd chosen was adjacent to those of the other three humans and, as I went into the hall, Frank came out of his cabin. He looked at me inquiringly and asked, "What just happened?"

"I don't know. I'm on my way to check it out."

"Do you want me to come along, in case you need help?" He was still suspicious of the Sunnys.

I decided that it might not be a bad idea to have him come. It was the first action that I'd seen him take that indicated any independence of thought. He'd previously focused his actions on satisfying Erin's orders and guarding her safety. This might be a good chance for me to get to know him a little better. I figured I could use all of the allies I could get.

"Yeah. Maybe you'd better come with me. It wouldn't hurt and you can make sure that everything is going well," I agreed.

"Look, I know what you think. It's not that I don't trust you, but I've made a promise to Erin to protect her. I know she's unreasonable at times, but what can you do?" He shrugged and gave a grin, indicating that he sometimes found it hard to put up with her, too. I didn't ask, but I suspected that he enjoyed the challenge. He was always nearby whenever she was out of her cabin. He certainly took good care of her.

"Frank, you don't know me, but I want you to know that I need for the four of us to stick together. This is a very risky raid we're making and it's one that I wouldn't have voluntarily chosen, but we got transported to Oberon by accident. It's kind of like it was meant to be that way. I've been communicating with the Sunnys and I'm convinced that they are our best friends in this effort. Their people are enslaved and they think we're their only hope of changing that. I've got a wife and child on Earth and I'm going to do everything in my power to ensure their safety."

He nodded, solemnly and replied, "I'm with you, brother." He held out his hand and I gripped it. We looked into each others eyes and I read a sense of well-meaning honesty in his aura as we touched.

Turning down the hall, I continued, "Besides, this isn't unpleasant. We've got food, it's warm and we've got a good place to sleep. It could be a lot worse."

"How long do you think this ship will take us to get to their planet?" he asked, coming back to the issue at hand.

"They gave me an estimate, but I really couldn't understand their measurement. I don't think it will take too long; maybe a couple of weeks – " We entered the bridge and I forgot what I was going to say.

The view through the wrap-around glass was very strange. There were stars directly ahead, but the nearer ones seemed to move in a curve towards us. It was kind of like being at the bottom of a funnel while water was being poured down the sides. The stars accelerated in our direction and became elongated and appeared to turn into colorful streaks as they passed our sides. The beauty of the view was enhanced by the fact that they changed colors as they flew by, becoming noticeably red-hued as they approached the back edge of the viewing port.

"Dis the faster-than-light travel!" Whistle was sitting nearby and had noticed our stunned amazement. "We get der soon now."

He added an unexpected comment that made me wonder again how the FTL drive worked. "Is like what you call surfing. We ride the universe waves. Dey very fast."

I realized that the constant background hum of the EmDrive had ceased and that was the change that had woken us. The FTL system didn't seem to make any audible sound at all. It was dead quiet in the ship. The only effect was the disconcerting visual distortion of space as we traveled. It apparently was 'very fast' indeed.

"We might as well go back to sleep," I turned to Frank.

"You go ahead. I'm going to stay here and watch the light show. It's amazing," he replied.

"OK," I paused and then added, "remember that these guys are our friends."

"That's not necessary. I'm committed to this game," he chided me.

"Sorry. I just can't help worrying about everything," I shook my head deprecatingly.

"Don't worry about it. I'll let you know if anything happens and I'm not going to frighten the little guys again," he put his hand on my shoulder and gave me a push towards the door. "Now go on back to sleep."

I decided that I had to trust him. There really wasn't much choice about it. The four of us were locked into the voyage and we had to stick together. Besides, I was still sleepy.

Just as I was about to enter my cabin, Erin stuck her head out of her door. I sighed and turned to see if she was going to pitch another fit, but she seemed calm.

"What's going on?" she asked.

"Nothing, really. We transitioned to faster-than-light speed and it woke me up. Frank is on the bridge watching the ship and he'll wake us if anything happens that needs our attention.

"Then it's alright. If he's out there, I mean. He's very trustworthy," she nodded her head as if trying to convince me. "It's just that this is so strange – " She paused and then added, "I know I've been difficult, but I'm frightened and lonely."

Now, I'm not too good with women. I like them, but I've never been able to really understand them. My mental abilities helped, but I'd developed a personal ethos that mostly kept me from reading my companion's minds unless it was an emergency. I didn't exactly read her mind in this instance, but her intent sort of soaked through and I slowly realized that this was an invitation. My thoughts immediately went back to my wonderful wife. I'd just left Liz a few days ago and now this complication came up.

I decided that my best approach would be to deliberately misunderstand her, "I'm lonely, too, and this is a frightening situation. It's not like humans have ever gone on an interstellar voyage before. But, remember, this isn't so bad. We've got food and a place to sleep. The Sunnys are our friends and this ship travels so fast that we'll be there and back in a very reasonable time."

I smiled at her and entered my cabin. Just before I shut the door, I turned to her and added, "Now, go back to sleep for a while and I'll catch up with you over breakfast."

She sighed and turned back into her room. I made sure her door shut, before shutting mine. Once I was inside my cabin, I sent a mental image to Whistle of him waking me if anything happened. I received a sense of confusion for a moment. He hadn't realized that I didn't have to be facing him to communicate, but then his thoughts cleared and I received an image of him opening my door if he needed help. That was good enough. I terminated my contact and laid down. Sleep came quickly.

Chapter 14

The next days went by slowly, but we managed to get through them without any major problems. Frank had noticeably warmed up to me. We had a number of interesting conversations about football and also about his life after the EMP.

I don't know where the Sunnys slept, or even if they slept. They seemed to be always hovering around in the bridge area or in the cafeteria. The four of us humans sat watches in the bridge, but it was mostly just to have something to do. There was nothing going on except the interminable distortion of the stars as they slid in towards us and turned into colorful streaks as they flew by.

I alternated sleeping, eating, and sitting on the bridge with exploring the ship. Frank sometimes went along with me, but he found the low overhead disconcerting and preferred to stay on the bridge or in his room. Ted, taciturn as always, slept as much as possible. Erin spent the preponderance of her time watching the stars and trying to talk to the Sunnys. Her behavior towards me was cool. She seemed to be angry about something, but I really couldn't figure out what it was. Perhaps she was worried about what the Warlord would think about her taking off into space and ignoring his requirements. It didn't compute to me and I just ignored her as best I could while I concentrated on other things.

Frazzle approached me about her. He didn't understand why she kept referring to taking the ship back to Earth. He was focused on helping his people with our aid and didn't care for her wanting to turn the ship over to her leader, the Warlord. Besides we weren't going to Earth at the moment.

There was an inter-species gap in comprehension there and it made him unhappy.

I tried to reassure him that she was just uncomfortable in her own way and reaching for a resolution to the situation that would most benefit those she cared about. His response was, "You help we the way you say and we help you get rid of the Great Ones in your system."

That was satisfactory to me. By now, I had come to consider the Sunnys' friends and allies. They couldn't engage in violence even if their survival depended on it and that made them even more worthy of protection. I was counting on their mastery of technology to provide a large boost for humanity and to help us rid ourselves of the Pug-bear threat.

I happened to be standing on the bridge, watching the streaming stars flow by, when we approached our destination. One particular, reddish star centered itself in the view. The stars had been gradually elongating and moving past us, but this one didn't elongate, instead. it grew rapidly in size and brightness. We must have been slowing down because the streaming effect of the nearby stars gradually ceased as we approached the red one.

As I watched, the ship made a sort of minuscule shudder, and then the view changed. We'd dropped out of FTL travel and were back in normal space. The sub-light EmDrive kicked on, creating a low, not unpleasant sound in the background. We continued moving towards the red sun at a greatly reduced speed. There was no hurry since I hadn't fully formulated what I wanted to do there, other than gather information and possibly help the Sunnys in some way.

Frazzle turned from his seat at the command console and motioned to me. I could sense that he was in doubt, so I made mental contact.

"There's a lot of radio communication going on in the system," he thought. "From the conversations I've picked up, some of my people are trying to break free of the Great Ones' mental control. They're in spacecraft and are trying to reach a ring of asteroids that circles this star. It's like the belt that circles yours, although it is much denser."

"There usually isn't much happening here. The Great Ones don't seem to worry about being attacked since my people are the only ones that have spacecraft. Even if they are watching, we're too far out for our wave-front to have reached the planet. We don't make much of a target. The ship does create a momentary flash when it drops out of FTL, but we came in far enough out to make it unlikely that anyone will detect us for many hours."

"I've been monitoring the comm chatter and it is all Sunny communications. It's old, not in our time frame, since it's all from in-system sources. The Pugs rarely communicate although they do monitor the local comm bands just to keep track of what we do. The Great Ones are sure we're under their control and don't worry about us." He paused in his thought stream and looked at the instruments.

I projected a question into his mind, "What about the Pugs? Won't they send out some kind of craft to intercept your people?"

"Perhaps. They do have a few shuttles that are armed. They normally use them against surface targets on worlds that are being enslaved, but they might be able to target our ships." He seemed dubious and ill at ease discussing potential violence.

"We'd better contact your people and see if they have any plan, other than to hide in the asteroids," I said this out loud for the benefit of Frank and Erin, who'd just come into the bridge.

"What's going on?" she asked.

"It looks like some of the Sunnys have gotten free of the Pug-bears and are trying to hide," I explained. "I think we should carry on with our comet idea. That seems to me to be the best way to disrupt any potential reprisal against them. We don't have any ship to ship weapons anyway."

"We haves a big anti-matter shooter in storage," Frazzle unexpectedly volunteered.

"What! Why didn't you say so before?" I was upset with him. I knew I shouldn't be. His people were so unreservedly pacifistic that it made me wonder how they'd ever survived. "Can it be mounted on the outside of the ship in such a way that we can control its aim from the bridge?"

The short answer I received was, "Yes." The long version required a lot of mental images and some mental squirming on his part. He didn't like to think of using the weapon against other intelligent life forms.

From his information, I learned that the weapon could be mounted the way I wanted. The problem was going to be getting the Sunnys to do the job. He thought that they could set up the mount and electronics with no problem, but I was going to have to install the gun in the cradle, myself. Arming a few of the short-range shuttle-craft was a task that the Pugs normally did. The Sunnys were unwilling to arm their ships and their resistance to the idea was practically disabling. The Pug-bears avoided the issue by having the Sunny technicians train the Pugs to install the weapons on the few armed shuttles they maintained.

Their stock of armed spacecraft was strictly limited. This lack of foresight could be attributed to the odd way the Pug-bears achieved their intelligence. The symbiont eggs they consumed were not very fertile and only attached to their brains rarely. This meant that the brain-enhanced Pug-bears were usually older individuals and, due to their aggressive natures, there weren't too many of them that lived out their entire one-hundred and forty-year potential lifespan.

The fact that there were few really intelligent ones paired with their history of dominance over all of the races they'd encountered made them complacent. They'd never had to face a serious challenge aside from the intractable denizens of the fifteenth world they'd attacked and those creatures were not technologically oriented, so they were very unlikely to achieve space travel. All told, I figured the Pug-bears had enjoyed success far too long. It was about time that someone slapped them around a bit. I wanted to be that someone.

With that in mind, I got Frazzle to start the other Sunnys working on installing the necessary superstructure and connections for the weapon. We inspected the anti-matter gun they'd had stored in the back of a cargo hold. It was wrapped tightly in opaque plastic, but when we'd cut the wrappings off, I was pleased to see that it was much larger and more robustly made than the shoulder-held versions. I looked at Frazzle, inquiringly, but he just shook his head and indicated that the Pugs had ordered it for some purpose that he didn't want to think about. I was pleased with it, though, it was large enough that it should do a lot of damage. I hoped that we could get it working before we met any serious opposition.

The anti-matter weapons generated a field that created either a continuous stream of discrete pulses or a single pulse of anti-matter particles. I didn't know how the mechanism worked, but the range seemed to only be limited by how many normal matter particles intervened between the muzzle of the weapon and the target. In space, there should be far fewer gas molecules to interfere, so the range should be much further. The weapons probably launched the anti-matter particles at a certain velocity, similar to a conventional rifle, but if the thing were mounted on the bow of a spacecraft moving at high speed, the effective velocity would be greatly augmented.

I was only speculating since the Sunnys refused to talk about the potential of the gun, but I hoped that it would be enough to give the Pugs and their masters a real surprise. The weapon wouldn't have as much range if it were used to target the ground from orbit. The density of the atmosphere would probably attenuate the anti-matter beam.

There were a lot of floating rocks conveniently located in the system's asteroid belt. These would all make very good Kinetic Energy Weapons. I wasn't above chucking a few smaller rocks down at strategic targets. Larger KEWs would make too much of a mess and probably kill some of the Sunnys; an outcome that I hoped to avoid.

The problem was that I didn't actually know how large a mass would do what. The physics was a little beyond me. I mean I could calculate momentum, but how do you know by just looking how much an asteroid masses? There were probably any number of ways to figure it out, but I didn't know any off the top of my head. In addition, once you've got the mass and the velocity, you know the force involved, but how do you convert this into a way to limit the damage of the impact? I thought it would be complicated by such things as atmospheric density, impact angle, and the type of target, but, hey, I'm basically just a guy who causes problems for the opposition. My best guess was to ask the Sunnys, except I couldn't tell them exactly what I had in mind.

This line of thought kept me productively occupied through the rest of the morning. I spent some time questioning Frazzle about the onboard computer capabilities, specifically about whether the comp could easily calculate orbital mechanics and velocities with the objective of placing a – I told Frazzle – cargo down at any set location. He answered in the affirmative. The comp could easily handle the math. However, he did sternly warn me that any valuable cargo would have to have some means of shedding velocity or it would be destroyed.

I brushed off this admonition. I had every intention of having the "cargo" destroyed along with everything in the immediate vicinity of the "landing." I don't think he actually knew what I had in mind. He didn't seem upset the way they usually did when I talked about harming other sentient life forms. In fact, he mentioned, of all things, parachutes as a means of landing.

I also asked him if there was some way to move a rock along with the ship. This nearly tore it because he immediately began cautioning me as to the potential destruction associated with high-V mass. I shrugged it off and finally got him to admit that the internal gravity system could be used to create a point gravity source outside of the ship. It was touchy, but he seemed to believe that a rock could be boosted to significant velocity by dragging it along behind an artificially created mass. That was what I hoped to hear and I slept well that night.

By mid-day, the Sunnys had completed the installation of the weapon mount and the electronics. The gun was self-powered and had the capability of firing about a hundred brief pulses or a shorter, continuous beam. After that, it had to be reloaded manually with another power pack. I asked them if that could be done remotely, but they informed me that they didn't have the equipment on the ship to create the required connections.

The problem then was in my hands. After some careful fitting and a lot of instructions from the Sunnys, I managed to get into a slightly modified Pug space suit. It was a combination of skin-tight fabric and a surprisingly small helmet that almost seemed like a mask. It made me feel claustrophobic, but since it provided a strong flow of cool air, I figured that I could put up with it for long enough to mount the gun.

We went to the cargo hold where the weapon was stored and here another problem became apparent. The eraser-rifles were lightweight, but this thing was much larger and far too heavy for me to move. The Sunnys had a cargo handler that could pick it up, but the exoskeleton was designed for only Sunnys to operate and they weren't going to carry the piece out to the mount.

After some thought, I had them tie a cable on the gun and simply drop it through the cargo hold door. We were all in pressure suits, so no problem there. They simply evacuated the hold, opened the door, and pitched the weapon outside with the cargo loader. It bumped gently against the hull and then floated off, free of the internal gravity field. It amazed me that the generated gravity field only covered things inside the ship. Once outside, the mass was still there, of course, but the weight disappeared.

I carefully moved out and snagged the weapon. My suit had some kind of adhesive soles on the boots and I could walk, albeit very carefully, on the side of the ship. It took a lot of careful pulling to get the mass started moving, but once it was, it continued easily as I gradually towed the gun up to the front of the ship.

It was my first chance to see what we'd been traveling in. The shape was like nothing I'd ever imagined. It was long and lean with a slim waist that sort of reminded me of a wasp. There were some large vanes attached to the rear portion of the hull. They didn't look aerodynamic and I knew the ship couldn't land anyway, so I assumed they had something to do with the propulsion system. I didn't know how it worked, other than there were actually two components, the sub-light EmDrive, and the FTL device.

The vanes were large and mounted solidly in heavy brackets attached to the sides of the ship. They weren't smooth looking like something you might see on TV prior to the Lucas spaceships. Their surface was covered with tiny spikes that slanted slightly aft. The vane color was a flat, dead black and I supposed that was necessary for effective functioning. The Sunnys' normal color preference was for bright colors, although the Masters didn't usually allow them to waste resources on aesthetics. They'd painted the insides of their personal spaces, where the Masters didn't go, in primary colors that reminded me of the ones favored by human children.

The slim waist expanded smoothly into the main body of the ship. There were mounts for detachable cargo holds or shuttles at the top of the waist. There was a single, boxy cargo container currently attached that was balanced on the other side of the ship by a sleek shuttle-craft that made human efforts look primitive and clunky.

Above the attachment mounts, the body of the ship rose in a slant to its full diameter and extended for a considerable distance until it gradually tapered to the bow. The bridge windows were obvious as I passed them and I could see my compatriots watching me closely. I waved cheerfully, although inside I was actually quite nervous. This wasn't anything my previous training had prepared me to do. Most recently I'd been living a primitive existence as a mountain man, so it was a memorable experience.

The gun mount was located exactly on the tip of the bow. The bow was covered with a heavily reinforced, dome-shaped plate that curved off towards the rear of the ship. Frazzle had explained to me that a deflector field was required to protect the ship from particle abrasion and rocks. The reinforced plate did double duty as a shield for any bits that managed to get through the field and also served as the main, I guess you could call it, antenna for generating the deflector field. It also made a great hard point for the gun mount.

I'd wondered if the gun would suffer damage from particles, but Frazzle had assured me that it was unlikely. The deflector field was a powerful application of their artificial gravity generator and it rarely allowed anything to strike the bow plate. I was dubious, but there wasn't any other choice that made as much sense for the mount.

As I approached the bow, I had to remember to start the gun's mass decelerating long before I reached the mount. It wouldn't do to try and just yank it to a standstill; it'd pull me right off the side of the ship. Likewise, I couldn't snag it by looping the cable around the mount. The gently moving mass would inevitably hit the end of the cable and rebound, possibly with deleterious effect. I didn't want to be knocked off the ship or caught in a bight of cable and lose an arm or leg and I certainly didn't want the gun to swing around and impact the hull or the bridge windows.

The gun was moving along smoothly, a little behind me and above, so I simply slowed down and let it catch up as I approached the bow. It drifted gently by, seemingly all innocent, but when it got to the end of the cable, it gave me one hell of a jerk. I rapidly shuffled forward, trying to keep my arms in their sockets, all of the while pulling backward to try and bleed off some of its momentum. I finally succeeded in stopping its movement just as I was beginning to wonder if it would simply pull me off the front of the ship.

Once stopped, it was a tedious and painstaking process to get the thing lined up with the mount, but I finally succeeded and clipped it into the aiming servos with titanium pins. The electronics, on the other hand, were easy to connect. There were a couple of rather ordinary power plugs and what looked for all the world like an old-fashioned Centronics parallel connector. That was it.

Mentally dusting off my hands, I retreated to the bridge window and gave the others the 'thumbs-up' signal. They dutifully applauded and I returned to the port, came back in through the lock, and hung up my suit after spending about ninety minutes on my first spacewalk.

Altogether, it hadn't been nearly as frightening as I'd thought it might be and I was pleased to have the ship armed. Just how effective the gun would be remained to be seen. I resolved to test it at the first opportunity on some innocuous target like a rock, especially a rock that couldn't shoot back before we got into a shoot-to-kill situation.

CHAPTER 15

The test opportunity came very quickly. We were still over ten light hours away from the occupied planet and we were traveling at a greatly reduced rate through a belt of rocks and debris. Apparently, the red star had undergone a very messy birth leaving behind a lot of navigational hazards in the system. This was one of the reasons the Sunnys had first settled on the planet. Along with plain rocks and water ice floating around, there were lots of metallic asteroids and the mining was good. They had a significant fleet of small mining craft designed for in-system use only; no FTL on them and only a small EmDrive unit that could move ore into orbit around their planet, where it could be refined, conveniently, in space.

Frazzle and I were the only ones on the bridge when the hull mass-proximity sensors (even though I had no idea how they worked and hadn't even known they were there) picked up a thicker clot of rock and dust almost in our direct path. I became aware of it when a chime rang and a series of lights lit up on the control console, causing Frazzle to make some rapid adjustments. As a result, the ship began to veer off its course slightly. When I asked him, he explained that the proximity detectors had indicated enough mass in our path to cause the deflector shield problems.

This was just what I'd been hoping for and I instructed him to slowly approach the mass. I told him that I wanted to see if we could clear navigation hazards with the bow gun. After a moment's shock at the idea of using the thing, he actually seemed to approve.

"Dat what you do then? Clear out rocks with anti-matter – that's good idea!"

I wasn't so sure that he meant it. He was probably just relieved that I wanted to shoot at inanimate objects rather than live ones, but I encouraged him to move closer to the rocks so that I could actually see them. I wanted to have a visual on the effect of the gun. This would probably be the only chance I had to check the improvised system out. Actual combat situations would undoubtedly be at long range and there would be no sign of a hit other than the disappearance of a threat marker on the computer display.

We moved close enough to see several large rocks tumbling in a kind of arabesque. They were moving together in a path around the star and had obviously done enough grinding to reduce the ones tempted to collide into small particles. There was a lot of dust and gravel moving along with them.

I sat at the fire-control station, a video display on the corner of the long bridge console. The Sunnys had mounted a joystick there. It had only a couple of buttons plus a trigger. They'd briefed me on its functionality and it was ridiculously simple to use. The stick moved the gun and the display showed target and range. One of the buttons activated a green laser designator and the other locked the system onto the designated target. The system was then armed and ready to fire.

The trigger would fire a brief burst for a millisecond if pushed and released. If pushed and held in, the burst would become a series of millisecond pulses, separated by a fraction of a second. It reminded me of a human ma-deuce in that respect. I felt instinctively that I could really hose down a target in the pulse mode.

Picking out the largest rock in the swarm was the work of a moment. The laser designator locked on and the gun began to track automatically. At this point, unless I moved the joystick in a large motion or thumbed off the designator, it would stay on target automatically. I watched the motion of the turret and barrel for thirty seconds or so. It worked just as advertised. The rock, spinning rather erratically, stayed right in the center of the video display where it was displayed in a lurid red color. The non-targeted companions showed in a light yellow.

I tired of watching the display and pressed the trigger. There was a slight delay as the anti-matter burst reached out to the rock. Then nothing. I was disappointed. The rock simply disappeared with not even a flash. I remembered that the eraser guns had much the same effect. We'd wondered why there was no explosion, only a crackling sound, but not having any other experience with anti-matter coming into contact with matter, I'd decided that was just the way it was.

The big weapon worked in the same fashion. No flash, no recoil – just a disappeared target. I took the joystick and sequentially destroyed the other elements of the swarm as Frazzle watched. Once they were gone, I held down the trigger and erased the gravel that remained. The space was clear.

I turned to him and said, "What is the range for the mass detectors attached to the system? I'd like to try it on a distant target."

The answer was a little more complex. The range varied depending upon the mass, as you might expect. We finally settled on a large rock that was about a hundred yards in diameter. It was traveling in the same orbit but was approximately a thousand miles ahead of us. The mass detectors had no difficulty sensing it, but here a problem arose. I tried and tried, but couldn't get the laser designator to touch the thing. It was just too far away for my relatively coarse movements to fine-tune the pointer.

After watching me fruitlessly try for a couple of minutes, Frazzle pointed out that the video display had a touch-sensitive function. He reached out and touched the image of the rock with a small forefinger and the laser instantly locked onto it. I was a little upset with him, but he acted as if he was enjoying my astonishment, so I let him feel good about the surprise.

When I pressed the trigger button momentarily, the image instantly reduced in size but didn't disappear. The laser designator continued to illuminate the remainder of the rock and I fired another pulse. This time, the entire target was destroyed. Considering the size of the target, I figured that even the first shot would have disabled a spacecraft, opening it up to hard vacuum and doing all kinds of damage to its systems. I was very satisfied with the weapon and, in fact, couldn't wait to get a chance to try it out on the enemy.

While I'd been happily shooting rocks, the ship had continued moving closer to the inner system asteroid belt. We could now hear the comm chatter and it was almost on our timeline, delayed by a matter of minutes, rather than hours. It was nearly time to make contact with the escaping Sunnys and to move on to the next phase of our attack. I instructed Frazzle to let them know we were on the way to their location and directly a startled-sounding Sunny voice came through.

I couldn't understand what was said, so I mentally tuned in to Frazzle's side of the conversation.

They were first alarmed at the idea that an FTL craft was returning, thinking it was under Pug-bear control, but after they got the message that we were rebels who were there to help them regain their freedom, they were very excited.

They were miners who'd been only minimally supervised by the Pugs. They'd been engaged in exploratory mining in the asteroid belt that was between their planet and the next one out in orbit, a smaller gas giant on the order of Neptune in size. The Sunnys had been planning an escape from the Masters for over a year and had made a break from their routine only a couple of days ago.

They had about twenty ships, but some were very small, only suitable for a couple of Sunnys and prospecting equipment. Others were larger delivery vessels that were used to haul the ore from the asteroids into orbit around their planet. They had set up orbital refineries in order to keep the waste products off of the surface. They periodically boosted the waste into a higher orbit, accumulated it, and then put an inexpensive, ionic pusher-engine on the package that would eventually shove it out of the system perpendicular to the ecliptic. The refined metals were transported from the orbital stations directly to their final destinations on the surface using larger matter transporters.

I asked Frazzle why they didn't use matter transporters to move the raw ore from the asteroid belt. It seemed to make sense to me, but he indicated that it simply wasn't as efficient as enclosing tons of ore in an artificial gravity field and towing it at low acceleration with an inexpensive EmDrive.

As I previously mentioned, their EmDrive was a considerably advanced version of a concept that we humans had already invented. It was first invented (on Earth) by British aerospace engineer Roger J. Shawyer, in 2000. The magazine 'New Scientist' ran a cover story on EmDrive in its 8 September 2006 issue. I'd read the article and knew that it was considered by many of our scientists to be a dubious device, but here the Sunnys were using a high-powered version to power their in-system travel.

Shawyer's version of the thing used a magnetron to direct microwaves into a metallic, fully enclosed, conic-shaped structure.. He calculated that the device would generate a directional thrust toward the narrow end of the structure. Some of our scientists maintained that it could not possibly work although the Chinese had created one that apparently did. Frazzle wasn't entirely clear on the action of their version of the device, but it apparently relied on some kind of interaction with virtual particles found in the quantum vacuum.

It looked like we were close to inventing it for ourselves, but our society was too concerned with what our politicians deemed important social issues, rather than trying to take steps that would get us off the planet, open up a wealth of new resources, allow us to do our own manufacturing in space and begin to protect us from possible calamities such as large meteor strikes or invasion by Pug-bears and the like. I was both proud of our home-grown research on the one hand and ashamed that we'd chosen to ignore easily obtainable advancements by retreating from space. We'd last gone to the moon in 1972 with the Apollo 17 mission, but before the first Pug-bear invasion and EMP event, the USA could barely get supplies up to the International Space Station and we had to hitchhike with the Russians if we wanted to get a person up there. That was all gone now, but the potential was still there, provided that I could somehow ensure that there would be no further invasion attempts.

In fact, if I could bring the Sunnys and their technology into contact with humans, I hoped that we might find common ground and create a union that would be beneficial to both species. We could fight, while they wouldn't or couldn't. They had technology that we sorely lacked. Maybe there was hope there for the future.

All of those considerations aside, the Sunny miner fleet was fleeing to their asteroid belt. The Pug-bears basically didn't care what happened to groups of Sunnys as long as they continued to get supplies, but the loss of the entire fleet of haulers and prospectors had shut down the orbital refining operations and put a crimp in supplies to the planet.

The Pug-bears needed the raw materials sent both to surface manufacturing facilities and their only orbital shipyard. They currently had two FTL vessels under construction that were intended to facilitate their expansion to additional solar systems.

Their drive to expand and dominate was their primary motivation. They didn't really utilize many of the elements of an established society on planet. The feral young lived as animals and even the ones that had been infected with the symbiont and gained intelligence preferred a solitary, hunting life.

Unfortunately, from the Sunnys' perspective, their primary prey on the planet was the Sunnys themselves. It was not a pleasant life for them.

The miners had been planning on leaving in their ships for some time and the few that were not mentally controlled by the Pug-bears finally had screwed up their courage and made the break. This action was improvidently ignored by the Pug-bears at first, but when the raw materials ran out, they had been forced to take action and ordered their local force of Pugs to take the few armed shuttles that were in the system and hunt the Sunnys down.

Altogether, the situation was really strange to my mind. The Pug-bears, for all of their superior mental power, essentially acted as primitives with no really good understanding of strategy. Sure, they could make good use of the Sunnys' technology, but they didn't plan things out the way humans would have. The Pugs were war-like but didn't cooperate well with each other, since their society had evolved on a planet where resources were scarce. They tended to direct their aggression towards their fellows, competing for status and mates, even when food and other necessities were plentiful.

The whole mess was really just a cosmic fluke that had come together in the right combination to allow the Pug-bears to expand and control their empire of planets. They'd been lucky not to run up against another species that had space technology and the aggressive constitution to oppose them. I resolved, for the hundredth time that I was going to change that situation.

Chapter 16

It took another twelve hours for us to close in on the Sunny fleet. We finally came to a relative stop in space, near a large, chaotic mass of tumbling rocks and water ice chunks. Their ships were scattered around the general area, although we couldn't see many of them. They had been maintaining what they considered were safe distances between their ships, in case the pursuing Pug force located them. From the Pug comm chatter and the miners' long-distance mass-detectors, we saw that the Pug shuttles were slowly moving through the in-system side of the asteroid belt. This meant that they were scattered out about five light minutes from our position.

Whistle had been running the comm system and was very worried about the Pugs' pursuit. He eventually turned to me and told me, "Dere fives of them shuttles. Dey all got shooters mounted on them and we afraid they'll find us."

Once I'd straightened out the number and confirmed that he really meant there were only five, I was a little bit relieved. My next thought was to find out about the 'shooters.' I asked him what they were and how did they compare to the big anti-matter gun on our ship. He was starting to get the idea that I meant to fight and it was hard to get him to concentrate on finding out the answer. However, he finally got confirmation from one of the ore-hauler pilots that the Pugs' weapons weren't comparable to ours. Our large gun had been created specifically to bombard the Earth from space, in case we proved resistant to their initial modes of attack.

Two of the shuttles were armed with smaller anti-matter projectors – on the order of the familiar eraser-rifles – and the other three had plasma guns. I asked about those and found, to my surprise, that they were simply more powerful models of the tripod-mounted weapon I'd seen the Pugs use on Earth. I hadn't known what it was and in my naivety, I'd simply called it an electro-bolt gun. Of the two, though, I would far sooner face that than the anti-matter weapon. The plasma bolt would burn metal, but it would take several shots to cut through our hull, while the anti-matter weapon would be a one-shot killer if it hit a sensitive area of the FTL ship.

The Pugs had separated their shuttles widely around the inside of the asteroid belt, having little idea of exactly where the Sunnys were located. The shuttles didn't have the long-distance mass sensors that the mining craft did. Their primary purpose was to destroy planetary installations and to intimidate close-range targets. The Pugs had used them effectively to destroy primitive civilizations on at least two other planets that were now occupied by Pug-bears, but they'd never used them against other spacecraft.

I knew that I wasn't a space-combat expert, but I figured that I could come up with some sort of strategy that might give us an advantage. I asked Frazzle where the nearest shuttle was located and he immediately brought up a visual display that covered about a third of the asteroid belt, showing our location, the scattered mining craft, and a target about twenty light seconds away, heading towards a heavy cluster of asteroids on our side of the belt. The cluster it was headed for was close by astronomical standards, but still about five light seconds from our location.

I decided to view the asteroid belt as a clock-face with the star at the center. This orientation, though strictly limited to two dimensions, gave me a slightly better perspective. If we were at twelve o'clock on the dial, the shuttle was moving towards the one o'clock mark. I directed Frazzle to calculate an intercept course with it so that we'd reach its approximate position as it approached the cluster of rocks.

His hands shook as he set up the course and then started the EmDrive. The ship rotated quickly and then moved off in the requisite direction. I powered up the weapon system and watched the display for any indication of the shuttle's mass. The detector on the weapon trigger was not as sensitive as the true long-distance ones. Frazzle kept me informed as we approached the shuttle. His display showed it easily, but he didn't think the shuttle had a corresponding capability. He indicated that we'd only have a problem when we got close. I hoped that he'd be pleasantly surprised. I was planning on our gun's longer range and I didn't intend to give the Pugs a chance.

The EmDrive didn't have a huge amount of acceleration, but it added up quickly, so it was only about fifteen minutes until I was able to see the Pugs' shuttle on my display. I wanted to get closer. I was nervous as anything, this being the critical test of the weapon system. I didn't want to chance missing. That would, at the minimum, give them an opportunity to call their fellows and spread the message about our presence.

We were still accelerating and as we got closer I asked Frazzle to shut the drive down. I judged we were moving fast enough and hoped that I hadn't waited too long. I didn't want to overshoot their position without getting off several shots.

Right in the middle of this tense point, Erin and the two guys came into the bridge and asked me what was going on. They'd been in a sleep period and had just come from eating breakfast. There wasn't any intercom system on the ship and I had judged that it would be fine if they weren't aware of what we were doing. My explanation was terse as I was distracted, "Fighting – don't bother me!"

On finding out that we were going into combat, they came over to my station and hovered around behind me, adding the stress of an audience to my nervousness. It all worked out, though. As the shuttle's marker slid towards us, I touched the screen, designating it with the targeting laser. A few seconds later, the shuttle-craft made an abrupt turn and headed in our direction. That laser had gotten their attention and they were coming to check it out. The only effect their turn had was to head them directly into our anti-matter pulse. Shortly after they turned, their mass disappeared from my screen and Frazzle let out a kind of yell, "You dissolved dem! I, I, I sad, but, but happy too!"

He was torn about the situation and I could sense a great disturbance in his mental aura. He certainly recognized the danger they posed to us and he was relieved that it was gone, but he still regretted the necessity of destroying them.

"OK, Frazzle, we're going to turn the ship to intercept the next shuttle," I hoped that he wouldn't balk at this and I reinforced it with a reassuring mental projection. However, he'd been forced to do disagreeable things by the Pug-bears before and, while reluctant, he turned the ship in the direction that the long-distance detector indicated. The next shuttle was about five light minutes away, counter-clockwise around the asteroid belt. It was almost directly in the center of the belt and we needed to move quickly to reach it in a reasonable time. The EmDrive proved capable, although we were going far faster than I judged safe considering the navigation hazards posed by dust and rocks.

The deflector shield got a workout. There was a nearly constant stream of dust bouncing off of it, creating a glowing plasma from the impact. The glow spread out from the edges of the shield area and trailed off at the periphery of visibility offered by the bridge windows. Frazzle turned to me and said, "Das fast as we should go in dust."

It looked like it would be about thirty minutes before we reached a reasonable distance from the second shuttle, so I told the others to watch and get me if anything happened. I was hungry and I'd determined to take a short break to get some food.

Erin came with me back to the cafeteria. She hadn't bothered me since I'd ignored her invitation. On the other hand, she'd acted as if she were a little hurt. I got the impression that she wasn't used to rejection, her being the rejector rather than the rejectee was more the rule in her experience.

"That was great, Dec!" she enthused. "You shot them down with no problem! How many more are there?"

"There are four more enemy shuttle-craft in this system according to the Sunnys. I'm hoping that we can get them cleared out with no trouble. Our gun out-ranges theirs and I don't think that guy even knew we were there until he sensed our targeting laser."

"What will you do then?" She'd changed her perspective on the situation, tacitly admitting the fact that I was in command. I didn't know if she'd done it intentionally to let me know that she'd abdicated her attempted control or if she was unconsciously adjusting.

"I've been planning with the Sunnys and I believe that our best tactic will be to try and free the ones on the planet. They don't have much hope for their population surviving much longer. From what we heard from the miners, the Pug-bears have been greatly increasing in number and the feral ones have been eating as many of the Sunnys as they can catch," I explained. This was a sensitive subject, given her apparent devotion to the Pug-bear in Denver, but she accepted my statement with no quibbling.

"How can you free them?" In that way, at least, she reminded me of Liz. Direct and to the point.

"I've got an idea. I haven't been able to tell the Sunnys about it as yet. I'm not sure how they'll react, given their aversion to violence. I think I can sell it to them as a possible solution that will give their people a chance without the necessity of a direct attack on the Pug-bears."

"What do you mean, 'a direct attack?'" She was puzzled. By now we were sitting on the floor in front of the bank of food machines and I was eating. The Sunnys did have seats in the room, but they were far too small for us. I thought that I'd have to have Whistle do something about that if I eventually had the opportunity.

"It's complicated..." I paused, thinking how best to explain. "The Pug-bears lay eggs that hatch into a spider-like form. The spiders are wild predators that will kill anything they can get. They grow up to be wild Pug-bears with no intelligence. However, if they eat a certain parasite egg, it lodges in their brain and their skulls grow. The parasite merges with their brain in some way and that makes them intelligent."

She interrupted, "Like the one in Denver. I understand. Are the intelligent ones friendly?"

"No, far from it. The intelligent ones are all dead set on taking over the universe and killing every other form of life they find. The one you have in Denver is the only one I've heard of that cooperates with humans in any way."

"Well, it kills prisoners, too, so maybe it isn't as friendly as I thought it was..." she said.

I realized that its influence over her mind was gradually fading. It was, after all, an inexperienced member of its race that had received its symbiont, but not any of the racial knowledge that was normally imparted by older members of its species. It was unaware of the species' plan for universal dominance and it was mostly unaware of the techniques for dominating other sapients' minds, making things up as it gained experience.

"Erin, I think that you're probably right about it," I met her eyes. That was a mistake. She reached out and took my hand. "Look," I said, as I showed her my left hand. The ring that Liz had placed on my finger had been obvious the entire time, but now I held it out for her inspection.

"I'm married. I mean, I consider you a friend, but..." I kind of trailed off. I hate it that I'm congenitally unable to deal with these sorts of situations.

"That's OK, Dec," she slowly let go, "I understand, but... you know we're a long way from home here and we might never get back."

"True," her statement didn't seem to call for anything else.

"Just remember that I'm your friend," she said quietly, looking hard directly into my eyes. I just nodded in response.

I thought, belatedly, of the plan I'd started to explain. "Oh, here's what I was going to say before. The Pug-bears' eggs do best in dry climates. I've seen them hatch in moist environments," I was thinking of the nest in Carlsbad Caverns, "but most of them rot before hatching if the humidity is too high. The Sunnys' planet that we're headed for has a belt of desert around the equator that provides the perfect place for the Pug-bears' eggs to hatch. I've got the idea that we can tow a water-ice comet to their planet and drop it into the desert area. That should greatly increase the humidity and keep the eggs from hatching. The net effect should be higher humidity, fewer Pug-bears and, I hope, a climate that the water-loving Sunnys will like."

She looked dubious, "Can we tow a comet? And, if we can, how are we going to locate one?"

I started to explain, but Frank poked his head through the door and said, "We're getting close. You'd better come and shoot this one pretty quick."

That broke that discussion up. We ran back through the transporter and I arranged myself in front of the weapon system. I was almost too late. Time had flown by as I talked to Erin. As I adjusted the joystick and scrolled the video display until the shuttle was in the center, I mentally chastised myself at getting so involved trying to explain my actions to her. We were closer than I'd planned and the shuttle-craft had obviously sensed us. It was turning our way and accelerating on an intercept vector.

As I locked the laser designator on the enemy, Frazzle exclaimed and pointed at his display which was flashing red. I glanced out the bridge window and saw a glowing ball of energy in the near distance. It was rapidly growing larger. Before I'd had a chance to even think, it flashed past. We were obviously in range of their plasma cannon and had they not been so anxious to get off a shot, they might have hit us with that one.

In response, my fingers tightened and our weapon fired. It was guided by the computer system and couldn't miss at that distance. It would take a few moments for the pulse to strike them, but I was already marking a second kill on my slate.

The proximity detector suddenly registered the absence of their mass. It had been a hit. I looked at Frank and Erin and mopped my brow, "That was closer than I'd like!"

"What?" they both asked. Neither had seen the plasma bolt go by.

"They took a shot at us and it was close," I responded. "It's my fault, I shouldn't have taken so much time eating."

Erin looked embarrassed since she knew that I'd spent most of my time talking to her, but she didn't say anything.

Frank, on the other hand, just smiled and said, "Well, they didn't hit us. You got them and that's all that counts. I learned in football that the only thing that counts is getting the ball over the goal line. Close isn't worth talking about."

I appreciated his viewpoint. It actually made me feel better.

As we were talking, Frazzle was listening in while he was monitoring the long-distance mass detectors. After Frank had spoken, he turned to me and said, "De others must'a got a message. Deys all coming in our direction."

I turned back to my display and didn't see anything, so I got up and stood behind the command chair. Frazzle's display was more elaborate and much more comprehensive than the limited weapons display. Using his, I was able to see the three remaining shuttle-craft. They were located at widely separated points near the in-system side of the belt, but they were all heading towards us. I realized that I'd have to change my tactics. There would be no more sneak-up and shoot them when they didn't expect it. I had to actually figure out a way to combat them all at once.

Frazzle was doing some calculations and said, "Deys gonna arrive at about the same time. At least one of dem will have anti-matter weapon."

He was correct. I didn't know what the first shuttle was armed with; it hadn't had an opportunity to show us what it had, but the second had definitely been armed with a plasma weapon. That left a minimum of one shuttle with anti-matter – possibly two. This was going to get interesting and not in a good way, either.

Chapter 17

The way the enemy were arranged, they were going to come at us from three points of a triangle. If we accelerated towards one, we might have a chance to deal with him individually before he had reinforcements. I asked Frazzle to head at maximum acceleration towards the nearest shuttle. We were shortly moving ever faster in its direction. The remaining two showed suddenly evidence of turning to try and adjust to our new trajectory, but they were playing catch-up, due to the distances involved.

I didn't know if the long-distance mass detectors were current with our timeline or if they lagged behind. Frazzle reassured me that they used some form of quantum wave analysis and their information was only a fraction of a second behind current positions. I relaxed a bit since the geometry of the situation was playing out in our favor.

The shuttles on Frazzle's display suddenly lit up in red, all at about the same time. He became agitated and yelled, "Watch outs! Deys shooting!"

They had coordinated their shots to intercept our path. In response, I ordered him to put us into a gradual turn towards the second nearest shuttle. As the ship began to veer off its course, I aligned the weapons display and locked the laser designator on my original target. It was headed straight for us at its maximum acceleration and I recognized that the pilot might not be able to swerve fast enough to avoid a long-distance shot. Just as the shuttle began to move off of my display, I triggered the gun. There wasn't any flash or sound and I belatedly realized that I missed the recoil of a human weapon. It was sort of anti-climactic – to shoot an all-destroying pulse and not to have any evidence to show that it had been shot. Funny what you think of in situations like that!

As soon as the pulse was away, I centered the designation display on the next shuttle. By then it was apparent that it was one of the plasma cannon-armed ones. Once again I could see the bolt coming from a long way away. The glow of the plasma moved far faster than the actual charge and it gave you a hellish view of what was about to hit you. This guy was a good shot, too. The damned bolt hit us right on the bow! There was a flash and the deflection field strength meter red-lined. The field held, though, creating a brilliant aurora display as the plasma streamed over the edges, safely far from our ship.

Frazzle was rapidly flipping switches and keying instructions at his station. I yelled at him to turn towards the final shuttle and fired my weapon at the same moment, hoping that the laser designation and computer system would retain the second target despite the plasma blast. He complied and our ship began to loop around in a wild turn.

I realized belatedly that both of my first two shots had been accurate. Frazzle gave an excited and shrill whistle and I turned to see what had disturbed him. He was pointing at the proximity display. It only showed one shuttle left. We were winning!

We continued to turn towards the final shuttle, but suddenly the main boards lit up in red again. Frazzle started entering commands rapidly and our acceleration slowed drastically. I linked into his mind since I had no confidence that his speech was up to the task. He was working hard to re-route the ship's power away from one of the propulsion vanes. The remaining Pug had hit us with an anti-matter bolt and it had just grazed the third vane, destroying the outboard section. The remainder of the vane was about to meltdown due to the excess power that was flowing into it, but Frazzle got it shut down rapidly with no additional damage.

Now it was a simple shooting duel. They had nearly as much range as we did, although we were shooting a much larger and more powerful pulse. I scrambled to get the computer display locked down on the enemy, who was by now, gyrating wildly in an attempt to avoid our counter shot.

It was difficult; he was swerving around so much. The only good thing about it was I figured he couldn't aim very well while going through such maneuvers. I worked my joystick and finally achieved a lock. The laser designator fixed on his craft and he began even wilder swerves as he sensed the targeting. We were still closing at a high rate of speed although our velocity increase had slowed considerably as a result of going to two-thirds power.

I watched the guy try to shake the laser-lock as we approached. It was no use. He couldn't do it. I continued to wait, wanting to make sure of my shot.

We flashed by a group of rocks that were innocently orbiting each other in their path around the star. As we did, I was startled to see about half of them vanish. I realized that the Pug was still shooting at us! He was moving too wildly to aim accurately, but a shot fired randomly could still hit us and if it hit us directly, it might destroy our ship. I triggered off an extended burst of pulses. No single shot this time. I wanted to send enough his way that even if the first pulse didn't hit him, he'd have a deuce of a time avoiding the follow-ups.

Shortly after I removed my finger from the trigger button, his display marker disappeared. I turned to the others and yelled, "I'm an Ace!"

They looked puzzled and it was a bit of a come-down for me. I had to explain that five aerial kills were what it took to be called an Ace. They still didn't get it, so I shut up on the topic and shut the weapon system down.

Frazzle reported that he'd gotten the power re-routed and there was no additional damage to our ship, but because of the hit, it wouldn't be able to go FTL until we'd been repaired.

"Where can we repair the damage?" I asked.

"Oh, dats easy. Deres a ship-yard orbiting the planet. Deys vets at fixing ships. We can get fixed there."

Despite my initial thought that he was suggesting that we would go in and get neutered by the 'vets,' I agreed that we should head that way.

I asked him, mentally, if there would be a problem with the Pug-bears at the repair facility. He thought that there would be a large contingent of Pugs and that would be the problem. Most of the orbital stations only had one or two Pug-bears in residence at any one time. The creatures preferred to stay on the surface where they could hunt and exercise their feral instincts. They were more comfortable there and probably would not be easily found to come up in a shuttle.

I thought that we'd have to do something that would discommode the Pugs in order to give us time to arrange the necessary repairs. Looking over Frazzle's shoulder, I noticed that the mass-detector showed a large group of rocks just a few degrees off of our path. I pointed at them and asked him to match their velocity.

It took some doing, but he eventually got us slowed down and into position about fifty klicks away from the rocks. Some of them were stone, but most of them were composed largely of ice. This was just what I needed to carry out my bombardment plan. It took some doing, but I finally convinced him to close in on one of the larger ice balls. It was rotating slowly and had a lot of large rocks in it, held together by what appeared to be water ice.

We shot the targeting laser at the object and the spectrum of the emitted gasses showed that the ice was nearly pure H_2O. The next thing was to capture the object. That wasn't as hard as I'd feared. Frazzle was able to extend the artificial gravity field outside the ship and he created an intense gravitational point source that was powerful enough to move the kilometer-in-diameter ball of ice toward the ship.

I didn't want it too close, so I asked him to set course for the equator of the planet and to arrange to drag the ball behind. This was going to be just like cosmic bowling!

The ship wasn't able to accelerate rapidly due to the damaged vane and, even if it could, the mass of the ice was so great that it slowed us down considerably. Nevertheless, we made progress towards our target. We were now far past the in-system side of the asteroid belt and had about five minutes light to go to reach the planet's orbit. It was coming around the sun towards us. Frazzle took a look and said that it was just getting into summer, based on the polar inclination. I didn't know about that, but I thought that it might be going to be a very wet season for them.

We accelerated the ice ball to a few miles per second in its path towards the planet. I thought that would be fast enough. I didn't want to destroy the target, only soak it down. We stopped accelerating and maintained a steady progress. It was going to take us hours to get into position, so I suggested to the others that we take a break.

Now, it might seem that all of this combat had taken a long time, but it was less than an hour since Erin and I had been speaking in the cafeteria. Neither of the other two evinced a desire to break away, so I went off to get a drink and use the bathroom by myself. They might be able to sit through my inaugural space combat with no need to relieve themselves, but the closer I got to the toilet facility, the more I needed to go. I guess I wasn't as cool a character as I tried to pretend.

I took the time to eat some more in the cafeteria. Whistle kept me company and we conversed a bit about how the ship might be repaired. He stated that it wasn't unknown for ships to strike rocks when passing through debris zones and the shipyard was set up to handle any repair. The only problem would be to get past the Pugs and controlling Pug-bears.

I thought that meant direct, on-station intervention by us humans. The only way I could see us getting the repairs done was to actually take the station and kill all of the opposition. I asked him how many Pugs would be on the facility and his mental image was discouraging. The station was quite large and maintained living facilities for over a hundred Pugs. They were mostly used for labor, being stronger than the Sunnys, but they were also armed and could prove to be a force that would be hard to overcome. I asked him for the layout and his description gave me an idea.

The station rotated slowly along its central hub with its six arms making it look like a starfish. The various groups of aliens maintained residential space complete with artificial gravity in separate arms. The central hub was set up with a grapple system on one end to allow smaller ships to dock there for light repair work.

The Pugs lived in one of the arms, the resident Pug-bears reserved two for their exclusive personal use and the Sunnys lived in one. The other two were warehouses for the inventory of ship parts and also provided docking space for the five shuttles.

The facility was prepared to repair anything from our starship to mining craft, so fixing our damaged vane wouldn't be a problem. It was also the site where two additional FTL ships were being assembled. These were in synchronous orbit with the station, but not always attached. The Sunnys normally shuttled parts and assemblies over to them with small, one-person tugs.

The miner's comm reports indicated that one ship was just getting past the skeleton stage and the other was now ready for EmDrive and FTL system installation. It still was a long way from completion, since the habitat systems and the control interfaces were yet to be shipped up from the planet's manufacturing centers. Neither was ready to fly, so they wouldn't pose a problem with our docking at the station's hub.

I discussed the station with Whistle and convinced myself that I understood the system well enough to know how to get rid of the majority of the Pugs. I'd simply destroy their residence arm with the anti-matter gun. Most of them remained in the arm unless they were engaged in repair work. As long as there wasn't any ship currently docked that was undergoing repair, the Pugs could mostly be counted on to be in their residence. There they maintained an atmospheric gas mixture that was more felicitous to their biology than the one that the Sunnys and Pug-bears found healthful. I remembered how the atmosphere of Earth would actually kill the Pugs. This meant that the creatures that I most needed to dispose of would be clumped up where I could get them all easily.

Meanwhile, we were approaching the planet and we had to do some maneuvering. It was a lot more difficult since we were towing a huge mass of ice with our power down by a third. The whole process wore me out. It took several hours to get the ship into high orbit around the equator of the planet, but Frazzle finally did it. He'd had some help from some of the other Sunnys who'd spelled him for a bit, but he was a real trooper and handled the majority of the operation himself.

We were orbiting in the opposite direction of the planetary spin. We could see the desert area between the coastal mountain ranges clearly. There were lots of clouds on the seaward sides of the ranges, but the air over the desert was uniformly unobstructed by clouds. We were going opposite to the spin and the landscape moved quickly below us.

It was simple to turn the ship and decelerate a bit. This dropped our orbit. Once we'd moved down a couple of hundred miles, we really braked, slowing the ice ball down correspondingly. As we started to lose altitude, I told Frazzle to release the gravity field. He must have known what I was going to do. He was by no means easy to fool, but he did balk a bit about dropping the mass on the planet. I reassured him that it would break up and fall as rain, ending on the desert.

He hadn't quite put two and two together, so he was amazed at my intent when I explained to him that the water would cause the Pug-bears' eggs to fail to hatch, thus alleviating a lot of the pressure on the Sunnys. It wouldn't do any harm to the adult Pug-bears, unless they happened to drown or be hit by some of the rocks embedded in the ice, but I figured they'd be set back considerably by the loss of their breeding grounds and crop of eggs.

He turned off the point gravity source, leaving the ice ball to slowly fall on its own as we accelerated back into higher orbit,. I'd planned better than I knew because it rapidly lost altitude during two orbits. It was moving against the rotation of the planet and the instant it hit the outer edges of the atmosphere, the ice began to break up.

Meanwhile, I had Whistle on the comm unit and he was able to contact the resistance organization on the surface. The Sunnys hadn't much of a resistance, mostly taking passive actions that would slow the Pug-bears' actions just a little bit. However, they were quite excited to hear that we were going to help them.

While we were dropping the ice ball, the rest of the Sunnys had assembled in the bridge's stadium seating and held a quiet discussion as they watched the operation. They finally reached a decision and just after we released the mass to drop, they announced that they wanted to transport to the surface and help the resistance.

They had the fortitude to directly address me and explain that they'd been considering trying to capture the human members of the crew and turn them over to the Pug-bears. They seemed embarrassed and they were definitely sorry they'd doubted our intentions.

They now believed that their best option was to leave the ship to help their fellows resist the Pug-bears. They thought that perhaps they could provide some assistance to the locals. They'd been discussing tactics and thought they could help best on the planet's surface. I was relieved since I still detected an aura of doubt surrounding them. We would be left with just the two original Sunnys and they'd proven themselves to be good allies.

Frazzle and Whistle made arrangements and it wasn't long before the group left the ship, moving down to the surface through a single transporter that had been kept hidden from the Pug-bears.

I wondered at this since the Pug-bears were capable of reading the Sunnys' minds easily. I didn't understand how they'd managed to keep secrets from the creatures. It turned out to be a sad story involving dedication and deception. There weren't enough Pug-bears on the surface to constantly monitor the entire Sunny population. The Pug-bears kept largely to themselves as long as the Sunnys continued to follow orders and provide material necessities and hunting targets. The Sunnys involved had all made up their minds to resist to their last breath and they'd sworn to kill themselves if they felt they were in danger of having their minds read. They'd followed through on it too. They all carried poison capsules that contained a nerve poison that would stop their minds instantly upon ingestion.

There had been a number of them who had eaten the poison the instant they were faced with a Pug-bear. The Pug-bears didn't care. If the Sunnys toppled over and died, that might be strange, but as far as they were concerned, Sunnys were interchangeable. Only recently had the oldest resident Pug-bear become concerned. The things were intelligent but naive. They'd never faced serious resistance and it took them a long time before they started to realize that there might be something going on.

Nevertheless, the transporter had been built and kept secret and the other Sunnys left the ship through it on their way to provide aid and direction to the planetary population. They were going to need it.

As it fell, the ice ball broke up in a spectacular fashion, spreading out in a huge cloud of spray. We could see fiery tracks as the embedded stones separated and fell, burning their way through the atmosphere. The surviving stones created havoc all along the desert strip completely around the globe and I was glad that we'd carefully targeted the inter-mountain region. No Sunnys lived there and they were unlikely to suffer much from the meteor fall. As it was, the impacts caused earthquakes and tsunamis that raced away from the shores on both coasts. The rain followed the stones down, falling as chunks of rapidly melting ice and tons of water that dropped along the desert area. I don't think the planet had ever experienced anything like the flood that covered parts of the desert strip. In ten more orbits, the show was over. The desert strip was covered by heavy clouds and there was nothing to be seen.

The surface Sunnys reported that some of the Pug-bears were raging around their cities, but most of them had hustled up into the mountains, heading for their breeding grounds to see what was happening. It was raining all over the globe now, except for the higher latitudes near both poles.

The Sunnys thought that the Pug-bears might be distracted enough to leave them alone for a considerable time. Their main problem was that there were

Pug troops in most of the cities and those creatures were now leaderless and acting aggressively.

I had Frazzle suggest that they try to ally with the Pugs. I also directed him to tell them to create mass-triggered auto-cannons. These would be traps that would only shoot when they sensed the larger mass of a Pug-bear. Since they could be computerized, the Sunnys could console themselves with the idea that they hadn't actually pulled the trigger.

Frazzle looked at me quizzically and said, "Me don't likes de way you thinks, but this maybe the only way to get rid of them. So, could it be alright?" He was trying to puzzle out the calculus of violence. It was natural for humans, but not for his race.

"Yes. It is alright!" I told him. "It's an old and perpetually bothersome problem. You usually can't defeat force without using force of your own. One of our ancient leaders once said, 'You can't make an omelet without breaking eggs.'"

My wisdom was confusing to him. He shrugged his shoulders and asked, "What's an omelet?"

I was speechless. He normally caught my meaning and I'd reached the point of forgetting that he wasn't some odd-looking human. It was good to remember that he was as alien to me as the Pugs, although a lot more friendly. I replied, "Never mind. Our next step is to get our ship repaired. Will you place us in a docking orbit for the space station?"

Chapter 18

A s usual, Frazzle was sitting at the command station. He ran some
computations, then entered a couple of commands and we started to
change orbital altitude while moving into a slow curve that would
eventually place us in an overtaking orbit, where we'd come up to the station
from behind.

The orbital station was not a happy place for the Sunnys and now it was
even worse than normal. The two resident Pug-bears had finally realized that
we had dealt them some very severe blows. Some of the station Sunnys had
locked themselves in their residence wing and were trying to avoid being
mentally coerced to open the doors, while the Pug-bears were rampaging
around angrily in the hub area. The Pugs were staying out of the Pug-bears'
way. They might not be very smart, but they at least knew when to keep out
of sight.

The Sunnys had a low-power comm unit in their residence that they used
for local communication in the immediate vicinity of the station. It was
often used to send messages over to the crews working on the two FTL ships.
There was an entire complement of Sunnys on both FTL ships and they
were very worried. They were afraid to go back to the station, due to the rage
of their Great Ones and they were starting to run short of air. They were
working entirely in hard-vacuum due to the skeletal and incomplete stage of
construction of the ships and they were begging their compatriots on the
station to send more air over to them.

We had about forty minutes before we would be closing on the station and
that seemed like it probably wouldn't be enough. I asked Frazzle if he could
hurry our approach. He ran some more calculations and then turned the

EmDrive on again. It had been shut off and we were coasting along in the right orbit. Turning it on increased our speed and boosted us to a higher orbital path. He ran the drive for a few minutes and then caused the ship to rotate around so we were approaching the station tail first.

I complained at this since the bow-gun wouldn't be able to be used in this position if it came to shooting. He informed me that he'd brake as we got close and that would allow us to drop into the correct orbit ahead of the station. Then we'd be pointing directly at it. He thought that if he was able to slow us the exact amount needed, the station would gradually coast up to us. Of course, that didn't solve the problem for the construction crews.

When I raised that objection, he turned to me and raised one finger in a very human gesture of admonition, "I planned on dat, Dec. We got a shuttle on dis ship and Whistle be a good shuttle pilot."

I suddenly remembered seeing the shuttle attached to the waist of the ship, opposite the attached cargo pod, "Can the shuttle carry air to the workers?"

"Yes, it no trouble," was the reassuring answer.

That left me to worry about the main problem: the one that hadn't changed since I'd decided that we needed to dock to get repaired. How was I going to deal with the two Pug-bears and the contingent of Pugs? The answer to the Pugs might be to simply shoot a hole in their residence. If I could do it without burning the entire wing off and damaging the station, it would give them enough of a problem to keep them busy. I hoped it would mean that they wouldn't recover enough to bother us.

The main gun was too powerful to dissolve a little hole. It was more likely to destroy that whole arm of the structure, destabilizing the station and throwing its rotation off. That was exactly what I was afraid of. It would mean that our hopes of repair would probably vanish. As a result, I kept mulling the issue over in my mind, searching for a better solution.

Frazzle was a truly great pilot. He delivered exactly as he'd promised. In about twenty minutes the ship was easing into orbit a few hundred kilometers in front of the oncoming station. That's when the weak aspect of my plan showed up. I suddenly realized that the arms of the six-armed structure looked more or less the same; I mean the residence ones. The arms that held supplies and shuttles had numerous docks and extensible crane-like structures for loading and unloading and were easy to distinguish. I noticed a connecting tube between two of the residence arms, but I was unsure what that was for.

In any event, I couldn't distinguish the Sunnys' habitat from the two arms preempted by the Pug-bears or the Pugs' single arm. I looked around the bridge for help, but the only one there was Frazzle and he was busy monitoring the navigation display; directing the ship. My fellow humans were off in the cafeteria and I didn't know where Whistle was at the moment.

I had to find a way to determine which was which. We were rapidly approaching the station, or rather, the station was rapidly approaching us. We'd slowed slightly and climbed into a higher orbit that would allow the station to pass within a kilometer below us. It was now about a hundred klicks away and coming up on our position. I was getting desperate. I couldn't randomly shoot. Killing the Sunnys would be disastrous for us. We needed their repair expertise too badly.

I was hovering around behind Frazzle mulling the problem over when Whistle walked in and asked me what I was doing. I was so distracted that I'd completely missed his arrival. When I explained that I was trying to figure out how to determine which arm of the space station held the Pugs, he asked an obvious question. It was so obvious that I'd overlooked it.

"Why you not use mind talk? De Pugs think about fights all the time."

Of course! That was it. I sank into a meditative trance, extending my perception outward as I did. I could sense the Sunnys and humans on the FTL ship and then, at a distance, a mass of thoughts became slowly clear. I opened my eyes and focused on each successive arm as the station slowly rotated below us.

The two arms with the resident Pug-bears were obvious. There was hardly any mental activity other than a sense of intelligence overlaid with ferocity coming from each of the two. Their two habitats were side-by-side and were linked on their out-board ends by a flimsy tube-like bridge that allowed them to privately visit back and forth without having to go through the hub of the station. The tube was something that I had noted, but I hadn't realized what it meant. I could possibly kill both of the Pug-bears by simply dissolving the bridge unless it had air-locks.

My mental search next located the Sunnys' habitat. The mental aura from it was entirely different; lighter and, considering their miserable situation, happier in some undefinable way. That meant the Pugs' habitat was immediately to the spin-ward side of the Pug-bears.

Figuring out the target had been a piece of cake! I was embarrassed that I hadn't thought of it myself. I mean, I'm the mental/Psi expert! I realized that I still had a lot to learn about my mental gifts. I had an unfortunate tendency to only use them in familiar ways. It was as natural as anything to sense a herd of elk or other wildlife, but in the unfamiliar environment in which I found myself, I was more likely to rely on the limited senses I had used since birth.

The space station would pass directly below us in about ten minutes. I sprinted for the transporter and hit the cargo dock running for the racks of spacesuits. I'd previously placed a couple of the eraser rifles nearby with the idea of possibly having to repel borders.

The suit I'd worn to install the main gun was arranged and waiting for my next use. It took almost all of the available time to get it on and sealed. As soon as I could, I grabbed the rifle and activated the cargo port. The atmosphere evacuated into a storage tank, just as it had before and the port opened slowly. It seemed like it was even slower than the last time I'd gone outside of the ship, but perhaps that was just my nerves.

I climbed over the edge of the port and walked partway around the waist of the ship. The station was already a little past us but the Pugs' arm was just rotating upwards to its nearest orientation. I aimed carefully and then held the trigger down for a long burst. I was rewarded with the view of a jet of air and condensing moisture that shot out of a neat hole in the arm.

It was too far away for me to see how large the hole actually was, but I'd definitely holed the thing. I was able to make out the vapor of the exhausting gasses and then I saw a few clumps of matter that flew out also. I suddenly realized that these were Pug bodies. The hole was large enough for them to fly through. I shook my head, trying to get over the idea that I'd just massacred the whole mess of them. Then I remembered how I'd seen the one in New York chewing on the bookstore owner's throat. I didn't feel so bad after that.

As an afterthought, I burned a couple of holes in the Pug-bears' residence wings. The result was about the same: a jet of gas and condensing water vapor. I hoped that the Pug-bears were having fun with that– I was struck with a wave of mental unease as the two of them unleashed their ferocity at the one who'd dared to destroy their habitat. It was paralyzing in its intensity. I'd previously fought off a single individual, now two of them were engaging in a rare cooperative effort. I could barely think for a moment, but then my mental defenses kicked in.

It was kind of like catching a disease. Your immune system remembers how to combat it and so did my mind. I parried their attack and waited, content in the knowledge that their air was going. Their attack became more intense and then almost frenzied. It reached a peak and then rapidly subsided and I knew with a certainty that they'd both expired.

I extended my senses to the space station again and found a sense of disorganization and confusion along with a few stray thoughts of violence. The Sunny crew was probably completely aghast at the destruction of their en-slavers. It would take them some time to reorganize and understand that they'd been freed. The violence? I couldn't sense very well, but it appeared that some of the Pugs were scattered around outside of their habitat and had survived. We'd have to deal with these.

Right now there were other problems that were more pressing. The Sunny FTL construction crews would soon be out of air and that was the most urgent issue. I turned to head back into the cargo bay. As I did, I caught a glimpse of red glows on the station's arms. The gas venting had destabilized the station and the Sunnys were now firing attitude adjustment thrusters to smooth out the movement. They'd gotten organized quickly, then.

Once back in the ship and having returned to the bridge, I found the other humans watching the station through the large window. Erin turned to me with amazement in her eyes and enthused, "It's really amazing! I really haven't felt like we were in space until I saw that rotating thing pass between us and the planet."

"Yeah. It's really advanced over what we managed to build on Earth," I said, somewhat bitterly. I was feeling inadequate as if the human lack of advancement reflected poorly on me personally.

"What were those plumes of white fog that came out of the arms a while ago?" she asked.

"That was me. I shot holes in three of the arms to vent the atmosphere. That got rid of most of the enemies on board."

"What! Where were you? You didn't use the nose gun. We came in here and Frazzle said you were gone somewhere to do something he didn't know."

"I went out on the hull and used one of the anti-matter rifles. It was the best thing I could come up with, but I think it will mean that we can get our ship repaired without a lot of fighting."

"Oh, Dec! We could have helped," she seemed concerned. "You took a huge chance going outside again."

"Yeah," added Ted. "I'd like to get a chance to go out, myself."

"You probably wouldn't fit in any of the available spacesuits, big guy!" I hoped that he was becoming more friendly. He'd been very reserved, almost to the point of hostility and this was the first sign of enthusiasm I'd seen him give.

Whistle interrupted, "We gots to get close to the ships dey building! Dey needs saving now! No times for shuttle."

I looked at Frazzle, but he was already maneuvering our ship closer to the two skeletal structures. We were about five hundred meters from the nearest one and closing slowly. Across the gap, I could see a cluster of thirty or so Sunny-sized figures in suits that were hanging onto the naked ship skeleton. They were all on the side closest to us and were waiting until we got close enough. I realized that they were going to jump across the gap and the cargo bay door needed to be opened again.

Whistle was already heading for the transporter to the cargo bay. I sent him an inquiring thought and received a blurred picture of him opening the port. As I said before, they were right on top of almost everything; the only thing that set them back was violence.

I could tell when he opened the bay door. The waiting Sunnys suddenly all launched themselves directly towards us. I was worried that they'd just bounce off the hull and drift away, but I'd forgotten the gripping surface of their suit's shoes. The ones that didn't fly right into the open port, landed on their feet and we could see them walking to the port in a video display that Frazzle had belatedly turned on.

He was still busy maneuvering the ship on around the FTL's skeleton and towards the second, more nearly finished ship. It was drifting in orbit about another half-klick away. Having the two close together made it easy to transfer workers and equipment back and forth. They had a limited number of crew and they needed to make the best use of each worker's skills with little downtime caused by remote job sites. It didn't take too long before the second group of construction workers arrived and the cargo bay door shut. Some of them were very short of air and it was a big relief for all of the Sunnys to be aboard. The whole crowd suddenly started coming through the transporter onto the bridge.

They were a widely varied crew with pelts of different colors. The place practically filled up with them. The stadium seating was shortly filled, leaving about half of them standing in the space behind. The other three humans and I had retreated to the corner of the command station near the gun controller. The noise was incredible and I suddenly realized that the Sunnys had a funny smell. I hadn't noticed it with the few that we'd encountered before, but these guys had been in their suits for a long time and their natural odor had built up. It wasn't as bad as a comparable group of humans would have been, though. They smelled kind of like a field of freshly-cut alfalfa hay with a little bit of fermentation added. Altogether it was not unpleasant.

Whistle came forward to just behind Frazzle and took command. He made a series of whistling sounds and clicks. Once he had their attention, he launched into a lengthy speech, the import of which was that we were here to free all Sunnys from the Great Ones and the Chosen Ones, their soldiers. He told them about how we could use violence to accomplish things they could not and how we'd systematically destroyed the Pugs' shuttlecraft and gotten rid of the ones that were on the space station. He pointed out that our FTL drive was damaged and we needed all of the cooperation of the workers to repair our ship.

There was some discussion back and forth during which some of them argued that they might be better off if they turned us over to the Great Ones. He quashed that idea quickly, pointing out that they would be far better off if they worked with us to free their species from the Great Ones' domination. We'd already changed the humidity level of the planet below, rendering the Great Ones' breeding grounds unusable and we had suggested ways they could resist them.

It was a long discussion, but they eventually agreed that we were allies and they'd repair our ship. Frazzle moved us into an intercept with the station. He'd been communicating with the Sunnys on the station and had found that there were still some Pugs and a third Pug-bear that were locked in the cargo arm. They'd been taking inventory with a small group of Sunnys. When I'd holed the station and it had realized that I'd killed most of its compatriots, the Pug-bear had attacked the Sunny inventory crew in a fury. Fortunately, two of them had been near the air-lock, had jumped through and locked it from outside, trapping their enemies. Then they'd promptly gotten as far away from the lock as possible to avoid the Pug-bear's mental control. It was a younger one and apparently didn't have the range or depth of control that an older one would have.

We'd have to take care of the remaining Pugs and the Pug-bear. It looked like Frank, Ted and I would shortly get a chance to fight.

Chapter 19

F razzle informed me that the older spaceships did not carry transporters and had to physically dock, so the space station had a docking attachment that mated with the FTL ship's cargo bay. This meant that we could actually travel through a tube without having to wear spacesuits. That was convenient since there were none that would fit the two big men and I thought that I'd really need their assistance to get the remaining Pugs rousted out of the storage area in which they'd been trapped.

The Sunnys had a transporter installed in the space station, but it was an early one with only one possible destination and the link was dedicated to the planetary surface. When I found out about that, it gave me pause for thought. There was no telling when the Pug-bears might send a large force of Pugs through to take back the station. I immediately brought it up to Whistle and he inquired of his friends on the station.

The answer was reassuring. They'd disabled the transporter when they'd realized that we were going to attempt to free them. As our attack progressed and showed signs of succeeding, they sealed off their side of the portal and also disabled the station-to-ground comm to prevent the Pugs from calling for help. I wondered if the Pug-bears had sent mental summons for assistance before they were killed by the depressurization of their habitat wings, but it didn't seem likely. They'd spent almost all of their final moments trying to attack my mind.

The lone surviving Pug-bear seemed to be a younger one without the experience and survival knowledge of the older ones. Even so, it was highly likely that it would eventually get the idea that it should ask for help from the surface. I realized that we'd need to act fast or we might be faced with a squadron of Pugs coming up in orbital shuttles. We'd destroyed the system-capable shuttles in our first space battle, but there were a number of less-capable cargo-lifters that were able to boost into orbit. These could carry out a limited mission that would allow the Pugs to reinforce the remainder of their station crew.

We started down the docking tube as fast as we could. It was an amazing experience. The Sunnys obviously had some tricks with chemistry that we could learn from. The tube was a seamless plastic extrusion. It was almost perfectly transparent with a slight blue tinge and it made a wide and smooth corridor from our port to that of the station. There was enough air pressure in it for us to breathe, but it was colder than anything.

Whistle let me know that the tube was extruded from the station on demand. It was formed from a quick-hardening plastic that could be vaporized by an electric charge when it was no longer needed. The system worked perfectly. We glided down the tube to the light mounted by the station port as if we were some kind of ungainly birds. The two big men whooped and waved their arms in exhilaration. Erin simply clung to my ankle and kept her mouth tightly shut with an expression on her face that seemed to signal incipient nausea.

Once we reached the station end, Whistle entered a code on the panel and the lock opened releasing warm air and humidity into the tube. The tube walls were immediately covered with frost as the humidity condensed and froze into crystalline patterns. We scooted through the lock and the door cycled shut. The air was warmer; a good thing because I was shivering and I could tell that Erin was really suffering. She looked half-frozen, but she perked up a bit when the warm air struck her.

We were immediately confronted with a group of Sunnys. They were waiting just outside the airlock in the hall and they drew back in alarm when they spotted the four of us humans coming through the door. Whistle was leading and he hastily assured them that there was nothing to fear. After he'd finished, the one that seemed to be their leader began a long welcoming speech. After about a minute of this, I interrupted and asked Whistle to tell them that it was imperative that we take care of the remaining Pugs. This elicited considerable discussion along with mixed approval and revulsion at the violence they knew would ensue. The upshot was that one of them led us down a corridor that took us to the hub of the station. From there, it was obvious where the Pugs were holed up. There was a large crowd of Sunnys sort of dithering around in front of the arm's closed airlock. There were three other closed locks also and I presumed that these were shut due to our holing of the habitats beyond.

When the waiting Sunnys saw us, there was a cacophony of whistles and clicks and the crowd parted in the middle to provide us access to the closed door. There was no vision port in the door, but the control panel held a view-screen that was operational. Whistle had one of the others turn it on and we were treated to a view of the resistance we had to face. The Pugs were grouped down the hall behind the airlock and had barricaded themselves behind a number of boxes. This view caused a lot of consternation among the resident Sunnys. After some conversation, Whistle let us know that the boxes contained highly sensitive and fragile electronic components for the two spaceships that were under construction.

Apparently, the young Pug-bear that the Pugs were protecting was smart enough to assume that we'd need these components, thus making them a better barrier. I was wondering what to do about that, having no idea if we actually needed the contents of the boxes or not, when Whistle pointed out something very obvious.

I can only assume that continued contact with me and my "violent" ways had started to influence his thinking. He actually came up with a suggestion that, if not directly violent in itself, obviously led to a lot of destruction.

"Deres another airlock behind Pugs. You shoot hole in outside of this place, they have to go back into the other lock."

In his own way, he was very devious. If we could force the Pugs to retreat without harming the equipment, we might be able to come at them with a little more advantage, especially if we moved rapidly in the confusion caused by the loss of pressure in the hallway. The situation as it was wouldn't resolve quickly. They could probably sit inside for longer than I wanted to wait outside.

It was only a matter of a few minutes for me to get into a pressure suit and into one of the arms that I'd already holed. Since it was already evacuated, I simply burned a man-sized hole in the outer hull with an anti-matter rifle. I then carefully climbed onto the outside of the hull and walked around until I was standing on the side nearest the storage arm. From that vantage point, I could easily see the location where the Pugs were waiting. The arms were rather narrow near the hub of the station, since the only thing there was the two airlocks. Once beyond the airlock section, the arms gradually expanded to contain a larger volume, so large, in fact that it couldn't be accommodated nearer the hub.

The Pugs were clustered in the narrow area and as soon as I had assured myself that I was facing the correct arm, helped by seeing Whistle peering out the adjacent view-port located on the wall of the hub between the arms, I dissolved a small hole in the airlock's hull. I knew that it had gone through since there was a steady stream of rapidly condensing air and frozen water droplets shooting out. That was good enough. I returned through my hole and the airlocks back into the hub as fast as I could.

The Pugs were in considerable disarray, a few were trying to block the hole by throwing pieces of flooring and other materials at it and, in fact, they'd been somewhat successful in slowing down the leak. The others were cycling through the airlock behind them as rapidly as they could. It was too small to hold many of them at once and it looked as if it would take a couple of more cycles for them all to get out.

There was still some air in the space, although it was leaking out quickly. I didn't know if there was enough for a human to survive, but then I remembered that the Pugs preferred a different gas mix than humans. I didn't know if the big guys and Erin could make it through the area. They didn't have space suits, so that meant that the first one in would have to be me. Without waiting for an invitation, it looked like the Pugs were too busy to issue one, I cycled through the lock, weapon at the ready.

The air inside was thin according to the HUD in my suit, but breathable. I motioned for the others to come on through and began to shoot the remaining Pugs at the same time. With the anti-matter rifle, beginning to shoot an organic target and finishing shooting it was almost instantaneous. A simple pass of the muzzle over the visible Pugs was sufficient.

Erin, Frank, and Ted came through the lock and we sprinted for the other lock. It was open with the remains of a couple of half-dissolved Pugs lying on the floor. I'd dissolved a little of the wall and the door itself, but not enough to affect the functioning. We cycled through and started shooting the instant the door cracked open. It was not a moment too soon. The Pugs were just starting to get organized. As it was, we caught them unawares and most of them went down immediately. A couple of them managed to run down the hall away from us and duck around a corner. I sighed. It looked like they'd have to be hunted down individually; a dangerous task.

We'd just finished checking the destruction and assured ourselves that there was no resistance left when the last Pug-bear came tearing around the corner followed closely by the two Pugs. It had decided that we might be more susceptible to an all-out attack than some hide-and-seek hunting game. It paired its charge with a mental attack at the same time. I was able to easily deflect its effort, but my companions were all stunned into inactivity.

As soon as the two Pugs came into view, they started shooting splinters at us, but by then I'd gotten the eraser rifle up and simply burned through the Pug-bear horizontally in a slicing motion that also left the two Pugs without mid-sections. None of their shots had done any damage, but I inwardly shuddered at the possibility of seeing my companions struck.

I turned and they were just starting to blink their eyes as if coming out of a deep slumber. Erin's eyes immediately opened wide as she saw the Pug-bear's remains.

"Oh, Dee! You got it! And, and we were no help. I was somewhere far away, hiding from something that frightened me! It was like a bad dream where you're being chased, but it faded out. How did you kill them?"

"I've learned to fight off their mental attacks," I didn't want to get into a long explanation. I'd already told her that I had that sort of ability.

"Hey, Man! It's a good thing you can fight that stuff! I couldn't move. It was like seeing about five defensive linemen running at you at the same time; you don't know which way to run for a moment." Frank had been affected differently, obviously, but had now recovered. "What's next? What do we have to do now?" he asked.

Ted was quiet, simply passing his hand over his eyes a couple of times, then looking alertly around. I checked our immediate area for anything I'd failed to notice. There was a long hall with a T-shaped crossing at the end. The enemy had come running around the right-hand corner and their remains were lying near the intersection.

I said, "We probably don't have to do anything else in here. I think we've gotten all the Pugs unless there were some others that stayed back somewhere." That statement decided me. We'd have to physically clear the arm unless there was another way to do it. I started to walk down to the intersection but then changed my mind again. I returned to the airlock and started to press the cycle button to open the door. My action was interrupted by the door cycling as Whistle came walking blithely through, acting as if he hadn't a care in the world.

"You get dem all!" He had a definite tone of triumph in his voice. "Dere no other creatures showing in the life monitor at the door." He waved his arms vaguely in the direction of the airlock to emphasize his meaning.

"You have sensors that can tell how many occupants are in a wing?" I asked.

"Dat correct! We know they all gone," he said.

"OK. Have the station Sunnys start repairing our ship as fast as possible! I don't know how much time we'll have. The Pugs could have called for help when they realized what we were up to." I was fearful that there might be an Ansible on the planet that could instantly alert the enemy to send FTL reinforcement. The possibility made me nervous and I wanted to be ready to go. I had a feeling that it was urgent that we have our ship in good fighting order.

Whistle turned to the airlock to get the other Sunnys organized. When we arrived, the hub was empty except for the five of us. Whistle led us to a lounge area that held some of their food machines. There were none there that were specifically tailored for humans, but we could eat some of the Sunny food and we did so, seated on the floor.

Chapter 20

The Sunnys worked rapidly, but it still took around one hundred hours for them to detach the damaged FTL vane from our ship, pull an entire vane off of the most nearly complete FTL ship, maneuver it over to our ship and gently shove it into place with small one-person tug vehicles. We watched closely from the station's hub. The video screens in the command center were capable of magnifying the view and we could easily zoom in to watch details as fine as a Sunny working on bolts alongside the main mounting bracket. The whole operation reminded me of some sort of futuristic ballet. The small tugs flying around, sometimes working in pairs and sometimes working at seemingly cross-purposes seemed an apt counterpoint to individual Sunnys jetting around with their EVA packs and belts of hand-held tools. It was intricate and confusing to the four of us humans, although I was the only one who was really interested enough to watch most of the time.

The two big men had somehow come up with a pack of cards and they spent much of their time playing Gin Rummy for stakes that were unknown to me. Erin spent time watching me watching the Sunny operation, but she also spent a lot of time apparently sleeping in her cabin on the station.

The Sunnys had hospitably given each of us a private cabin in an exterior wall of the station hub. That way we were close to the action for our convenience and, probably, more easily observable for the Sunnys' convenience. They still hadn't developed the degree of trust that Whistle and Frazzle exhibited.

About halfway into the repair process, I got nervous about being separated from our ship and decided that we'd be better off if we left the station and camped out on board. Some of the ship's power was shut down for the repairs, but the habitat area was still warm and the atmospheric recycling was chugging along. It would have made no sense to vent the ship or let it cool down. A lot of the work had to happen inside service access corridors and tubes, so the Sunnys kept things running. Accordingly, we moved back into our usual cabins on board. It might have been a little premature, but the move made me feel much better. At least I could shoot at any attacking vessels that might show up, even if we couldn't run until the repairs were done.

There was another situation that was developing as time passed. The contingent of Sunnys that had left the FTL and transported to the planet surface had somehow set off a perfect storm of resistance against the Pug-bears' rule. They were greatly aided by the comet strike. There was rain all over the planet for days as the excess water cycled through the atmosphere.

The desert area was ruined for the Pug-bears' purpose of egg hatching. There were rivers and shallow seas in the inter-mountain region and the Pug-bears were rampaging around like feral animals in total disregard of their grafted-on intelligence. They'd initially all dashed up to the breeding grounds, but now they were filtering out, coming down the mountains to decimate the Sunny cities, killing any Sunny unfortunate enough to be caught outside the protective shields and water barriers.

The Sunnys from our ship had spread out to various locations on the planet and were coordinating the setting up of motion-sensing auto-cannons. None of them were very happy about the process, but they'd somehow gathered up enough fortitude to carry out the task. I thought that their feelings were somewhat shielded by the fact that they weren't actually pulling the triggers, themselves. The Pug-bears were doing a good job of that. They'd rush a cannon installation repeatedly until they'd figured out a way to get by its defensive fire and then they'd rip it apart; a task that they were easily strong enough to accomplish. The best part was, they often lost several individuals to the gun before they were able to swamp it. The numbers seemed to be rapidly working out in favor of the Sunnys and I was pleased, as were Frazzle and Whistle.

The two of them kept busy talking to their former shipmates, making suggestions about devious ways to install the auto-cannon traps. When it came to raw brainpower, the Sunnys were more than a match for the Pug-bears. Their only failing was their extreme vulnerability to mental control.

Once I recognized that, I resolved to try and do something about it. I spent a couple of hours working with both of them, trying to see if I could somehow set up a barrier in their minds that would protect them from Pug-bear control methods. It was not much use. Frazzle did develop a small amount of resistance that was facilitated by his ability to do higher math in his head. When he focused intently on working out an equation, he was able to simply ignore my attempts at low-intensity mental control. However, if I put a bit more effort into it, he would lose the ability to focus and then rapidly succumb.

He was eager to learn, though. "You keep trying on me, please! Me wants to be free of their mind controls. I learn some resistance and maybe with practice, I learn more. Dec, you keep trying on me, please, please!" was the way he put it.

We continued to work at it, spacing our efforts out over time, so as to not become over-tired. I didn't have much hope of him mastering the process, but I figured that any improvement was a hundred percent better than what he'd started with. Erin was a frequent observer of our efforts. She had developed the somewhat disconcerting habit of watching me when I was busy. Without looking, I'd sense her attention when I was observing the repairs through the video display and also when I was working with Frazzle.

Eventually, she asked me if I thought that she could learn to defend against mental control. The idea of working closely with her gave me pause. I had, of course, worked with Liz and my son. Also with Rudy, but I had an emotional bond with all of them. Frazzle was no problem for me. His very alienness kept me from becoming too involved. I'd had little success with my friends in Grand Lake, though. Working with other humans was best facilitated by strong empathy and, for me, that meant I had to love them at some level. I didn't want to feel that way about Erin. Somehow it felt like I'd be cheating on Liz.

On the other hand, I really needed all of my allies to have as much strength as possible. Erin wasn't too bad in a gunfight, but she really didn't have the killer instinct that Liz or the two football players had. I eventually came to the conclusion that we'd be better off if I was able to train her to some degree.

She was all for me training her and wanted to start the instant I suggested it, but I wanted to wait until the next wake period. I thought that it would go better and more smoothly if we were both rested and fresh. In a way I was right, but the whole training thing didn't work out the way I'd hoped.

We met in the cafeteria the next morning. The Sunnys were still working on attaching the vane to our FTL ship. By now they'd reached the point where most of the work was internal; connecting the sub-systems to the main power supply along with all of the control systems. Whistle informed me that it would take at least another twenty-four hours for them to finalize the adjustments, reprogram the ship's computer to take account of the slightly more efficient vane and its modified control subset, and then to test the connections. After that, we'd be free to take the ship into FTL when needed. I thought that I'd better do what I could with Erin now since there didn't seem to be any foreseeable free time in the near future.

She sat down cross-legged on the floor directly in front of me. I rested my back against one of the food machines and began to take her into the trance state that I'd found worked best for this kind of thing. As I mentioned, I'd never really had great success with this sort of training except with Liz, Michael, and Rudy. Things started getting out of control immediately. Despite my prior manipulation of Erin's mind, when I briefly implanted the control mechanism to overcome her objections to my leadership, I hadn't connected with her on a deep level. It was like jumping into a whirlwind. Her mind was quick and didn't focus on any one thought for long before moving on to any of a number of possible conclusions. This level of activity was different to me and it gave me a problem for a while until I was able to get more deeply in touch with her.

Somewhere in the process, I became aware that she was gazing into my eyes with her lips parted slightly. She had deep green eyes and I hadn't really noticed them before. She was – I paused, startled. She was hijacking my mental flow in some way. I tried to redirect the mental relationship, but no matter what way I attempted, she somehow managed to start the whole thing sliding into a sexual mode. The woman was more adept at psychic seduction than I was prepared to handle.

I had to continually back up and try to get us on a more business-like basis. In the process, I managed to give her some degree of resistance to the most common Pug-Bear control thoughts. I'm not sure how I did it, but I could tell that she was learning how to resist them. The main problem was that she was more or less simultaneously learning how to get around my defenses against being seduced. I finally broke out of contact and realized that I was sweating and breathing rapidly. She was in no better condition.

She stretched and looked at me with eyes that spoke volumes. Her gaze was of a "come hither" variety and I felt the urge to comply, but suddenly my conscience spoke up and I got a bad case of guilty feelings. I was committed to Liz and wasn't going to change anything, no matter how much she pleaded or how attractive she made herself.

As if sensing my change and I guess that we were in rapport enough that she did, she let out a disappointed sigh and smiled, half-embarrassed. "I'm sorry, Dec. I've never known anyone like you before. You're just so straightforward and trustworthy and I...," she paused. "I want that in my life. I know that you're committed to your wife and that's what I want for myself. Maybe – no, I guess I'll just have to try and live with myself. Things could change."

She added this last thought somewhat hopefully, but I wasn't sure if she meant that she'd find someone else or I might change my mind. "Well, this session was informative for both of us. I guess we're more in tune with each other now," I said somewhat inanely. "What I mean is that I'm sure that you picked up at least some techniques that will help you resist mental control in the future."

I wanted to back out of the situation gracefully. I started to stand up and realized that I was still breathing heavily. I turned away quickly and headed for the door. As I walked, I added, over my shoulder, "I've got to go check on progress with the repairs." I felt like a complete fool in any of a number of ways.

She just smiled knowingly and answered, "I'll see you later."

I was really glad to see the furry, alien countenance of Frazzle as he glanced my way when I entered the bridge. At least with him, there was only an open friendliness with no other possible complications. I felt a lot more at ease with the operational and strategic problems at hand.

"How long do we have before the ship will be finished?"

"Bouts done now, Dec," he chirped.

I was mostly used to his patois by now and it was starting to sound natural to me. I hadn't been noticing his odd use of our language for days. I'd developed a sort of mental translation program that simply filled in the blanks and smoothed over the mistakes in his speech.

"OK! That's good news," I answered.

"We can goes quick," he said. "Where do you want to go?"

That was the question. The situation on the planet below was gradually calming down and we couldn't help there anyhow. We just didn't have enough force to make a difference.

Now, that was a thought! Force! That was what I'd been lacking during the entire invasion period on Earth. Despite having the armed FTL, as good as it was, I felt like I desperately needed more warm and (hopefully) fighting-ready bodies on our side. How was I going to get them?

Chapter 21

The weather had been gradually warming up as spring progressed into summer. It seemed like it had been an eternity since Dec left. Michael and I were lonely and missed him terribly, but we were managing. The homestead was a comforting place. Dec and I had put a lot of ourselves into it and I knew every inch of the cabin, yard, and outbuildings. They gave me a reassuring feeling of familiarity every morning when I got up and began the day's routine.

I started by making breakfast for the two of us. That usually involved getting Michael to help make pancakes; something he loved doing. They became very artistic when he made them. He'd show me an indiscriminate blob and tell me it was a dinosaur or a whale or whatever. His imagination was always working overtime and I was proud of my little boy.

Once breakfast was over, we gathered the eggs from the chicken flock and tended to our milk cows and horses. The large animals were normally penned in the barn at night and released to graze in the area during the day. There was plenty of grass in small clearings along the creek and they didn't have to wander far in order to get enough to eat. Both cows and the three horses knew enough to come back when it grew dark.

There was always a possibility of bears or cougars and smaller predators. I didn't worry much about the smaller ones. They were unlikely to pose a threat to the livestock. There had been a rumor of some wolves moving into the area. So far that's all it was, a rumor. I kept my .243 near the front door and carried it along if I had to travel any distance from the cabin. It wasn't too heavy a rifle, weighing in at around seven pounds, but it still got in the way at times. Nevertheless, I felt better when I had it nearby.

I also carried a smaller 9-millimeter semi-automatic pistol that I strapped to my calf. This was just about the first thing I put on when I got out of bed. Before the alien attack and the EMP, I was always armed when on the job, but I would never have thought of carrying at all times. Our lives were different back then. The aliens had made us realize that we were far more vulnerable to violence than we'd thought. Security was now uppermost in everyone's mind.

I spent part of each night renewing the mental wards around the homestead. Dec had taught me to visualize a protective zone that would gradually increase anxiety in any predator that dared to try and come in. It seemed to work, but I wasn't as good as him and it took more effort for me to keep the barriers up. Even so, I looked forward to going to bed, not that I was worn out with work, but because I could sense Dec's presence best when I was just on the verge of sleep. I'd be in that warm, safe state, just before dropping off and I could feel him occupying his side of the bed, even though I knew he was off across the mountains. As long as I could sense his presence, I knew that he was safe and would eventually come back to us after he stopped the aliens again.

Occasionally, we would speak when I was dreaming. It made me wonder if it was a dream or not, but I finally realized that we were actually communicating on some level. This realization was greatly strengthened when I was wondering where the leather punch was. My horse had hooked his halter on a pine stub and had broken the cheek strap. We had plenty of cured leather in the barn and it only took me a short time to cut a replacement. The only problem was that the leather punch was missing from the toolbox. I needed to poke some holes in the strap in order to attach it to the remainder of the halter and pushing an old nail through the leather just didn't seem to make as smooth a hole as I would have liked.

It was nearly dark by that time, so I decided to wait until morning when there was better light to aid my search for the missing punch. We had supper and I got Michael to bed, did my own nighttime routine, and crawled under the covers. I was asleep and had been for a while when I became aware that I was standing outside and Dec was beside me. He placed his arm around my shoulders and kissed me. I turned to him and held on as tightly as I could. He felt so good; I'd really missed that.

At one level I knew I was dreaming, but on another level, the experience seemed very real. He put his hands on my shoulders and said softly, "I've got to go now. I'm busy with battle preparations, but everything is fine. The leather punch is on the cross beam to the left of the barn door. It's slipped down in a crack where it's difficult to see."

Things faded out and became fuzzy at that point. I tried to cling to him, but he faded out also and I drifted off to a restless sleep. It didn't seem like it had been over ten minutes when the rooster started his morning bragging. He made a good alarm clock, but this morning I was tired and resented his telling the world that he could beat up any other rooster that came around. I kicked around under the covers trying to get back to sleep, but then I remembered Dec telling me about the punch. That did it! I couldn't go back to sleep until I checked to see if it was where he'd said it was, so I got up and dressed. Michael was still sleeping when I slipped out the door and went across the damp grass to the barn.

It was dim inside and the space smelled of warm animals. All three horses nickered at me and stomped their feet as I let them and the cows out for the day. The barn faced the east and the sun was just starting to provide enough light coming over the mountains for me to see in the interior. I walked over to the door and there it was, exactly where Dec had told me. I pulled the punch out of the crack and looked at it as if it were some kind of ghost. It was a little spooky. He'd known right where it was and I was holding confirmation that my 'dream' hadn't really been a dream.

I was just finishing punching the necessary holes in the strap when Michael came out onto the cabin porch and called to me to come and make breakfast. I carefully put the punch back in the toolbox before returning to the cabin.

We were running a little low on some necessary items, so about noon, we rode into town to go to the store. Michael and I had gathered up the few things we wanted and were waiting to pay. There were a couple of girls in front of me, buying some beans and flour. While Molly weighed the items, they conversed and I couldn't help but overhear them talking about William Smith. It seemed that both of them were infatuated with him, but one had convinced herself that he was interested in her in return.

I knew William slightly. He'd always seemed very nice to me. Some of the men didn't hold much stock in him and Dec had always been non-committal about him. On the other hand, I had a positive view of the man. He always smiled and greeted me politely, tipping his hat, which was something a lot of men didn't do. We'd only had a few chances to converse, but he was amusing and seemed interested in what I had to say.

The two girls finished their business and left. Molly gathered my items together, tallied them and I settled with her, using some junk silver coins. We'd started out using paper money, but a lot of it had worn out. The problem was partially solved when one of the townsfolk had rather grudgingly pulled out a couple of bags of silver coins that he'd been hoarding.

"I never thought I'd be trading these in under this kind of circumstance," he said. "Always thought that the government would just fold by printing too much paper money and I was convinced that these silver coins would retain their value." They had and, by now, they'd spread all over the area and had become one of our easier means of exchange. Of course, we also bartered like crazy.

We had only just arrived back at the cabin when I heard a horse neigh across the creek. It was about as good a warning as someone honking a car horn. I turned and saw that it was William Smith and one of the other shepherds, a man that I didn't know very well. They rode into the barnyard and when I greeted them, a little cautiously, William responded by asking me if I'd seen a couple of stray sheep.

"Hi, Elizabeth, Randy, and I are looking for a couple of lambs that got away from our herd last night. We're grazing them about a mile over the ridge to the west and our count turned up short this morning. We trailed them in this direction, but the tracks faded out and there's been no sign of them. I just thought that maybe you'd have seen the strays."

"No. I've been in town and we didn't see anything on the way in or on the way back. Nothing this morning before we left either."

Randy spoke up, "We've lost a few head to some kind of critter, maybe a lion or a wolf, and we were hoping to find these two before they came to a bad end."

"No. I can't help you with the search. Sorry!" I was about to dismiss them, but William changed the subject.

"How are you doing since Dec's been gone? Everything alright?"

I didn't want to dwell on the fact that Michael and I were alone, but now that he'd asked, I had to answer, "We're doing OK. There have been no problems that I can't handle and we've been able to keep the predators off of our chicken flock, so things are going well. Thanks for asking."

His eyes grew serious and he stopped smiling. He looked earnestly at me and said, "Elizabeth, if you ever need anything, anything at all, you ask me. I'd be honored to help you with any problem. It bothers me to see a woman and child alone out here. The world just isn't as safe as it used to be."

"Don't worry, William. I'm a good shot and can handle myself." I wanted him and especially Randy (who didn't look as reputable) to know that I could take care of protecting myself.

"Well, what with your husband missing for weeks now, I still worry about you. Just call on me if there's ever any need." He tipped his hat and the two rode off into the trees on the other side of our yard.

"Mommy, what did those men want?" Michael came walking down from the porch with a curious glint in his eye.

"Oh, Honey, they were just looking for some sheep that are lost."

"Well, there's no lost sheep around here and they need to go far away to find them," he said with a frown and a four-year-old's total assurance that he was correct.

The rest of the day went by slowly and it gradually clouded over. By nightfall, a light drizzle was falling, so we went to bed early. I was awakened in the middle of the night by a commotion near the barn. The horses were whinnying and the two cows were making some noise also. In between our animals' sounds, I could hear something running, then the bleat of a sheep in distress along with some snarling.

I jumped out of bed and grabbed my rifle and one of the flashlights. We'd been very careful about preserving the batteries, but the light would barely shine across to the barn after all of this time. I quietly cracked the door and looked outside. It was still raining and everything was misty. As I watched I saw a sheep bolt into the center of the barnyard, closely pursued by a dark shadow. It let out a loud baa as it was pulled down. The shadow seemed to hover around the throat of the sheep as it kicked and struggled. I aimed carefully and turned the flashlight on after I'd gotten the rifle lined up.

It was a wolf and it jumped and then glared at me, its eyes shining a bright green in the light. The rifle cracked, shooting out a large ball of brilliant flame that blinded my right eye from the flash. I'd kept my left eye closed and immediately switched, closing my right and opening my left. I'd hit the wolf and it was kicking in the mud beside the sheep. There was nothing I could do for either of them at the moment and I didn't want to go out there anyway. I was spooked and thought that there most likely would be more wolves nearby. I didn't want to try shooting them in the rain with a bolt-action rifle that only held four cartridges and with only a dim flashlight, so I closed and barred the door.

Michael was standing right behind me with the butcher knife in his hand when I turned around.

"Baby, what are you doing out of bed?" I was shocked.

"I didn't want anything to get you, Mommy. I got the knife just in case."

"That's my brave little boy! Now let me have the knife and you get back to bed. It was a wolf and I killed it, so there's nothing to worry about now." He dutifully climbed back into his little bed and I pulled up the covers under his chin.

"Mommy, can I have a rifle when I get big? I want to be able to kill wolves that scare me, too," he said, his eyes large in the darkness.

"Don't worry, Michael, you'll be able to take care of yourself and until you can, I'm here to protect you."

"I love you, Mommy!" he said softly, already falling back to sleep.

I just wished I could relax so easily. It took me a long time to go back to sleep. I spent a while reinforcing the wards around the homestead and hoping that the other wolves would stay away.

It turned out to be a vain hope. I don't know if the wolves were bold or my ward making just wasn't very good, but when I looked out in the morning, the sheep had been mostly eaten. The wolf's carcass was still there, lips drawn back in a death mask, but the sheep was just a puddle of blood, some bone fragments. and a scattering of muddy wool. The other wolves must have sneaked in and devoured it while I slept. They had certainly been quiet about it, too. That made me feel very insecure.

Along about noon, William came riding back through the yard. He was dripping wet with the drizzle and water ran off his hat and oilskin duster as he hunched over the pommel of his saddle. He came up to the porch as I stepped out.

"Good day, Elisabeth. I see you found one of my lost lambs. The other one is up in the trees over there about three hundred yards or so." He seemed dispirited.

"It was wolves. I shot one, but that was the only one I saw."

"Where's the body now?" he asked, looking around.

"I've already skinned the thing. The skin is nailed up in the barn and the remains are in the trash pile out to the left of the barn. It was a big, black male wolf, but it didn't look like it was very old." I was proud of how much I'd gotten done.

"There's a fair-sized pack of them that's been hanging around. I think I'm going to have to move the flock to the south pastures on the other side of town to get away from their range. That will mean I won't be able to check on you very often," he said.

"Don't worry about it, William, I'm capable of taking care of myself," I replied, feeling as if we'd just had the same conversation the day before.

"Well, that's true. You taught that wolf not to come around, but I still worry..." he trailed off, shaking his head.

"That's kind of you, but we're really OK. Now you probably ought to get your flock moving, if you're going to be on the other side of town any time soon. It's already noon."

He rode off and paused to wave at me, just before he entered the trees. I had a sinking feeling that he'd left me all alone for a moment. Then I realized that I was really thinking about Dec. I wished with all of my heart that he'd come back and soon.

Chapter 22

The summer slowly wore on. I still had a connection with Dec and it was comforting to sense him every night. However, I was beginning to worry. It had been a month since he'd left and I didn't want to face the oncoming winter without him. There were preparations to be made and the only time to make them was the summertime. We'd always worked like oxen during the long summer days. I did my best and some of our friends from town came out at times and helped, too, but it didn't feel as if I was making much headway in my preparations.

The wolves hadn't shown up again, but I'd had a problem with some kind of varmint getting at the chickens and had lost several hens to it. This further reduced my confidence, since I was working as hard as I could to ward the place, but it seemed to be losing effect. I just wasn't as good at it as Dec was and, without his help, I was losing what ability I had.

Late one afternoon, I was splitting some wood for the stove and I decided to tackle a large stump with twisted grain. We'd pulled the thing out of the creek last summer and it'd been sitting around waiting for Dec to get to it. For some reason, I decided that I'd just take out my frustrations on the chunk and I started in with the ax. I'd gotten the ax buried in the end, but then the grain was so tight that I couldn't get it worked out again. After wiping my forehead, I got the wedge and the sledgehammer and carefully started the wedge in the split caused by the ax. I figured I could tap it in and that would release the ax. After that, I wasn't sure if I'd continue with the stump or pick out some easier wood to split.

Anyway, the wedge got stuck too. I banged it with the sledgehammer as best I could and ended up burying it in the wood to the point where there was nothing to even hit with the hammer. The ax was still stuck, so I pounded on it a bit and only succeeded in driving it deeper. The whole thing was frustrating and I couldn't see how I was going to get enough pieces of wood to even cook supper. I dropped the hammer and stepped back, wiping my forehead. Hearing a noise, I looked up and saw William coming across the creek. He rode up to me and shook his head at my predicament.

"Elizabeth, you've just got everything stuck and you're going to need some help," he said as he dismounted. He took the sledgehammer from the ground at my side and swung at the ax head in such a way that it instantly tilted over. Another swing and the ax was free. Then he carefully used the ax as a wedge, tapping it into the log with the hammer until there was a loud "Crack" and the grain suddenly released. The wedge came out and with a few hard swings of the ax, the stump split in half.

"There! That's how you do it," William said kindly, handing the ax back to me.

"Thank you! I wasn't sure if I was going to have a warm supper tonight or not," I exaggerated.

"Why don't you get your stove going and let me chop some more kindling for you before I leave?"

"That's very nice of you William, I'd appreciate that." What else could I say?

I went in and started the stove, shooing Michael up to the loft to play with some of his toys and stay out of my way while I started supper. As I did, it occurred to me that I should ask William if I could fix supper for him.

He readily assented when I asked, stating that he was actually quite hungry, not having eaten since dawn. It took me about an hour and he chopped wood steadily all of the while. When I finally had the food on the table, he was standing in front of a huge pile of kindling, easily enough for a couple of weeks.

"Wow! I'd forgotten what a man can get done!" I exclaimed.

"It was my pleasure," he said with a smile.

He washed up and we sat in the kitchen and had a nice meal. Michael was on his best behavior, looking out the corners of his eyes at the unusual spectacle of a man in our kitchen. Once the meal was over, William hung around while I got Michael in bed. Then he sat beside the boy and told him a long, involved story about catching some fish in Grand Lake. Michael listened carefully and finally dropped off to sleep.

"Well, Elizabeth, I'd best be getting on. I aim to ride into town and stay at the hotel for the night," he said as he stretched and stepped towards the door.

"I'm sorry, we don't have any available guest quarters, Mr. Smith," I answered. "The best I can offer you is the haymow." We did have a guest room, but it was currently being used for storage and sewing projects.

"No. That's quite alright. It's not too far into town and I'll be more comfortable there. And, you know you can call me William, Elizabeth." He met my gaze and I could see that his eyes were warm and sympathetic. "Are you still doing OK out here by yourself?"

"Well, yes, but it does get lonely sometimes with just the two of us," I answered. I don't know why I encouraged him, but it was true, I was lonely. He was gentlemen enough not to think it was some kind of invitation, though.

"I'll stop back by in a few days to check on you. Maybe you'll let me take Michael fishing. He seemed to like the story I told him."

"That might be nice," I said as I ushered him out the door. After a bit, I could hear his horse clop off towards the stream. That was followed by the sound of the water splashing around the horses' hooves as they crossed on the way into town.

It was a long night and it wasn't helped by the fact that I couldn't seem to sense Dec except for a little bit as it got near dawn and when I did finally start to feel his presence, it was as if he were very far away.

It so happened that I needed to go into town a couple of days later. Michael had been playing in the cabin and had swung a stick that he'd adopted as a sword and broken one of our lanterns. These were oil lamps and he knocked the chimney off the one that sat on the table. He was sorry and I wasn't very upset. After all boys will be boys. After a discussion of why we shouldn't play with sticks inside, which he attended to carefully with his eyes suitably wide, we headed for town to see if there might be a replacement available somewhere. It was by no means a guaranteed thing that there would be another lamp available. Supplies were very sparse. However, this was Saturday and some of the townspeople had taken to having a combination get-together and flea market on Saturday afternoons. I suspected that the social aspect was more important to most of them than the financial part.

Once we got there, I was talking to a couple of the ladies and trying to control Michael at the same time. He was excited and wanting to get into everything. I didn't want him running off or breaking anything else, so I was trying to hold his hand, much to his distress. Suddenly a shadow appeared at my side and I turned to see William standing close.

"Elizabeth, it looks like you've got your hands full there," he chuckled as he spoke, indicating that he understood how much of a handful a four-year-old could be. "Why don't you let me take the boy over to the lake and see if we can catch a fish?"

I was tired of the fight and also I wanted to have a sensible conversation with some other adults, so I agreed, "If you're sure that it'd be no trouble for you?"

"Not at all! I know just how to keep him interested for a while. If you get done before we come back, I'll have him over by the town dock." The two of them walked off hand-in-hand, Michael looking up at William with admiration in his eyes.

Nellie waited until they were out of hearing and then exclaimed, "I never thought that man would do something like that!"

"What do you mean?" I asked.

"Well...," she hesitated, drew a breath, and then decided to continue. "He – I mean, I've heard that he is kind of wild if you know what I mean?"

"No, I don't. He's stopped by and helped me a few times and he's always been friendly and shown me every sign that he was trustworthy."

The two ladies looked at each other with a sort of knowing glance.

"What is it?" Now they had made me curious. Whatever it was, I didn't think that it could be too bad.

"Let's just say that he's been playing the field with the single women in town," replied Maria. "Some of the girls have been competing for his attentions, but I've heard that he seems to have taken himself off the market recently. It really disappointed a lot of them. A couple of them were convinced that he was close to proposing," she drew a breath and continued, "but I don't think that was really a possibility. My opinion is that he's probably got his eye on some female somewhere and they're just out of luck."

"Yeah," interjected Nellie. "Maybe you'd better watch out. You might not realize it, but there's been some talk about you, what with your husband gone missing and all."

I didn't like that one bit! "No, that's not something I want to even discuss. I happen to know that Declan is fine," I was exaggerating a little, but I hoped that I wasn't deceiving myself, just in order to feel better and keep my spirits up.

Nellie smiled sympathetically, "Anyway, you should probably see about getting some other men to stop by and help you a little bit more. That would put a stop to some of the gossip."

Now it was gossip! I tried to reassure myself that it was just a small-town sort of thing. I responded, "I'm not a widow and won't be! Dec knows exactly how to take care of himself and I'm confident that it won't be long before he's back."

"Nevertheless, I'll send Jim out to cut some wood for you sometime this next week," she answered.

I drew a deep breath, "Thank you, Nellie! That would be very appreciated." I was going to say something else, but I happened to glance at a table with some miscellaneous junk that was just a few yards away. There was a perfectly fine lamp chimney sitting there and it looked like it might be exactly the right size. "Please excuse me. There's something over there I might want to buy."

It was the work of only a couple of minutes to get the chimney. It had a small chip on the top edge and I used that to work the price down a bit. Having finished my business, I waved to the ladies and set out for the lake. As I rounded a building, I could see the two of them sitting side-by-side on the end of the dock. Michael turned as he heard my steps on the wood, jumped up, and came running, screaming excitedly about the fish he'd caught and how big it was. William followed up with a couple of smaller trout on a stringer.

"...And, I'm going to eat it for supper!" my son yelled, pointing at the stringer.

"I guess I'll just have to plan on cooking fish, then," I smiled down at him. William came up and I paused for a moment, thinking about the ladies' warning. "Thank you, William! It was really nice of you to keep him interested while I got some things done."

"No problem!" he responded, "I'll be happy to take care of him anytime you need help. We're best buddies!"

"We sure are!" enthused Michael.

"I've got to get back to the house." I decided that I'd better go before I gave people any additional grounds for gossip. "Thanks, again, William."

Michael, of course, wasn't ready to let it go at that, "Mommy, can William come for supper? Please?"

Now I had to come up with something and I opted for a tried and true excuse used by women throughout time. "No, Honey, Mommy's got a headache and doesn't feel like having company." William looked concerned, but I just waved at him and we headed for the horses. I took a deep breath and decided that maybe he was just being friendly and helpful, but an undercurrent of instinct or feminine intuition told me that it might also be more than that. It was flattering in a way. Here all of the younger girls wanted the guy and, I had to admit that it was true, he'd been paying a lot of attention to me. For about the ten-thousandth time, I wished Dec would come riding over the hill.

I dreamed about Dec that night. He was close to me in bed and, although I knew it was a dream, it seemed as if he was hovering over me, supported by his arms. I was breathing rapidly and moved my legs in anticipation and excitement. It had been so long. He began to lower himself down onto me and I felt a warm flush of readiness. Just as he was getting closer, his face blurred and slowly faded out in the manner of dreams. I tried repeatedly to get him to come back, but it wouldn't work. I was simultaneously aroused and disappointed. No matter what I did, in my dream, he wouldn't come back.

Finally, I saw a figure approaching me as though through a fog. I breathed a deep sigh of relief and thought, "It's about time!" It got closer and closer and then a face appeared. I thought that it was Dec's, but then it morphed into that of William and the shock startled me wide awake. I had no interest in him! Why had his face appeared? I was, to put it mildly, horrified.

I sat up, still breathing rapidly, my heart pounding so hard that I had to put my hand on my breast to try and slow it. I realized that I was still aroused and a surge of anger at Dec came over me. How could he go off and leave me – us alone?

The next instant I realized how wrong that anger was and I felt equally guilty. Dec was everything that I'd ever wanted in a husband, strong, capable, extremely loving. and devoted. It was very confusing and my mind was in turmoil. It took until near dawn before I could go back to sleep. Even then, it wasn't restful. I tossed and turned and kicked the bed covers into a knot. I was so twitchy that Jefferson finally jumped off the bed; something he normally was reluctant to do.

When I finally awoke, it was past time to get up, but I'd come to a conclusion and had resolved to try and discourage William from coming by again. I knew one thing for certain: my resolution would meet with the full approval and approbation of Jefferson. He'd never taken to the man. The cat usually simply disappeared before he reached the house, only showing up after he'd left. I wondered if maybe our cat knew or sensed something that I couldn't. Just as I'd learned to rely on his alien sensing ability, perhaps I'd better take a cue from him and avoid William.

But, the facts remained the same. I was a woman, isolated from my nearest friends by a few miles and the world was far more dangerous than it was only a few years before. I had to try and protect my son and our homestead from predators of both the four-legged and two-legged variety. As I thought about it, I realized that for the first time in a long, long time, perhaps since I'd become an adult, I was fearful and not at all sure that I could cope. I missed my husband, terribly and in addition, I was so lonely.

Chapter 23

There was a continuous low clanking from something that the Sunny repair crew was doing. I'd been in my cabin for several hours; how many I didn't know, but I hadn't been able to sleep despite lying horizontal and keeping my eyes closed. I was still worrying about my insight. I needed more force, more fighters on our side. I wished for about the hundredth time that I could simply call Rudy and his men, but then I remembered that many of them had died in the prior run-in with the Pug-bears. I wasn't even sure that Rudy had survived his hair-brained attempt to get to Miami. There was no way to know.

One thing I felt good about was having the spaceship repaired. I felt pleased with myself for having figured out how to arm it, too. I didn't know if anyone would ever hear about it, but I'd more than survived my first space battle, despite one of the Pug's shuttles nearly scorching our gun off the bow. Suddenly a thought hit me. What if they'd actually hit our gun? We'd have been out of business and forced to run. There was no other replacement weapon of that caliber on board and besides, the gun we had needed to be recharged manually. That was a huge oversight that I'd neglected to rectify. I jumped up and ran out to the bridge.

Frazzle was sitting at the control station, as he usually was. I don't know when he actually slept. "Frazzle! Are there any other big anti-matter guns like the one we put on the bow?" I gasped, trying to catch my breath as I came through the entrance.

"Yes, dere two more. Dey were made for the other two ships being builded."

"Where are the guns now? Here in orbit or on the surface?" That was a rather critical piece of information. I doubted that the Pug-bears would willingly send them up to me if they had them. If the Sunnys had them, they were probably too busy and maybe needed the weapons themselves to create auto-traps.

"Dey in the station supplies arm. Does we need them?"

"Yes, I want to mount them on the lower edge of the habitat space, above the waist of the ship. We can put one on each side and that way we'll be able to deal more effectively with multiple attacks at once."

He frowned at the idea of combat, but slowly nodded his head in agreement. I had a momentary thought that I might be assigned to one of the lower levels of Hell for perverting these innocent, non-violent creatures' thinking.

"Also, the gun we have on the bow has only a limited capacity before it has to be manually recharged. I'd like to see if we can connect the power supply to the ship's power. That way, we won't have to worry about running out of shots in the middle of a bad situation. Can you see if the workers over there can set up mountings on the sides of the ship? I don't expect them to actually mount the guns, though. I can do that like the last time."

"Well, some of dem have put guns on the Pugs' shuttles. Pugs get tired of doing it themselves and make us, so some can do it." He looked distressed at the thought.

It was another thing to hold against the Pugs. I didn't like the Pug-bears, but they were so alien and feral acting that they often seemed to have no more mercy than an animal, despite their empathetic mental control ability. The Pugs, on the other hand, were at least civilized to the degree of an iron-age society. True, their lives were short, brutal, and exclusively focused on fighting for status, but I still had the thought that they could probably understand enough about the Sunnys to treat them better. The Sunnys were very special in my mind. I was unaware of any other group of people that were so non-violent by nature. Humanity certainly didn't have an analog for them. Even non-violent religious sects didn't compare. The Sunnys not only objected to and refrained from violence, they were almost fully incapable of thinking about it.

"Frazzle, let's get them working on the other mounts and see if they can figure out how to link the power supplies up to the ship. Also, get the other

two guns out here to our ship. If we have to run from some force that the
Pugs might bring against us, at least we'll be able to finish mounting them
ourselves."

"OK, den!" He'd adopted some of our colloquialisms.

After we'd had that conversation, I returned to my cabin. I was still tired and
hoped to get some sleep. I'd handled one aspect of force multiplication.
Additional firepower would be very helpful and might make the difference
in our survival in case of any additional space battles. Unfortunately, I still
wanted more fighters. I continued mulling that over, even going so far as to
contemplate returning to Earth to try and recruit volunteers. It didn't take
long for me to reject that idea. I could see myself trying to run a recruitment
campaign for some of the Eastern Slope Warlord's fighters. It didn't seem
like that was one of my better ideas.

I finally came around to a thought that I'd had before. It had originally
occurred to me when we were first trying to stop the invasion, years ago. Liz
had found a booklet detailing the planets dominated by the aliens and
showing their projected targets, of which Earth was next on the list. The
fifteenth planet in the booklet had some kind of creatures or civilization that
had apparently fought off the Pug-bears' invasion. At the time, I'd
mentioned to Liz that perhaps we might consider allying ourselves with
those creatures.

She'd been quick to point out that we didn't know anything about them and
the old statement, "The enemy of my enemy is my friend," often proved to
be wrong. The enemy of your enemy can as easily become your enemy, too.
There's no hard and fast rule on this point, obviously.

So, that left me with the rather desperate idea that maybe we could go to
that planet and see if we could find out how the residents had stopped the
Pug-bears. Maybe they wouldn't want to ally with us, but perhaps we could
still learn some things from them that would help. I couldn't see what else
we could do. The Sunnys on the planet below were barely holding the Pug-
bears off and the outcome was dubious despite our comet-water-bomb
tactic.

There was no way I wanted to inject our tiny force of four humans into that
situation. We'd simply get killed without accomplishing anything. We could
try to drop some more things on the Pug-bears' heads, but they weren't
centralized anywhere. They didn't live in groups and were distributed across

the mountains. The only reasonable target had been their breeding grounds and the comet had taken those out. Dropping random rocks was just as likely to hurt the Sunnys as the Pug-bears. I was reminded of the military adage that you can't take and hold ground with air-power alone.

I finally came to a decision. It was the enigmatic fifteenth planet. That was the only place I knew that offered a possibility of finding fighters that could help shut down the Pug-bears' expansion plans. I didn't like it much, but that was it. At least I was confident that my mental abilities would let me communicate with the creatures there. All we needed was for the guns to get mounted and to take on some supplies. With that thought, I finally fell asleep.

Mounting the two extra guns didn't take more than five hours. The Sunnys were able to weld the mounts in place and then used their tugs to haul the guns out. They apparently had no problem making the connections and linking up the control interface. My idea of hooking the weapons to the ship's power supply wasn't much harder to implement either.

There were access ports scattered across much of the hull that allowed various tools to be hooked into the power. The welding had actually been powered by the ship through these ports and it was a simple task to co-opt three of the power ports for the guns. The most difficult one was the initial gun, mounted as it was on the bow-shield plate. The nearest power port was under the rear edge of the shield, where it was out of the way and protected from any stray rocks that managed to get through the deflection field. The Sunny engineers allowed as how they couldn't easily run a cable through the shield plate. It was some hyper-dense material that was almost impervious to cutting or drilling. Instead, they ran a heavily armored cable from the power port to the gun. The cable was exposed across about twenty meters of shield and could be vulnerable there, but they managed to leave the gun's normal power pack in place as a backup system. That meant if the cable was cut, we'd still have about a hundred shots before we couldn't use the gun any longer.

I thought that was probably good enough. I couldn't imagine needing to shoot that much, but then I was a novice at this sort of thing, too. I felt better about the other two guns. They were mounted right on top of the power ports and their mounting shielded the ports to a high degree. They would be harder to knock out unless a well-aimed shot hit them directly.

On the fifth day after arriving in orbit and taking the space station, we said, "Goodbye," to the station Sunny crew and moved off a reasonable distance with a few brief pulses of our thrusters. Frazzle laid in our course to the fifteenth planet.

It was a longer journey than the first one we'd taken to the Sunny planet. Our new destination was roughly at the far end of a triangle from Earth. Visualize Earth as being located at the right angle corner of a right triangle. Then the planet where we now were would be located at the nearest corner to Earth. This new planet was located at the end of the hypotenuse of the triangle, a line that ran from the Sunny planet to planet fifteen. The journey would take roughly twenty-one days to complete. The leg back to Earth from the fifteenth planet was shorter. That leg of the triangle was about fourteen days.

I didn't actually know how far the systems were from each other. I still hadn't been able to sensibly discuss distance with either of my Sunny friends. There was something about the concept that seemed to go against their worldview. We could communicate better when discussing time from one point to another. They didn't get it when I tried to divide time into velocity and distance. It was, I guess, all space-time to them.

They knew exactly where the Pug-bears' system was, though. It was a fairly short distance perpendicular to the plane of the triangle I just described. The Pugs' planet was only a short hop away from that of the Pug-bears. The two were located in a loose binary system. The stars circled each other in a stately pavane at a distance of a couple of light-years. As sisters, they had much the same chemical composition, a fact that probably accounted for some of the alienness of the two races. I learned these facts during the latter part of our voyage to the planet of the Pug-bears' only failure – unless you could consider the Earth a failure, but the outcome there was still in doubt.

We spent the first part of the voyage ensuring that the new systems and weapons were in working order. There was no way to actually engage in target practice with the new guns while we were at FTL velocity, but I had Frazzle set up simulations on the main computer and then download them into the weapons control systems. It was cumbersome, however, it worked well enough that I felt reasonably assured that the systems not only worked but that I could simultaneously control all three weapons. I spent several hours engaging simulated targets and eventually learned how to set up the system to fight three enemy ships simultaneously and then transition to the next three within a few milliseconds of firing at the first targets. Erin, as usual, was a close observer.

She was somewhat startled on the fourth day when I asked her to take over the weapons system.

"Are you sure, Dec? I don't know anything about space-guns," she demurred.

"Look, Erin, I might be injured or somewhere else and someone needs to be able to help defend us. I'd try Ted and Frank, but neither of them has any interest in this type of fighting. I've already asked. Ted never got interested in computer games and Frank says that he only understands two-dimensional football strategy, so they're not going to be the main candidates for this. That leaves you, so please sit down and let me run you through the operation."

I did my best to train her and it turned out that she was really a natural at this sort of thing. She, too, had never been interested in computer combat games, but the idea of being able to defend her life seemed to make the learning experience far more important than simply playing a game. She was very quick on picking up the controls and it only took her a few tries to begin to master the strategic aspects of targeting. It was a little more complicated than that, but, in my limited experience, I judged that she'd almost caught up with me in terms of skill level after a day of training. Thereafter, we took turns posing different scenarios for Frazzle to program, trying to come up with something that would cause the other person serious problems and, hopefully, cause them to have to improvise and come up with a new strategy for a firing solution. If it hadn't been so serious, it would have been fun.

It did bring us closer together and taught each of us that the other could be relied upon to give their best in a fight. She seemed to accept that we weren't going to develop a romantic relationship, but a couple of times, I caught her looking at me with a thoughtful gaze that seemed to have more than a little sexual heat. At least, the practice kept us busy in a productive way. Frank and Ted simply played cards most of the time, save for the times when they decided to work out or attend to their weapons.

We finally dropped out of FTL speed about sixty light minutes from a hot blue star. There were a large number of planets circling this sun at a fair distance. The closer ones were mostly on the order of Mercury; hot and burned up, in-conducive to any life. Our destination was farther away from the star than I would have thought, but the Cinderella zone was, by necessity, a long way out. Frazzle assured me that the temperature there was bearable for humans, but he still thought that we'd find it very hot.

We had to approach carefully. The Pug-bears had left a small orbital station guarding the planet. Whistle thought that there was always a small contingent of Pugs and a few Sunnys on the station. Their task was to keep watch for any kind of activity from the planet. Apparently, the Pug-bears had been so upset by their unprecedented defeat there, that they wanted to make sure that nothing ever came up from the planet's surface.

Sitting behind Frazzle in the bridge, I asked the obvious question. Why hadn't they used kinetic energy weapons – rocks – and bombed the crap out of their enemy? He gave me a long, involved speech dealing with some philosophical concept covering the undesirability of violence and how that meant the Pug-bears did the correct thing by giving up on the planet.

I finally tired of his circumlocutions and tried to pin him down, whereupon he gave me a more direct answer. It turned out to be due to the same reason that I hadn't been able to bomb the Pug-bears on the Sunny planet. There were simply no cities or concentrations of force to target on the planet below. The possibility of simply using a huge KEW to rid the planet of life had fortunately not occurred to them.

We approached the planet on the opposite side from the orbital station, hoping that we could get close enough to figure out how to take it down without having to destroy the thing. I didn't want to kill the Sunny crew, even though I could care less about the Pugs. The problem was that I couldn't have a station full of Pugs with unknown offensive capabilities hanging around while I landed on the surface of the planet in what might prove to be a vain and foolhardy attempt to recruit the locals into my self-defined war.

I was sitting, pondering the problem with my chin resting on my hand, when Frazzle alerted me to a pleasant development. He was in contact with the Sunnys on the station and they'd informed him that there was only a minimal crew on-board. There were six Sunnys and only four Pugs. The best part was there were no Pug-bears currently in residence. The facilities were very limited and the Pug-bears didn't care for the lack of space. The last remaining Pug-bear had been picked up by the periodic supply ship a long time ago. The Pugs mostly left the Sunnys alone and had delegated the daily operations to them so there was little chance that the Pugs would even hear that we'd entered the system as long as we transported onto the station. They would certainly notice the fact that a large ship had docked if we tried that. I also didn't want the presence of the guns attached to the waist and bow to give them ideas.

There had been other Pugs stationed with the four remaining ones, but they'd lost shuttles during their infrequent patrols. The station normally had three atmospheric-capable shuttle-craft, but they were now down to one.

One shuttle had been lost when the crew had landed at the abandoned fort while bombing the natives. They'd abruptly gone black and had never come back on the air. The second was lost when the last patrol got caught in the local equivalent of a hurricane. The pilot hadn't realized exactly how high the storm system rose into the atmosphere and had flown into the top edge of the eye and been caught in turbulence. Since the Pugs weren't exactly what you would call expert pilots, he'd been forced down and after some intermittent communication from the surface, that shuttle had gone off the air. The Sunnys presumed that both of the crew were now dead. They didn't think that anyone could survive down below for very long, due to the ferocity of the local animal life-forms.

The immediate result of our contact was that I interrupted Frank and Ted's card game, got them loaded up with their weapons and we transported over to the station with Whistle. The local Sunnys were a little dubious when they first set eyes on us, especially on the two big men, but Whistle calmed them down and they led us rapidly through the core of the station to the Pug's habitat arm. This station was configured with three arms; one for the Sunnys, another that was reserved for the Pug-bears, and the final, atmospheric-controlled one in which we were planning on going Pug hunting.

We cycled through the unguarded airlock and moved quietly down the hall followed by Whistle and one of the local Sunnys. The local guy informed us that the Pugs would most likely be in the larger space at the end of the arm. That space was designed to provide the residents with a simulation of their own planet, complete with the correct gravity, atmosphere, some prey animals, and plant life. If it was representative of the Pugs in general, I already knew that I wouldn't like it.

The end of the hall had a large set of double doors that evidently served the purpose of keeping the native animal life under control. It wouldn't do for the creatures to somehow find their way out to the main part of the habitat.

We prepared ourselves, first shooing the Sunnys back a safe distance down the hall. They quickly retreated and hovered nervously around a couple of doors that they could easily duck through. As we were ready to attempt our entry, Whistle came dashing down to where I was and grabbed onto my arm with both hands. "Dec, you watch out! Dey's maybe seen you," he motioned vaguely towards a camera lens stationed near the upper left of the double doors. There was a red, flashing light by the lens and I immediately understood that indicator to mean that the system was actively being used.

Without waiting another instant, I shoved Whistle out of the way and motioned to Frank, who happened to be nearest. He hit the double doors, slamming them open and nearly tearing them off of their hinges. As he went through, he dropped to the floor and began to slide sideways towards some nearby cover.

The room was so full of plants that you couldn't see how large it was. There were some muted animal noises in the background, but nothing nearby. There was no sign of any Pug activity. The leaves were still and the animal noises faded out rapidly as they evidently sensed our alien presence. I ducked in turn and moved around the left side of the opening. There was a large plant with huge leaves directly in front of me and I started to slip into its inviting cover. As I did, I noticed that some innocent-looking tendrils that were attached to the stem of the plant were quivering and starting to move slowly in my direction.

That didn't look good and I quickly backed off. I'd previously encountered an alien plant in one of the aliens' domes that could shoot harpoon-like weapons and I didn't want to give these tendrils a chance at me. I was looking at them when Ted jumped around the corner and crashed directly into the plant. The tendrils responded instantly by wrapping around every part of him they could reach. He let out an exclamation and rapidly made a couple of passes with his sword.

Fortunately, the tendrils were no match for the sharpened steel and after a couple of more swings, he was free. "Man! That hyped-up vine has got a strong grip!" he exclaimed. I glanced at him, pausing in my scanning the undergrowth. He was looking at his left wrist where I could see red welts where the tendrils had begun to cut right into his skin.

I whispered loudly, "Ted, Frank! Watch out for those things and any other plant that looks suspicious. The Pugs are at home here and know what's up; we don't!"

Frank had a wide-eyed look on his face and simply pointed at the nearest plant to his location. It was also one of the tendril-bearing ones and the tendrils were all stretched out at maximum extension, straining for a grip on him. He seemed to get a grip on himself and replied, "Yeah! Tell me something I don't know!"

In return, Ted shushed us with his finger over his lips and indicated a direction by pointing with his chin. I focused on what he was watching.

It wasn't immediately obvious, but I gradually made out the broken-up outline of a Pug concealed in the bushes. I finally saw that it was watching the doorway and hadn't yet located any of us. There may not have been any Pugs in the immediate vicinity of the doors, since this one, at least, hadn't seen our arrival.

I slowly pulled out my eraser-pistol. This would be the first time I used it in combat and I wanted to be extra careful to make the shot count. I need not have worried. The anti-matter burst struck the bushes and Pug leaving a gaping hole where his midsection had been concealed. One down.

At that moment, Frank jumped up and threw a large knife, something I hadn't seen him do previously. Obviously, the two guards were far more capable than I'd thought and I'd already figured they were deadly.

The targeted Pug staggered out of the bushes with the knife sticking through his throat. It took a couple of steps and then I shot it with the pistol. Two down.

I looked at Frank, who was back down shielded by some bushes. Ones that had no tendrils that I could see. He motioned violently towards my left and then ducked as a couple of splinters ripped through the leaves over his head. I'd known that it wasn't going to be that easy. There were only two Pugs left, but they were hunting us as hard as we were hunting them and the terrain was to their advantage.

We kept still while Frank let out a moan as if he were struck and dying. After about thirty seconds, I could hear some rustling in the leaves and a Pug came slinking out from behind a tendril plant. He passed Ted's position without seeing the guard. That was a big mistake. The long sword flashed out and detached the Pug's gun hand from his arm. The creature let out a scream and turned towards Ted, who was now standing, recovering from the swing. The sword came back up from the stroke and curved around in a neat parabola, cleaving the creature's neck. Three down.

The last Pug evidently preferred survival over valor. I suddenly heard a body moving rapidly away from us and then a door open on the left bulkhead. We dashed over and found that the door he'd run through had a window. Looking through, I could see the Pug looking back at me with a snarl on his face while he tried to activate some kind of touch panel on the wall. That wouldn't do at all!

I tried the door, but it was no good – locked! The eraser-pistol was next and that removed the barrier from between us. I ducked so as to be able to aim at the Pug and shot him. His head dissolved, but as it did, I could hear the sound of some gas coming into the habitat from overhead vents. It was hissing and I could see a faint cloud starting to descend. We wanted no part of that, whatever it was, so we beat a hasty retreat back through the double doors and pulled them shut.

Whistle was waiting to inform us, "Dats capture gas to knock out animals in the habitat. You might have been hurt by it, so good you gets out."

That said it all, except for the fact that we now had total possession of the station.

Chapter 24

O ur next step was to see about descending to the planet's surface. There were a number of things to accomplish first, but I delegated most of them to our two Sunnys and headed back to my cabin on our vessel to take a nap. I don't know what it is about action, but, if given the chance, I usually feel much better if I take a nap afterward. We all stopped in the galley area and had some food and then I told the others to leave me alone for a few hours.

Meanwhile, Whistle had availed himself of the sole remaining shuttle that was attached to the station. It was considerably larger than ours and offered plenty of space for our entire group. When he had that moved and safely attached to one of the docking stations on our FTL's waist, Frazzle fired up the EmDrive and shoved us into a much higher orbit. We were now traveling in an equatorial orbit along with a lot of rocks and dust; almost enough debris to comprise a rudimentary ring system. We'd approached the planet from one of the poles and avoided the ring, but now it made a good place to store the ship while we went and found out what we could about the inhabitants.

Frazzle was going to stay with the ship in case it required moving. I didn't expect any company. The Sunnys on the station had indicated that it would be months before their relief was due, but you never know about things like that. I figured our ship would be safer if it were parked somewhere where it was unobtrusive. I most certainly didn't expect Frazzle to fight the ship if any Pugs came calling. In fact, I gave him specific instructions to head out a few light minutes and find a place to lay low the instant the instruments detected any ship coming out of FTL in the system.

When I woke from my nap, the two guards had packed a full complement of weapons for all four of us humans. Whistle was also going down with us, but he only would carry a light pack with food and miscellaneous supplies for himself.

We boarded the shuttle through the short and cold docking-umbilical and arranged ourselves in the seats as best we could. The seats were a little tight, especially for the big men. The Pugs were notoriously narrow in the hip area. I had to wedge myself into a seat and even Erin filled her seat tightly, although her posterior was trim. Whistle took the pilot station, but before he sat down, he made a disgusted noise and spent some time scrounging around in a cabinet before he came up with something like a towel. The Pug pilot had been a slob and there were stains all over the pilot's seat. Whistle carefully covered the seat with the fabric and gingerly placed himself on top with a prim expression on his furry face.

Once we were strapped in, he detached the release and the shuttle floated free with a jerk due to the pneumatic launching mechanism. Once clear, he activated the engine. The Sunnys' shuttles used a form of the EmDrive design and were limited to in-system travel. However, they were still plenty fast. It didn't take us more than an hour to settle into low orbit around the mysterious planet. He maneuvered into a lower orbit, then rotated us and began a braking sequence. When we'd slowed enough to initiate atmospheric entry, he rotated so that we were looking forward again. Then he tested the atmospheric controls.

The shuttle wasn't at all like one of our conventional airplanes, but it did have some control surfaces that used aerodynamic shapes. These checked out and Whistle turned to me with one of his rather charming expressions (I'd taken to identifying it as a human-like smile since it seemed to serve the same purpose), "Decs, we set for going down. All's OK–"

He was interrupted by the shriek of an alarm and a video display flashing with pulses of yellow. He turned back to the controls and punched a few buttons. "De motor's having problems. De lazy Pugs don't maintenance it and it's – " There was a muffled explosion and the shuttle lurched.

Frank shouted, "What's happening?" The other two just held on and looked at the flashing screen.

The shuttle's interior power flickered, went out for a moment, and then came back on, but the interior lights were now only about half as bright as they'd been before.

Now I was getting worried, "Whistle, what's wrong with it?"

"De motor locked up! We have control powers, but no motors," was his succinct explanation.

It looked as if we were still in the landing business, but it was obvious that we'd have to do some repair work before we saw orbit again. If things were too bad, we might have to wait for help from Frazzle. Thinking of that, I activated the communicator and called him.

"Frazzle, we've got engine problems and may not be able to take off again. If we make it down in one piece, I'll call you to come pick us up with the smaller shuttle."

"I have to make two trips to get all. I can do dat with no problems," was the quick response.

Having a potential rescue close at hand calmed everyone down and left us only one item to worry about – the landing.

Whistle did a good job piloting us down. He got into contact with the station and they sent us the location of the original landing on the planet. The Pugs had set up a large camp and there was the possibility that there was still an active transporter at that location. It had been powered down and disconnected from the power system in an excess of caution. The Pug-bears didn't care for the way they'd been treated by the locals and wanted no chance that they'd be able to transport themselves off the surface. Even so, they hadn't destroyed the transporter equipment and there was a possibility we'd be able to get it going.

We were now in the outer edges of the atmosphere and it looked like it was going to be a wild ride down. The planet definitely had weather and we could see huge storms with clouds that extended nearly as high as we were. Whistle made every effort to fly around these obstacles, but as we descended, he finally ran out of options and had to fly through the edges of one. We were gliding without power, so he couldn't fly around it.

It was every bit as bad as it looked. We were banged around, tossed, lifted up thousands of feet in a few seconds, and then dropped even further the next minute. There came a point where the shuttle was knocked completely upside down, causing a tearing noise from outside. It was so loud that it could be heard over the roar of the storm winds. We'd lost one of our stabilizers and the craft became even harder to control from that point.

Everything comes to an end, though, and this was no exception. Thanks to the skill of our furry pilot, we glided in a limping sort-of way out of the other side of the clouds into a bright, sunlit area with clear skies.

Whistle took a deep breath and turned to me, "We a long way from where we want to be. De Pug landing station is way over the horizon and we too low to get there."

"How close can you get us?" I asked.

"Depends. If no more storms, I maybe find up-blowing winds and we glide closer or not. I don't know."

He turned on a Doppler scanner that would help him locate updrafts and headed for a low line of hills in the distance. We coasted lower and lower.

By now, the surface was beginning to be visible and it didn't enhance my confidence. It was a combination of veldt and heavy jungle. The jungles were clustered around slow-moving, wide rivers meandering across the terrain. Every so often, the rivers would spread out and create a swamp-like lake. As we got lower, we could see clouds of large, flying creatures skimming over the swamps.

We'd descended to the point where Whistle was picking out the final details of where he hoped to land us. We were moving across a flat veldt a few miles from a river and he was aiming for a gap in the sparse trees that covered the landscape.

The last few seconds seemed to last forever, but we finally struck and it was rough. We hit, bounced, skidded sideways, hit a tree trunk with one of the lifting surfaces which ripped off, and then finally came to rest heeled over on our left side. Everything was quiet for a moment, except for the ticking of over-heated metal that was beginning to cool.

We were down on the planet that I'd set out to visit, but it looked like we weren't getting off anytime soon. If Frazzle didn't come and get us, we had an estimated hundred miles or so to walk to the Pugs' original landing site. When we got there, we'd have to try and get the transporter going or call

Frazzle for a pick-up. Right now, it didn't seem too hopeful for us. The power was mostly off in the shuttle with only some sparks that came at random intervals from the control panel. The emergency lighting was still on, though, so we could see enough to get around.

I looked at Whistle. His fur was mussed and he'd sustained a gash across his forehead that was leaking a pale, but still reddish-colored blood down over his left cheek. He tried to give me a cheerful look, but it failed. Instead, he looked like a sad puppy dog with mournful eyes.

The others were watching me in shock. "Are you guys all OK?" My question was designed to get them moving. I could see that they were unhurt and the cabin hadn't been breached despite the crash landing.

Erin was the first to get a grip on herself, "Yes, I'm OK, but are we trapped here?" She looked understandably worried.

It was a good question and it made me realize that my mind had fixed itself on the trauma of the crash. I wasn't thinking clearly myself as yet. I grabbed the communicator and tried to raise Frazzle.

It didn't work. Whistle tried it, then made some adjustments, but couldn't get anything but static. "De antenna builded into shuttle body and maybe it's breaked," was all he could come up with.

In response, I made a mental effort to shake off the shock of the bad landing and the even worse situation we were now in. I reached out and patted Whistle's right shoulder, "We need to get that cut closed up. You're bleeding all over your fur."

He put his left hand on mine and seemed to sort of shake himself. The next minute, he was more cheerful. "We gots to get de door opened. De electrics make smoke that's bad for us. Need fresh air pretty soon."

Belatedly, I realized that he was right. There was a thin haze of acrid smoke coming from behind the control panel displays. I made my way over to the hatch, but the automatic opening mechanism wasn't working. The power to it was off or had failed. The mechanical unlocking lever still worked, though, and I slid it to the Open position. There was a little click and the hatch opened slightly, letting the pressure inside equalize.

Fortunately, the external pressure was about the same as what we had been maintaining inside the shuttle and we were spared the problem of decompressing, at least. I suddenly realized that the shuttle's gravity generator was off. It was usually set to maintain about three-quarters of Earth normal. What with the crash, I hadn't noticed that I was feeling a little heavier, but I had just realized that I was standing on a deck that sloped downwards and that wasn't right. When working, the gravity generator always kept the deck level under our feet no matter the orientation of the shuttle.

I hopped up and down experimentally. Erin saw this and sarcastically commented, "What? Are you trying to jump for joy or something?"

"No, I was trying to check the planet's gravity." My answer seemed to embarrass her and she turned her head away, but not before I could see a flush start across her cheeks.

Whistle interrupted before she could respond, "We gots good gravity here. I checked whiles we come down. It's OK and air is OK too. Dat not be our problem." He went silent for a moment.

"What is the main problem we have, Whistle?" I asked. I figured that he knew more about the planet than he'd previously said.

He made a kind of indecisive humming noise and then spoke, "Eeee... I don't know much 'bouts de creatures here, but dey supposed to be very fierce and dangerous. We have to walk long ways. Better bring all de guns for protect us." He shivered and then added, "I scared!"

"Don't be frightened," I didn't know what we were up against, but being afraid wouldn't help. "We'll bring all of the guns and we'll protect you carefully."

"Dat good," was all he said.

With his reassurance about the air in mind, I pushed on the hatch. Here another problem arose. I couldn't move it more than a few inches. It was either pushing against something outside or had been warped in the crash. I shoved hard and then paused to breathe deeply. As I was starting to shove again, a big arm came across my chest and Frank pushed me out of the way. He got under the hatch, which was partly above us, and braced his shoulders on the bare metal. He took a deep breath and then I could see the veins on his forehead pop out as he shoved hard with his legs. The hatch let out a skreeking sound and moved a little bit. Ted came over to help and after a brief discussion about how best to arrange themselves, the two pushed in unison and the hatch opened wider and wider, then released and flew back against the outside of the ship with a loud bang. Whistle jumped at the noise.

I poked my head out and looked around. It was nearly dark. The hot, blue sun was a small speck, low against the horizon and the shadows were very long. There was a hot wind blowing and the noise of its passing was loud in the grass-like plants that surrounded our crash site. There were some shadows that looked remarkably like trees in the near distance. Over the wind, I suddenly heard a distant sound that was undoubtedly caused by the local animal life. It was loud and sounded dangerous to me.

I turned back to the others, "It's nearly dark out there. We'd better stay in the shuttle until morning when we can see what we're up against."

"Maybe we'd better shut the hatch," Erin pointed out, worriedly. "We don't want anything to come in while we're sleeping."

"That's a good idea. Maybe we can pull it partially shut. We'll still need ventilation to keep the smoke down," I said.

Frank and Ted managed to somehow pull the hatch mostly shut after some effort. I took a safety harness and tied the hatch locking mechanism to one of the mounts for the control panel in order to give us some degree of security. Then we set about finding a way to make ourselves comfortable for the night.

We finally got arranged in the remains of the cabin. Erin was stretched out against the side farthest from the hatch on some of the seat cushions. Frank and Ted had each found a space that was large enough for them to relax.

I'd gotten Whistle's bleeding stopped and he was curled into a little ball near the control panel, which had finally stopped smoking. As for me, I was sitting in a seat, keeping watch on the hatch and listening to the wind.

It was gusty outside and I could hear it through the cracked-open hatch. We hadn't been able to fully close it, since it was warped out of shape from the impact. The crack allowed me to hear the high wind as it howled around the damaged shuttle. The sound rose and fell, creating a sense of menace, adding to the worry I already felt about being stranded on a strange planet with potentially deadly inhabitants.

As I sat there, I gradually sank into a drowsy state wherein I was puzzling over how to get back out into space. My thoughts on that subject became disorganized and faded out. Then I realized that I was standing outside of my cabin back on Earth. Then I was inside somehow, but I didn't remember passing through the door. I realized, dimly, that I was in an out-of-body state, and as I understood that, I moved rapidly to the side of our bed. Liz was lying on my side of the bed, sleeping. The moon was shining brightly through the window and I could see the tracks of tears dried on her cheeks. I reached out and stroked her hair and she murmured softly and shifted her position. A faint smile came over her face and I was given to understand that, at some level, she understood that I was with her.

We weren't in direct communication. I'd tried to contact her several times, but there seemed to be some kind of distance attenuation of our connection. I understood that the level of connection was essentially instantaneous, no matter the distance since it was related to quantum entanglement, but it somehow decreased in strength the farther away I was from her. I didn't know why; all I knew was that I wanted with all my heart to hold her physically. I climbed into the bed and lay down in a spooning position with her. As I did, she sighed and snuggled a little closer – I was jerked back to the shuttle instantly in a state of alarm. There was a definite sense of danger in the wind and as I listened, I could hear a soft scraping as if something was scratching or clawing at the shuttle-craft. The scratching ceased and there was a low moaning noise that was partially lost in the wind. The next instant, a large claw appeared in the hatch crack. The claw was joined by two others and they slid back and forth searching for some purchase on the metal of the port.

Whatever it was outside, it must have been huge, since the claws were at least six inches in length. The hatch was almost that thick. The claws hooked on the edge of the hatch and the thing pulled, actually causing the shuttle to shift a little. I heard a gasp and saw Whistle looking at the claws with terror written large on his furry face. A part of my mind noted with passing interest that I'd become so familiar with the Sunnys that I could read their body language and expressions.

The claws pulled again and I decided that was about as much of that as I wanted to put up with. The thing had started to re-position itself so it could pull on the hatch rather than the side of the port and that might give it more access. It seemed to be easily strong enough to break the webbing that we'd used to tie the hatch shut.

I moved carefully closer, drawing my anti-matter pistol from its holster. I didn't want to dissolve the hatch, so I positioned myself directly under the crack. The thing outside obviously saw me. It began to moan loudly and intensified its effort to rip open the hatch. It got its claws hooked in the lip of the hatch door just as I shot through the crack at what I could see of its arm. The anti-matter passed through the crack, striking the creature's appendage. There was an incredibly loud scream as the shot took effect. The creature staggered back and the hatch was jerked wide open, snapping the webbing as if it were strings. Two large, clawed fingers dropped through the opening, landing on the floor where they flexed independently. They'd been detached by the anti-matter as it burned through the arm of the thing.

There was a huge thrashing sound outside as if the creature was struggling to reorient itself. Then Frank let out a warning shout in response to the thing shoving its muzzle into the gap. It was large enough that it couldn't fit entirely. The edges of the port kept its mouth from fully opening, but it stuck out a long, purple-colored tongue covered with spike-like teeth and octopus-like suckers. This appendage slopped wetly onto the floor and began to swing wildly back and forth, nearly striking my leg in its search. I fell backward and ended up wedged between a seat and the wall of the shuttle. The tongue slithered close to my foot as I tried to reach the pistol which had been knocked out of my hand. One of the suckers latched onto my boot and the entire purple mass of tissue moved instantly towards me.

As more suckers clamped onto the toe of my boot, Erin came scrambling over the intervening seats and dove into the crack where my gun had fallen. She came out shooting and both the majority of the tongue and the end of the thing's snout disappeared. The remains of the snout jerked out of the port, leaking a pale, watery fluid that was evidently the creature's blood. There was a loud scream, followed by receding moans as it stumbled off into the darkness and high wind.

I kicked the end of the still attached tongue off of my foot and stood up, "I owe you big time for that, Erin!"

She smiled and said, "Maybe someday I'll be able to collect on that debt."

Drat the woman! No matter what happened, she seemed to be able to make it into a sexual innuendo. It wasn't what she said so much as it was the way she said it. I shook it off, thinking that at least she liked me enough to flirt even in the current dire circumstance.

We pulled the hatch shut again and retied the fragments of webbing. It wasn't very strong, but it might hold against something that was smaller than the mystery beast had been. The rest of the night went by with no sounds and no intrusions other than the hot wind.

CHAPTER 25

We collected our supplies and did our best to distribute the weight according to the relative strength of each person. Whistle couldn't carry even as much as Erin. I loaded up a considerable weight of food and weapons, but Frank and Ted really packed it on. They each carried about twice what I felt was reasonable.

The sun was up and rapidly heating the veldt when we pushed through the hatch for the last time. There were huge depressions in the ground that I realized were the footprints of the mystery creature and there was a trail of dried blood along the path it had taken in its retreat. After looking the huge footprints over and speculating on the predatory nature of the beast and the likelihood of encountering another of its species, we got our bearings and set out towards the site of the Pugs' deserted station.

The route led over the veldt towards one of the rivers. We could see the wall of vegetation rising up in the distance. Judging from its height, there was plenty of water there. The veldt itself was hot and dry with a brittle, sandy soil and sparse, grass-like plants that grew in clumps interspersed with a low, thorny shrub. Ted brushed against one of the thorns and exclaimed loudly.

"Those things are poisoned! It barely scratched my arm and it burns like fury!" He was rubbing the tiny scratch as it puffed up and turned red.

"Let me see it!" I commanded.

"What can you do? It's a scratch and it's already swelling up. What I want to do is to neutralize the poison that must be in there," he stated querulously.

"Maybe there is something I can do. At least let me try," I responded, grabbing his thick forearm.

He let me inspect the scratch, then I tried something that popped into my head. I hadn't previously thought about using my mental abilities to heal something, but it came to me that perhaps I could have some impact on the poison.

I took a deep breath and sank into a quick, trance-like state, still holding his arm. After a minute or so of visualizing my connectedness with the entire Universe, I focused on the little scratch. It was unclear at first, but then I sensed something in the scratch that didn't belong. I concentrated and realized that it was the molecules of toxin from the thorn. There was a fine strand of material that had been shed from the tip of the thorn and it was definitely antagonistic to Ted's skin. It was slowly releasing a thin stream of molecules that his cells shrank from. I realized that was the poison and mentally visualized the molecules migrating to the surface of the scratch. In a little while, I could sense them moving out of his body. The wound was weeping lymph and I wiped the thin fluid away a couple of times. By the time I'd wiped it off a third time, the swelling was noticeably smaller and the inflamed area was turning back to his normal skin color. I brought myself out of my meditative state and released his arm. His eyes were large as he looked at me, "It doesn't hurt at all now! What in the Hell did you do? That was really spooky!"

Frank, who had been watching closely over my shoulder let out a snort, "He put some voodoo on you! Now you'd better be careful or he'll turn you into a zombie next!"

"Aw, come on, now!" Ted complained, waving his hand in the air. "It's as good as new and I don't believe any of that zombie stuff anyhows." He betrayed his concern and false bravado by looking at me and asking, "You're not going to try and zombie me are you, Dec?"

"No, I don't need zombies, I need you with all of your senses on full alert and ready to fight. I did a mental trick that I didn't know I could do. It's related to my ability to speak mentally and I'm not sure how powerful it is. I probably couldn't heal you of a serious injury." I turned to the others, "Let's be careful of the plants. Obviously, they can harm us, so steer clear of any thorns or sap. In fact, let's try and not brush the things at all." This last was a vain hope. The looming jungle in the near distance looked very thick.

We proceeded, walking carefully and also watching for animal life. It wasn't long before we saw some deer-sized animals. They were browsing on the thorn bushes and their heads popped up as soon as they saw us. They weren't as wary as a mule deer, probably because we were so strange to them, but they weren't going to let us get close, either. They rapidly retreated as we walked nearer. We never did get close enough to make out fine details on them.

Eventually, we came to the edge of the veldt. It gradually transitioned from grasses and thorny scrub into a series of taller, palm-like cycads or something analogous and then into some true giant trees. These were similar to hardwoods on Earth and they rose like columns for thirty feet or more before the first branches occurred. The shade under them was so dense that only the hardiest, under-story plants survived. Nevertheless, there was no easy pathway through.

We eventually found what was obviously an animal trail and followed it as it wound through and around the massive boles. It meandered in the general direction of the river and I judged that it was a safe bet that it would lead to a watering place. As we rounded a corner in the dense undergrowth, we saw a sparkling glint ahead in the darkness. It was the blue sun flashing off the water as it rippled in the wind.

We all had our weapons out and ready as we approached the water. I'd cautioned the others that predators usually found watering places ideal for ambushing prey and we didn't want to be jumped without being ready to respond.

There was a muddy bank covered with animal prints as we came up to the water. The river was choppy from the wind and it was wider than I'd hoped. We weren't going to get across easily at this location. I looked both ways up and down the current. There was a shadow downstream that looked sort of like a beaver dam. I figured if it was similar, it would be what was blocking the water's flow so that it formed a wide pool in front of us. While I looked, Erin carefully stayed in the shade of the trees with Whistle. Frank stood beside me as Ted continued on, gingerly stepping across the mudflat, trying not to sink in. He was largely successful since the mud had dried in the brilliant sun and had formed a hard surface covered with cracks.

Ted was a couple of yards from the edge of the water when it happened. There was something in the water and I only became aware of it mentally at the last second. Its mind was so still that it seemed as if it were a frog. I'd sensed frogs before and they had next to no mental activity. This was the same. I sensed a sudden intention in the mental currents and shouted out, "Get back!"

Ted turned and started back to me, but he wasn't fast enough. There was a huge eruption as the pool exploded outwards and a hideous creature that seemed to be all shark-like jaws lunged out and snapped its mouth closed on him. He had time for an agonized shriek as it shook its head. The violence of the shake and the sharp teeth shredded his body. His shoulder and arm came flying past us along with a heavy spray of blood.

I tried to bring my gun up to shoot, but before I could stop shaking and get it aligned, the creature popped back into the water carrying the remains of our friend. Frank and I looked at each other in agony and then dashed back to the tree line. I stopped and searched for Ted's mind, but there was nothing there. He was dead and it had only taken a couple of seconds.

We hid behind one of the forest giants and tried to pull ourselves together. Erin was crying and I ended up holding her as she cried herself out. "He was one of my only two friends in the world," she sobbed. "I hate this place! Why, oh why did you bring us here?" She paused in her crying and looked at me with the beginnings of anger in her gaze.

Frank stepped up and put his hand on my shoulder, "It was too fast. None of us saw it coming, Erin. It was just Ted's time, I guess. We've faced death many times protecting you and in battle. This was so fast, it was a good way to go. I don't think he had time to suffer."

"I'm sorry I couldn't sense the thing," I said. "It had next to no mental presence. It was just about like a frog or maybe a crocodile and it was so fast! We can't cross the river here. We've got to find somewhere that is shallow and not very wide." Whistle nodded in agreement at this last thought.

It took us some time to regain our composure. When we did, we moved downstream towards what I thought was a dam. It was rough going and it wasn't helped by the sadness we all felt at the loss of Ted. Even Whistle seemed depressed. His naturally buoyant nature normally made him the best of companions, but now he was downcast and quiet. After he'd processed the event for a while, he told us, "I sad. You humans are my friends and I liked Ted. Dis is a bad place for us all. We got to get off dis planet as soon as we can." He paused, then added, "I want Ted back."

Erin had recovered enough to comfort him a little, putting her hand on his shoulder while she said, "We all want him back, but his spirit has gone on now. Maybe he'll watch over us from wherever he is."

The little Sunny seemed to take some comfort in her words and livened up enough that we started to make better time. He'd been so down that his steps had slowed until he was barely moving and we hadn't the heart to try and speed him up.

We finally came to a clearing where there were a large number of stumps. They looked for all the world like a beaver had felled the trees and that strengthened my belief that we were approaching a dam. I didn't know if the trees had been dropped by the creature that had taken Ted or something else, but I kept my anti-matter rifle ready just in case. However, nothing bothered us as we threaded through the field of stumps and passed through a narrow lane between some larger trees. At the end of the lane was the dam.

It extended all the way across the water and there was a well-defined animal trail across the top of the structure. We set out across and made good time crossing. As we walked, I noticed a slight ripple in the water, paralleling us, but I didn't mention it to the others. I just kept my rifle in the ready position with the muzzle pointing roughly at the ripple. Nothing came of it and we weren't attacked. We reached the end of the dam, climbed down a steep jumble of logs, and re-entered the forest on the far side of the river, following the same game trail.

In a mile or so, we came out of the trees onto a long, sloping veldt that climbed towards a high range of hills or small mountains that were probably twenty miles away. We kept up a quick pace and by the time the sun was going down, we'd approached them closely enough to become entangled in a welter of hills and rocks. We continued walking in the long twilight towards an obvious pass over the mountains.

Erin finally moaned and said, "I can't walk another step. I've got to stop here and rest or I'm just going to collapse."

I mentally reprimanded myself for forcing her to walk the last couple of miles. I'd been subliminally aware that she was exhausted, but my mind kept dwelling on things that I might have done differently so that we wouldn't have lost Ted.

The same hot wind was still blowing as we made a camp, sheltered in between two, huge boulders that rested on each other. The crack we were in was deep and I judged that the mystery beast of last night might not be able to reach us if it or one of its relatives showed up. I figured that the one from last night was probably too injured to travel much, but there still might be more of them around or other dangers that we were completely unaware of.

It was a long and restless night. Several times I was wakened by my mental wards being probed. I'd set up the same type of wards that I used around our cabin back on Earth and they seemed to work, but some of the local creatures kept coming around and moving closer to our location than I appreciated. I guessed that they were just curious, but they might have been trying for an easy meal, too. They moved into the warded area and then retreated as the sense of unease from the wards hit them. The constant activity kept me mostly awake and I was glad when the dawn came.

Chapter 26

The day broke suddenly. The sun was so bright that its rays illuminated everything from the instant it started over the horizon. There were long shadows cast by the rocks and the hills, but we could see easily as we got ready to start. We ate some rations and headed out, moving up towards the pass.

The way grew steeper and steeper. I felt that we were lucky that the gravity was perhaps a little less than Earth normal. Weighing less, despite our time in lower artificial gravity, helped with the climb. We strung out in a line, Frank following up behind Erin, who followed Whistle and me. Whistle sometimes got a little too close on my heels and I had to explain to him that it might not be safe, since if I slipped, I'd surely knock him down as I fell. He'd back off a bit, but the next time I would look, he'd be right behind me again. I took it to mean that he was very nervous about our safety.

We kept on steadily until about mid-day as I judged from the shortness of the shadows, there was no glancing at the sun. You couldn't move your eyes within forty-five degrees of the brilliant orb; it was just too bright and you risked your sight looking in its direction. You might not have been blinded if you happened to look directly at it, but, as we each found out inadvertently for ourselves, a brief glance dazzled you and left your eyes watering and unable to see accurately for several minutes afterward. After experiencing that brightness, we each carefully kept our line of sight close to the ground.

The moment the sun was directly overhead corresponded almost exactly with the moment that we crested the pass. The view was magnificent. The mountainside descended in a vast, smooth slope and gradually blended into the omnipresent veldt. The tree-lined paths of rivers were visible in the distance and there was one large area that was covered in heavy vegetation. I took this to be a swamp. Unfortunately, it was directly in our path. By this point, I thought we were about forty percent of the way there, so with luck and if the swamp was not too difficult, we might be reaching our goal sometime towards the end of the day after tomorrow.

The way down the mountain was almost designed for easy walking, but after an hour of holding back on the downward slope, my calves and thighs were burning. Going downhill was harder than it seemed. We finally came to a flatter place that was covered with broken rocks. It looked as if they'd fallen or rolled down the hill behind us. As we were crossing this area slowly, necessitated by the numerous, rounded stones, the incessant wind shifted direction and blew down the mountain from behind us. When I glanced back, I could see a huge storm, like the one that had caused us to crash in the first place, building on the far side of the mountains.

Without warning, a very strong gust of wind struck us. It was falling off of the sides of the storm, and rolling down the mountainside only increased its strength. It was easily hurricane force, knocking both Erin and Whistle off their feet. Frank leaned backward slightly but kept his feet easily. As for me, it staggered me, but then I didn't weigh as much as the big man. He had a hundred pounds on me and the extra weight really helped him resist the wind.

Within five minutes of the wind strengthening, the first rock came rolling downwards at a high rate of speed. I could see that it was being followed by numerous others and the wind wasn't slowing. In sudden alarm, I shouted to the others that we had to find shelter. We crouched behind a massive boulder that was conveniently nearby and listened to the rocks bouncing off it and to either side of us. After about ten minutes of this, the wind died down somewhat and the rockfall slowed to the point where we felt safe to proceed.

We hurried out of the area of fallen stones and eventually started up a low grade on the other side of a valley. There were only a few rocks that had blown up this high, so we'd probably made it clear of the unexpected hazard. We came over the side of the valley and descended into a large, depressed-looking area of land.

This was shaped like a bowl and was surprisingly full of small trees. A brief distance into the grove found us in an open meadow area. The normal grass plants were there, but there was some kind of a battle going on at the far side of the grassy area.

We could see a cloud of dust and hear various snarls and screeches coming from the spot. We got our weapons ready and rapidly moved through the grass to a position of better vantage. As we approached, I tried to sense what was going on from a mental perspective, since the dust-obscured most of our view.

Mentally, it was confusing. It was as if there were a curious doubling of thought. One part was clearly rational, but quite angry and the other part echoed those attributes very strongly. If it hadn't been for the temporal factor – the stronger thoughts were echos, so the first ones must be the originals – I would have sworn that there was only one creature and it was having a fight with itself.

The wind picked up again as we neared the site and suddenly the dust blew away. There were two creatures engaged in a battle to the death. The one that I found most familiar was a green-striped, tiger-like beast with no tail and a smaller, secondary pair of arms folded out of the way against its chest. The primary arms were hugely muscular and had very deadly-looking claws which it was attempting to use to get free of the other animal.

The other animal was as close to the legendary hydra as I'd ever hoped to see. It had a number of thick tentacles with both eyes and a lamprey-like mouth on the end. There was too much action to count the tentacles, but there were at least seven or eight. One of them was lying on the ground below the tiger's feet, mostly detached by a bite that had severed the main muscles. It was far from dead, though. It was still snapping its many circular rows of teeth and thrashing around.

With one of its thrashes, it managed to latch onto the tiger's rear foot eliciting a roar of pain and rage. With the roar, the mental activity increased and I was able to understand that the tiger was the original source of the thoughts. Somehow the tentacled hydra was echoing the tiger's thoughts.

As I realized that, one of the rear hydra heads that were holding back from the struggle swiveled towards me and I had a momentary shock. Instead of the two animals, all I saw was Liz standing there smiling at me. She motioned with her arm as if to beckon me to her side. I shook my head and looked again. There she stood in the midst of the dust cloud waving her arm.

Suddenly the image of her faded and I was able to see the two animals again. The tiger had just severed a second tentacle and the one which had been focusing on me was now trying to wrap around the tiger's neck.

I sent a thought towards the tiger to break off of the fight and it jumped hard in response but was unable to break free. Not wanting to injure it, I pulled out my splinter-gun and carefully aimed at the slime-covered body of the hydra. It had come out of a den and was still partway in the ground. The leverage of its body in the hole gave it more strength than it would have if it were fully exposed.

There was just a moment where the tiger flung itself to one side and the hydra's body was more fully exposed. I fired a single splinter into the slimy flesh. The poison-covered projectile was spectacularly effective. It instantly dissolved a large hole in the thing's side and a noxious black fluid came gushing out. The heads all hissed in dismay and simultaneously released the tiger which staggered back and landed on its haunches in a sitting position. It immediately recovered and jumped away from the hydra's lair.

The hydra was not doing well from the effects of the poison, but it had the energy and presence of mind to know who had caused its injury. The remaining heads focused on me and I was instantly under a multi-pronged mental attack that immediately threatened to overwhelm my defenses. The space in front of me was filled with images that I recognized were ripped from my memories and I could barely stand, so great was the confusion in my mind. My consciousness retreated and things became black for a moment.

Then there was a merciful cessation of the attack and I gathered myself to fight back realizing as I did that the hydra was no longer a threat. Frank had used his anti-matter rifle and disintegrated all of the heads and most of the body. It wasn't a moment too soon, because I had been on the verge of going completely under.

I stood there looking in shock at the remains of the mind-controlling beast. Then I became aware of another, weaker, mental voice that seemed to come from the sides of my head. The tiger thing was looking at me and rather clearly projecting thoughts of gratitude, although there was a kind of prideful, prickly air about them.

I gathered my wits and thought back at it, emphasizing that we were friendly and not interested in fighting. I told it that I'd realized that it was fighting for its life and I'd decided that it needed assistance.

"Not much!" I received. "I was defeating the vision beast." It turned and started towards the edge of the clearing.

"Wait!" I sent. It stopped and turned towards me. As it did I observed that its motion wasn't cat-like at all. It was more of a simulation of an earthly tiger than a true cat. I decided on the instant to refer to it as a "Sim-tiger."

"What?" impatiently. It looked over its shoulder as if it were late for an appointment.

"We need help, ourselves. I was hoping that you'd at least give us information." I sent.

"I can do that," it rather grudgingly admitted. "You did help me with the vision beast after all."

It came close to me and I could hear Erin and Whistle gasp in fear that it meant to attack.

"What kind of creature are you?" it was inquisitive, and I suspected that it had always intended to find out more about us. The feigned leaving was a show to ease its ego and show us that it was truly independent. In that hiding of its interest, it was more like a cat. I had an image of Jefferson that popped into my mind and on a whim. I sent it to the Sim-tiger.

It generated an instant surge of interest. "What's that creature? It looks somewhat like me, but it has a tail."

"We're from another world and that creature is a valued hunting partner of mine," I intended to emphasize the equality and partnership that Jefferson surely felt.

This statement caused the creature to narrow its eyes, "You're not like the ones that came earlier that we killed. You seem both stronger mentally and softer in your body. What are you? Do you mean to try and take our world away like those others?"

For an answer, I envisioned a Pug-bear and a Pug. These images garnered a hissing snarl, "So, you know them! Are you teamed with them?" It crouched as if to spring, gathering its haunches under its massive body.

I hastened to explain, "No! They have attacked our world and I managed to stop their invasion, but now they're coming back to attack us again. I found out that some creature on your world had fought them and won. It must have been your people. We came here to find out what you did and to seek assistance in fighting them."

"My people do not work with others!" The response was vehement. "We are the people of the grasslands and forest edges and we kill what we want and go where we desire."

"In that, you are very like the creature that I showed you, yet he and I have a strong affinity for each other and make a good team. If you won't help us, perhaps you'll at least give us information. That would be very greatly appreciated," I tried to emphasize our need as I sent this last thought.

It paused, then yawned widely, showing an impressive set of teeth and leaving no doubt that it was entirely a carnivore. "I have decided that I will give you information about how we defeated the invaders. If they are coming back to your world, they must think they can defeat you. Although they cannot defeat us, they may decide to try after they defeat you. If I help you, perhaps you'll defeat them and we won't have to put ourselves at risk, killing them again."

This was direct and to the point. I realized that the Sim-tiger was, in many ways, a primitive. It didn't seem terribly interested in falsehoods. It said what it thought directly, although it apparently had a rather large ego associated with its fighting ability. I had detected a hint of intense interest when I said that I'd stopped the Pug-bears and I suspected that it was not quite so confident as it appeared.

"We had a problem with our spacecraft and it lies over the mountains, broken and unable to fly. In order to leave your planet, we must go to the invaders' landing site and try to use some of their left-over equipment," I explained. "We've had some problems with your world." I sadly sent an image of Ted's demise.

It paused as it received my thought that Ted had been a fierce fighter and we hadn't known anything about such a creature until it grabbed him.

The Sim-tiger's next thought was a little more sympathetic, "I can see how you're upset, losing a friend and good fighter. You're like young ones of my people. You have no experience of our world and need guidance."

I nodded weakly. This might yet work out. I sent it some images of the attack of the mystery beast at the shuttle wreck and that got its attention fully.

"You defeated the night-stalker? It retreated from your location? That never happens! Once they set their sights on prey, they persist until they've eaten it. There is no escape from them, even for us," he sent with a definite air of respect for our demonstrated fighting ability. "There is no question! I will help you and you will tell me what you know! This can be a good partnership for both peoples!"

The Sim-tiger was enthusiastic. It had taken some time for it to accept us as potential allies, but now I seemed to have given it the right idea. It turned back towards the woods and, looking over its shoulder at the rest of my party, sent, "Let's leave this place. The vision beast stinks and we have a long way to travel to reach the camp of the invaders."

Chapter 27

The Sim-tiger set a rapid pace at first, but then finding that Whistle and Erin were having difficulty keeping up, it slowed. As we exited the small forest in the bowl-shaped depression and started out across the veldt, it kept pace with me, walking companionably nearby. This gave us time to exchange information.

I had no difficulty mentally communicating with the Sim-tiger, but when I tried to summon Whistle to come up to where we were, I realized that I couldn't sense him. I stumbled in my stride and shook my head as if to clear it. I tried to push my senses outward and found that everything was muffled. I hadn't realized it immediately after the vision beast's attack, but something about the assault had damaged my mental ability. I was, for the first time in years, mentally blind and I didn't like the feeling. In fact, I felt like I was missing a major part of myself. I tried to rationalize the feeling. I'd lived the majority of my life with my mind unawakened and this was no different, but I'd become so dependent upon my mental senses that it was as if someone had put a blindfold on me. It was extremely disconcerting.

The Sim-tiger had given me his name a few minutes before my upsetting realization. I tried to explain my difficulty to Kasm. His response wasn't very reassuring, "Many times the victims of the vision beast do not recover their voice or senses. It is very strong and even I was ensnared by its wiles."

The vision beast captured prey by reading its mind and sending an image of the thing that the intended victim most desired into its awareness. The prey then usually walked right up to the hydra and was devoured. I remembered seeing Liz before I shot the thing and it attacked with its full mental strength.

"What did it show you that allowed it to lure you up to it?" I asked.

I received a sense of anger at my question mixed with overtones of extreme grief. After a moment, Kasm answered, "My mate was killed by a night-stalker a year ago. I was thinking of her as I crossed the meadow and suddenly there she was..." He paused, "I was stupid. I knew she couldn't be there, but I came too close anyhow."

That was a very human-like emotional response. It looked to me like we had a lot in common with his species, at least mentally. Physically, he was about twice my weight and very muscular and solidly built, though he wasn't designed for speed.

I tried to make him feel better, "I, too, saw my mate as if she were standing right in front of me. If I'd been alone and on my own world, I would have walked up to her also."

"Is your mate dead?" he asked.

"No, but she and my son are all alone in a wild place and I'm worried that the invaders are coming back. They may be in danger," I sent.

"You must protect them!" He was concerned, "I can see that it is fate that brought us together and I must help you. I have no one here and will never have anyone. We mate but to one during our lives. If your mate is in danger, I will help, even to the point of going with you to fight the invaders. I detest them!"

"I'm duly grateful for your aid," I answered. Then I turned the conversation back to my mental disability, "You say that many do not recover from this type of blinding?"

"That is correct. My people depend upon our mental communication ability and those who lack it are banished from our society. They live solitary lives in the wilderness," he looked at me, speculatively and then continued, "How do you communicate with me and yet you say you cannot use your mind?"

"It's strange. I have no difficulty understanding your thoughts, but my ability to sense animals and also to speak to my compatriots is lost. I hope that it will come back to me..." I trailed off, thinking of what life would be like without my ability.

"It may come back, although I've never heard of it happening. You are strange to me and you may have strange abilities." He seemed uneasy and obviously decided to change the subject, "Unless I'm greatly mistaken, you are using weapons that belong to the invaders. Is that correct?"

"Yes, we captured many of their weapons and, in fact, the spaceship that we used to travel here belongs to them. We captured it." I received a sense of renewed approbation from him. Then I asked something that had been bothering me, "How is it that I can understand your thoughts? You do not know my language."

His answer was simple, yet complex, "You can understand the thoughts of animals, can you not?"

"Yes, but their thoughts are simple and related to food or danger," I responded.

"True, but you have also been able to understand the thoughts of your friends," he added.

"That's correct, but they speak my language, so I thought that was how their minds worked."

He snorted, "In many ways, you are like a cub. You are very strong mentally, yet you do not know the first thing about mental talk. Know this, then. Rational beings are able to communicate rational thoughts. I have no spoken language, yet I could communicate with the alien invaders just as I communicate with you. You have had no problem previously communicating with your small, furry friend, have you?"

"No, but I assumed that was because he spoke my language before I met him," I answered. I had to pause for a moment as I walked around a thorn bush, but then I continued, "So, you would have me understand that all rational beings can communicate with thoughts. Now that I think about it, my mental ability was awakened by the attack of one of the alien invaders; a most powerful one. Most of my people do not have this ability."

"Yours must be a strange race," he commented.

"Perhaps to you, but not to me," I mentally added a sense of humor.

He responded in kind, "Funny. My race would be strange to you also."

"Will we meet others of your kind?" I wanted to be prepared if this were likely, but he seemed to avoid my question for a moment. Then he countered my question with one of his own.

"Tell me about your mate and son," he requested.

"They are – " I paused in horror and then exclaimed, "I can't remember what they look like!" As I strained to recall, I realized that large portions of my memory were foggy. The dream beast's attack was still affecting me in ways that had yet to fully materialize.

"Your memory is blurred, is it not?" Kasm asked gently.

"Yes! It's as if I'm trying to see through a dense fog!"

"That sometimes happens when the vision beast is particularly powerful. You are suffering one of the worst effects of its attack. You may recover your memories, but you will have to work at it. It is only the most powerful memories that are blocked. Unfortunately, they are also the ones that are most important to the individual. Your species may be able to fight off the effect," he paused, suddenly uncertain, "I don't know enough about your kind to say."

I had been thinking quickly and desperately, trying to inventory my memory banks to see what was missing. Then I realized that I probably wouldn't know it was missing. It terrified me in a way that I'd never felt before. The thought of gradually losing my memories was worse for me than being killed quickly. I took several deep breaths to try and calm my panic.

Erin saw that I was upset, although she didn't understand what about. She came over to me and put her hand on my arm, concern showing in her face as she asked, "Is there anything wrong, Dec?"

"The ropy-armed creature has damaged my telepathic ability and also fogged my memory!" I agonized. "I'm afraid that I won't remember who I am!"

She didn't say anything, but put her arms around me and held me in a gentle hug.

Kasm had walked on and after a moment, I broke free, wiped my hand over my face, and followed. Perhaps it wasn't as bad as I'd thought. I remembered that I had a wife who loved me, even if I couldn't see her face in my mind. And, I knew I had a son named Michael, so that was something. I just had to work at keeping my memories going somehow.

We continued in this manner, Erin walking by my side, Frank, and Whistle following, and Kasm leading. After about thirty minutes, Kasm dropped back and looked at me, "Have you recovered your memory?"

"Not much. It's still blurry," I admitted.

"It may take days for the effects to settle, so don't worry. You may have sustained less damage than you think. Meanwhile, we have a problem," as he thought this, he directed my attention to a copse of trees that we were approaching.

"Can you sense anything in the trees?"

I tried, but nothing came to me, "No, I'm not able, now."

"There is a night-stalker lying up in them. It is aware of our approach. They do not like to attack during the day, but this one is hungry and I believe that we will have to fight. Are your weapons ready? If they are not, our best recourse would be to run as fast as we can and hope that it is blinded by the sun."

I checked my rifle. It held nearly a full charge and was ready to go. I shifted it in my arms, nervously and then asked, "Is it going to show itself or will it try to ambush us?"

"No, it comes now," was his response.

There was a crackle of brush and the taller trees that were farther back in the copse waved wildly. Suddenly, I saw the thing's monstrous head moving in our direction as it broke through the tall trees and shoved its ponderous body through the shorter ones.

We were about two hundred yards from the copse and it was coming rapidly, walking with long strides on all fours. The front arms were nearly as long as the hind legs and the entire beast must have topped twenty thousand pounds. It looked to be forty feet or more in length and its gray-skinned skull was perhaps a quarter of its length. When it realized that we could see it, it let out a shrieking roar and accelerated rapidly.

As it cleared the tree-line, all three of us, Erin, Frank, and I fired our rifles. The anti-matter weapons worked as well as they normally did and the beast's head, shoulders, and a large section of its chest disappeared. The corpse dropped with a thunderous crash that I could feel through the soles of my feet. Simultaneously, Kasm, who'd been preparing to run to the side, sent out a mental exclamation of amazement.

"Your weapons are amazing!" he thought. "Those things are almost impossible to deal with. My people just avoid them when we can."

He paused and then sent, "It wasn't alone. Be ready."

There was a loud blatting noise that came from the trees and we shifted nervously in response. Shortly, some of the bushes moved and we got ready, but I paused as I sensed Kasm's amusement although he didn't send me any thoughts.

A lighter patch of gray showed through the bushes for a moment and then I realized that it was the snout of a baby night stalker. I say "baby" although the creature probably weighed at least six or seven thousand pounds. It was at least as large as the largest African elephant. We kept our weapons aimed at it as it shuffled slowly up to the corpse of its mother and snuffled sadly around it.

"Kasm, should we kill it?" I thought that it might be a good idea. That would make one less of the dangerous things, but Kasm took the opportunity to let me know that his people had an ethos regarding their planet and all of its life-forms.

"No. Let it be. It is old enough to survive on its own and it will soon forget its loss. It is not a good thing to kill unnecessarily. All life has an equal right to existence. Who is to say which is more important, you, me or that little one? If someone claims to have the right to assign importance and judge which lives or dies, that is the first step towards tyranny. In the experience of my people, none can claim omnipotence."

I couldn't help it. I was minded to compare his people's idea about the baby night stalker's right to life unfavorably with the arrogance of humans before our civilization was mostly destroyed by the Pug-bears' EMP. We, as a species, have always been more than willing to assign lesser value to others' lives. Take the numerous instances of genocide that our kind have perpetuated or the wholesale disposal of unborn babies for convenience. I didn't want him to know these things about us; I felt ashamed and I thought that we wouldn't measure up to their standards. After an uncomfortable moment, I lowered my weapon and the others followed my lead.

Kasm had been studying me and he sent, "I felt that you were worried about my judgment of your people." He paused as I started to send a denial and then looked away before continuing, "Our people have not always lived up to this ideal, either. Our stories tell of times when clans fought other clans and whole bloodlines were destroyed. It is nothing to be ashamed of. I think that all peoples must go through this at times. It is not what you've done in the past, but what you've developed into and how you act in the present that matters."

The Sim-tiger was a true philosopher and I resolved to try to win his respect. I indicated that we should go and started moving to the left in order to give the bereaved baby plenty of room. The others trailed behind. We hiked on around the outside of the grove of trees and continued across the veldt. We could hear the baby night stalker's blaating cries carried downwind to us for a long time. It eventually stilled or we got too far away to hear it any longer.

Chapter 28

T he day wore on. It was shorter than an Earth day since the planet had little axial tilt and rotated rapidly. The days and nights were each about ten hours long. It was getting close to dusk when we called a halt to our trek. Kasm had led us to a rocky area where there was a large outcropping with one particular rock that poked into the sky like a large thumb extending out at a shallow angle from the ground.

He indicated that we should spend the night on the thumb-nail. The access was gradual, but the back of the stone narrowed so that only one of us could clamber up at a time. According to Kasm, his people often used the rock as a lookout. He had determined rightly that we weren't nocturnal creatures and would need to rest during the dark hours.

"You need not worry about being approached. We are high enough that even a night-stalker cannot reach us and the back of the rock is narrow enough that I can defend against anything foolish enough to try and climb up," he sent along with a hint of an attitude of superiority.

I realized that he normally wouldn't worry about holing up for the night. He could rest anywhere since his senses would alert him to anything that approached his location. Nevertheless, I decided to tell him a little more about us. "We normally sleep through the entire night, but we often have animal partners that will awake us if there is any problem. Our weapons allow us to deal with most surprises."

"There will be no surprises tonight," he responded as he carefully selected a comfortable spot on the rock and lay down facing the route we'd climbed up.

I sat down and as we ate some of our rations, I took a moment to study our green-striped companion in the last rays of the fading light.

As I'd mentioned before, he was somewhat similar to an earthly tiger but stockier with a shorter back. From his movements and from watching him as we traveled, I realized that his spine was less flexible than one of our cats. This probably meant that he wasn't as fast a runner, proportionately. However, I definitely didn't want to race him. His legs were heavy with muscles and I judged that in a fight the blows of his fore-paws would be deadly. Both hind and forefeet were armed with semi-retractable claws of a respectable size and as a result, he seemed to have no difficulty climbing the rock on which we were laid up for the night.

Perhaps the most immediately noticeable thing about him was his rather lurid color scheme. He was covered in narrow yellow and green stripes. Under the bluish sun, they sort of faded together and the net effect allowed him to blend into the grassy areas of the veldt perfectly. I could see that he would be almost invisible, even to a direct glance, if he were careful in his choice of locations.

The stripes worked well in the jungle also. The green blended with the vegetation and the yellow looked like brief rays of light shining through the upper story of leaves.

As if the colors weren't enough, his major difference from our mammalian forms was that he had an extra set of arms. I don't know what else to call them. They were attached to a secondary socket on his shoulder blades that was located behind the sockets for his forelegs. The socket was a little lower than the foreleg socket and he normally held his second arms tucked up against his chest where they were out of the way as he traveled.

The second arms were also muscular, but less so than his legs. The interesting part was that the toes were rather elongated and, while not prehensile, they were flexible enough to provide him with a degree of manipulation ability. I'd seen him toying with a small stone that he'd picked up as he lay down and he could use his paws (I guess you'd have to call them hands) quite well.

While we ate, I asked him about his extra arms, "Kasm?"

He looked inquiringly at me but didn't say anything.

"I'm curious about some of our anatomical differences," I started. "All of the furred animals on our planet have four limbs, like me. I'm interested in your two additional arms."

He considered for a moment and then answered, "I can see how you might be envious, but you've made up a little for your lack of hand-arms by walking on your hind legs and converting your forelegs to hand-arms. I don't see how you live without claws, though. Those little flat things on your fingers are poor excuses for weapons."

I responded, "Well, we don't fight that way. Our fighting with each other normally involves various types of blows and kicks along with joint manipulation and techniques of throwing opponents to the ground."

"That wouldn't work if you were fighting me. You must be helpless against naturally armed predators," he observed.

I struggled to explain our use of weapons in a single thought, "That's why we rely on weapons. Our kind developed weapons early out of necessity and I guess you could say that we've made a virtue out of our helplessness."

He snorted and gazed down at the base of the stone. There was a pack of wolf-sized creatures snuffling around the place where we'd ascended. They, too, had the second set of arms, but theirs were used simply to augment their gait. They finally came to the conclusion that we'd climbed the rock and stared up at our location. Kasm stood up and stretched, then looked meaningfully down at them. In response, they made a low chittering sound and rapidly retreated into the darkness of the bushes.

Kasm sent, "The scavenger-beasts will not bother us. They would never challenge one of my people," he looked at me and seemed to somehow laugh, "but they might try to see what you taste like."

"Thanks for the warning. I don't think they'd like our taste and we certainly would resent them trying to eat us. Will they return?" I said as I stood and unhooked my gun-belt, pausing momentarily with my weapon in my hand as I looked down towards where they had disappeared.

"No. They have gone elsewhere to seek out food. They cannot climb the stone and it wouldn't do them any good if they could. I believe that, between the two of us, we are more than a match for any beast on this world," he sent, then he had a sudden thought. "Do you think that I could use one of your weapons?"

He stood and came over to my location stretching out his near hand-arm for my inspection. I looked it over and he wiggled his fingers. They were easily capable of holding the grip of my handgun, but, lacking a thumb, he would have some difficulty with the weapon.

"Here, hold this and let's see if you can use it," I said. I removed the power pack to forestall any unfortunate incidents. Then I handed over my anti-matter pistol. He took it gingerly.

He rather clumsily arranged it in his hand the way I would normally hold it, his four fingers curving around the front of the grip and holding it tightly against his leathery palm. I reached out carefully and asked, "May I arrange your fingers correctly?"

He signaled assent and I lifted his top finger and placed it on the firing stud; the weapon didn't have an actual trigger. "You have to grip it with the other fingers and use this finger to actuate the mechanism. When you depress this small stud, the device will destroy anything directly in front of it. The basic and most important rule for its use is to never point it at anything that you do not want destroyed."

He was able to pull the stud back and it made a slight click, but the weapon was pointing directly at Erin and Whistle as he did. I was glad I'd removed the power pack, but it gave me an opportunity to reinforce the point, "It looks as if you could use the weapon, but, if the power pack was in it, you would have just destroyed two of our party accidentally."

"No," he responded, "I was intentionally pointing it at them to see if I could keep it steady as I depressed the stud."

That seemed callous, but then I got the sense that he was embarrassed by his faux pas and was just covering up. "That's all right. There was no harm done. If you promise not to point it at any of us, I'll put the power back in it and you can see if you can shoot that thing that is climbing up the rock towards us." I pointed at a creature that looked like an anaconda equipped with numerous sets of clawed legs. It was like a cross between a snake and a centipede, but with a toothed mouth that reminded me uncomfortably of the thing that had eaten Ted.

"Now that can climb and it is a nasty fighter," Kasm said as he held the weapon out to me.

I replaced the power pack and handed it back. He accepted it like a pro and carefully aimed at the centipede-snake which had reached about the halfway point up the rock ridge. He depressed the firing stud and the snake and some parts of the rock disintegrated. Without saying anything, he took the weapon in his other hand and passed it to me.

"That was a good shot," I congratulated him. "I believe that your ability to use our weapon has been very successfully demonstrated."

"Yes, but it is almost too easy to kill," he complained. "Doesn't such ability predispose you to kill without thinking much about the act?"

"I don't think so. I mean, it might in some individuals, but I personally try to avoid killing unless it is a last resort."

"There!" he thought triumphantly. "You have shown that you, too, have an ethos about life. You just didn't express it well before. I believe that in many ways, we are quite similar."

I replied, "I think that we are also. It is the basis for what we call friendship. That is a relationship where each is willing to aid the other."

He responded affirmatively to this thought and re-composed himself on his look-out point, "Then, friend, I will watch the night and you will sleep. Tomorrow, we will reach the invaders' fort and there you will be able to see what you can do."

The rest of the night was uneventful and I actually slept quite well. There is something about direct mental communication that makes it difficult to conceal one's intentions and I knew that he meant us well and could be relied on to alert us if there was any problem. I awakened once to see Kasm, his head on his paws, gazing meditatively out over the starlit horizon.

Chapter 28

I kept guard while the humans slept. Dec was an interesting creature. His mind was extremely strong, despite the damage inflicted by the vision-beast. I wondered what the next day would bring and then my mind gradually slipped into a reminiscence. I recalled events in my earlier life.

It was the most cherished day of my life. I wouldn't give up those memories for anything. It was the day my intended had finally agreed to become my full mate. Keta and I had been born in the same year. We had both studied under the same teachers and we had grown up together. True, she had often favored Rakutan who was my main rival in both the hunt and in the eyes of the fighters of our tribe, but she had chosen me.

You must understand that we, the people of Tukoli, our beautiful planet, do not call ourselves by a particular name. We are just, "The People," the only creatures on the planet capable of rational thought. While it's true that the stench-beasts live in communal hives and cooperate to a certain extent, theirs is not a rational level of mentation. They have in-built, instinctive behavior patterns that lead them to defend their hives in group action, but they do not think. No other animal upon our planet can actually think as we do. You might object to this statement by mentioning the vision-beast. It has a high degree of mental power and can easily entrap prey by mirroring the prey's inner desires back to it. However, that is simply a predatory action that requires no deeper level of understanding.

We are the people blessed by Tukola, our wonderful, blue sun. It gives us life. Its heat drives the storms that bring the rains. The rising heat on the plains causes the wind that is the primary part of our weather. The wind may be hot, but it provides us with a degree of cooling during the hottest part of the day. It blows the scent of our prey towards us and ours away from our prey.

We speak mentally, but we do not have a communal mental life. Each of us is separate and individual unless we choose to become as-one, an action that only mates take and sometimes not even mates. Each mated pair has that option. They can blend their mental lives together into an inextricable wholeness. Some do not go that far, either through fear or because they aren't that tightly bound.

It is a fact that we mate for life, yet some of our mated couples act as individuals save in the matter of creating and raising young. Others make the blending step and become almost a different level of creature. They are the ones who give us a higher level of guidance. My parents were such a couple, yet Keta's parents were not tightly bound.

She knew that I desired her, but I believe that the example of her parents caused her to hesitate. She spent her early life being friends with all and not exclusively with one male. This was the usual way that non-bonded individuals acted. They would eventually mate with another when their season was upon them and that mating would lead them into an unmovable pattern wherein they would only mate with the one that they had first chosen.

Our life is hazardous and we are often injured or even killed by other animals or accidents. Those who do not bond mentally will survive the death of their mate with little problem. Those who do bond mentally normally do not survive their deceased mate by many days. Something in them just breaks and they cannot go on – usually.

I thought of Keta and me growing up together. Both of us mastered the skills necessary to hunt our prey and to live in happiness on this, our world. My only worry during our youth was that she seemed to often favor my rival, Rakutan. He was as large as I and perhaps, truthfully, more skilled at hunting. I did not like him, because his judgment was often too hasty. That habit of being quick to decide often led him to take risks that were unnecessary and had, at times, led him to endanger others of our tribe.

His poor judgment once caused him to attack a baby night-stalker, thinking that he could slip in and kill it before its mother knew what was happening. He was leading a small group of other youths and two of them were killed by the mother before they could get away. He did not manage to kill the baby either.

When pressed about this mistake, he airily stated that the others had come along of their own volition and their fate was not his responsibility. This was one of the reasons I did not like him. The other was the favor that Keta often showed to him. I believe that he assumed that she would be his.

On the other hand, I had desired her companionship throughout my life starting at an early age, although I was not sure that she valued me.

As we became adults, I grew strong and heavy with muscle. My razor-sharp claws and strong teeth were weapons that I learned to use with great efficiency. I was the best fighter in the tribe and the second-best hunter behind Rakutan.

The day came when I was hunting a borbori, a large and dangerous grass-eating animal that is armed with an unlikely set of sharp tusks. I had followed it for a good fraction of the morning and had made sure that it was laying up in a thicket at the edge of the jungle. I made use of the wind and carefully scouted out the best way to attack the animal.

I'd decided to wait until it came out for its mid-day feeding and then to jump it from behind a clump of grass that bordered the only path into the thicket. I was lying there, waiting, when I detected an incredibly alluring odor blowing downwind. It was Keta and she'd come into her first season. The wind also blew the scent of Rakutan and this was something that I could not countenance. I thought for a moment about what to do, but the two were rapidly approaching my position.

I stood up and then I could see that she was running before him and he was herding her away from the resting place the tribe had taken the night before. A certain amount of coyness is usual among our females, yet it seemed as if she were running much harder than she would have if she wanted to be caught. Nevertheless, he was the fastest in the tribe and was gaining slowly.

As I stood up, she sighted me and turned directly towards me. I sent a warning, "Watch yourself, there is a borbori here!"

She swerved a bit away from the direct line she'd been on that would have taken her right in front of the area I'd indicated and that swerve almost allowed Rakutan to catch her. She looked at me with an appeal and sent, "I cannot allow him to catch me. It must be you and no other!"

At that moment, the borbori, alerted by the scent and sound of their headlong approach, came rushing out of the thicket and stopped with its hair standing out all over its body. It looked huge and angry and it immediately sighted Keta. It let out a deep snort and charged directly towards her.

The sudden appearance of the massive creature coming directly towards him caused Rakutan to reverse directions, calling out as he did for Keta to run behind him. I'd known that he was lacking in judgment, but now I also knew that he was a bit of a coward, too. To give him credit, the borbori was a monster of its kind, and its popping out without warning would have frightened almost any creature.

Nonetheless, Keta simply swerved out of its path and continued in my direction. It focused upon her as she approached and altered its course to strike at her. By now, I was moving as fast as I could and as the borbori neared her, I launched myself desperately at its hindquarters. I managed to hook my claws into one of its thighs, tripping it. It went down and rolled, coming back in a fighting position with its tusks aimed directly at me. I leaped high and just passed over its thrust. As I did, I lashed out with one paw and caught the rock-hard hide that covered its fore-shoulder. That grip held and I whipped around and yanked it over on its side again. After that, it was just a matter of biting, avoiding the tusks and wrestling the animal around until I could catch its throat in my jaws.

As I finished the kill I became aware of Keta rubbing against my body and her thoughts were ones that I cannot in decency pass on. It was too intimate. Suffice it to say that we became mated and bonded that day. As I say, it was the most memorable day of my life and I think about it often, wishing that I could relive the happiness of that hour.

When we returned to the tribe, bearing chunks of borbori, Rakutan had told the elders that we'd both been killed. From that time onward, he bore the name of "Deserter." As one who ran away from members of our tribe in the face of danger, he gradually drew apart and eventually left, opting to live a life of solitary wandering.

The memory of that wonderful day is always poisoned by the memory of Keta trying to defend our child against the charge of a night-stalker. We'd been traveling along the jungle's edge and one of the invaders' flying craft had approached. Since they seemed to delight in shooting at my people, we'd set off at a fast run and descended into a nearby valley for cover. The craft had disappeared, but as we'd rounded a corner in the boulder-strewn cleft, we'd stumbled upon a resting night-stalker. It hadn't fed recently and was immediately after us. Those creatures don't stop until they've caught their prey or are convinced that it's unobtainable. Our people normally avoid them, but we'd been distracted by the flying thing and had made a fatal mistake.

It cornered the three of us in a rocky vale. We were backed against an unclimbable cliff and trapped. I'd attacked immediately and had been thrown by the creature, landing upon a ledge of the cliff, dazed and unable to even stand. I did, however, have a good view of the night-stalker smashing and devouring the only two beings that I loved.

I believe that I went insane then. I was so stunned that I could not move and the sight of their deaths was more than I could bear. One moment she was an intimate part of my thoughts and the next there was a huge void as if the center of my being had been ripped out. There was nothing there! And, nothing there where my child had been either!

I don't know what happened next. I eventually became aware that I was limping across the grasslands in a direction away from our tribe. I knew both my mate and child were no longer alive. The only thing I could sense was their absence and a great sense of futility filled me. I wanted nothing more than to die myself.

This state persisted for days and I became weak. Finally, I stumbled upon the carcass of a recently deceased food animal that had broken its neck in a fall. The smell of its body was more than I could bear and I ate and began to regain my strength. Over the next days, I hunted and rested and recovered. My mind was still a place that alternated between madness and sanity, but my body was becoming what it had been before the attack.

I had no desire to see any members of my tribe and so I wandered for many days, through the seasonal change from warm south winds to hot north winds. I tried repeatedly to come to grips with my loss. As the days progressed, my sense of failure and loss faded into the blur of simple existence.

I was walking across an open clearing, thinking of Keta when I saw a movement on the far side of the area. I raised my head and then shook it to clear my eyes. It was her! I called, "Keta!" but there was no response. Even so, there she stood looking at me with her beautiful eyes. I instantly ran towards her. As I approached, I could see that she was preparing to greet me as she'd always done in the past. I dashed up and horribly was caught by a damnable vision-beast. It had indeed been too wonderful to be real!

I started trying to sever its many tentacles and was having some success, but the things are very hard to kill. While you are biting one head off, the others clamp down and tangle your legs with their incessant writhing. It was beginning to look as if I might not escape when there was a sudden puffing noise from in back of me and something struck the beast's body. It moaned and released me all at once and I leaped out of its grasp.

The next thing I knew was that it mentally attacked a strange creature standing with others of its kind. The vision beast's attack was not unknown to me. If enough of the arms are left on before they die, the vision beasts can mount a stunning mental attack and this one was very powerful. I sensed the creature's startled response and then was amazed as it parried much of the attack.

That was how I met Dec and his group.

He was mentally very strong and I found his aura attractive. After we'd been together for a day or so, I realized that he was somehow filling a void in my mind where I'd been left empty from the death of Keta. I didn't explain that to him, but his mind subliminally clicked with mine and gave me a renewed sense of purpose.

I resolved not to leave him and his small group. They'd somehow become important to me and I sensed that I could live again by accepting his quest as my own. In addition, we had a common enemy – the invaders who had tried to take our world. From what I understood, Dec offered my people a possibility of destroying those evil creatures and I wanted to become part of that effort. I felt that saving my people would somehow make up to me for losing Keta. I knew it was irrational, but there it was, anyway. I was staying with him.

Chapter 30

I was awakened by a buzzing sound that rapidly approached. I opened my eyes just in time to flinch as some kind of medium-sized flying creature sailed just over my nose. It was supported by what looked like four wings, although they were blurred from the speed at which they were beating. I rolled over and jumped to my feet in alarm. We were in the middle of a whole swarm of the things. They were circling around the rock thumb, both above and slightly below our location. Kasm sent me a rather amused thought, "The flyers won't hurt you. They are fruit eaters and are just returning from their nightly feeding."

The flying creatures apparently nested underneath the edge of the thumb-shaped rock on a series of ledges that lined the overhang. They took turns diving under the rock and gradually the whole flock disappeared as they found space on the ledges to land.

With this start, our day began. Erin had been lying fairly close to me with Frank on her other side. Whistle was huddled in a little ball near a rocky outcrop that provided him a little shelter. They had all waked to see the aerial circus and now they clustered around me as we shared some of our provisions. I asked Kasm if he wanted any of our food, but he disdainfully turned his head to the side.

"It doesn't smell good to me. I'll catch something after we get on our way." He somehow managed to send an implication that our provisions couldn't possibly be edible.

I responded, "Our food is balanced to provide us with all the nourishment that we need, but I agree, it doesn't have a very good taste, even for us."

"You must have a stronger stomach than me, then. If I tried to eat that stuff, the way it smells, it would make me sick," he admitted.

The morning went much as had the prior morning. We clambered down off our perch and began trekking through the grassland and thorn bushes. The sun rose rapidly into a clear sky. It was hot and the same, hot wind was blowing, causing the grasses to bend down in waves as the gusts passed. The wind was loud and gusty, making me a little jumpy since it made it harder for me to hear. Nevertheless, I realized that both Kasm and, to a lesser extent, Whistle had more acute hearing than humans, so I kept giving them quick glances to assure myself that they weren't alerting to any threat that I couldn't perceive.

At a certain point, Kasm slipped quickly away into the grass, seeming to disappear as his camouflage blended in more thoroughly as he moved away. A little while later, there was a commotion behind some shrubs about a quarter of a mile away. A dust cloud rose and was quickly blown away by the wind. He came back about fifteen minutes later with an air of satisfaction for having gotten his morning meal. I never did find out what it was that he'd killed.

As the sun rose higher, it heated up. Along about noon, we crested a low hill and saw a jungle in the near distance. Kasm sent, "That is the location of the invaders' fort. We'll have to travel through the trees for some distance to reach it. There are hostile creatures that live in the branches, so warn the others to stay away from the higher trees and especially away from those that have hanging tangles. The creatures live in the tangles and they can eject noxious fluids to splash on the unwary traveler."

"Poison?" I asked.

"Not for me. I don't know about you. But, the fluids smell awful and won't wash off for days," was the not-too-reassuring response.

We continued and eventually reached the border between the veldt and the outlying reaches of the jungle. The jungle's edge was heavy with brush and lower growth interspersed among the short trees. We had to force our way through this, although Kasm seemed to have an easier time of it than we two-legged creatures. He managed to find spaces to move through, simply pushing the dense brush out of the way with his muscular shoulders. We were more careful, remembering the lesson imparted by the poison thorns.

After passing through the jungle's boundary, the going became easier and we threaded our way through the taller trees. The branches were heavy and the shade was so dense that the undergrowth was much thinner here. Even so, it posed a bit of a problem, until our cat-like guide began pacing down an animal trail. This was considerably easier for us to follow, although it wound around, back and forth between the trees in a kind of a crazy fashion, as if the creature or creatures that created it were unsure about where they were going.

After following this winding way for about an hour, Kasm paused and looked over his shoulder at me. Ahead, the trail passed near a massive tree that was nearly obscured by long hanging tendrils of some kind or other. They were matted together and I could see animals that were nearly the size of Whistle clambering over the surface and popping in and out of holes in the mat.

Just as I saw the creatures, they apparently saw us, since they set up a loud, clamorous alarm that consisted of shrieks and loud, obnoxious grunts emitted through a bulbous proboscis. Each of the grunting ones held an arm behind itself and scraped it repeatedly across its back. When each creature had gathered enough of the sticky mess that it had excreted onto its back, it would hurl the whole handful in our direction.

A few of the missiles landed nearby. Fortunately, we were at the extreme edge of their effective throwing distance. From the stench that emitted from the near misses, we were easily persuaded not to approach any further. We backed up along the trail and forced our way through the thinner underbrush in a wide detour around the tree. A few of the creatures showed that they weren't restricted in their range to just their home tree. They followed us at a distance, jumping from branch to branch with admirable agility.

As they got a little closer, they noticed Whistle for the first time. They set up a series of barking noises and more came streaming through the branches from the home tree. They all had their eyes fixed upon him and as the newer arrivals saw him, they began to make hostile barking noises also. I tried, but couldn't sense anything of their motivations, but it was obvious that they didn't like his looks at all.

The whole group came closer, barking and grunting as they wiped their backs. I looked in Kasm's direction for instructions, but he'd disappeared. This was, I decided, more than enough from these obnoxious beasts.

Moreover, it looked as if they were all preparing to hurl stink bombs at once and I didn't want to think of the effect it would have on us. The odor from the near misses had been tremendously awful. A direct hit would be unimaginable.

I pulled out my anti-matter pistol and caught a glimpse of both Erin and Frank pulling theirs. We all fired at once, sweeping the disintegrating beam of anti-particles across beasts and trees alike, trying to wipe the whole mass of them off the planet. It mostly worked. A few stink bombs landed close to us, one almost splattering Frank's feet. The remaining creatures were so dismayed by the sudden disappearance of the branches and their fellows that they fell back some distance. There they set up a more alarmed type of barking and I could see hundreds more of them popping out of the matted tree in the distance and jumping through the branches in our direction.

I pushed my pistol back into its holster and unslung my rifle. A long burst of anti-matter caused most of the matted tree to crackle and disappear. This was too much for the survivors. They let out a series of horrified shrieks at the destruction of their home and presumably the rest of their tribe and fled back towards the now greatly reduced tree. Only the far side of the tree remained. The matted area had been largely dissolved on the nearest side and I could see chambers and structures now exposed to the daylight.

As the creatures swarmed back onto the tree, it gave out a large cracking noise as the top half broke off and toppled over onto the remains of the matted structure. This caused the outraged beasts to shriek even louder.

Kasm suddenly poked his head out from under a large bush to my left and sent, "This way, and hurry. The stink-beasts will come looking for vengeance if we wait here too long."

We followed after him as fast as we could and finally could hear the shrieking no longer. I hoped the things wouldn't think to follow after us and was reassured when Kasm let me know that they wouldn't follow if they couldn't see us.

Kasm found another animal trail that went generally in the direction that we wanted and we resumed our meandering progress. I couldn't see the sun due to the thick overgrowth, but sometime in the later afternoon, we came out into a large clearing and saw the remains of the Pugs' fort.

The clearing was starting to fill in with bushes and tall, thin plants that were normally shaded from the sun. It looked like the open area would be completely impassible in another year or so. We followed a trail through the bushes and eventually ended up next to the outside wall of the compound. The bushes grew up against it, but we were able to work around the edge and so came at last to the main gates. They were open, one hanging on by a single hinge and leaning at an acute angle.

Inside, the area had been paved with some kind of hard-surfaced material that looked like rock-melt. It was cracked and plants had gained a toe-hold in the surface. We spread out, carefully investigating the area.

There were the remains of a shuttle-craft here. I explored it anxiously, but, from the first, it was apparent that it would never fly again. There was just too much wrong with it. Part of it had been severely damaged by an explosion that had blown through the hull and destroyed the engines.

Kasm was following along with me and I asked him, "Did your people do this?"

"Yes, we managed to steal one of the small bomblets the aliens were using against us and turned it against them," was his response. "They didn't consider the possibility that we would be smart enough to set a trap for them."

"What kind of bomblet was it?" The only small bombs I was aware of were the anti-matter ones that were like our hand-grenades in size and they were far too powerful to have caused this relatively minor damage. If one of them had been used, there would be little left of the entire compound.

It turned out that the Pugs had been using some kind of anti-personnel bombs that scattered small explosive devices throughout the area where they were dropped. These would lie inert until disturbed by a living creature. The resulting explosion was large enough to destroy the victim and any others nearby. Kasm's people had managed to get one of these explosives placed under the edge of the shuttle's open port so that it went off when the Pugs boarded and started to close the port door. The result was devastating to the Pugs. The shuttle was effectively destroyed and the remaining Pugs had been forced to escape by using the transporter to the orbital station.

They'd set the transporter to automatically turn itself off after they went through in order to keep Kasm's kind from following them to the station.

Kasm said that some of his tribe had tried to activate it again, but had not been able to figure out the power supply.

As we were discussing this, Frank came out of an open door in a nearby structure and called for us to come. He'd found the transporter. Whistle and Erin came jogging around a corner and beat us to the entrance where Frank was standing. Together we went to see if this would be our way off of the surface.

CHAPTER 31

I was feeding the chickens when I realized that I was obsessing. I tried to keep my mind on what I was doing, but I kept circling around to the same thought: It seemed like it had been forever since Dec left. It was nearing the end of our short summer and the days were becoming cooler. Along with the coming of the cooler weather, a problem had arisen. We heard that the Eastern Slope Warlord's gang had retreated to Denver. They'd been up in the Estes Park area, but something had happened and now there were reports of Pug-bears and Pugs coming from the nearby homesteaders. The Eastern Slope gang had apparently been given a stinging defeat by the Pugs and had moved back down the front range to their primary position where they were preparing to fight.

There had been no Pugs in our area, but a few Pug-bears had found their way into the Grand Lake region. They were ferals without any intelligence. They showed no signs of the symbiont-imparted cunning that made them superior to the Pugs.

Our local organization had made short work of the ones that had shown up. As soon as someone reported one in their area, the men would track it down and destroy it. We'd lost a number of animals to the nasty things and a couple of men had succumbed to their poison also, but we felt we were holding our own.

Michael and I were doing fine. Our few animals stayed close to the homestead and I was able to protect them from any marauding predators. Jefferson helped also by alerting me to anything amiss. These days he was staying close to the house where he could pop through the cat-flap for safety.

I guess that he was feeling a little less secure, although how he knew about the Pug-bears, I don't know. There had been none in our immediate area.

We usually went into town on a weekly basis and our friends stopped by at least once every few days. This gave me a feeling of community and a little additional security.

My primary consideration was that it was now a little over three months since Dec had gone over the mountains and I'd somehow lost the ability to sense him. I tried and tried and it was like there was just a vacancy in my mind where he'd previously been constantly present. I know that this sounds like I'm crazy, but I'd come to depend upon my developing psychic senses and his absence made me desperately worried.

My worry became worse when I started counting the weeks since my last period. I was not only late, but I'd missed twice. I had become very slim; living as we did. I sometimes didn't eat enough; I just didn't have any appetite and as a result, I occasionally missed a period. I'd come to view this as normal, but then I realized that I'd missed twice in a row. I stood in front of our full-length mirror in the bedroom, lifted my dress, and looked critically at my stomach from the side. I was definitely showing a little swelling. When I realized that, I knew that Dec had left me with a present from some time before he rode off.

I was happy, but this added to my worries. Well, there was nothing for it, but to begin to prepare. I started to save up extra wood, realizing that I wouldn't be able to cut as much in the latter stages of winter. I also started to plan on building up additional stores of food. I hadn't told anyone as yet. I wanted to wait until I'd missed again. I figured that, due to my slimness, I wouldn't be able to conceal my state from Mollie and my other women friends beyond that time.

The thing was, my pregnancy and the intrusion of more Pug-bears into our area made me aware of just how vulnerable we were. I had a young son to protect and I'd have a new baby in six or seven months. If Dec didn't come back, I just didn't know what I'd do. My first pregnancy had been difficult during the final trimester and I'd not been able to do much. If this one was going to be the same, I was not sure that I'd be able to manage by myself.

I thought that I might have to move us into town for a few months. We could probably move in with Mollie and her husband for a while. I really didn't know what else I could do. Dec's absence both physically and mentally weighed heavily on me during the day and even more during the nights.

Jefferson was the one bright light. I'd come to depend on him as a kind of early warning system. He would always let me know if there was anything problematical around. Coyotes were no problem. He'd come through the flap and then look back at it with an expression of disdain that I'd come to associate with their presence.

Wolves and larger predators were different. He'd continue across the room, perch on the kitchen table, and hiss at the door. That was my signal to get my rifle and peer out the door in case the creatures were minded to make a pass at our livestock.

We did have a cougar in the area, but it mostly stayed away from our homestead. I didn't know how Jefferson would react to it, but I presumed that he'd be very wary. The big cat wouldn't hesitate to take him for lunch if it could catch him.

My resolve to discourage William hadn't been tested. He'd been busy in the hills a considerable distance on the other side of town all summer. I'd heard that the main flock of sheep was being grazed down there and, since he'd been placed in charge of all of the herders, he hadn't found the time to ride by our place. I was just as happy with that. I had a funny feeling about him. He'd been nothing but kind to us and seemed to like Michael, but when he was around, I felt that he was perhaps overly interested in me. Despite Dec's absence, I felt that all men should respect my husband and my status as his wife.

The weeks passed and I missed my cycle again. I was definitely expecting and my body slowly began to prepare me for the event. Dec was still missing and I felt totally alone. It was a disconcerting feeling that was shortly to become worse.

It was during the first colder period of the year when our neighbor, George, who lived up near the old border of Rocky Mountain Park came riding by in considerable haste. I was chopping wood when he came through the trees. I dropped the ax and put my hand on my rifle until I recognized him. Michael was playing in the house, so I didn't have to worry about him.

"Hi, George!" I called. "What brings you this way?"

"Hey, Liz," he responded, riding closer at a fast pace. "I'm on my way to town. There's a problem and you'd probably better get your stuff together to evacuate."

"What's going on?" I was alarmed.

"I was up on the hill to the east of my place. You know, the one that gives a good view up the mountains towards the Divide. It was clear and I had my binoculars. I saw something and, when I focused on it, I saw a group of Pug-bears and some two-legged creatures coming down the old asphalt road towards the park entrance."

"The two-legs must be Pugs," I guessed. "They would be the only things that would accompany Pug-bears. No humans would be tolerated by the things. Where do you think they were headed."

"Well, it looked like they were just following the road, but that will bring them into town eventually, and on the way, they'll pass close to your place. You know the old road is just a little more than a mile away," he responded.

I didn't know how acute the Pug-bears' senses were, but I suspected that they wouldn't know we were out here unless they saw a column of smoke from my cookstove. On the other hand, they might not stick to the road and they might also be exploring the trails that led off the road. It was clear that we lived where we did. The trail from the road was well-worn and showed that we passed that way often.

"George, how long do you think we have before they show up here?" I was mentally calculating how rapidly we could evacuate.

He rubbed his chin thoughtfully and answered, "Maybe several hours. They were way up when I saw them and I don't think they were moving very fast. I'm headed into town to alert people. If I can get enough men together, I intend to ride back to the park gates and try to stand them off there. We can't afford to have them come into town."

"You'd better get on, then. I'll start to pack and get us ready to move into town, if necessary." Turning, I headed towards the house, but then I realized that I'd forgotten my rifle, so I came back to pick it up, blushing in embarrassment at my oversight.

George looked at me critically and then I saw a change pass over his face. "Liz, I don't mean to pry, but are you expecting?" He was blushing at his forwardness but seemed to think that my status was important enough to pry about.

"Yes. It happened two or three weeks before Dec left," I answered. "I've been working to get ready."

"You'd better get your son and get on into town, then. I wouldn't want to bet on what those critters will do as they get closer and you aren't in a condition to take as good a care of yourself as you might be. Now, don't you be worrying about your livestock. I'll keep an eye on 'em."

His way of putting it was a little crude, but, frankly, I appreciated his care, so I thanked him and walked back to the house as he rode across the yard and crossed the stream.

We packed quickly and rode into town a couple of hours later. Molly agreed to put us up in her spare room in back of the store, so that was fine.

I was in front of the store when a large group of men, led by George and the Sheriff headed up the road. They were all heavily armed and I waved at George as they went by. They were on their way to the park gates to try and intercept the Pug-bears.

About an hour later, we could hear a distant rattle of gunfire echoing through the hills. It was faint, but the park gates were several miles away. The battle continued for over an hour and gradually died out with a few sporadic shots echoing across the trees. I was one of a group of women who stood on the street and listened. More than a few of us were also armed. If the enemy made it through the men, they'd find that the town was equally heavily defended.

Another hour went by interspersed by a few single shots. We figured that the deer hunting rule held true here also. If you hear one shot, that's one dead deer. If you hear two shots, there's maybe a dead deer. Three shots usually meant that the deer got away. In this case, I realized that the Pug-bears were harder to kill, so a multitude of shots probably meant that a Pug-bear was the target.

Eventually, the men began to straggle back into town. Their story was horrifying. There had been thirty-one of the townsmen that had gone up the hill. Only nineteen came back down. The rest were all dead. It was horrible, the mourning and wailing from the women as they found out their husband or intended hadn't survived. There were no wounded. The aliens' weapons either missed completely or killed. There was no halfway status.

By then, there were a lot more men who'd gathered in the gazebo park and they were all ready to set out to recover the bodies. The survivors of the battle assured us that they'd killed every alien that had come down the mountain, so we thought there wouldn't be a problem riding up there. However, it was getting on towards dark and none of them even seemed to be thinking about that factor. They were just getting organized and ready to head out. I thought that they had better wait until morning. There was no point in trying to rescue any survivors; there weren't any. Having a large group of armed men wandering around worrying about alien attacks in the dark wasn't a good idea. They'd be more likely to shoot each other than do any good.

With that in mind, I stepped out into the street in front of them and got their attention. After arguing a few minutes, I won my point and the guys resolved to wait until the morning. It was a long night.

The next day, they rode up to the site. Hours later, they came back with several bodies. Some of the killed had been hit with anti-matter weapons and there were no remains. It was a hard time for the town. We had a mass funeral and tried to cope as best we could. It got so bad in town, that Michael and I moved back out to our cabin. I couldn't take the mournfulness of the place. The only good that came of the battle was that all of the aliens had been killed and the remainder of the population was more prepared. They'd formulated a battle plan and had stationed look-outs on the park access road. It was unlikely that the aliens would catch us by surprise again.

Shortly after that episode, we got word from a traveler that the aliens had come down to the Denver area and there had been a huge battle there, as well. There were enough of the creatures to take part of the Broomfield area and hold it for a while. There had been extensive house-to-house fighting required to drive them out. The upshot was that the Pug-bears and Pugs controlled Boulder and its environs while the Warlord's gang patrolled just south of that town in sufficient force to keep them at bay, at least for the time being.

I didn't know where the things were coming from, but there were apparently plenty of them. Of course, their weapons were far more effective than our rifles and they were harder to kill, so it didn't take too many Pugs to keep our guys busy.

A couple of days later at our homestead, Michael and I were by the wood-pile. I'd enlisted his aid in stacking kindling and he was helping, somewhat. I was splitting a log when Michael drew my attention to William, who was riding across the stream.

His horse clopped up to us and he swung down, tossing the reins over the saddle.

"Hi there young feller," he said, greeting Michael who responded with a large smile. Then he turned to me with a long glance. "Hello, Elizabeth."

"Hello yourself," I answered. I could see that his eyes strayed down my body, pausing at my breasts and continuing down to my slightly rounded stomach. As he saw my condition, his pupils narrowed momentarily.

"It looks like you're in a family way," he observed. "Your husband still not back, I understand?"

"No, William, he's still not back, but I'm hoping that he will be soon." What else could I say? I didn't know where Dec was, but I truly wanted him back with all my heart.

"Are you going to be able to cope through the winter in your condition and without your man?" William asked.

"I'm sure I... we'll be alright. I've been preparing. I've got a lot of wood stored up and we've got plenty of supplies –" I started to explain, but he interrupted.

"Don't worry, Elizabeth. I'll make sure you're taken care of." Something about his attitude was proprietary and a little off-key as he added, "I like your son and I'm sure that I'll like your new baby as well."

This wasn't going well, I decided. It seemed like he thought he had some claim on me and my small family. I resentfully said, "Well, don't worry about it. I'm well set and my friends from town check on me often."

Seeing that I was angry, he changed his attitude and tried to make it seem as if he was just concerned.

"That's good, then. The sheep have been moved back into this area and I'll be staying in town a lot more. I'll be happy to check on you more often. You can depend on me."

I responded, somewhat mollified, "OK, thanks. Now, I'd better get back to my chores. Don't let me keep you."

Seeing that he was being dismissed, he decided to accept it gracefully and said something about having to go check on a new shepherd who had just been hired. He swung back up into the saddle and started off. Then he paused, turned back to me, and said, "A beautiful woman like you with a family, shouldn't be left alone out here. It's too dangerous. I'll be sure and stop back by often."

I waved and grabbed my ax as he rode off. I wasn't too happy about the way this visit had gone, but I couldn't see what he'd really done except to seem concerned. I didn't know why I was upset with him.

I returned to splitting kindling and wondered again when Dec would be back. My mind turned to thinking about the worst possibilities. If Dec didn't return, I would either have to move into town or get someone to help me out here.

What if Dec never returned? I couldn't sense him. What if he were dead? The thought was horrible, but it persisted. I tried to be reasonable about it. I had a son and would have another child. I'd need help. The land was far more primitive than it had been before the aliens had exploded the EMP. A single woman with two children would be in danger.

I'd need a man around – I dropped that thought like a hot potato. It didn't bear thinking about. Everything would be fine and Dec would return; but when?

Chapter 32

M ost of the Pug-bears that faced the Warlord's gang were ferals and ended up being used as shock troops by the normally subservient Pugs. We heard via the inter-mountain grapevine that the ferals were fierce fighters, but not noticeably intelligent.

The Pugs, normally the front-line cannon fodder, seemed to be running the assault, but were less aggressive than I expected, probably due to the absence of their intelligent masters. As a result, the front range invasion seemed to be at a standstill.

I'd told the townspeople that the Pug-bears needed the symbionts in order to reach their full potential and the word had gotten over to the Warlord's people. We were in a somewhat cooperative relationship with them by now. The antagonistic status of the recent past had been modified by having the aliens to fight. Every human cooperated when it came to killing the invaders.

I'd mulled over what I knew about the invaders from their first attempt. The Pug-bears that bore the symbionts were the brains of the operation and they seemed to have a fierce determination to make the Pugs fight. However, the Pugs weren't very good as organized fighters, in spite of their physical toughness. They lacked a sense of strategy. Their idea of a good fight was to rush out in a group and then start shooting. Their problem with this tactic was our side were notably good shots. For their part, though, their weapons were more deadly than ours. They either had a miss or a kill with the splinter-guns and the anti-matter weapons were enough to keep humans hiding. As a result, our side had evolved a strategy of mass sniping and then rapid movement to avoid the return fire.

Every now and then a group of Pugs would come over the pass and descend towards Grand Lake. We'd managed to kill all of them that presented themselves, but some lone Pug-bears had found their way past our blockade.

These awful creatures posed no collective threat, but they were a constant problem for the ranchers and sheep-herders in the area. Not only did they kill lots of livestock, they were a menace to any human they encountered. They were mostly impervious to hunting rifles unless they were of magnum power and loaded with solid and heavy bullets for lots of penetration. Even then, you had to hit the things through gaps in their natural armor. A high-caliber bullet would just bounce off of their backplates.

The best place to aim was at their neck, below the armor, or right down their throat. They had a habit of raising their heads and staring at you while opening their mouths that made it possible to hit the sweet spot in the back of their throat if you were calm and aimed carefully. A shot down the gullet usually made them considerably less interested in eating you.

Michael and I remained at our homestead. I depended upon Jefferson to alert me of any intrusions and, for the most part, he was reliable. The only times he was distracted were usually at night when some other Tom would drop by for a fight or an argument over a female in heat. Jefferson always settled those issues quickly, though.

The other Tom would vacate at a full run, often with a chewed-up ear and always missing clouds of fur. Jefferson would court the female, do his best to ensure that more of the local cat population bore his signature orange coat, and then pop back through the cat-flap with an air of satisfaction mixed with a smug look of superiority on his face.

He always wanted to lie on the bed after such an escapade, but I had a problem with that concept. It was because he was often bleeding from a variety of scratches and I didn't like to have my covers stained. My normal strategy was to wake up when I heard the sound of cats cussing at each other. The noise would rise to a crescendo and after the other cat fled, he'd come inside. I'd catch him, sponge off any bloody patches, and dry his coat.

He submitted to this treatment happily. I think that he believed that my ministrations were the natural order of things. He seemed to think that I could take care of any wound. In the back of my mind, I dreaded the time that would inevitably come. He'd get older and become less adept at his fighting and I could see that he was too bull-headed to back off. I just hoped that my medical skills were up to the challenge when the time came.

One windy night, I heard the usual catfight noises. A series of yowls and counter-yowls mixed with screeches. Before the fight had gotten really started, Jefferson came flying through the flap and leaped up on the bookcase with every hair standing out. I could hear the other cat let out a loud screech that terminated suddenly in mid-cry.

This didn't bode well and I jumped out of bed seizing my heaviest rifle. Dec had taken his beloved Win-mag, but I had an old .338. I hated to shoot the heavy thing. It had a roar like a thunderbolt and a kick that made my shoulder sore for a couple of weeks. In addition, it was almost too heavy for me to handle, but I kind of liked that feature, since it helped with the recoil. It was a bolt action and held a couple of cartridges in its magazine in addition to the one in the chamber.

With the rifle and a flashlight, I cautiously looked through the window near the door. Just as I did, there was a horrible moaning noise that set the short hair on my neck standing straight up. It was a sound that I'd never forgotten; a Pug-bear. There was a scrabbling at the cat-flap and the thing's taloned arm came through and felt around on the inside.

Finding nothing in reach, the arm withdrew, casually ripping the flap out of its hole and leaving an open space that the creature shoved as much of its face into as would fit. It obviously sensed us and I suddenly felt a mental compulsion to open the door and come out. The level of desire to go out rapidly mounted and I found myself with my hand on the thick piece of steel that barred the door.

That shocked me, but what was worse, something pressed against my hip at that moment and I realized that Michael was trying to open the door with all of his might. He didn't have anything like the resistance that I had to the alien's mental compulsion and had been completely snared by the creature.

Behind us, Jefferson sounded his battle cry from the top of the bookshelf but didn't make any effort to come down. I shoved Michael away, but he came right back to me and clawed at the barred door.

Dropping my rifle and the flashlight, I grabbed him with both hands and rushed him over to the bed. It was the work of seconds to roll him tightly in the covers and then wrap one of Dec's belts around the bundle. As I buckled the belt, he began to cry in gasps and sobs, wriggling as he still tried to obey the Pug-bear's compulsion.

The alien was hungry and it drew prey to it with its mental powers. It suddenly pulled its head away from the cat-flap and the door shook as it shoved its heavy bulk against it. Dec had built the door out of heavy and well-seasoned oak boards and I always kept it barred at night since he had gone. The Pug-bear's shoves rattled the door in its frame, but it held.

The sounds ceased for a moment and then the creature jammed its head through the kitchen window. The glass shattered and let in the ammonia-like stench of the alien along with a gust of cold night air. I screamed and jumped to my rifle. I fumbled the safety off and got positioned with the flashlight in my left hand, held against the front stock.

When the light came on, the Pug-bear moaned and renewed its thrusting against the window frame. There were only a few shreds of glass left, but the frame was too small to admit the thing. Its bulky carapace wouldn't fit through the opening in the logs. It didn't seem to realize that and continued to try to shove its way into the room by brute force. This was obviously a feral without the symbiont. Its mental attack was too weak to be anything else and an intelligent one would have quickly understood that the only way in was through the door.

I carefully aimed and squeezed the trigger. A huge ball of flame shot out of the muzzle, blinding me as the rifle kicked hard and I lost my balance and sat down on the floor. I could hardly hear for the ringing in my ears caused by the concussion of the high-powered round in the confined space, but after a moment, I made out the high-pitched screams of the Pug-bear. I'd hit it somewhere in the neck area and it had flipped over onto its back on the porch and was thrashing around.

Mindful of the possibility of some of the alien's venom having gotten on the broken glass, I pulled some boots on and carefully climbed up on a chair, well away from the window. I didn't want to just go over and look outside. If it were still able, it could easily stick a poison claw in me if I were that close.

From the vantage of the chair, I could see the thing was lying partway off the porch with its head pointed away from the house. Its feet were scrabbling wildly in the air, but then one of them hooked the porch rail and spun the creature, still on its back completely around and off of the porch. Once on the ground, it managed to slowly right itself and face the window.

I knew it was injured. They usually were able to come off their back rapidly. This one was moving slowly but wasn't yet out of the fight. I shakily climbed down located the rifle. Once I'd ejected the spent round and chambered a fresh cartridge, I climbed back on the chair and then up onto the table. The Pug-bear was still moaning, but with a higher-pitched overtone to its sound. The harmonics from its call seemed to be specially designed to strike fear in humans, although I knew they were not used to us as prey.

Wincing as I shouldered the rifle, I aimed at the hateful thing's opened mouth and fired a second shot. The results were even worse than the first shot. I was blinded by the flash and I dropped the rifle as the table collapsed. It wasn't designed for that kind of stress and I pitched off and banged my head on the side of a cabinet.

It was maybe a little later. I was aware of me moaning inside my chest, but I could hardly hear anything. Jefferson was crouched on my chest licking at my cheek, apparently trying to help me recover my wits. I pushed him off and sat up, foggily realizing that he wouldn't be down off the bookcase if the Pug-bear were still a threat.

I rubbed my head and gradually climbed to my feet, holding onto the cabinets for stability. The flashlight hadn't gone out and was still shining on the far side of the room. I picked it up and checked Michael. He was wrapped in the covers with his head out and a strained expression on his face. I kissed him and was alarmed when he didn't respond. Even so, I had to make certain we were safe before I investigated further.

I retrieved the rifle for the third time, reloaded, and approached the window. By glancing out, I could see the carcass lying on the ground by the steps. My second shot had done for it.

I located a lantern and lit it. In the yellow flame from the wick, I swept up the broken glass into a pile near the window. I was afraid to touch it. If any of the alien's venom had been dripped on the glass and I cut myself, it would be my end. They were that deadly. The things liberally dripped venom from their claws and teeth when they were in a fight and it was almost a sure bet that some was spread around on the cabin floor.

I retreated back to the bed with the rifle and the lantern. Unwrapping Michael seemed to take forever. He was unhurt physically, but he was unresponsive. I sat there holding him with Jefferson crouching by my side.

After a time, perhaps a few minutes or even so much as an hour, I had reached a calm state and felt ready to try and contact his mind. I carefully extended my mental touch. He was locked into a small compartment that radiated fear to the point of blind unreasoning panic. I began to work at calming him.

By dawn, we hadn't moved much, but he was now responding although in a sleepy way. From his words, I knew that he really didn't remember or comprehend what had happened. That was probably a good thing because I was still trying to deal with the horror of the night's events. If he didn't remember, perhaps he'd recover quickly.

It was maybe ten in the morning; the sun was shining brightly and the cabin was a bit warmer. I'd wrapped us in all of the covers to keep warm and just recently I'd had to remove part of them. My ears were still ringing and I couldn't hear too well, but Jefferson alerted and I quickly unwrapped, lifting the rifle from the floor. Then I heard a series of loud curses from outside. Glancing through the window, I saw a horse tied to the porch rail, then there was a thunderous pounding on the door.

I unbarred the door and it was shoved open. William came pushing through and grabbed me in his arms before I could so much as raise my hands.

"Elizabeth! Elizabeth! Are you alright?" His eyes were dark with concern. He glanced around the cabin, taking in the scene. "I was riding by and I saw the dead Pug-bear by the porch. I was afraid that you were – you were – " He drew a shaky breath and kissed my forehead, "I was afraid that you weren't alright. I should have known better. You're the most capable female I've ever known."

I gently disentangled myself from his embrace. It was obvious to me that he cared about my safety and I appreciated that, but his arms around me were a little too intimate. I turned and righted the chair from the floor, then sat down, placing the rifle on the floor as I did.

"I'm OK, William. The Pug-bear is dead and it didn't hurt us. I don't know what I'm going to do about that window, though. Oh! And the blasted creature destroyed the cat door too!" I realized that I'd been in almost a state of shock. His presence forced me back into a more normal mode of thinking.

"I've told you, you shouldn't be out here alone!" William's eyes flashed and he looked at me angrily. "Even though you killed that thing, you could have been injured. You need to be in town or…" here he paused, considering his next words. He shook his head as if to reassure himself that he was right and then continued, "you need a man here with you to protect you."

I didn't want to argue the point and Dec seemed very far away right now, so I just nodded. He was correct in a way. I was rapidly coming to the conclusion that I'd have to move into town and take advantage of Molly's hospitality, at least until spring or until Dec returned. William, however, chose to take my nod as assent to his latter point and added, "I'm available. I know that it hasn't been very long since your husband left, but you've got to realize that he's not going to be coming back. No one could fight those things alone and live. There hasn't been any word of him from the Warlord's people and they've had all they can handle fighting the aliens. No, he's not coming back. You'll need another man. I'd be honored and I promise to care for you and both of your children."

I was taken aback. I'd known that he was interested in me, but this amounted to a proposal. I wasn't interested. I was still Dec's wife, but I realized that the country was wild and my children needed security. I wasn't going to be able to cope alone, especially as my pregnancy progressed. Somewhat offended, I said, "I'm married to Declan and I'm confident that he is still alive. I appreciate your offer, but it's – I just can't think about such a thing now. I'm going to see about moving into town for the winter. I'd appreciate your help, especially if you'd drop by here and keep an eye on things. I don't want any squatters moving in while I'm away."

He drew a deep breath and prepared to argue, but then he just sighed, "Please forgive me if I put too much pressure on you. I would be really happy if you'd agree to marry me, but I can wait until you satisfy yourself that Declan isn't coming back. I'll keep an eye on the house, here, and I'll help you move into town. I hope that you'll let me come by and see you often in town. I want to keep an eye on you also. You're too independent for your own good, you know."

I didn't like his patronizing tone, but I understood that he really was worried about me, so I just smiled and said, "I'll be happy for the help."

I reasoned that I could deal with him dropping by to visit me later. I didn't want my town friends to think he was courting me, but I thought I could keep it on a business footing if I just concentrated on having him report on the status of our homestead.

By the end of the day, we were safely moved into Molly's spare room. William had been a god-send and had overseen every aspect of getting us packed, boarding up the cabin, and moving us into town. I was exhausted and I was sure he was also.

My major concern was that Jefferson had vanished. He didn't care for William and I was sure that he wouldn't move into town either. I planned to ride out tomorrow and see if I couldn't locate him. At the least, I'd fix the cat door and make sure there was plenty of food and a warm place for him to nest during the cold nights.

As I laid down beside Michael's warm, snug, little body in Molly's feather bed, I reflected on where Dec might be. I had lost contact with him and that didn't reassure me. What if he were injured or ... killed? What would I do then? I sank into a restless sleep.

Chapter 33

Whistle had looked over the transporter mechanism carefully by the time night fell. We'd set up a temporary camp in one of the vacant buildings. It was a simple box-like structure with a sliding door and no amenities, but it gave us some shelter from the incessant wind. We, the humans, I mean, were just about worn out by that wind. It was hot and blew almost continually. Even here in the jungle and inside the walls of the Pug fort, the moving air managed to curl down over the waving trees and gust across the grasses and weeds.

Kasm had come into the hut, but let me know that he didn't like the feeling of being confined. He said that as long as the wind was blowing, he wanted to enjoy it. I guess the old adage that "One man's meat is another man's poison," goes double when the other is an alien.

I was trying to put a good face on things, but failing miserably. Whistle's report hadn't been favorable. He'd first thought that the transporter might work. There was some power stored in the accumulators that had caused it to flicker and attempt to sync up with the transporter on the station, but then the power was exhausted and the mechanism became inert once again.

When he looked more closely, he found that the transporter power supply was completely burned out. The reactive pile had overheated and melted through the bottom of the containment structure. The damage was minimized somewhat since they had built in some form of damping material that stopped the reaction. It had worked, but too late. There was no fixing the unit.

He did mention that the Sunnys on the station would know that someone had tried to link the transporters together. There had been enough power to start the linkage and the electronics on the station would record the attempt.

"Maybe dis will be enough of a signal for them to come and get us," he hopefully suggested, ignoring the fact that they didn't have another shuttle-craft available unless Frazzle showed up.

By nightfall, there had been no response from the station. It looked as if we were indeed stuck on the planet. We settled down in the hut while Kasm prowled somewhere outside. Frank immediately went to sleep and Whistle went into his sleep-like trance state. The Sunnys didn't exactly sleep according to what Frazzle had told me. They slowed their metabolism and it looked as if they were sleeping, but their minds continued to work. They used this state to concentrate on problems and it was one of the reasons their race was so technologically adept.

I had been sleeping for some hours, but then had wakened mulling over my problem. I was still suffering from the vision beast's attack and my memory hadn't gotten any better, nor had my psychic senses. There were large foggy areas in my mind and I was still struggling with them, hoping that I could find a clue or clues that would lead me back to myself as I'd been before the mental injury.

It was funny that I could communicate with Kasm, yet none of my other abilities were active. I could remember being able to sense other minds, but I couldn't do it now. What was worse was the selective damage to my ordinary memories. I could remember having a wife and, I thought, a child, but I couldn't picture them and even had difficulty remembering her name at times.

I'd gradually gotten sleepy again. I was lying there on the edge of sleep, drifting lightly in a hypnogogic state and almost ready to drop off, when Erin slid over to me and pressed against my side with her arm around me. That woke me immediately.

Erin's body felt warm through her thin shirt and I found myself inadvertently responding. I placed my arm tentatively around her and wondered as I did if I'd encouraged her or had some kind of relationship with her before my injury.

She whispered to me with her head held slightly over mine as she leaned on her elbow, "Dec, we're stuck here on this planet. I'm afraid that we'll never get back to Earth. Our past lives are gone and we have to make our way forward as best we can together."

She made some sense, at that, but I hadn't given up yet. We might be able to figure a way to use the shuttle or perhaps Whistle could rebuild the power supply. I had a habit of never giving up. As I thought that, I realized that it was a memory from before. Some things just popped through the fog. I looked up at Erin's outline and realized that her hair was brushing across my face. She'd lowered her head and we were face-to-face. I could feel her breath on my lips as she whispered, "I don't want to live and die here alone. Together we can find a way to survive and, and I want you – " She lowered her face and our lips met for the first time.

It was not unpleasant and my breathing accelerated, but then the fog in my mind cleared. It was because the arousal I was feeling put me in touch with a memory of Liz bending over me in much the same way. It was confusing and I turned my head away.

Erin sighed in frustration and then said softly, "You'll come around to my way of thinking eventually. We're stuck with each other and that's the truth, even if you don't like it."

I pulled my arm off of her and rolled slightly to my right. As I did, I answered, "You may be right. I'm not sure how we're going to get out of here, but I haven't given up yet." I was redirecting the conversation. I didn't want to hurt her feelings and somewhere in the back of my mind, I realized there was a possibility that I might have to give up on getting back into space. That meant that I'd have to live with her one way or another; the prospect could be far worse, I reasoned. Then something hit my mind and I asked, "What about Frank?"

She shook her head, "He's always been there for me, but I don't think he has a romantic bone in his body. All he thinks about is fighting." She paused and then drew closer, "No. You're the one I want!"

She moved to kiss me again. I indecisively moved my head away and then turned back toward her. If we were stuck here, I – Kasm's thought hit my mind suddenly, "Quit whatever you're doing in there and get out here! Some of my people are entering the fort now! I must greet them and I want you with me so there will be no mistakes."

I jumped up and grabbed my weapons. Erin sat up and scooted on her behind up against the wall, drawing her rifle across the floor from where it was lying by her pack. Frank and Whistle both woke and, in an instant, Frank was up with his sword in his hand, ready to fight.

"What is it?" he hissed.

"Kasm alerted me that some of his people are outside. You stay in here! He only wants me to come out," I explained in a low voice.

"Dec, it could be a trap!" Erin interjected. "Do you trust him?"

"With my life," I snapped. I thought how could she not trust him after what we'd gone through? Then, I drew a breath and realized that none of the others had been party to my conversations with Kasm. As far as they knew, I could be deluded into thinking I was talking with a wild animal that was setting us up as dinner guests. I guessed I couldn't blame them for worrying that we might be the main course.

"Don't worry," I answered, more calmly. "Kasm and I will meet these others and see if we can come to some sort of agreement with them. We'll need more help if we're to survive."

They didn't say anything else and I took that as assent. Opening the door, I slid out the crack into the wind. Kasm was waiting by the side of the hut.

"Come with me," he commanded.

I stumbled a bit in the weeds and he stepped closer and said, "Place your hand on my shoulder. I know you can't see well in the darkness." He could have taken my hand with his manipulating arm, but it wasn't a gesture that he seemed to use. Together we walked rapidly towards the gates of the fort. He slowed as we rounded the wrecked shuttle and then I became aware that we were surrounded by a large number of slightly glowing pairs of eyes. I could make out the dim bulk of the Sim-tigers' bodies. There were a lot of them hidden in the darkness. I could sense Kasm's tenseness in the ripple of muscles along his shoulder.

The newcomers must have been silent. I could sense nothing of their thoughts, but then Kasm sent, "Greetings. This is Dec and I am going to help him." It was as if I was listening to one side of a telephone conversation.

I couldn't hear what they said, only his responses. My lack of psychic sense was frustrating.

He sent, "No. He is the enemy of the invaders. They invaded his world also and he came here searching for allies to fight them."

There was a pause while they apparently discussed that concept among themselves, then Kasm answered an unheard question, "He saved my life from a vision-beast and he and the other two of his kind have killed two night-stalkers that we encountered."

He was stretching the truth a bit. We hadn't met him when we shot up the first one, but I guessed it made a more dramatic story. The conclave went on for nearly half an hour with Kasm arguing that they should help us. Some of them seemed disposed to be helpful, but one group apparently didn't want anything to do with us. Harming us never came up, so I thought to myself that they were at least reasonable and realized that we were not responsible for the Pugs' attack on them. It could have also been due to the description of our weapons' abilities that Kasm gave when he elaborated on the death of the second night-stalker.

Eventually, it became apparent that some of the Sim-tigers had silently backed out of the group surrounding us and had left. I wondered if I were regaining some of my psychic abilities because the air was less heavy as if I could sense a lessening of pressure or presence as they left. I hoped that I was starting to recover and this was a sign of it.

Shortly after they departed, the wind commenced blowing harder in its pre-dawn pattern. Kasm and I were sitting near the wrecked shuttle and the others were sitting or lying around us in the weeds. I suddenly realized that I could make out their forms more easily. It was nearly dawn.

We'd not only survived the meeting with the Sim-tigers, we now had secured the cooperation of a significant number of them. Kasm had actually convinced them to agree to travel back to Earth with us and fight the Pug-bears. We were ignoring, for the moment, the fact that we might not be able to return. However, during the night as the conclave progressed, I'd realized that we did have access to more shuttle parts. There was our wreck and perhaps we could salvage enough from the two crashed ships to get one going well enough to reach the space station. This idea heartened me greatly, although it would prove to be difficult to transport the heavy parts over the distance that we'd traveled. I reasoned that we could possibly do the job with the help of the Sim-tiger clan.

As the light brightened, Kasm let me know that the remaining Sim-tigers were going to hunt and he was going with them. While they were gone, I filled the others in on the meeting, and then, after breakfast, Whistle and I went to look at the shuttle and the transporter again. He'd been thinking about our crashed shuttle also and had come to an even more feasible idea than mine. If we could remove the internal systems reactor from our crash and somehow move it over the intervening miles, it would be able to provide enough power for us to fire up the transporter for a single trip, as long as it wasn't carrying much mass.

He and I would be able to go through and then we could, hopefully, somehow arrange to get the others up to the station and into the FTL. Whistle seemed to think that he could return along with some kind of larger power supply. It would have enough strength to allow the transporter to make several fully-loaded runs. This, in turn, would let him and some of the station Sunnys come down with the parts to repair the main power reactor, and. then we'd be in business. We could transport both ourselves and a large number of Sim-tigers up to the FTL ship. It would hold about fifty or sixty of them and I was intent on taking advantage of their agreeing to come and fight the Pug-bears in our solar system.

From their description of the fighting that had gone on during the attempted invasion, the Sim-tigers were more than able to destroy Pug-bears. Being accomplished telepaths, they were immune to the Pug-bears' rather primitive (by their standards) mental compulsion and, even more wonderfully, they had proven to be completely immune to the Pug-bear venom.

They were stronger than the Pug-bears, although they weren't as heavy. They could flip the creatures on their backs and then, ignoring the poison claws, they would claw through the lightly armored nerve-plexus that was the weakest point of the creature's external anatomy. When I inquired about the Pugs, Kasm explained, "As long as you can ensure that they can't shoot at us or bomb us from the sky, we can fight them on the ground. We learned how to ambush them when they were here and it's easy. Their senses are not as sharp as ours and our camouflage allows us to remain undetected until they are too close to avoid a charge."

That sounded hopeful. I was beginning to believe that we might clear the Earth of the invaders if we could solve the problem of getting back to the space station. We agreed to start for our wrecked ship the next morning.

CHAPTER 34

We had left the fort and were entering a large clearing in the jungle. There had been no problems and no alarms. There were nearly sixty of Kasm's clan with us and other creatures stayed far away. Kasm assured me that even a night-stalker would hesitate to attack such a large group of his people. I hadn't been looking forward to a renewed acquaintance with the stench-beasts and I was quite glad that we had such a large force.

I'd started to pass through the last vestiges of the smaller forest growth that lined the edge of the clearing when Kasm came crashing back to me and shoved his shoulder into my waist.

"Get back! Get back! There's a flying craft coming this way fast!" he sent.

We ducked under some cover as we heard the engines of a shuttle-craft approaching. It was flying rapidly and heading directly towards the fort. I didn't know who was flying it or where it had come from, but it was either Frazzle or some Pugs that had shown up from somewhere.

We turned and headed back down the trail towards the fort. Some of the Sim-tigers sprinted on ahead and quickly disappeared along the trail. I set out at a pace that I knew I could hold for the several miles that we'd traveled. Frank, Erin, and Whistle dropped rapidly behind and I signaled for Kasm to detail some of the clan to guard them.

It was a long run, but as I neared the fort, Kasm sent, "You can slow down now. The invaders landed next to the damaged shuttle and then incautiously came out to look around. They must have sensed the transporter's partial start-up and come to see what was going on. It was a big mistake for them to come out of their strong point. They're all dead now. The ones that ran ahead of us caught all of them and killed them. They had no chance to even get off a shot."

I was greatly impressed. The Sim-tigers were much better fighters against the Pugs than were humans. They'd make great allies if I could get them back to Earth. I didn't know if there were any more of the invading aliens on Earth, but there certainly were some on Oberon. Once we cleared out that force, we could transport through to Estes Park and clear out any remaining invaders there. Then I'd have my hands full working out an alliance between the human race, the Sunnys, and the Sim-tigers. I had the notion that I could cobble together a coalition that could be aimed at the Pug-bears' occupied planets and somehow stop them permanently. It was just a passing thought at the moment, but I knew in the back of my mind that the Pug-bears would continue to be a problem as long as they had access to space travel. They had to be stopped somehow, even if it came to dropping KEWs on their planet until they were extinct. One larger rock accelerated to a sizable fraction of c would probably do for the Pug-bears' home planet and that of the Pugs, but I had yet to figure a way of getting the Pug-bears off of the Sunny planets without killing the Sunnys in the process. My comet attack had been moderately effective from the reports, but I had left before I knew how the revolution came out.

When I arrived at the fort, I immediately investigated the Pugs' shuttle. It was a vastly different model than the ones I'd seen previously. Those had been smaller ships, suitable for only a small number of passengers and capable of strafing or bombing runs. This one was a cargo carrier that was easily capable of holding a hundred or more Pugs or humans. If Whistle could fly this hulk, our problems were solved. We could load the whole mess of us, Sim-tigers and all, and fly back to the station. Of course, there was the question of where these Pugs and their large shuttle had come from. If they had a shuttle of this size, it must have come in on a correspondingly large FTL and there were probably a lot of Pugs now running around on the orbital station.

There was no sense waiting around for them to come and check on what had happened, assuming that they had the capability. When the stragglers had arrived at the fort, the slowest of which was Whistle, I rushed him into the shuttle before he'd even had a chance to catch his wind.

He looked it over and said, "Dec, I never fly a craft like dis, but it's mostly computer-controlled. I can get us up."

"What I want to know is where it came from," I said.

"If I calls up to the station, it will alert dem that we're coming up and their crew is dead. Do you want me to call anyway?" he asked.

"No. We'll fly up and act as if we're their returning crew. If they call us on the communicator, we'll just pretend it's not working and hope they let us dock." I was thinking hard, trying to improvise. If we could dock, I intended for the Sim-tigers to rapidly kill all of the Pugs on the station. I'd take a smaller group of them and attempt to take the FTL ship in which they must have arrived.

I outlined my thoughts to Kasm about what we needed to do and he explained to his people. I was worried about their response to their first shuttle flight, but it was a non-event. They proved to be far more adaptable than I'd anticipated. They took to space as if they were meant to be there.

As we approached the station, I could see that there was a huge FTL docked there. The ship was roughly twice as long as ours and I assumed that it must be a second-generation vessel. The Sunnys always seemed to be intent on creating something better, even when they knew the end beneficiaries would be the Pug-bears. The ship was big enough that it would have no difficulty carrying the shuttle we'd captured. Judging from its size, it must have brought a very large crew to the station. That didn't bode well for our small force, even augmented as we were by the Sim-tigers.

As I'd hoped and partially expected, the Pugs made no effort to hail us, leaving the docking arrangements to be made by the station crew of Sunnys. The Pugs and Pug-bears were basically primitives in their thinking. They had no reason to suspect that any other forces would be traveling in space and they acted as if their operations were totally secure. This was a weakness that I'd learned to expect and I also wanted to keep in my mind as an object lesson. Never make assumptions that impact security. The unexpected can happen and you can be caught unaware.

The Sunnys on the station called us, expecting to contact the Pug crew and when they found that we were in possession of the craft, they were shocked and amazed. They'd apparently given us up for dead.

Whistle had to do some fast-talking, but he convinced them to conspire with us on our surprise docking. To give them credit, they weren't hard to convince. Their only reservation was they were worried about retribution should the Pugs dominate in the coming conflict. They were also, of course, unhappy about the incipient violence, but they'd reached a point of fear where their survival instincts had kicked in, making the thought of dead Pugs more bearable.

The large ship had arrived with only a skeleton crew, so that was a relief. They'd previously stopped at another system and dropped off their main complement of Pug fighters. The Sunnys there were not behaving very well and must have required some intimidation. There was a crew of only twenty Pugs and four Pug-bears that were left to come in on the big ship. It arrived piloted by only a couple of Sunnys. They'd started out the flight with more, but the Pug-bears had killed several of them for amusement.

They'd extended their voyage to this station to relieve the Pug watchers that were stationed here and to check on the station and the status in general. It was fortunate for us that they did since it had made it possible for us to capture their shuttle.

I had a foggy idea that I'd told Frazzle to go somewhere if the instruments detected another ship coming. Since our smaller ship wasn't docked or nearby, I hoped that was what he'd done. I didn't like to think about the possibility that the Pugs had captured him and our original vessel. When I mentioned this to Whistle, he assured me that he'd already asked the station Sunnys and they'd indicated that Frazzle had left the instant they'd detected the traces of the big ship exiting from FTL status.

The station crew thought that there had been plenty of time for him to get away. He'd been traveling under EmDrive power which was difficult to detect at a distance. That sounded good to me, but they hadn't heard from him since. The incoming ship had deviated from its direct path for an unknown reason and they were suspicious about that. I hoped that it didn't mean that he'd been intercepted.

They hastened to warn us about a new, second-generation Ansible system that didn't rely on the gravity of a planet. It could be used from a lighter-weight platform, such as a ship. We didn't want to risk trying to call Frazzle now. Even given the Pugs' lack of foresight, it would be too chancy. They might just have someone monitoring the FTL's new quantum comm system and pick up our call.

The short-range system we were using to communicate with the Sunnys' docking coordinator was a simple radio system. Monitoring those bands wouldn't give enough warning to be useful. Anyone using them effectively was already within a few light minutes and could be on top of you quickly. On the other hand, the quantum system was essentially instantaneous. We'd destroyed the older model on Oberon before we left for that reason.

Following instructions from docking control, we gradually approached the station and moved into an intercept trajectory that would dock us on one of the two available arms. The large FTL had attached to the third arm. It threw the station's rotation out of balance, but the Sunny crew was compensating by using the FTL's EmDrive engines and maneuvering thrusters. It was wasteful, but apparently, the Pugs didn't care. It didn't put them out in any way; the Sunnys would just have to make adjustments.

We approached slowly, Whistle working at a high rate of speed at the board. Matching up with the station's spin and having to compensate for the perturbations due to the sporadic adjustments made by the massive FTL was difficult. There was a lot of chatter back and forth between Whistle and the coordinator, but we ended up gliding into contact with no more than a slight shudder and a clash of metal as the docking clamps engaged.

Kasm's forces instantly unstrapped and were ready for action. It made me appreciate how nice it must be to have enough natural weapons not to have to load up with guns and reloads. The second the hatch had equalized and I swung it open, Kasm brushed by me, followed by a long stream of his compatriots. The two Sunnys who had been on the other side of the port whistled cries of alarm. Whistle popped his head through the hatch, under my arm. and let out a series of clicks and whistling noises at which they quieted. They'd been pushed against the wall by the Sim-tigers' rush and they held totally still, immobile in the grip of near panic, despite Whistle's reassurances.

Frank and I were loaded and ready to go also. We followed the last of the cat-like creatures down the arm to the hub of the station. They'd been moving so fast that there was nothing there save a few savaged Pug carcasses and one overturned Pug-bear. The latter was still moving its legs feebly in reflex actions. Without getting too close, giving due respect to the toxic nature of its claws, I looked at the bottom of its carapace. There was a series of deep gouges there that cut right through the natural armor at its thinnest point. Despite the flow of its blood, you could see that a thick cable-like nerve plexus had been severed. I pointed it out to Frank who studied it carefully.

"If I could turn one of these things over, my sword would do as good a job on the bottom," he observed.

"Yeah. But that's the problem. How do you get close enough to them to turn them over without being struck?" I responded.

"I dunno, but it's good to know that they've got a weakness somewhere," he answered, turning his back and walking toward the nearest hallway.

It led to the docked FTL and we could hear the sounds of conflict coming from the opening. It was mostly caused by the Sim-tigers growling, but as we approached, I could hear the hissing speech of the Pugs. They'd holed up behind some piled-up boxes and were standing off Kasm's group with anti-matter pistols.

This seemed to me to be a highly undesirable strategy. It was more than likely that they'd eventually shoot a bolt that would hole the station. We didn't have suits and weren't prepared for vacuum fighting. When we reached a point that gave us a view of the situation, I could see that Kasm's force was crouching in the lee of an open pressure door. The edges of the door showed eroded spots where they'd been struck lightly by the anti-matter beams. Luckily, the Pugs only had a few of the handguns and weren't shooting very much. The small weapons only carried enough charge for a very few, low-power shots, and the Pugs were trying to make their limited ammunition count.

Whenever a Sim-tiger would expose himself, a Pug would try to shoot him. The result was a sporadic barrage of anti-matter beams that flew down the hall, hissing lightly as they reacted with the molecules in the air until they attenuated and disappeared. We stopped at a slight curve of the hallway and peered around the corner carefully. Judging that I could hit the Pugs' cover with my rifle without doing irreparable damage to the station wall behind their position, I triggered off a very brief burst. The boxes crackled and disappeared along with pieces of the defending force where they were unlucky enough to be struck.

As soon as I'd shot and the damage was done, Kasm and company hurled themselves through the gap in the boxes. There was a lot of ruckus and a couple of Pugs jumped up and tried to run, but were quickly brought down by the tigers who simply and efficiently crushed their necks or skulls with a single bite. It was over in short order.

Since I'd only seen one Pug-bear, I sent an inquiring thought to Kasm and he responded, "That's the only one of them we've seen. The others must be in their ship."

I was about to ask about the other arm of the station when a small group of Sim-tigers brushed past us from behind. They'd gone exploring down the other arm but had found nothing but a couple of frightened Sunnys who were coming up to the control center in the hub. The Pug force was localized near their vessel and we'd killed all of them we could reach.

As I was taking stock of the situation, the lights by the airlock between us and the FTL flashed yellow and there was a wrenching clash of tortured metal. The FTL had pulled away without even bothering to undock from the clamps. This was very bad. There were enough aliens left on the ship to force the Sunny crew to take off. I'd hoped to capture the huge craft, but now, although it was unarmed, it was free to leave the system and also to call for reinforcements.

I turned to Whistle, who'd just arrived. His smaller legs couldn't carry him as fast as we moved and he was always late to the party, although I thought that he was also being very careful not to get in the way when his violent friends were fighting. "Whistle, quick! Go and call Frazzle. See if you can reach him and get him to come pick us up. We might have a chance if he can get here before that ship goes into FTL. If we can catch up to her, we can either capture her or shoot her lights out."

He turned dutifully and ran back the way he'd come. Kasm and I followed while Frank stayed behind, checking on the dead Pugs, just to make sure they really were dead.

As we ran, Kasm told me that the Pugs had managed to kill several of his people due to the constricted nature of the fight. "I don't want to fight where we can't use our natural advantages again," he sent with an overtone of anger in his aura.

"We'll have to ensure that you aren't faced with this type of situation in the future. If we can fight on the surface of a planet, your people can use their natural speed and camouflage. There is one potential battle that we may have to engage in where we'll be limited to this type of environment and that's a base on one of the small moons in our system. There is little atmosphere and it's deadly cold, so all life is restricted to a series of domes," I responded. Speaking to him was almost becoming like thinking to myself.

We'd gotten close and I wasn't observing some of the amenities with him any longer.

"You'd better see if we can just blow the domes up! I really don't like losing my friends," was his measured reply.

I agreed, but the potential presence of Sunnys in the domes was a problem. Perhaps we'd be able to get them isolated somehow before we attacked.

We arrived back at the command center for the station and I asked Whistle to try and contact Frazzle on the Ansible. A short time later, we were in contact. Frazzle had taken the ship sun-ward and moved into the shadow of the next planet in.

It was a small ball of rock, baked by the intense rays of the blue sun. He'd set up an orbit that kept him mostly in the cone of shadow cast by the planet. This kept the sun's rays from overheating the FTL and also made it difficult for the ship to be picked out by any sensors since the mass of the planet behind it provided enough noise to cover the relatively small signal from the ship.

I was still in awe over the long-range comm system. It was far better than radio since there was no lag in our conversation. I instructed Frazzle to start heading our way. Using the EmDrive's maximum acceleration, he could be close enough to our location for the transporter system to work reliably in a little over an hour. Now it was a race to see if he'd pick us up with enough time left to pursue the Pug-bears' large ship before it reached light speed and became unavailable.

CHAPTER 35

We didn't make it. The Pug-bears' ship exited the system and the station crew detected the faint, but unmistakable signature of its entrance into FTL status shortly before Frazzle got near enough for us to transport aboard. I was exasperated! Now, what were we to do? There was a distinct possibility that the large FTL would return within a few weeks fully loaded with Pug fighters. I doubted that they'd attempt to land on the planet, but they would surely re-take the station. Frazzle and Whistle agreed with me and Whistle wasted no time in convincing the five remaining station crew members to come with us.

This group consisted of a mated couple and three single females. The females all had brindled coats. They ranged from a dark gray background to a tawny, almost reddish field over which a series of blotches and spots were scattered. I'd learned that all Sunny females had multicolored coats while the males were uniformly a single color with possibly an accent color across their stomach or face. It made the sexes relatively easy to differentiate. I certainly couldn't tell any difference physically, save the females were slightly more robust. The couple were older and two of the females were their daughters. The other, reddish-coated one was unrelated.

I sent Whistle and a couple of the Sim-tigers to launch the large shuttle-craft that we'd captured on the planet's surface. It was a really convenient size for larger groups, whether they were men or aliens and I didn't want to leave it behind. Whistle was to head for the FTL and match up with it, docking on the second set of grapples. The FTL was set up to carry two rider-craft. Now, if only the grapple arms and claws were standard and would hold the new shuttle. Whistle thought it would work, but he wasn't sure.

As soon as Frazzle had our ship within a reasonable distance for transporting, one which ensured that we'd introduce no errors into our transcribed selves, we began to stage through. The transporter on the ship could hold a maximum of four of us and that delayed things considerably since we had over sixty individuals to move. The ship continued in our direction and we all eventually got on board. Whistle and the other shuttle arrived about an hour after we got the Sim-tigers settled into cabins.

When they arrived, we got good news. The larger shuttle had the same docking system as our smaller one and there was no problem attaching it to the big ship. When asked, Frazzle told me that the FTL had more than enough power to transport the additional mass. That was a real blessing, as now we had both smaller ships and that nicely increased our transportation capability.

The Sim-tigers weren't much of a problem. Blood-related groups preferred to sleep together, a fact which ended up allowing us to fit several into a single cabin. The ship was almost large enough to accommodate everyone. Erin offered to give up her cabin and bunk with me, but I forestalled her by rooming with Frank. She was disappointed and made no effort to hide it, even going so far as to try and bribe Frank to trade with her. Fortunately, he calmly said that he was happy where he was and that was the end of it.

Frazzle turned the ship outward towards the edge of the system's disk. There was no sense in hanging around near the station. We moved out on EmDrive power without accelerating too rapidly. After everyone had gotten settled and briefed on the facilities, I called a meeting with Kasm, a couple of others of his group, Frazzle and Whistle, and Erin. Frank expressed no interest, saying, "Just point me at a fight and tell me who to kill and I'm fine with that. I don't want to be involved in strategy. I trust that you'll make the right decisions."

We met on the command deck and hashed out the possibilities for our next move. I initially suggested that we return to the Sunny system that we'd dropped the ice bomb on, in order to see how they were making out with their revolt against the Pug-bears. Frazzle and Whistle were in favor of this, but Kasm pointed out that we were not ready to attack on a planetary scale.

He was correct and his blunt statement that there were too few of us made me realize that there was little we could do for the Sunny revolution. Aside from dropping some additional KEWs on the widely dispersed enemy, there was no additional action that was feasible for us. It's one thing to engage in small groups and quite another to take planetary-scale action. We needed to focus on those choke points in the enemies' organization that would allow us to make maximum use of our small force.

We ended up by determining that our best action would be to head back to Earth and stop the second wave of the invasion there before the Pug-bears built up a large force on the planet. Then we'd try and recruit human fighters to help free the Sunnys. We still needed more ships, but since we had the only armed FTL in space, I thought that we'd probably be able to capture others that we encountered. With that in mind, we set out to return to Earth on the most direct route.

We'd arrived at the Sim-tigers' planet by traveling along two legs of a triangle. Rather than retrace our journey exactly, it was far shorter for us to return along the third leg, but Frazzle informed me that it was still going to take about three weeks. There was a large and thick dust cloud that blocked the direct path and we'd have to circumnavigate that. Passing through that much dust in an FTL state would be risky. The FTL system was rather delicately balanced and the presence of so much external mass might interfere with our wave-form. I didn't understand his whole explanation, but I was happy to agree that we needed to avoid the risk. He laid in the course and accelerated and in a fairly short time, we entered into the FTL state.

Keeping the Sim-tigers amused proved to be my primary concern. They didn't intend to be difficult, but they were used to traveling daily and covering a lot of ground in their wandering life on Tukoli. After a couple of days listening to Kasm complain about being bored, I resorted to asking Frank to demonstrate swordplay to them. This was a great hit and resulted in requests for swords. The ship did have some bar-stock in the mechanical shop and Whistle was able to fashion some crude swords that they could practice with. We took every effort to ensure that no injuries occurred, but there were a few bruised heads and arms from the exercise. I'd been foresightful enough to have the blades wrapped with a kind of rubber-like material that was available in a rope form and that provided enough cushion that clumsy strikes were mostly blunted.

After some days of practice, the Sim-tigers started to develop their own style of fighting. It shortly became far more deadly than I'd foreseen. The extra weapon, paired with claws and teeth greatly increased their options for strikes. They were mostly disdainful of our handguns, but the swords really seemed to fill a perceived need in their minds. We put together a crude model of a Pug-bear and they made good use of it. The primary problem was that we had to almost constantly repair the thing. They'd run past at full speed and slash at the legs as they went by. Inevitably, the legs would break or be knocked askew by the force of the blow and the model would topple over. Then the Sim-tiger would dash around to an advantageous position and strike at the nerve plexus with either the sword or a convenient paw full of extended and razor-sharp claws. The way they were going, I almost hated to turn them loose on the Pug-bears; that is if I hadn't hated the nasty things so much.

At the same time, I took it upon myself to teach classes in map-reading, orientation, and sit-rep techniques. It had never occurred to the Sim-tigers that it might be a good thing to have a standardized reporting technique and the idea caused a lot of discussion among them. I was still unable to communicate with any of them, having to impose on Kasm's goodwill as a translator. I was relieved when he stated that he was learning as he translated and didn't mind the work.

Erin had been a veterinarian and briefed small groups on the anatomy of earthly animals including humans. I was able to get Whistle to discuss what the Sunnys knew of both the Pugs and Pug-bears and that proved popular since The People fully believed in the concept of know your enemy. I reasoned that it couldn't hurt to have educated my forces. They were certainly capable of killing any earth life if they could defeat the Pug-bears in combat. Having them understand just how vulnerable the locals were might keep them from inadvertently injuring people who were on our side. At least, that was my hope.

I did my best to avoid being alone with Erin. I think she got the idea that I was avoiding her; on more than one occasion, I caught her giving me a speculative, hurt look. I didn't want to mislead her. We were on our way back to Earth and even though I couldn't remember much about my wife, I did know that I was married and didn't need the complication of a relationship with the fiery red-head.

I found that I had enough time to spend hours in my cabin, alone, meditating and concentrating on rebuilding my damaged memories. The fog was mostly gone now. I could clearly remember everything that had happened since the vision-beast had injured me. By concentrating, I could remember much of what had gone before. In fact, I felt that I was nearly back to normal functionality with the exception that my memories of my wife and child were very fuzzy.

I was meditating on this issue during the early part of a sleep period when it hit me! Kasm had indicated that the vision-beast would take the most desired memory and amplify it back to its victim. He'd been thinking about his deceased mate when he was snared. I'd been doing the same thing in some way. I remembered suddenly that the vision-beast had shown me a view of – Liz! I could remember her name! Apparently, the damage done by the creature in its death throes was focused on that entry point it had used to gain control over me in the first place. It was no wonder that I was having problems with my memories of her. I felt that I'd made a major step. Maybe I couldn't remember what she looked like, but I'd remembered her name! I was quite pleased with this progress.

The next day, over breakfast, I could still remember it. Erin came into the cafeteria area, selected some food from one of the machines, and then sat down beside me. Rather unthinkingly, I began to explain to her my struggles to remember. When I got to the point about remembering my marriage to Liz, I glanced up from my plate to see a stricken expression pass over her face.

"Erin! I didn't mean – " I started, but she interrupted me.

"That's OK. I know that you've been suffering from your memory problem. I just hoped – I mean I just wanted to be helpful. I'm glad you can remember something!" She abruptly stood and carried her tray over to the disposal chute, then walked rapidly out of the room.

I watched as she left. She was trying to act nonchalantly, but I could tell that my partial recovery had hit her hard. She looked like she was hurrying to get out of my sight before she broke down in tears. I felt like a complete jerk over the situation. Thinking about it, though, I felt somewhat angry. Why did this have to happen to me? I really hadn't tried to attract her and I wanted the best for her. I knew that I found her desirable, but my conscience wouldn't let me follow up on that as long as there was a chance that I could be reunited with Liz. With our impending approach to Sol, that began to seem more and more likely. I sighed and then left for the bridge.

About midway through the voyage, Frazzle came to me in the cafeteria, "Dec, how do humans mate?"

That set me back a bit. I thought that he'd been to one of Erin's classes, but I was fairly sure that she wasn't covering such things. I considered and then decided that I'd better get some clarification about what he was getting at. "What do you mean?" I asked. "Are you speaking of the physical action?"

"Oh! No! Dat's not it! I mean, Sunnys have a big celebration of all the group when a couple decide to bond and we don't have enough of us to have a proper party on the ship." He seemed to be a little embarrassed. "Also, a family member gots to give the boy to the girl. I don't have no family on the ship."

It suddenly came through to me. I'd noticed that the single Sunny girl had been spending a lot of time hanging around the control deck when Frazzle was there. He wanted to get married!

I asked carefully, "Could a friend, even if that friend was a different species, act as a family member in such a case?"

His eyes sparkled, "Dat would be wonderful! Dec, would you do that for me?"

"Of course, I would! I'd be greatly honored to give you to her and as for the party, I'm sure we can invite the whole ship. Everyone's in need of entertainment and even the Sim-tigers would probably be glad to attend." Just as I said that Kasm and one of his compatriots entered the room. They were apparently arguing a fine point of swordplay, but Kasm immediately turned his attention to me, having overheard my last statement.

"Attend what, Dec?" he sent.

I hadn't actually sent that out directly to him in the manner I used when we communicated, nevertheless, he'd somehow overheard my thoughts, or ... another option occurred to me, he could understand English.

He overheard that thought and sent back, "Not well, but I'm learning. It helps that you both think the words and speak them. I'm able to glean the meaning and the sounds are starting to make sense to me. Now, what would we be interested in attending?"

I explained and I could sense that he was amused and pleased at the same time. He walked over to Frazzle and looked him over carefully, much to Frazzle's consternation. Then he turned his head to me and sent, "Tell him that we'd all be pleased to attend his bonding party. We do something similar and I want to be the first to wish him a long and fruitful life with many children."

The party was held in the loading dock since that was the largest space on the ship. It went well and, although I was nervous about it, I seemed to do well in my official role. The other Sunnys showed their approbation by whistling and stamping their feet and the entire group of Kasm's people made the deck shudder with a collective roar after the ceremony was complete. Erin and Frank both congratulated Frazzle and Mrs. Frazzle – we hadn't settled on a human name for her as yet, but we were leaning towards "Red" simply due to her predominant color.

As the group broke up and went back to their normal hang-outs, I noticed that Whistle was leaving with both of the other two single females. He had an arm around each and they were whistling and I would have sworn, giggling, if they made such a noise. I wondered if he'd be getting married next or if he was still playing the field, small though it was. I noticed Erin grinning at their backs as they left. She came over to me with a smile and said, "I've always liked weddings. Never been married myself, though. I guess I just never found a man I could respect." She paused, looked at them, and then glanced rather coyly at me and added quietly, "Until now."

I put my arm around her and gave her a weak hug, then disengaged and headed back to my cabin. I was flattered and confused by her attention. I had a wife, I kept telling myself that, despite my foggy memory. I thought that I'd been very happy with my family. I just wished I'd regain both my memory and my psychic abilities. The incident put a nasty crimp in my mood. I'd been happy for Frazzle, but I spent the sleep period in a kind of restless half-sleep, worrying about my mind, my marriage, and what I was going to do about Erin's obvious attraction to me.

Frazzle was back in the control room the next day with Red. She hung over the back of his seat and they seemed to be always touching. It was almost silly, they acted like two kids with their first crush. We gradually got back to our normal activity pattern, although Whistle seemed to be hiding out somewhere most of the time. I thought that he was spending time with each of the two other available females alternately, but I didn't actually check up on it.

In such a fashion, we whiled away the days until we exited from FTL far from the sun in the vicinity of the Oort cloud. Frazzle didn't want to exit too close to Uranus and he felt the debris in the cloud would provide some shielding against possible detection. We proceeded towards Oberon under EmDrive and arrived there after several hours of travel. Once again, we approached from behind the planet. The Pug-bears weren't overly watchful, but there was no sense challenging them directly, either.

We took up an orbital path that would allow us to slowly move to the side of the planet occupied by Oberon. We were nearer Uranus' surface than Oberon's orbit and our ship would be masked from any of the moon base's quantum sensors against the noise of the planet. We'd be easily visible to telescopic observation, but there was little likelihood of that. The invaders weren't interested in enhancing their scientific knowledge by observing the planet. The Sunnys might be, but they were mostly too intimidated by their en-slavers to volunteer any information to the Pug-bears. We were gambling and hoped they'd try hailing us first if they actually noticed that we were catching up to the moon's position.

As soon as we had a good view of the moon, we could see that it was now covered with far more domes than before. Many more of the aliens had evidently arrived since our departure. They hadn't wasted time while we were gone. In addition to the numerous new domes, there was an FTL vessel trailing the moon in its orbit around Uranus. When we detected this new ship, my plans changed rapidly. I suddenly wanted to capture it in the worst possible way.

The single ship I commanded was nice, but in order to carry the attack to the Pug-bears we'd need additional vessels. I had been intending to attack the domes, freeing the captive Sunnys and destroying all of the Pugs and Pug-bears. Now, my focus was on first capturing the additional ship.

We were meeting in the control room, the humans, Kasm, and all of the Sunnys. I was trying to reach some consensus on the best way to capture the ship. Suddenly Frazzle and Red both exclaimed and we turned towards the video screens.

The new FTL was accelerating and leaving orbit! We'd possibly waited too long to attack. The ship was moving out quickly, but it looked as if it wasn't directly leaving the system. Instead, it was heading sun-ward. After running some quick calculations, Frazzle said, "Deys heading most likely for the moon base of the biggest planet. Maybe we can intercept them there."

It looked like they were heading for Io. We maneuvered to drop back in orbit until Oberon passed out of sight around the rim of Uranus. Once we were hidden from direct view, we accelerated out at right angles to the ecliptic, then began to gradually turn so that we'd come towards Io from outside of the orbital plane. Frazzle turned on the EmDrive unit to its highest acceleration and we traveled rapidly towards our goal. It was still going to be hours, but from his calculations, the other FTL wasn't traveling at anything like our velocity. We'd reach Io a little before they would, despite our much longer trajectory.

About midway in our pursuit, we determined that they were headed for Europa rather than Io. The two were currently on the same side of Jupiter and that had confused Frazzle. He had been operating under the assumption that they were headed for the old Io base, but he suddenly remembered that the Pugs had also set up a small installation on Europa.

As we got closer, Frazzle tuned the comm unit to listen in and determined that the other ship was in touch with some Sunnys on the moon. From the chatter, it seemed like the FTL's bridge was manned by Sunnys as was the Europa approach control, so Frazzle took a chance and interrupted.

His call created a considerable amount of startlement on the others' parts, but they eventually got things straightened out. Both groups were frightened by the newly arrived Pug-bears and Pugs. The Sunnys on the FTL had suffered from the same poor treatment as had the ones we'd rescued previously. Many of them had been killed on their voyage, leaving only a skeleton crew to fly the ship. There were some Pugs on Europa, but they mostly kept to themselves, leaving the Sunnys there to run things. The Pug-bears had never been to that base since it existed solely to extract some dissolved minerals from the subsurface ocean. The Sunnys had determined that the Europa ocean held a high concentration of some essential mineral nutrients that both the Pugs and Pug-bears required and they'd been forced to set up a small extraction and distillation plant.

Both the FTL's Sunny crew and those on Europa were pleased to hear that we were nearby. The FTL was carrying a large number of Pugs, but no Pug-bears. We'd have to figure out a way to neutralize that force if we were to take the ship.

After some discussion back and forth, the FTL Sunnys simply invited us to transport on board, provided we could quickly suppress the Pugs. We prepared a boarding party and all met in the hold to take our turn in the ship-to-ship transporter. Whistle had tuned it carefully to the other FTL's unit and we began to move through in groups of eight. Kasm insisted that his people compose the first two transporter loads. He didn't want to be insulting, he said, but they could probably have all of the resistance under control before we humans could get organized. I didn't disagree, having seen his people in training. They were very fast.

We went through in our turn to find that there was just a small group of Pugs that were left alive. They had locked themselves in a service closet and the Sim-tigers were making sure that they stayed inside. Kasm had rounded up the two Sunnys from the control room and had them in the hall near the service closet when we got there.

Not wanting to damage the ship in any way, I decided to speak to the Sunnys about opening the closet, but they had no English, so we waited until Whistle could make his way over. Once he arrived, the problem was shortly solved. The three scampered down the hall to a panel and opened it. They stuck their heads inside and busied themselves for a moment, then pulled out to have a face-to-face discussion. This evidently was productive, because one of the two new Sunnys leaned into the alcove and began to rewire some circuitry while Whistle and the other one watched carefully over his shoulders. Suddenly Whistle pointed at me and I spun in time to see the closet door's lock turn from yellow to blue.

Everyone moved out of the direct line of fire and I shoved the door open with my foot. There was no response. Finally, I peeked around the jamb, bending down near the floor. There were four Pugs inside, standing near the back wall with their hands opened at chest height. They were obviously unarmed and didn't seem to be interested in a fight.

I was unsure about capturing them. I didn't want to be burdened with the obnoxious creatures, but it occurred to me that if we treated them well, we could send them through a transporter link to Europa to convince the ones there to also surrender. As long as there wasn't a resident Pug-bear to force them to fight, they might see the futility of resistance, despite their fractious nature. With this in mind, we started to move them into a cabin that could be secured from the outside. I sent Whistle along with a guard of Sim-tigers to see to that task.

Unfortunately, it didn't work out well. Whistle came dashing back to me after about five minutes. The Pugs had somehow managed to access a storage locker they passed and had armed themselves. There had been a brief, intense fight and all four of the Pugs were now dead as was one of the guards.

I was very unhappy about the loss of one of The People and resolved that when it came to Pugs, the rule in the future would be, "Take no captives."

Now that we had the new ship in our possession, Europa was next on the list. The resident Sunnys were on the comm begging us to come and get them. They'd had enough of the conditions and also of the contingent of Pugs that were stationed there. We used the transporter in the new ship and came out in one of the smaller domes on the surface. The Sunnys were frightened of us, having never seen anything like our crew, but, once again, Whistle proved a superlative mediator. He had them calmed down and transporting up to the FTL in a few minutes.

The Pugs were all in a larger residence that was located a few hundred yards away. Rather than waste our time on fighting and possibly taking losses, I contacted Frazzle and together we worked out which dome it was. We evacuated from ours, in case my calculations were wrong – I didn't want to run the risk of eradicating ourselves – and then Erin took a shot at the Pugs' dome with the bow gun on our armed FTL. She was deadly accurate and the dome, along with a portion of the local landscape, simply ceased to blemish the moon's surface.

I was contemplating the desirability of going back and trying to figure out how to separate the Sunnys on Oberon into a single location so we could zap the other domes when Whistle came to me with an interesting piece of information. The dome we'd just left had a second transporter link that was tuned to one in Estes Park!

In the back of my mind, I'd been trying to figure how we'd return to Earth. True, we could fly the FTLs into orbit and we had our original shuttle-craft to land with along with the larger one. I could bring all of the Sim-tigers down with the larger one alone. The new FTL we'd just captured was missing its rider shuttle. On the other hand, it would be even better to simply transport into the heart of the enemies' territory unannounced.

My disability continued. My psychic senses had not cleared up and my ordinary memory still wasn't cooperating fully. I did remember that the original transporter that I'd come through from the park was a single connection one that wouldn't allow us to connect with the ship's transporter. The local Sunnys informed us that the Pugs had set up a couple more of the units in Estes Park. These were advanced units. One of these third-generation transporters was currently connected to the Europa portal, but both had the ability to receive from any source that could match their digital-handshaking code sequence.

Knowing that the Pugs had reached Estes, I assumed that they'd chased off any humans that were there. I fervently hoped that they hadn't gotten much farther than that in their second invasion. The newly rescued Sunnys didn't know, but they had heard reports of heavy fighting that was holding up the advance.

We moved both ships into orbit around Europa, transported our entire force over to the newly captured ship, and then moved down to the sole remaining dome on the surface. I'd decided to use the transporter there to jump to the Estes location. We staged our main force, consisting of fifty-three Sim-tigers, three humans, and one rather reluctant Sunny in the dome, decided on our transport order, and then we were ready to begin to take the fight through to the surface of Earth.

Frazzle had taken charge of both ships and agreed to bring them into Earth orbit. He thought that he and Whistle could figure out a way to hack the handshaking code and re-tune one or both of the ship transporters directly to the Estes Park transporters. This part of the plan assumed that we were successful in our counter-invasion and could capture the Estes equipment.

If Whistle proved incapable of hacking into the Earth-side transporters, Frazzle would fly down in the smaller shuttle and bring enough tools and parts to make the linkage work. We would have the FTL ships, the shuttle,s and a way back and forth from the surface. It was a good start if we could do it. Now all we had to do was to go through and kill a mess of Pugs and Pug-bears.

Chapter 36

Once again, Kasm insisted on using his people as the spear-point of our attack. I understood his reasons but didn't feel it was fair that we humans were taking a secondary role in the counter-attack on Earth. Nevertheless, I ended by deferring to him. His people were excellent fighters and with the addition of swords to their imposing natural weapons, I was forced to concede that they were the most logical choice. I resolved to come through immediately after their first group. If they ran into any trouble facing armed Pugs, I wanted to be there with my anti-matter weapons to help out.

Frank got me aside and essentially said the same thing, "Dec, you and I'd better go through right after those cats. We can shoot and they're likely to get pinned down by some of those Pug things. If we go through in the second transporter load, we can be in a position to help out." He placed his big hand on my shoulder and added, "Promise me that you won't let Erin go through until we've got the buggers laid out. She'll want to get in the fight and I don't want to have to be looking out for her while I'm concentrating on killing Pugs. I just couldn't take it, if she got hurt."

"I agree," I said. I was a little surprised at the depth of emotion he showed. I hadn't realized that he cared about his charge so much. "I'm going to tell her that she should hang back with Frazzle and Red. They will need some human advice if anything happens to us. She'll have to get them to try and destroy the Pug-bears' settlements in the system. If we lose, I want her to drop a KEW on Estes. If it kills everyone on the front range, it will be bad, but we've got to get rid of the Pug-bears for the sake of humanity."

"What about your wife?" he asked.

"We live in Grand Lake, over the Divide. If the KEW were aimed precisely, it might not do too much damage over there... at least, that's what I hope," I concluded lamely. I looked away from him. I found it difficult to think about the damage that could be done with just one sizable rock. If they were still alive and in Grand Lake, my family might easily be vaporized.

In less time than I'd planned, the Sim-tigers had arranged their first transporter group and were in the machine and ready to go. Frazzle had shown us which of the control buttons activated the link to Estes. Kasm looked out at me, winked, and pressed the button with his hand-arm. There was a flicker and they were gone.

Immediately, the second complement of his people moved into the chamber. Frank and I shoved our way into the room, too. Making sure that all were safely within the door frame (the chamber was an open one with no actual door), I then activated the system.

We came out in the Stanley Hotel. The second-floor hallway we exited into was empty, save for the bodies of several Pugs. There were battle sounds coming from the ground floor and we wasted no time in making our way downwards.

We came down the broad staircase and emerged into the lobby. It was a mess. Dead Pugs everywhere and to my pleasure, not a sign of even an injured Sim-tiger. The fight had moved out of the building and was now going on in the front. Our tiger friends dashed out the front entrance and rapidly ran down the staircase to the front lawn. The first group of our allies was just now chasing a batch of Pugs across the lawn towards a stand of spruce trees. The Pugs were running at a surprising rate, but the Sim-tigers were much faster. When one of them caught up to a Pug, it would either slash with a sword or rake a paw-full of claws across the unfortunate alien. I remembered that the Pugs were unable to live in our atmosphere without their skin-tight bodysuits and respirators. The slashes cut through their suits, even though they were tough enough to withstand small-caliber bullets, and the Pugs immediately dropped, convulsing as whatever it was in the air began to dissolve their flesh.

Just as the front of the Pug group entered the grove of trees, four huge Pug-bears came tearing around the right edge of the grove. They collided with two of the Sim-tigers, who had not seen them coming and the cat-like creatures were bowled off their feet. The Pug-bears piled on their fallen enemies and began to rip at them with their full complement of deadly claws. The other Sim-tigers jumped into the fray and both sets of aliens made a confused, heaving mass for a few seconds. One of the Pug-bears was actually thrown several yards out of the pile, landing on its back. It was missing a couple of legs on one side and seemed to be having a hard time regaining its feet. It finally started to get up, but by then, I'd gotten my anti-matter rifle arranged and dissolved half of its carapace.

The mass of fighters heaved and then broke into clumps, rapidly resolving into two separate struggles. The last two Pug-bears started to run but were quickly halted. One was faced with three Sim-tigers, while the other was pulled down by a Sim-tiger that had somehow leaped onto its back. Two of the late-arriving Sim-tigers had caught up and were circling round the confused Pug-bear, looking for an opening. It was slashing wildly with its claws, as was the other Pug-bear. This was where the swords came into their own. The tigers simply slashed the legs off whenever they were presented with an opportunity. It didn't take long for them to immobilize both Pug-bears. Then they carefully flipped each individual over and severed the vulnerable nerve plexus on their bottom side.

Frank and I were still running towards the group but had only covered half of the distance by that point. The fight had gone down fast. One lone Pug came racing around the left side of the trees pursued by the only Sim-tiger that had continued chasing Pugs when the Pug-bears attacked. He was shortly pulled down and dispatched.

We arrived at the scene of the carnage and were met by Kasm. He was extremely angry and worked up by the fight. The two Sim-tigers who had lost their feet due to the Pug-bears' charge were both dead and he didn't like it one bit. He was so angry that his fur coat was standing out, bristling in all directions and I thought for a moment that he was going to jump at us. When his eyes met mine, he calmed noticeably and sent, "You're late! We killed these, so show us where the rest of them are hiding. Our blood demands vengeance!"

"We'll find them soon enough," I spoke aloud. "We'll have to do some scouting to see what's up around here. I've got no idea how many of them have landed and they could be spread out over a large area by now. Keep alert! We don't want them shooting at us from a distance. An ambush could be very bad."

We'd defeated the first group of them that we'd encountered, but it had been months since we'd left Earth and there really was no knowing how many had transported down during that time. The rest of the Sim-tigers arrived and we spread out to search the hotel grounds and the rest of the town. There were a few Pugs that showed up, walking down the road from the Park, but they didn't last long. The Sim-tigers weren't in a mind to take captives.

The question of where the invaders were was answered surprisingly by a human. The Sim-tiger scouts came herding a tired-looking man up the street from the southern edge of town. Something about him looked familiar; his stride seemed like one I'd seen before or maybe it was the way he carried himself. I couldn't place it though until he got close enough for me to see his face. It was Joe! The last time I'd seen him, he was with my friend Rudy and the Shoshone leader, Freddy Stormbreaker. They'd been the final survivors of our strike team that had disrupted the Pug-bears' invasion a little over four years ago. We'd separated; they'd gone off on what I thought was a wild-goose chase to Miami and Liz and I had gone over the mountains to Grand Lake.

As if a key were turned, a large chunk of my locked mind opened and memories of that time came flooding out. I remembered the desperate fighting we'd gone through and the despair that we'd felt when the Pug-bears had exploded the EMP that had driven our entire civilization back to a seventeenth-century lifestyle. I'd been sorry that Rudy had chosen to head to Miami. He'd sworn an oath that required him to go there. It might not have been binding on other people, but Rudy was always a man that could be relied upon to keep his word. I never thought I'd see any of the three again.

"Joe! I can't believe it's you after all this time!" I enthused. "What happened to Rudy and Stormbreaker? And, what have you been doing with yourself? You look like you've been ridden hard and put away wet!"

He smiled tiredly as he answered, "I've been fighting alongside the Denver group, trying to keep the Pug-bears out of our territory. Rudy is down in Denver with the Eastern Slope Warlord's advisers and Stormbreaker is probably over in Grand Lake with his wife, looking for you right about now. If you're going to play twenty questions, I've got some for you too, like where'd you come from and what are these green-striped cat-things? That's just a starter, so don't think I'm going to quit there!"

He was the same old Joe! Mildly sarcastic and a little prickly when he was unsure of the strategic situation.

"Listen, these are Sim-tigers and they're our best friends right now! They can kill Pug-bears so fast it makes it seem like child's play! They hate the Pug-bears and have agreed to help us in return for our help in making sure the nasty things are never a threat again. We're allies and I've got another set of alien allies also, but they're not fighters. They're flying the spaceships right now."

"That's nice – Whoa! – What spaceships?" he stuttered.

"Oh, just the two Faster-Than-Light ships that I've captured from the Pug-bears, that's all." I was having fun looking at his expression. "But, really, Joe, we need tactical information desperately right now! Where are all of the Pugs and Pug-bears and what strength do they have? We intend to wipe them off the Earth if we can, but we can't find any more than the few that were here."

"Don't fret about it, Dec. The main force of Pugs along with a number of Pug-bears is holed up in downtown Boulder. It's been deserted for some months since the aliens invaded again, but we, I mean the Warlord's army, have mostly kept them contained in the center of town. We control the south side of Boulder, up to just past the University and the Pugs have set up their front line along the Pearl Street Mall. We've been sniping back and forth for weeks. The Pug-bears don't seem to be doing much raiding or much of anything else. We know there are a few with the Pugs, but we haven't seen them for quite a while."

"So, what are you doing up here? Your main force is stopped in south Boulder you say, so how did you get all the way to Estes?" I thought I knew, but I needed for him to tell me.

"We sent out a number of scouts to see how far the invaders had come, whether they had spread out north of Boulder and if there were a lot more in Estes. I don't know where the other guys are, hope they haven't been caught, but I've been up on the Peak-to-Peak highway. Not on the highway, you understand, but in the general area. I finally worked my way down through Allenspark a couple of days ago and I was poking around the outskirts of Estes Park, looking for any aliens and trying to keep a low profile. Apparently, I wasn't as successful as I'd hoped, cause a couple of your stripey friends jumped out of some bushes, grabbed my gun, and, well, here I am!"

"Are there any Pugs or Pug-bears between us and Boulder now?" I asked.

"Dec, I've been up in the hills as I said and I can't say for sure, but I think they are all located down in Boulder. There could be some in Lyons, but I don't know any more than that. What are you going to do?"

"I think I've got a plan," I replied. I'd been working it out as we spoke. It was improvising, but we didn't have a very large force and I didn't think fighting a pitched battle against Pugs, possibly armed with advanced weapons was a good idea.

I got Kasm's attention and started to explain, "Here's what we can do. We'll head down the front range towards Boulder. It'll take us a couple of days to get close. The Sim-tigers will serve as a scouting force and will eliminate any small groups of enemy as they go. We'll be right behind with our anti-matter guns – Uh, eraser-guns, Joe." He'd looked puzzled, but my use of the old name that we'd originally used, made him smile and nod.

"Then, assuming that we can get the Eastern Slope Warlord to cooperate, we can squeeze the Pug forces in towards the center of Boulder. If that works, I've got a nasty surprise for them. One of our spaceships carries a large anti-matter cannon and I'll get Erin to take out the center of their forces. I think she can do that in a single pass in low orbit. That should soften them up enough for us to make a coordinated attack from both sides and hopefully wipe them out."

I was proud of myself for thinking of this, but there were a lot of "what-ifs" involved. The Pug forces could evacuate up Boulder Canyon or simply retreat into the foothills or even move out to the east in the direction of Longmont. I was hoping that the Warlord had enough people to blockade the other ways out of the town.

Joe nodded, "I think we can make that happen. If I can get a little rest, I'll be ready to head back to the Warlord's area and I'll take a message from you. I think I can get Rudy to advise him to do what you want. He is awful bull-headed, though. I'm also tired and it's a long way back down there from here and there's a lot of rough terrain to cover, too."

"I'm sure that I can help with that also," I smiled, bragging. By now Frazzle would be partway to Earth orbit and he could fly the shuttle down, pick us up and we could fly to Denver.

Joe just shook his head as I explained. He did look very tired, but I wasn't through with him. "So, did you get to Miami?" I asked.

He sighed, "It's a long story, but to make it short, yes. At least Rudy and I got there. Stormbreaker stopped at a small town in Oklahoma. He took up with a Cherokee woman and they ended up getting married. They came back with us when we came back through from Miami."

"OK, but what happened in Miami? Did Rudy find Mick's sister?" I wanted to hear the whole story, but it was obvious that he was reluctant to relive it.

"We had a hell of a time getting down there. I don't want to even think about the things we had to do on the way down or back and it wasn't worth it! Mick hadn't told us that his sister had a pacemaker. She had some kind of congenital heart defect and they'd installed a pacemaker – lousy things! She died within an hour of the EMP going off – her friend told us. She suffered for an hour and then just died. The EMP destroyed the pacemaker or reprogrammed it or something. What a waste!" He shook his head regretfully. "It took us six months to get down there and we stayed there for a couple of years, but things didn't work out very well. Too much disease, not enough food, and too many gangs. We finally decided to come back."

He continued, "I don't mind telling you that I thought about it quite a bit before we started back. There really were some nice-looking women in the Miami area, but the local gangs were bad, too. The trip back was difficult. It took nearly a year. Walking when we had no cars, stealing cars and gas when we could. Food was hard to come by and we had to work at avoiding local militias and scavengers. We hid out a lot, just waiting for some group or other to move out of our way. As it was, we were ambushed three times before we picked Stormbreaker and his woman back up. Rudy got shot up bad in the last one. His left arm will never be the same; blew out a big chunk of his muscle. Anyway, I'm glad I decided to come back with him. One man alone would never have made it. If we hadn't met up with Stormbreaker and his woman, I don't know what we would have done. Rudy was hurt and couldn't fight well, so having two more with us really helped. We talked about you a lot. We figured that you'd most likely be in some serious trouble somehow. It does seem to follow you around." He laughed, then continued, "Anyway, when we finally got into Denver, we checked around and decided to hook up with the Warlord's group. They're good people, mostly. They were fighting the Pugs and needed our knowledge, especially when the Pug-bears started showing up."

He paused and looked around as if to reassure himself that our location was secure, then he continued, "Sorry, I just have to keep checking for ambushes. I've been in the woods for so long now that I'm nervous in a town like this. I was up in the Allenspark area; there were no Pugs there, but a couple of Pug-bears had been through. There are a few folks that live around there and they're plenty scared. I figured that I could sneak by Estes and hike over the pass to see if I'd get lucky and find you. It wasn't part of my job – Rudy had just asked me to scout out the Pugs, but it felt like I was close, so I decided to try, then your stripey alien friends caught me. I thought I was done for. They almost make the Pug-bears seem cuddly. Where did they come from, anyway?"

Joe had never been one to talk so vociferously before. I guessed that he had been by himself for a long time as he scouted or maybe it was just relief at finding me and realizing that the Sim-tigers were friends.

"They fought the Pug-bears' invasion of their planet to a stand-still. When I found that out, I wanted to have them as friends and, as you can see, it worked out nicely." I waved my hand vaguely at the small group of Sim-tigers that were resting nearby. "Now, I'm sorry to make you walk some more, but let's go see about getting a ride down to Denver."

It took us some time to hike back to the Stanley, but only a few minutes to transport up to Europa, then jump from there to the FTL. It was just Joe, Whistle, and me since Frank stayed in Estes to help back up Kasm's group as they started south. We needed him there to coordinate the attack if nothing else.

We got to the ship and I immediately took Joe to my cabin and got him settled in. I think he was asleep before I exited the room. I walked down the hall, grabbed some food, and then headed for the bridge. Frazzle leaped out of his chair when I came in. Red shyly hung back, but he dashed over to me and stretched his short arms around my middle in a hug.

"Dec, I glad you came back. We been worried about you. De Pug-bears are bad fighters and I'm glad you're OK!" Frazzle was practically unintelligible, he was speaking so fast.

"I'm glad you were worried about me, but I'm just fine. We've cleared out the enemy from around the transporters and we know where most of them are located. I'm going to need to fly down to a place on the other side of them and organize a force to fight them. The Sim-tigers will drive them into that force and then – " I was interrupted by another hug from the other side. As I glanced down at the slim arms that crossed my chest, I said, "Hello, Erin."

She loosened up her hug but didn't let go, so I turned to face her, gently disengaging her arms as I did, "Glad to see you. We're fine and we've got the Pugs just where we want them. They're holed up in Boulder. I'm going to set up a pincers attack and compress them into the Pearl Street Mall area and then signal to you. I'll need you to make a pass across the area with the bow cannon. If we're lucky, that will take care of much of the problem."

She acerbically replied, "What a greeting. Here I was worried about you! You're all business aren't you?" She paused and showed me that she had been listening. "What if we aren't lucky? I could miss and hit your forces or you, you bone-head! I couldn't take it if that happened!"

"Don't worry, we'll be observing from the shuttle-craft and I'll make sure I'm out of range when you fire," I reassured her.

"OK, but I'll need specific coordinates for the shot. Will Frazzle set up the fire-control computer for us?" She was thinking ahead.

Frazzle wasn't too happy about it, but by now, he'd lost a lot of the inability to consider violence that he'd originally had and he agreed to make sure that the shot struck where I wanted it. It was up to me to send him the exact location, though.

A few hours later, Joe and I were located in the shuttle. Whistle was piloting and we were trying to make the best of the small space. It was a tight fit for the three of us, but we managed to survive until we landed near Mile-High stadium. That was the site of the Warlord's main headquarters. I'd pointed out the Pearl Street Mall as we flew over Boulder and Whistle had recorded the specifics of the location for later transmission to Frazzle.

Joe and I climbed out of the shuttle to face a large group of bizarrely-dressed fighters. They favored buckskin and there were a number of fur caps of various sorts gracing their heads. The most important thing was they were armed with a large number of well-used firearms that were all pointing at us. Joe glanced at me and whispered, "I don't know these guys, so – ."

I looked at the holes in the ends of the muzzles and smiled my most charming smile.

Chapter 37

J oe carefully held his hands up, showing his empty palms. As he did, I
heard someone in the back of the group surrounding us yell, "Dec!"

It was Rudy! The next instant he came charging through the front line of
men and suddenly we were hugging each other and pounding on each
other's back. I noticed that his left arm seemed to be locked and relatively
immobile. I put my hands on his shoulders and pushed him back to look in
his face. He'd aged more than the four years we'd been apart. I glanced at his
arm and he said, "I've been through a lot since I saw you last. My arm's never
going to let me be as good a fighter as I used to be."

"Aw, Rudy, even with one arm tied behind you, you're more than a match for
most guys," I wasn't flattering him, only being honest.

"Not anymore, Dec. I caught a bullet and the scar tissue has locked my arm
in a right angle. I can't extend it and it makes it really hard to shoot and
fight. I've been busy advising the Warlord. He's a good guy. Name is Jake."

"Jake," I said, "Is that all? No high and mighty titles or anything?"

"It's what he goes by," he replied. "He must have a last name, but I never
heard it. He doesn't go much for formality or titles, but he's a capable
organizer and that's mostly the reason that Denver has done as well as it has.
We'll need to have you meet him."

I asked, "I heard he was pretty stern, especially with prisoners. True?"

Rudy responded, "He has to maintain order, and a lot of the people who survived are, shall we say, hard-headed." His eyes strayed to the shuttle-craft. "What do you have there? It sure isn't a human craft! What have you been doing?"

"Look, Rudy, I've got two spaceships that can take us to other star systems. One of them is armed and if we can get the Pugs pinned down in one location or squeezed up where they are in Boulder, my ship will make a strafing run and wipe them out. We definitely need to see this Jake. If he can get his people to attack, then my forces will attack from the North and we'll settle the Pugs for good." I didn't mention the exact type of forces I had. It just seemed too complicated and wasn't necessary anyhow. He was impressed enough as it was.

We got organized to go see Jake, leaving Whistle locked in the shuttle. I figured that he'd be safer there than walking around with us, especially when no one had ever seen anything like him before. Rudy led the way and we were shortly approaching the stadium command post.

The Warlord wasn't anything like I'd thought he'd be. He'd been in the Marine Reserve and was a fighter, but he also knew enough about how people worked to rule successfully over the Denver area and run a large contingent of fighters, some of whom were truly wild and undisciplined. He was a medium-sized guy with piercing eyes, longish hair, and an imposing presence.

We were ushered into his private quarters where we had an involved discussion. I explained my plan and enumerated my resources, including the nature of my allies. The idea of me bringing another couple of alien races to Earth didn't go over well at first, but I was able to gain a provisional acceptance for them. Both Rudy and Jake were willing to wait until they saw how well the six-limbed tigers fought. Joe helped with his description, but he really hadn't seen them in a fight.

Finally, we got down to the basic issue of territory and power. I could tell that Jake, not only wanted to do the right thing for the people under his command, he also wanted to keep their territory and keep himself in control. I explained that I had no ambitions towards control or expansion of my personal territory. To keep things simple, I claimed control over the Grand Lake area. We had more of a democracy there, but I thought that the folks wouldn't mind if I exaggerated my authority a little. Our meeting became much more cooperative when we agreed that we'd each stay on our own side

of the Divide. Grand Lake really didn't have enough resources to interest
Jake. He needed farm and ranch land to keep his large population fed and we
didn't have much of that. We agreed that we could trade back and forth and
that we'd cooperate in mutual self-defense and we would start by fighting
the Pugs and Pug-bears.

After hammering out details, we adopted my basic plan with only some
minor modifications. I was to go back and attack with my forces, driving the
invaders towards the south of Boulder. When the Warlord's people saw the
Pugs moving their way, they'd attack. They were going to reinforce their
front line quietly so that they would have far more force there than they'd
been using and that should allow them to stop the Pugs' advance and drive
them back towards us. They'd also cover both the high ground in the
foothills and provide a large force out on the flat towards Longmont to keep
the Pugs boxed into Boulder. This would prevent them from escaping our
trap. Once we'd compressed the invading force as tightly as we could, we'd
pull back rapidly just before Erin made her strafing pass. She'd be firing from
low orbit and Frazzle had calculated that they'd be able to fire the big anti-
matter cannon on burst mode for about seven seconds. I'd have them move
the ship into an east-west orbit right over Baseline Road in Boulder. That
would allow the cannon to strike at the east end of the occupied area and
traverse towards the west, with the burst ending as it struck the front row of
foothills. With any luck, it would catch our enemy by surprise.

All forces would then converge, wiping out any Pugs that remained. At least
that was the plan. We agreed to start the northern side's advance as soon as I
was able to return to Estes Park. Jake's people would begin sneaking
reinforcements up to the front lines immediately. We hoped to be able to
finish the battle sometime tomorrow. The exact time would depend on two
factors. The first was how fast we could bunch up the Pugs and the second
was how long after that time it would take for Erin to be in the right
position.

We shook hands and Joe and I left, Rudy coming with us as an escort back to
the shuttle. He was going to stay in Denver for the time being. His position
as strategic adviser was important to our success. Joe was going to come back
with me. He'd be in radio contact with the southern front and would act as
liaison.

When we got back to the shuttle-craft, I introduced Rudy to Whistle. Rudy,
at least, was very impressed with my furry little friend. They inspected each
other and then Whistle said, " You got a bad arm. We got advanced medical

device on the ship that might fix. When dis over, we get you on ship and see if your arm can be better fixed."

Rudy reached out his good arm, taking Whistle's small paw in his hand to shake it. "That's a deal. I'd be really grateful if my arm could be even a little better. It's not much use the way it is."

We climbed back into the tight cockpit and took off. In a few minutes, we were out of Denver and heading towards Estes Park at about a two-mile altitude. We landed with no problems and I briefed Kasm and his group on their role. They'd rested about as much as they wanted by then and they started moving out immediately. There weren't too many of them, but each was an accomplished Pug fighter and they could cover territory rapidly.

While we were gone, Frank had located a working farm truck and the three of us humans took it down the road towards Lyons. There we waited for the Sim-tigers to catch up. They'd spread out so they could cover a sizable front, but they were keeping pace with each other and in touch telepathically. Their mental communication gave them the ability to coordinate their movements precisely.

Whistle flew an observation pattern in the shuttle. If he located any of the enemy, he'd break in on Joe's radio so we could respond. It worked well. He located a few small Pug groups and the Sim-tigers attacked them, per my instructions relayed through Kasm, who was still the only mental contact that I could make.

We moved out of Lyons headed towards Boulder and rolled up a few more groups of Pugs and a couple of Pug-bears along the road into town. The Pug-bears seemed to be ferals, under the direction of the Pugs. At least they fought like they had no sense, wildly charging around and almost as dangerous to the Pugs as to the Sim-tigers. They were easily dispatched.

Things got stickier as we got into north Boulder. I don't know how many Pugs were there, but it was a large group, maybe several thousand. They were mostly armed with splinter-guns, though and those weapons were largely nullified by the Sim-tigers' natural resistance to poison and their speed and agility. Frank and I used our eraser-rifles sparingly to clear out strongholds the Pugs had set up in a few buildings, including the social services complex that was near the north end of town. I'd given Joe my eraser-pistol, but he stayed back with the radio and had no actual opportunity to use it.

The Pug resistance grew stiffer and stiffer as they retreated. We were bunching them up and there were more and more of them with a few actually carrying anti-matter weapons or the crew-served, plasma-bolt weapons. We lost a few Sim-tigers to these, but our allies were creative and flexible with their strategy. One or two would keep moving and showing themselves to attract fire, while others would circle the Pugs and attack from an unexpected direction. In this way, we gradually advanced throughout the night hours and into the morning of the next day.

Along about ten in the morning, Joe let me know that the Warlord's people were attacking. The Pugs had tried to break out down the highway and they had sprung their trap. We increased our pressure and by noon, the enemy was heavily concentrated in the downtown Boulder area. I didn't think that things could get any more favorable for us, so I called in Erin's strike. The FTL was still a little out of position, but Frazzle said that he could manage the firing run in about an hour, so we dug in and just tried to keep the Pugs where they were.

They must have had at least one knowledgeable military mind in their ranks. Someone on their side apparently got very nervous about their situation, because they tried to break through our northern front. There was some heavy fighting for a few minutes, but we were able to hold. Frank and I obliterated a couple of large groups of them with our anti-matter weapons. That was good for me. I mean "dead is dead" and I didn't care if we killed them or Erin did.

At exactly five minutes past one, there was a loud roaring noise that quickly passed from east to west. We couldn't see much, but what we did see was impressive. The buildings, trees, and everything just disappeared, taking the enemy forces with it. There was no smoke or dust. One minute there were buildings, the next minute the roaring sound, caused by vast numbers of particles crackling out of existence, ripped by and there was just a strip of raw earth. The ground level had been lowered several feet by the anti-matter beam and the strip looked like a half-mile-wide parking lot that neatly bisected the town. The pass was followed by a momentary silence and then a number of fountains of water shot up from severed water mains. I was shocked at the destruction. Attaching the gun to the ship's power had increased the output by an order of magnitude over the power pack.

We advanced carefully, finding only a little resistance. There were still a few Pugs that had been in positions nearer to us, but they posed no problems. I could hear gunfire to the south and realized that the Denver forces were also finishing off the remaining Pugs. Every so often a Pug-bear would come out of hiding and need to be dealt with, but the Sim-tigers were handling that easily. The Warlord's forces had a much more difficult time with the Pug-bears, but they, too, had developed ways to bring the tough creatures down.

By dusk, we'd finished the clean-up and I met Jake and Rudy in the center of the barren strip. The second wave of the aliens' invasion was effectively over.

Jake looked at Frank curiously and greeted him, "Hey, Frank! Good to see you. Where's Ted and Erin?"

Frank looked unhappy for a moment at being reminded of his friend, then answered tersely, "Ted didn't make it. Erin's flying the ship up there." He pointed upwards as he spoke.

"Why don't you come on back with me. You can have a position in my personal guard," Jake suggested.

Frank didn't pause to think it over. He answered immediately, "No. I think I'd like to stay on with Dec and the tigers. I'm getting along with those cats pretty well and there's still some stragglers to wipe out."

Jake shrugged as if it didn't matter, then turned to me to ask, "How about Erin? Are you going to keep her, too?"

I didn't want him to think that I had claim to her. I replied, "She can make her own decision as to where she wants to go, I guess. I don't know what she'll want to do."

His reply was somewhat foreboding. Despite being a better person than I'd expected, he was still the Warlord and had expectations that he wanted his people to meet. "She's got some explaining to do when I see her. I sent her up to Estes to see what happened there and she just went off, leaving my people to retreat when Pugs started coming through in force."

"It was an accident," I hastily replied. "We got caught in the transporter when it activated and ended up on one of the moons of Uranus. We've been working to get back all of this time."

"That may be, but I'm still unhappy with her. She was the leader of my group and she should have had enough sense not to get herself in the way of danger. She'll have to be demoted for that."

He had apparently already made up his mind.

Chapter 38

There were some Pug-bears that we missed. They had been breeding higher up in the foothills and had left many nests full of eggs that needed to be wiped out. The front range is a semi-arid climate and it was dry enough there for them to hatch. We put up a bounty for destroyed eggs and hoped that the local residents would kill most of the nasty things before they could hatch into the venomous spider-form that was so horrifying.

Some of Kasm's people moved into the front range. They found that they had a taste for the local mule deer and they enjoyed exploring in an area where they were on the top of the food chain. They also had the desirable ability to be able to smell out nests of eggs. There were still a few Pug-bears here and there, but we knew how to handle them now. They weren't much of a military threat without their Pug forces.

As days passed, the Pug-bears were gradually eliminated. They were mostly feral or only acted semi-intelligent. This puzzled me and I wondered if the symbiont that conferred intelligence upon them had not been brought to Earth or if they were totally missing this creature's influence upon their brain for some reason. That question was settled by a few autopsies of recently killed Pug-bears. The symbiont was present in some of them, but it was stunted. The longer the Pug-bears had been alive on Earth, the more likely the symbiont was to be stunted. Something in our environment was acting to suppress most of the symbionts. I couldn't figure it out, but there were probably some people around somewhere who could. I just needed to find them. Nevertheless, it was a blessing to find that the remaining Pug-bears were not likely to gain high intelligence for whatever reason.

I'd been anxious to make sure the Pug-bears didn't get a foothold on Earth. That had been my overt reason for hanging around the Boulder area, but in the depths of my mind, I was dreading going to Grand Lake. I was unsure about my relationship with a woman whom I barely remembered.

Erin and Frazzle had transported down right after the victory. Frazzle went back up to maintain the two spaceships until I could formulate what I wanted to do with them, but Erin and Whistle had stayed. She'd had a private audience with Jake and had come out pale and shaking. Thereafter, she'd stayed close to Frank and me. I got the feeling that she was done with her relationship with the Warlord. Whatever it had been in the past, it was no longer something that she wanted.

After I autopsied the Pug-bears and satisfied myself that the local people would probably kill them all before the winter started, I realized that I couldn't delay going home any longer. I set up a meeting with Jake to make plans and to say goodbye. Erin and Frank were going to come with me, as was Joe.

Rudy said that he thought he'd stay in the Denver area for a while, but would come over to see us later. He was looking forward to Whistle's promised medical treatment and they'd made arrangements for that. I hoped that it worked out well for him.

Whistle declined going with us to meet with the Warlord. He had some light maintenance he wanted to do on the smaller shuttle, so we left him working on it.

We went up to the stadium to meet with Jake and were waiting for him to finish some urgent business of some kind. Frank, Erin, Joe, and I were sitting in section A, row two, waiting for our turn with him when I suddenly felt the familiar paralysis induced by a Pug-bear mental attack.

It reminded me of the icy feeling that I'd had when the oldest Pug-bear had ambushed me on Titan. I was frozen where I was and my mind was under emotional pressure as the creature tried to assert complete control. I couldn't see the others, not being able to turn my head, but I assumed that they were snared also.

What I could see was bad enough. A huge Pug-bear with a greatly enlarged cranium was climbing over the railing directly in front of me, its velvety, concave eyes focused right on me. Suddenly the pressure it was exerting on my mind broke through with a snapping feeling and I could hear its thoughts. It was thinking to itself, not directing questions at me.

"How could this puny human have destroyed all of its fellows? It had been helping the Warlord, searching for a way to control the humans through him. It had been all alone and had thought the humans were its only chance for survival. Then it had sensed others of its own kind! It had gone up into the mountains and met them and there it learned that it was one of the master race! It had bred with them and left eggs to create more of its kind. Now, this puny human had ruined all chances of its domination. It was going to kill all of us and then leave, hoping to find some others of its kind still alive. They'd escape to the wilderness and breed more warriors there."

The pressure increased exponentially as it approached. I tried to pull my mind together, but the fog that had been there since the vision-beast attack seemed to swirl around and confuse me. The Pug-bear had rather stupidly come straight at me from the ground level and, as a result, it had to climb up and over the railing. It was hampered in this task by not having any means to actually grip the pipes with its claws and that was slowing it down.

I struggled frantically for a moment. My mind felt like it was going to explode. There was a blinding flash in my vision, paired with an involuntary full-body jerk as all my nerves fired. The air seemed to glow in the aftermath and then I remembered all at once. The fog was instantly gone! I knew how to deal with this creature. I created a mental bolt and sent it with as much force as I could. I commanded the Pug-bear to die with a powerful, single-minded thrust. My mental strike burned through its open mind like a hot knife through butter and it spasmed and then fell backward off the railing. The creature's mental attack ceased and I was suddenly able to move.

I jumped up and started to turn, meaning to run for my anti-matter pistol which I'd been forced to leave with one of the guards on the way into the stadium. As I turned, I was startled by a green-striped form that charged past me. Kasm had been late to our meeting and had just arrived. He'd sprinted down the steps from the mid-level concourse and now leaped over the rail, landing on the disabled Pug-bear. It was simple for him to rip out the vulnerable nerve-plexus on the thing's underside since it had landed on its back and had not been able to even start to right itself before he arrived.

I could feel it start to die as the nerves failed. Frank appeared at my side and Erin screamed. The threat was over as fast as it began. The Pug-bear had lived just long enough to rip open my locked memory and Psi ability. I could suddenly sense – Liz! She was in some kind of distress and I knew I needed to be there rapidly. I sent a mental message to Whistle, asking him to bring the shuttle to pick me up. He responded with a hint of amazement that I had regained my mental voice and instantly dropped what he was doing and headed for the shuttle-craft.

Jake came running out along with a group of guards. To save a lot of discussion, I simply grabbed his mind and shoved the whole series of events into it. He staggered, catching himself on the back of a seat, then he looked at me and said, "Go Dec! We'll meet later and get our business done. I'm sorry that this thing attacked you. It's been with us since the beginning and I thought it was adapted to life with humans. I understand that I was deceived. Go on and take care of your wife!"

The guards got out of the way as Kasm and I sprinted for the open area where the shuttle would land, Erin, Frank, and Joe right behind us. As I exited from the stadium, I could hear the sound of the rapidly approaching shuttle sounding like an extended thunder-roll in the clear air.

Whistle landed and I climbed in as fast as I could. Joe started to get in but was brushed aside as Kasm leaped past, crowding me against the side of the cockpit as he fit his bulky body inside. I started to object, but he forestalled my argument, "You're going to your mate and I'm going with you. I'm going to make sure that she's protected for you."

I realized that he needed this to help him heal from his own terrible loss, so I simply made room for him. There was no more room in the tight cockpit and I looked at Frank helplessly.

Frank and Erin stopped and he said, "Go ahead. We'll come over the Divide on horseback."

The hatch shut and we lifted off.

CHAPTER 39

It was frosty this morning when I went out to let the animals out of the barn. Michael was still asleep, but I'd been too worried to sleep much. I hadn't been eating as well as I should, mostly from stress and worry, but I was still getting large. My stomach poked out as if I'd eaten a small watermelon. I'd been bigger at this stage when I was carrying Michael, but that was when Dec was here to take care of me. Now, in his absence, I found that I worried about nearly everything.

True, my friends from town often came out to see me, but lately, even their visits had been stressful. Some of them had started hinting that I should move on, implying that Dec most likely wasn't coming back and that I should find someone else to help me cope with the new child. I thought that William had possibly put them up to it. He'd made it clear that he wanted me for himself. However, I wasn't anywhere ready to give up on my capable husband, even though I could no longer sense his mental presence the way I had been able to when he was near.

The one bright light in my situation was that our friend, Freddy Stormbreaker had come to town. Not only had he come, but he'd brought his wife! He had met and married a nice Cherokee woman somewhere in Oklahoma. He brought me news about Rudy and Joe also. They'd survived their journey to Miami and now were back in the Denver area working with the Eastern Slope Warlord, fighting the new invasion of Pugs and Pug-bears. The aliens had shown up in force a couple of weeks after Dec had left. They had been causing problems on the front range and there had been a number of pitched battles. At the moment, the invaders were stopped somewhere in the Boulder area, while the Warlord's people held Broomfield and Denver.

We were just thankful that the fighting hadn't come over the pass to our area except for a few abortive forays by small groups of Pugs and some roaming, feral Pug-bears. We'd dealt with all of these forcefully, leaving no survivors to report back to their main force on the other side of the Divide.

I'd been overjoyed to see Freddy. The last time I'd seen him was in Lyons where we parted ways after blowing up the alien's base on Titan. He had aged a bit, but then fighting your way across country in this post-EMP world was likely to do that. His wife, Virginia, was very nice and quite cute. It was easy to see why he'd picked her. I joked with him about why she'd picked him although I knew perfectly well. Despite his rough exterior, he was one of the nicest men I knew and he had the additional benefit, a virtue in this dangerous time, of being a deadly fighter. His presence in town even made me feel more secure out in our cabin.

Virginia and Stormy stopped by every couple of days to check on me and I was glad to see them, especially since they weren't the ones who were pushing me towards William. I was expecting them to show up around ten today. Stormbreaker had promised to take Michael out to harvest a deer. My son was now nearly five and Stormbreaker told me that he should start learning how to hunt, even though he wasn't old enough to handle a rifle. Apparently, Freddy had been trained to help clean and butcher deer at the age of four and felt strongly that, as he put it, even a paleface's boy should learn that stuff.

Now you may think that hunting late in the morning wouldn't be a good time to find a deer, since they usually move around at dawn and dusk, but it was the early part of the rut and they were distracted and less careful. Besides there wasn't much hunting pressure to the north of our place and the animals weren't as wary as a result, so I had no doubt that Stormbreaker would get one.

Michael woke and we had breakfast. He could hardly eat for excitement, but he finished and got dressed in some older clothes. I didn't want him to chance ruining any of his better things with blood. Along about nine-thirty, there was a hail from outside and I opened the door to find my friends on horseback just entering the yard.

Michael was out the door in a flash. He'd already gotten his pony saddled and he was up and ready to go quickly. Freddy looked at me and smiled, "Don't you worry, Liz. We ain't going to go very far. I scouted out a couple of likely places in the big meadow along the creek about a mile north of here. I expect that you'll hear our shot fairly shortly. I aim to enjoy myself teaching this youngster how to field clean a mulie. We'll pack it back to the house, here, to do the final cutting up. Virginia is really good at butchering."

Virginia smiled and nodded her head. She didn't speak much, but when she did, it was always about something worthwhile. Now, she looked a little worried and glanced at Michael. He'd started his horse across the yard, heading for the north trail. Stormbreaker looked at Virginia, nodded, and started after Michael. It was obvious that she had something to tell me and that they'd planned it out on the way up here.

"Liz, that William has been in town the last couple of days. I heard that he's been talking about how he intended to marry you and take over this homestead. Now, don't get me wrong, I know that you said that he'd been decent to you and helpful and such, but there's something about him that doesn't set square with either me or Fred. You'd best watch yourself around him. He's got some of the women in town talking about how lucky you are that he likes you, too. I think they're just jealous, though. Now, don't worry, we'll take good care of Michael."

She didn't wait for my reply, but turned her horse and kicked it in the ribs. It snorted and leaped forward into a fast trot as she hurried to catch up with the others. That was just her way. She'd keep quiet, but when she had something to say, she'd just let fly, not holding back. When she felt that she'd communicated what was on her mind, she'd go quiet again.

I sighed deeply. If only Dec would show up, that would stop all this nonsense. I missed him and I knew that I was going to need him even more in the months to come. I'd figured out that my baby would be due sometime in late January or early February. It was likely to be cold and we could be snowed in, so I'd either have to move into town if I wanted help or find someone to move in with us to help me through the laying-in period. I'd broached the subject with Virginia and she'd told me not to worry. She hadn't spoken to Freddy about it as far as I knew, but I suspected that they'd be willing to stay with us when my time came.

I went back into the cabin and busied myself with chores. It seemed like there was always something to do. I couldn't remember how it used to be, back when I was single before the aliens had destroyed our civilization. All I could do was marvel over how much harder it was to keep up our homestead than to track criminals. It was more than a full-time job.

I had finished washing clothes and was hanging them out on the line to dry when I heard a distant shot. The sound was carried down on the wind from the north and I stopped what I was doing to listen for a follow-up shot, but there was none. A single shot usually meant that there was a dead deer. Freddy was a good shot, so I expected that he'd be teaching Michael how to gut the animal during the next hour or so and that I could expect them back to the house sometime after lunch. I resolved to start early and fix enough food for four people since they'd probably be hungry.

I hung up the rest of the washing and walked back around the house. As I came around to the front porch, I almost ran into William. He had tied his horse down by the barn and had walked up to the house, not making any noise. He smiled at me and said, "Hello, Elizabeth. I wanted to come up and talk to you. We've got some business that we need to get settled." He stepped towards me as he spoke.

I'd originally thought it was somewhat charming, the way he always used my full name. It seemed sort of formal as if he was extraordinarily polite. Now, it just bothered me and seemed as if he were too tightly wound to relax. And, thinking about it, I didn't like the way he spoke my name. It was like he thought he had some kind of ownership rights over it.

"Hi, William. Now's not a good time. I've got chores to do and some cooking also," I replied, stepping past him and moving towards the cabin door.

"No. That can wait. I've waited as long as I care to for you to make up your mind to let me court you. We're going to come to an arrangement right now. Now, we can wait for a month to get married, but I want to be in charge here when you have your baby. I want it to understand that I'm the man of the house. You need me here to take charge of this place. It's getting run-down with just you working on it and you can't do much in your condition anyway."

This was just too much! I opened the door and then turned to block him as he started to come inside also. "Now, you just listen to me, Mr. Smith!" I tried to stay calm, but my voice was shaking. "I'm not marrying anyone. I'm already married and I'm happy with my husband. I'm not changing."

He brushed my statements aside, just waving his hand in negation as he argued, "Listen to me, Elizabeth! Your husband is dead! DEAD! He is never coming back. He's been gone for months now and that should be long enough for any woman to mourn. This place needs a man and I'm just the man for the job! I can make this holding into a real home. It could be expanded and be real nice with the right man working on it. There's plenty of women who'd jump at the chance to hook up with me! I've set my sights on you, though. When I first saw you, I thought that you'd be the perfect woman for me and I'm not going to take 'No' as an answer."

I was getting really angry and I could feel my face heat up as I responded, "Well, you're just going to have to resign yourself to it, because 'No!' is the answer. If you're so popular with the other women, go get one of them!"

I stepped back and started to slam the door in his face, but he kicked the bottom of it and stopped the swing. The heavy door hurt his foot. His buckskin moccasins didn't offer much protection for that kind of thing.

He cursed, "Damn it! That hurt! I came up here with good intentions to ask you nicely! Now, you're going to find that you can't turn me down! You're going to be my wife physically right now, even if the legal part has to wait for a while."

With that, he shoved me into the cabin, following as I staggered back. He grabbed my arm and visibly tried to calm down in an effort to make me more amenable. "I know you're pregnant and I promise to be gentle. There's no need to fight it. I've been with plenty of women and I know how to make you happy, even in your condition. Just relax and you'll see what a good husband I can be."

I tried to strike him. I used to be good at hand-to-hand, but he was faster and just too strong. Besides I was afraid of fighting too hard. My baby was at risk and I didn't want to chance being struck in the abdomen. I was thinking rapidly, trying to find a way out of this situation that didn't involve lying with him.

He was watching my face and could see that I was realizing that I didn't have any options. He started to smile and reached out to brush across my left breast. I took a deep breath and prepared to knee him in the groin, stepping forward as if I were yielding. He pulled me closer with a smirk on his face.

Just at that moment, I realized that there was something in my mind, a presence that was rapidly getting stronger. It was familiar, but it had initially been so faint and had strengthened so imperceptibly that it hadn't come to my conscious attention until this minute. With renewed strength, I smiled up at William, pressed my breasts against his chest, and raised my right knee as hard as I could. It made a thunk as it took him between the legs. He gasped and staggered back, falling to his knees. He doubled over with a groan and I started for the door.

As I passed him, he managed to grab the hem of my long skirt with a powerful grip. I tried to pull away, but he wouldn't let go. He was pale and gasping, yet he still managed to get out, "You're going to regret this! When I get better I'm going to take you and you're not going to like it."

I yanked hard and my skirt ripped, the waistband pulled free and I stepped out of the fabric and jumped for the door. I was so angry and frightened that I bypassed the rifle that was leaning against the wall nearby. I just wanted out of there right then. I ran out onto the porch, hearing William try to get to his feet inside. He was breathing very heavily and still groaning.

As I started for the barn, I heard a whining sound rapidly gaining in strength. It seemed to slow, although still approaching. Then I looked up and everything fell into place. The presence in my mind was Dec! He was in the flying craft that was hovering over the yard, preparing to land. I shrieked his name in excitement as the ship lowered to the ground.

By the time it had landed and the hatch had opened, I was preparing to climb up the side. The hatch opened and I staggered back as a huge green-striped tiger leaped out. It charged towards the house and I turned to see William standing on the porch aiming my rifle at the ship's open port where Dec was just climbing out. I screamed.

Before William had a chance to shoot, the tiger thing struck him. I don't think he ever saw it coming, he was so focused on killing Dec. The rifle flew out of his hands and landed on the ground and it was his turn to scream. It was horrible but quick. The tiger bit down and his scream suddenly broke off. William was dead.

I tried to recover my balance, but then I was suddenly wrapped in the strongest, most tender arms I could imagine. Dec's arms were wrapped around me as if he'd never let go! I was safe! His mental presence was strong and it was as if he'd never left. For the first time in months, I felt secure. I turned into his loving embrace and looked up into his infinitely deep eyes!

Epilog

I was so happy to have Liz in my arms again that I felt my heart would burst with joy! Then she turned into my embrace and I realized that we were going to have another child. I suddenly became aware of the love in her mind and a soft, baby presence that held the rudiments of consciousness. I knew instantly that the child would be a girl. Her baby mind was similar to that of Michael's before he was born, but there was a difference. She was already becoming feminine. I lost myself in their joint presence for a timeless moment.

Our mental melding was interrupted by Kasm, who directed his thoughts towards me.

"Dec, I can sense that you are happy and I'm glad!" He paused in his thought, then continued, "It's good that I was here, this one meant death! I could sense it in him."

I was jolted out of our linkage. I had been so intent on Liz that I hadn't really noticed what Kasm had done. William's neck was broken and red blood was still running out of his ripped carotid artery. As I looked, it ceased to flow. He was definitely dead. Then I saw the rifle. It shocked me. I felt like I was definitely slipping in my reflexes. Previously, I would have come out of the shuttle ready to tackle any challenge. Now, I understood how much Liz meant to me. I'd been so focused on her that I could have lost everything. I resolved to try to do better in the future. The world was far more dangerous now than ever before and I couldn't allow my love for her to interfere with my ability to protect her.

Kasm was still linked with me and acknowledged my series of recriminating thoughts with a loud snort followed by an unhappy thought, "At least you have a chance to continue to protect her."

I was instantly contrite and sent, "For that, I have to thank you. I'm in your debt. I only wish that I'd been there to help you when you needed it."

"There's no debt. You saved me from the vision-beast. I just want to work with you to finish off our mutual enemies. We cannot allow them to continue to threaten our worlds and those of the small furry ones."

I agreed. We'd need to do something about the Pug-bear threat. I felt instinctively that I'd first have to build up a force that could handle the two spaceships. That thought led to thoughts of Jake, the warlord, and those led to Frank and Erin.

Thinking about them made me realize how lucky I'd been. They'd been great assets during the past few months as had been the Sunnys. Maybe Erin was a little overly attached to me, but – I had a thought. Somehow my return to my normal mental state was making me retroactively more perceptive. It had been obvious for a long time, but I'd bypassed the knowledge. Frank was hopelessly in love with Erin. I knew without a shadow of a doubt that he loved her deeply, although he'd never volunteer it to her. He was intent on waiting for her to realize it.

I smiled. Perhaps I could help with the situation. I'd manipulated her mind before. If I could somehow just lead her to realize his feelings, maybe she'd forget about me. She knew I was unavailable and I knew she was beating herself up about it. Maybe a little surreptitious mental influence would be a good thing here. I didn't want Liz to feel as if she had a rival, either, even though Erin wasn't any threat to her.

Tentatively, I extended my mental touch across the miles we'd come in the shuttle. The two of them were already on horseback and headed for the Continental Divide. They were following us. I sensed Joe's presence with them, so I knew they were on their way here.

I sank deeper into Erin's subconscious thought pattern. There was a sense of loss and sadness as she thought of not being loved. Those thoughts were linked to images of me, but, as I explored her mind, I found a series of images of Frank helping and defending her. She felt grateful to him and that feeling gave me the key that I needed.

I rearranged the linkage in her mind so that the feeling of love was more closely attached to the emotion of gratitude. I didn't want her to consciously sense that I was manipulating her feelings, so I left it at that and detached from her carefully. That was all that I did. I still didn't like messing with the mind of a friend, but I consoled myself with the thought that I hadn't done more than provide a possible route for her to realize Frank's feelings. I just hoped that it would work.

About an hour later, as we were all sitting, or lying as was the case with Kasm, in the living room of the cabin, Stormbreaker, Virginia, and Michael arrived. They had gotten a deer, which proved handy. Kasm immediately appropriated the left hind-quarter and retired to the porch to eat. He was accompanied by a fascinated Michael. Michael had hugged me happily and then been immediately distracted by Kasm's alien body. Shortly after they went out, there was a bit of a commotion on the porch. I could sense Michael's alarm, but Kasm was giving every evidence of being amused. There was also an overtone of rather fierce anger tinged with curiosity. I couldn't figure out what was going on and I jumped up, alarming the others.

When I poked my head through the door, it was all clear. Jefferson had returned. He'd apparently left when Smith had arrived, having great disapproval of the man, but enough time had passed that he must have figured that William had left as, indeed, he had – in a permanent manner. We'd moved his body to one of the stalls in the barn, pending the Sheriff's arrival to check on the circumstances.

Finding another cat, and Jefferson was convinced that Kasm fit into that category, our Tom-cat proceeded to work up a proper case of indignation about the interloper feeding on our porch. When I came out, he was standing on the steps with every hair on his body sticking out and posed in an arch-backed, bristle-tailed, witches' cat stance, showing his profile to Kasm in a vain attempt to intimidate the six-limbed alien.

Kasm hadn't moved and was just lying there over the remains of his meal with a sort of pleased expression on his face. He could display more emotion than one of our felines and was doing so. When he noticed my presence, he sent, "This little one is a true fighter! I like him, but I'm unable to reach his mind to calm him down. Can you help?"

It only took a moment to show Kasm the ... I guess you could call it, "the frequency" of Jefferson's lightning-like flickers of thought. He'd missed them; they were on a level that he normally didn't access, even though once shown, he had no problem getting in touch with the alarmed cat. I didn't intervene. It wasn't necessary. Kasm shortly had Jefferson literally eating out of his hand.

Once convinced that Kasm was friendly and not threatening, Jefferson actually curled up next to him, accepted some scraps of meat that the Sim-tiger dangled in front of him, and then began to purr contentedly. During this process, I hadn't actually stepped through the open door. However, after Jefferson calmed down, I could see that his eyes strayed over to me. He squinted at me a couple of times before I got it. He was giving me the cold shoulder. I tuned to his thoughts, such as they were. He was not ready to forgive me for being absent so long.

I figured that I might as well take what was coming to me, so I walked out and set down cross-legged in front of him. He looked away for a moment and then audibly sighed, stood up, and faced me. Then he proceeded to tell me off in a series of yowls that left no doubt about what he was saying. "How dare you leave us all alone for so long. There have been all kinds of trouble here and I could have used the help. You should be ashamed of yourself!" There was more like that and I felt properly chastened. He finished and turned symbolically away from me. In response, I made a little 'churring' noise with my tongue and he turned back, looking surprised as if he'd just seen me. The next instant, I had twenty pounds of purring cat frantically rubbing his head on my chest and face, much to Kasm's amusement. I could also hear Liz laughing softly from her observation post in the doorway.

The big cat-like creature had understood every aspect of the emotions that were flying back and forth. He was probably more human in that regard than the Sunnys. As cuddly as they looked, they still didn't map as closely to our mental processes and emotions as Kasm's kind.

Once the delayed greeting was over, the others came out of the cabin and sat on the porch chairs. It was nice there, except for the still-drying bloodstain. Stormbreaker filled me in on his experiences with frequent glances at his bride for her approval, intermixed with a couple of appraising stares at Kasm. He ended by asking me if he could learn to communicate with the alien. I glanced at Kasm and noted that he could more than half follow the verbal aspects of the discussion. He couldn't understand all of the words, but he could tune to the emotions and those provided a good key, allowing him to understand the meaning of what was said.

"Stormbreaker, Kasm understands you already. He normally communicates mentally, but he's learned a lot of English from being around me. He just can't speak it though," I responded.

"Can some," rumbled Kasm in a deep growl. I was shocked. I hadn't known that he had the capacity to actually speak. His words were well-formed, but the growling tone made them a little difficult to follow at first.

During the next few days, the two seemed to bond and become close friends. I was all for that. We'd have to work together closely if we were to make an impact on the Pug-bear problem.

Whistle seemed to hit it off with Michael. At five years of age, Michael was only a little smaller than the little Sunny. Something about the Sunnys' nature seemed to fit well with the playfulness of a human child and they were usually to be found in roughly the same location. The way Kasm and Whistle fit in with a group of humans was very reassuring to me. There was certainly hope for the future relationship of our kinds.

We put Stormbreaker and Virginia up in the guest room, Kasm and Whistle stayed in the living area with Whistle sleeping on the couch. Kasm was content to curl in front of the fireplace with Jefferson. About half the time, I'd come out of the bedroom in the morning, still half asleep from renewing my relationship with my lovely wife, and find Michael either sitting with Whistle or actually curled up with his head on Kasm's side and Jefferson on his lap. It was like we were all one happy family.

Then the day came that I'd been worried about. Erin, Frank, and Joe arrived. They were escorted out to our place by the Sheriff, who'd been out a couple of days previously to take our report of Smith's demise.

Stormbreaker and Joe pounded each other's back in greeting while Erin hung back, seemingly somewhat reluctant to come forward. Frank had immediately strode over to me and shook my hand, but I sensed something in him that seemed like he felt guilty in some fashion. I finally tuned into their subconscious minds and realized as I did that my machinations had worked. Erin came over to me at about the same time and said, "I've got something to tell you Dec."

"You know that you can tell me anything," I responded, aware of the critical eye of my wife on me, as I did.

Erin looked away and I saw that she was blushing. When she turned back to me, she had gathered her courage and she looked at both Liz and me. "What I've got to say concerns both of you. I want to clear the air."

Liz looked at me with a long, slow glance that implied that I'd have some explaining to do when she got me alone.

Erin continued, "Mrs. Dunham, I want to confess that I fell for your husband. He was so competent and kind that I felt like I really wanted him. When I thought that we wouldn't get off of Kasm's planet, I was almost glad. I thought that I'd have him for myself that way. You see, I knew that I couldn't compete with you, even when his memory of you was partially lost, I didn't have a real chance."

She turned to me, "Dec, I know I was a pain, constantly trying to pressure you. You don't know how frustrating you were to me, though."

I started to answer, but she continued, "The most amazing thing happened, though. As we were coming over the Divide to Grand Lake, I had time to think back on my life and I realized something. Frank has been my bodyguard for years. Ted had only been with me for a few months, but it seems like Frank has always been there. I started to think about you, but then I suddenly understood my feelings better than I ever have. I realized that I love Frank. I've loved him for a long time, but I was just too proud and blind to allow myself to see it. I thought that I had some status in Jake's organization that would suffer if I hooked up with my guard. Jake no longer trusts me the way he used to and I don't care about that kind of status any longer. Mrs. Dunham, you've got a wonderful husband, but I think I've just found that I might have a wonderful future with Frank."

I looked at Frank. His heart was shining through his eyes. I'd known that he was devoted to her, but I had been too distracted to worry about their personal feelings during our adventure. It was obvious that he was extremely happy and I wished the best for both of them. I glanced at Liz and she beamed at me. I received a pleased thought from her that had to do with the fact that she'd always known that I was reliable and trustworthy. My wife wasn't one to hold grudges. She seemed to understand Erin's previous actions and wasn't offended that Erin had thought she wanted me.

It took several days for everything to begin to work out. Frazzle sent a message through the comm system to the Sunnys on Oberon. Since the Pugs didn't monitor comm traffic, relying on the Sunnys to report anything out of the ordinary to them, it was easy and safe. The Oberon Sunnys wanted to be rescued and were easily convinced to simply come through the transporter to Estes as soon as they understood there were no Pugs or Pug-bears left alive to punish them. Once they were through, we turned off the transporters. They were the only ones currently on Earth, so there was no chance that we'd be taken by surprise by a flank attack.

Fortunately, they had enough foresight to destroy the new Ansible communication system prior to their departure. I'd completely forgotten about that possibility. We'd destroyed the original one and I hadn't considered that the Pug-bears might have another. It had arrived on the larger ship that we'd captured. Its loss would eventually pose a problem for us since the Pug-bears used it to make supply requests on a fairly regular basis and the loss of contact would surely be noticed. We'd have to do something about that in the near future.

I wanted to try and salvage the potentially useful equipment that was on Oberon. According to the rescued Sunnys, there was a large weapons cache there that I thought would prove very useful provided we could get it. So far, I had been resisting the idea of making a direct assault through the transporters as too dangerous. I didn't want to simply shoot the domes with the anti-matter cannon either, so the Pugs and Pug-bears there went unmolested.

Eventually, most of the Sim-tigers moved into the Grand Lake area. They'd tracked down almost all of the adult Pug-bears and eliminated them. For some reason, there hadn't been nearly as many on Earth as I'd feared. Unfortunately, not all of the Pug-bears' nests had been located. There could still be some hatchlings that would cause rather severe problems in the spring.

The few surviving Pugs hadn't lasted long. They died when their respirator supplies ran out. They just couldn't live for long in our atmosphere.

We spent a lot of time arguing about the best way to solve the Pug-bear problem. Their natural aggressiveness combined with the Pugs' warlike society and the Sunny technology meant that they would never be good neighbors. Ideally, if they could be separated from the Sunnys and cut off from technology, they'd be forever restricted to their own planet. The Pugs might develop some more sophisticated technology of their own, but they too were caught in a biological trap. Their short life spans combined with a violent nature made it unlikely that they'd pose a threat very rapidly.

I discussed simply destroying their respective home planets with the others, but we were all resistant to the idea of genocide, even if the intended targets weren't friendly. We wanted a less destructive solution. There was also the problem of removing the Pug-bears from the Sunny planets they'd invaded. Dropping ice balls from space might help, but there needed to be a more elegant solution that wouldn't endanger the Sunnys.

We finally realized that we had a clue to the dilemma based on the autopsies we'd performed on the Pug-bears. The symbionts were apparently being stunted in their growth by some environmental factor here on Earth. We needed to figure out what that was and to do so, we needed some Pug-bears and symbiont eggs. I sent over the mountain to ask the Warlord if he'd place a bounty on Pug-bear eggs so that we might have some to study. Some of his people had found some of the wafers of compressed symbiont eggs stored in the Stanley hotel and we got our hands on a case of these also. We just needed a competent biological researcher to try and find the vulnerability and the agent that was exploiting it.

Once we'd worked through these difficulties, I needed to deal with our relationship with our eastern neighbors. We needed to come to an agreement with Jake about how we would jointly organize to fight the Pug-bears. That led me to realize that we'd have to also organize to start rebuilding. Jake was doing a good job, but he was running a sort of dictatorship and I thought that we'd probably be better off with some sort of confederation. That, too, was a problem for the future.

After sending some messages back and forth, I set up a meeting with Jake to get started with our counter-invasion plans. We agreed to meet at Estes Park in the Stanley Hotel as a neutral location.

Frazzle brought the larger shuttle down to Grand Lake and we all loaded up for the trip over to Estes. There was no sense taking horses when we had the ability to fly and Liz pointed out that the shuttle would be a great symbol of our power that would improve our stature, helping our negotiating position.

The flight was short. The shuttle-craft was designed for space-flight, after all, and had plenty of speed. Frazzle had us over the mountains and landing on the front lawn of the Stanley in just a few minutes. He shut the craft down and opened the hatch as a large group of people watched from the elevated front porch of the historic building.

Together, our diverse group, composed of Sim-tigers, Sunnys, and humans exited the shuttle-craft, coming out into the bright sun and crisp mountain air on the grounds of the Stanley Hotel. We walked across the unkempt lawn, headed for our meeting with Jake, the Eastern Slope Warlord, and his lieutenants. With any luck, we could agree on how to structure a strike force that would take the fight to the Pug-bears.

The End

Human Psychic Potential: A Brief Discussion

Some of the readers of the first book in the Gaea Ascendant series, The Time of The Cat, have written to me inquiring about the introduction of Psi powers towards the end of the story. At least one of the comments had to do with the fact that I had created a straightforward story with a normal (well, exceptionally capable) human hero and it stretched the reader's belief to suddenly give him extraordinary powers.

That is a fair objection. A major component of science fiction story-telling is to create a universe that seems plausible. This can be done in several ways. I chose the introduction of alien-originated technology along with malicious aliens. This is a possible, if rather unlikely, scenario that fits into a genre that has been explored before, thus giving the reader a feeling of familiarity. Another example of creating a believable universe is found in stories that attempt to extend the science of the current time and make predictions about the future. Although the predictions are often wrong and may appear hopelessly naïve after a number of years, the world thus created is easily controllable and the intended reader doesn't find it too difficult to suspend his or her disbelief.

The concept of "suspension of disbelief" can be characterized as agreeing to allow the author's world to exist in your imagination. This may be easy or difficult for the reader, but in either case, it is important for the author to create a consistent story that doesn't violate the rules of the created universe. You can blend genres such as in the movie Cowboys and Aliens, but you cannot suddenly have a cowboy pull out an Uzi and start blasting away without introducing another element into the story. Such an action would change the implicit rules.

In the case of The Time of The Cat, I seemingly broke the consistency rule. In the story, there is a consistent universe, albeit one with advanced science and alien life forms and suddenly the hero develops Psi powers. Is this fair or not? I believe it is fair and here's why:

If you've read the story, you might recall that Dec had placed considerable reliance on his "sixth sense" to warn of impending danger from the inception, so there was at least some warning that he might be gifted in that way.

Now, I'm not going to ask you to believe that Dec's story exists in a different world than ours, one that has different physical rules. I'm going to do something much harder. I'm asserting that psychic abilities exist within the human population of our world. Like all other abilities, they are distributed on a normal bell curve. Dec just happens to be an outlier on that curve, although he doesn't manifest his abilities until he is severely threatened.

There is a large body of research that proves (yes, I did say "proves") beyond a shadow of a doubt that humans have at least a rudimentary ability to manipulate matter with their minds. The PEAR lab at Princeton University has conducted millions of trials showing that humans can impact the time of decay of an atomic nucleus. Granted, the target is very small and the effect is tiny; the experimental subjects were able to influence the event by about two percent on average, yet the millions of trials conducted mean that the effect is statistically very solid. In short, it exists.

There have been experiments that show that cells removed from the cheek of a subject still respond to his emotions, even when separated by over three hundred miles. There have been experiments that show that people who meditate together form a bond that lets them respond to each other's emotions when they are isolated in separate, shielded, sound-proof rooms. In fact, there is a large body of experimental evidence along these lines that most scientists either willfully ignore (easy to do when it doesn't fit into your worldview) or are simply unaware of.

I'm not going to delve into other forms of evidence in this brief essay, other than to note that the CIA spent a lot of money on their remote viewing program. This program involved having a viewer sitting in a lab mentally view and describe a remote location without knowing either the location or its details. Surprisingly, the results were usually far above chance. Even more surprisingly, the researchers found that normal humans all had that ability and got better with practice.

When you consider that we float in a sea of virtual quantum particles and the very atoms of our bodies may be viewed as a special form of energy, it's easy to see the interconnectedness of everything. The recent theorizing about torsion waves that travel a billion times faster than light in the quantum plenum may lead to an understanding of quantum entanglement and instantaneous information transfer.

Energy may be thought of as a medium that can store information. If the quantum plenum may be viewed as a wave construct, then information must be stored in those waves, just as in a hologram. Since the Meta-Universe is considered to be infinite, it could store an infinite amount of information. Blending in systems and chaos theory makes it at least conceivable that such a vast store of information may have self-organized into a form of intelligence; perhaps one that is so far beyond our comprehension that it deserves the appellative "Guiding-Organizing-Design" originated by Dr. Gary Schwartz.

Be that as it may, as children of this information-universe, humans are inextricably woven into the information flow. To some extent, we sense magnetic fields, see "auras" beyond the scope of normal human vision, sense the gravitational pull of remote stars as well as our own sun and moon, and sometimes, to varying degrees, we know what other humans are thinking.

Far from changing the rules of our "normal" universe – the one in which Dec exists, I simply took his natural ability and magnified it greatly as his response to the mental attack of the old Pug-bear on Titan. It's not too difficult to think that a human with an extraordinary ability might be able to impart some of the techniques of this ability to others. The Pug-bear's attack opened Dec's mind and he was able to transfer that to a lesser extent to Liz and also, but even less successfully to Rudy. It seems to make sense to me that emotionally bonded couples would be more able to make such a connection. In the PEAR research at Princeton, emotionally bonded couples scored almost five percentage points higher on the task when working together.

So, that's my answer. In a nutshell, I'm fully convinced that psychic abilities exist and like other human abilities, it's obvious that humans can learn to use them and get better with practice.

In the second book of the series, Second Wave, Dec's psychic ability also plays a large part as you've just seen. I could say more, but instead, I'll just comment that you'll see more of Dec's and Liz's Psi ability in the following story: Confederation.

Namaste!

Eric Martell

Αβουτ Τηε Αυτηορ

Eric S. Martell set out to become a scientist when he was five. He has a PhD. in experimental psychology. When personal computers came along (way back in prehistory), he became adept with them and spent years in software design, working on projects that ranged from early childhood learning software to military training. He has been trained in various types of energy healing, is an expert in real estate investing and sales, and holds a black belt in Tae-Kwon-Do. He is also a pilot, scuba diver, guitar player, outdoorsman and is addicted to both science and science fiction.

Eric's science fiction books offer both believable science and compelling characters set against realistic action. They are carefully researched, and while his fictional science sometimes strains against the bounds of current knowledge, it is always plausible. His stories cover alien invasion in an apocalyptic setting, political structure, space travel, advanced weapons, quantum physics, hunting, war, romance, time travel, and alien worlds.

He's been published in a series of anthologies and has published many full-length science fiction novels. His writing goal is to provide his readers with stories they cannot put down, and he takes readers' suggestions seriously.

Notices about new books, free short stories, opinion posts, and preview pages for many of his books can be found on his author blog at **EricMartellAuthor.com**

I make every effort to ensure your reading experience is enjoyable. This involves multiple editing steps, interior book layout, design, and using a professional cover artist/designer. Even so, it is becoming more difficult to find readers. If you liked this book, please leave a review and tell your friends.

Reviews may be left on the platform of your choice or emailed directly to me through my blog.

Thank you,

Eric

E. S. Martell

Venice, Florida

2021

Also By Eric S. Martell